THE
HACKER

THE
HACKER
DANIEL SCANLAN

An Aries Book

First published in the UK in 2022 by Head of Zeus Ltd,
part of Bloomsbury Publishing Plc

9 7 5 3 1 2 4 6 8

A catalogue record for this book is available from the British Library.

ISBN (HB): 9781803289861
ISBN (XTPB): 9781803289878
ISBN (E): 9781801107822

Printed and bound in Great Britain by
CPI Group (UK) Ltd, Croydon CR0 4YY

Head of Zeus Ltd
First Floor East
5–8 Hardwick Street
London EC1R 4RG

WWW.HEADOFZEUS.COM

"The Seventy-first Spirit is Dantalion. He is a Duke Great and Mighty, appearing in the Form of a Man with many Countenances, all Men's and Women's Faces; and he hath a Book in his right hand. His Office is to teach all Arts and Sciences unto any; and to declare the Secret Counsel of any one; for he knoweth the Thoughts of all Men and Women, and can change them at his Will. He can cause Love, and show the Similitude of any person, and show the same by a Vision, let them be in what part of the World they Will. He governeth 36 Legions of Spirits; and this is his Seal."

S. L. MacGregor Mathers, A. Crowley, *The Goetia: The Lesser Key of Solomon the King* (1904). 1995 reprint: ISBN 0-87728-847-X.

1

A Realm of Shadows

I'm not handing them over 'til I'm sure you're good for it. DarkSend only, Ericka typed, eyes welded to her screens, the lone source of light, a bright pool that barely reached the walls of the borrowed ops room.

The response was instant. *I need them now. The boat will be here tomorrow. We agreed. You can't just jack the price on me. I got customers waiting.*

FBI Assistant Special Agent in Charge Ericka Blackwood cocked her head as she responded. She had to keep him talking, give him a chance to slip up. *That's too bad for you. These girls are still fresh. I can sell them anywhere. I'm not a fucking charity.*

Her partner Special Agent Tim O'Connell snorted from the darkness behind her, and she shot him a feral look over her shoulder. He glanced at his monitor, speaking in his thick Manchester-Irish accent. "We're still good. I don't think they've figured it out." He leaned in to look over her shoulder, placing a fresh coffee on the table beside her. The screen's glow highlighted his craggy features, the deep scar on his right cheek running from his beard to his hairline, bisecting his brow.

Without taking her eyes from the screen, Ericka leaned back reaching for her cup, tipping her head for a generous gulp, braced by the heat in her throat. "He's using the same VPN as this morning. The stream's clean. No precise location data. He's in the city somewhere, but that's as tight as I've got right now." She sipped again, waiting while their quarry typed his response.

The two local FBI agents craned their necks to see from behind them, watching the screens. One shook his head with a humorless smile; the other was still, grim-faced. They were in over their heads, forced to stand and watch since she and Tim had arrived at the FBI field office in Portland, Agents Ralston and Chung, pacing like wolves, waiting for a signal from the pack leader. Ericka and Tim had come straight from the airport and hadn't left the building since.

The text window flashed the target's response. *Isn't my rep good for anything? You got your cash last time. Why are you fucking with me?* Ericka nibbled her lower lip as she stared at the seized tablet lying on the battered table. It was hooked to her machines with several cables, like a dying patient on life support. No time to go through it and look for past deals, she'd just had time to break the device encryption. Twelve hours since the Oregon agents had arrested its owner, isolating the device so it couldn't hook up to anything. They had taken his 'shipment' of young women into protective custody hours before they were to embark for China via the Philippines. The man in custody was a local goon, little more than a trumped-up pimp. If they didn't flush the buyers out soon, they'd have to start over.

Ericka glanced at the locals. "How much longer do we have before his lawyer gets there?"

The taller agent, Ralston, glanced at his mobile and shrugged. Worry etched his face, an officer deeply invested in his work. He'd barely left the room since they arrived. "No more than an hour now."

As soon as his lawyer left cells and got his mobile back, they were blown. Ericka stared at Ralston, her mind racing through options, coming up empty. "We can't break their VPN by then and we don't have time to scour his data well enough to impersonate him believably for much longer. Anything you can think of about these guys that your prisoner would know?" Tricking him took information, whatever the source, she needed something. Breaking into their technology was just the first step; now she needed to peer into their heads.

Ralston leaned close as he spoke, the smell of stale sweat and coffee filling the air. "Nothing. He's not gonna spill. We didn't even know there was more than one local group selling until you cracked that thing." Ericka caught the wince—hard for this one to ask for help.

She slumped into her seat, turning to Tim where he leaned back in the worn, government-issue chair. "Think these guys sample the goods?" She cringed at her own mental image. They had nothing to lose. As soon as their target knew police had taken the snakehead goon down, he would vanish. It might be years before they picked him up again. Dark web middlemen were always the hardest, but it was what they did and why they were here.

Tim shrugged, leaning forward in his chair towards her. "Never heard of one who doesn't."

The question came from behind her. "What are you going to do?"

Ericka turned to answer the shorter agent, Chung, who sat on another table against the wall, arms folded across his muscular chest, shirt wet-stained in the armpits. She gestured with her chin towards the screen. "Shoot him a bait pic that'll send me his location if he opens it. Sometimes I can load software too. A long shot but I'll try and work them a bit first to whet their appetites." She leaned back, lifting her fingers from the keyboard. "Are any of the girls still in the building?"

Ralston nodded, still gazing at her screen. "Just the youngest, waiting for placement. She's the one who escaped and tipped us off. Gutsy kid. Why?" He turned to her, eyes narrowed.

Ericka stood up, tugging on her leather jacket, gesturing to Tim to stay on the monitors. "I need to talk to her. Does she speak English?"

Chung nodded. "She does."

Ericka gestured to him. "Let's go."

The girl was just a frightened child, delicate features hard, eyes projecting dread. Ericka sat on the edge of the coffee table across from the worn couch, stomach cramping. The social worker closed the door to the witness room with more force than was necessary, making the girl flinch. This kid could be no more than seventeen, wiping a tear from her cheek as she met Ericka's stare, wearing borrowed clothes so large they swam on her. Ericka forced a smile, knowing her probing blue eyes and hawk-like features could be intimidating. The harsh fluorescent lighting and stark, police station décor didn't help.

"I know this is hard, but I need your help. I'm Ericka. No one will know what you tell me. Do you understand?" The girl nodded, her expression unchanged. "Do you know anything about where you were going, what you were going to be doing?" Her gaze dropped to the floor, but the kid said nothing. Okay, she understood. "Will you tell me your name?" A shake of the head with an instant of defiant eye contact, shifting her weight. "Anything you can tell me about the men you were being taken to? There are other girls we need to help."

That got a reaction. Fierce tears welled up while the jaw set. "I know that. My sister left two days ago. When we came here they told us we would be cleaning in hotels, but we ended up working the trade. Now she's on her way to China, sold as a wife to someone in a shithole village who can't do better than very used goods like us." Flawless, accented English, very surprising.

"What's her name?"

"Bopha. She's twenty."

Ericka nodded. That was something she could use. "When were you to leave?"

"Our ship was supposed to be here tomorrow."

Ericka looked down, forcing herself to breathe, wincing at the matter-of-fact description of her sister's fate. The kid's look of naïve resolve brought it bubbling up, straining against mental discipline. A memory of her own sister now weathered by time and failure. She peered into the haunted brown eyes, forcing calm into her voice, gripping the girl's shoulder. "You'll see her soon." Ericka stood up, forcing a rigid posture, waiting until she was in the hallway alone to let go of the gasps.

* * *

Tim leaned back from the terminal as she strode into the room, shaking his head to indicate nothing had happened. Avoiding eye contact with the others, she dropped into her seat, typing fast. *These girls are worth the extra money. Two of them are really something special. Fuck, can hardly keep from helping myself. Bopha's little sister is one of them, a real beauty. Worth a fortune to your guy. Ask him.*

His replies were instant now. *Pussy is pussy. I don't need to ask him. He's looking in. Where they're going, they won't be beautiful long.* Chilled inside, Ericka could sense her prey eyeing the bait, salivating, craving it. Minutes passed. *But pretty affects the price for sure.*

The surge of adrenaline made her skin tingle and she shifted in her chair. The bastard was going to bite. The agents behind her let out the breaths they'd been holding. *She's eighteen, but she looks lots younger than that to me. Real skinny, like a schoolgirl.* She waited, muscles tense, working the mind of her prey, worried how long the answer was taking.

The flash of the text window caught her eye. *My guy wants to see pics.*

Ericka let out an explosive breath. They'd just been having a side bar. She typed again, a grim smile betraying her excited focus. She glanced at Tim as he nodded agreement. *Gimme a sec while I take some. Where do you want me to send them?*

An instant reply this time. *Usual drop box.*

She looked back to Tim, but he was already typing, searching the seized tablet. Two minutes passed. "There are six file transfer accounts on here. No idea which one he means."

6

They were going to have to take some chances. Ericka turned her head to talk over her shoulder to the local agents. "We don't have time to figure it out. I'll send to all of them assuming he wasn't smart enough to set one up as a tripwire. Let's hope he saved his passwords, I might not have time to find them." Her fingers danced over the console, using a copy of the tablet's data loaded into a 'virtual machine' on her computer. This software allowed her to mimic the tablet's digital profile using her own equipment, seeing what he would see on his own device. She scanned the data before uploading the bait and typing in the message window. *They're up, all yours.*

Tim turned to look at the locals. "We'll be able to tell when they take it."

Ralston pulled his chair tight behind Ericka, close enough she could feel his body heat on her back. "What will they see when they open it?"

Ericka answered without taking her eyes from the screen. "A fake error message telling them the file was corrupted during transfer. How fast it works or whether it does at all depends on what they've got loaded for security. It has a worm embedded in it. It will pull software from one of our servers, which broadcasts the bad guy's IP to us over the clear web, routed around his security. If we don't get anything in five minutes, we're done." She turned to look at Chung. "The first group went out of here on a boat two days ago. You'll want to figure which ships are possibilities and get the navy or the coast guard after them."

Tim slapped the table, his voice raised with excitement. "There's one. Running it now." They crowded behind his screen as he turned to speak. "Baxter building, main branch of the library. Using public Wi-Fi. Better get some locals down there and tell them to secure all the security video for the last three hours!"

"Shit! They've gone offline. Might have figured it out." Ericka drummed her fingers on the edge of the table. Ralston's eyes were wide as he stared at her. She scanned the drop box accounts, opening the one displaying completed file transfers. One showed a transfer to a contact, someone who called himself Tighty. She scanned the seized tablet again, not daring to hope its owner was that stupid. But he was. Two of his social media contacts used the same handle, likely the same guy. She opened an account and clicked on his friend Tighty. A grinning, corpulent face appeared in the profile pic. She let out the breath she had been holding. This is what it was all about—he could be in cells by evening.

She addressed Ralston. "This is probably one of your guys. No location though. I don't think it's good enough to run facial recognition software." Chung was on his mobile steering local police into Portland's main library.

Ralston's smile was forbidding as he stared at the picture, eyes hard, a sheen of perspiration betraying his excitement. He appeared to be breathing again, anticipating how this was going to end. "No need. Mr. Kang and I go way back. I was wondering just last week where he was going to turn up next."

Tim touched her wrist. "We're getting account data from this Kang guy, but he has location services turned off. Hoovered his credentials though. He must have needed to make a call. We've heated them up for sure."

Ericka blew out a sharp breath, fingers pounding keys, tension flooding out of her, sure of the bust now. "Well let's fix that." She opened a connection to his web account, toggling through the target's settings, changing and saving his selections. A few seconds passed before she gestured towards the screen showing GPS numbers. Done, she had him, oh yes. "Right in the middle of terminal six at the main docks, standing there now." The locals left at a run, both gesturing to no one as they shouted into their phones.

Ericka spun her chair to look at her partner, poking at him with her boot. "And that's that. That's all we can do for now." She stared at Tim, lounging back in her chair, a lioness whose latest kill lay cooling in the shade behind her. She turned back to her screen, concentrating on relaxing and bringing her heart rate down, resisting the urge to wipe the film of sweat from her face. She nodded towards the picture. "As soon as they scoop Einstein there, let's go home."

Back now from chasing garden-variety criminals in Oregon. The red-eye back to Virginia and her real quarry: following digital trails through cloaked servers and hidden pathways. Ericka pulled the dark strands of hair out of her face and stuffed them into her hairclip. Sitting in front of an array of dimmed monitors, she nestled into a non-government-issue chair, two small space heaters whirring, each covering half of the L-shaped station. Headphones and virtual-reality goggles rested on a gleaming surface, spotless like a high-end hotel lobby. Narrow ground-level windows like gun slits peered up at leafless trees. Their shared office smelled of dust and overheated electronics accented with the remains of fast food waiting for garbage day.

For some targets, dangle the bait, caress the ego, promise

the flesh or money they crave, and they lunge out, all caution forgotten. Amateur-hour predators unable to control their lusts. All their careful hiding, routing through proxy servers and cloaks of multi-level encryption lost when they step into the light to claim their prize. She sighed, remembering the video of the girls as light splashed on their wide-eyed faces when the hatch was pried open, coast guard flashlights illuminating their terrified features. She couldn't save them all but every single one counted.

They weren't all that easy. There were uncaught monsters below, master hackers, jihadis, digital specters. She had seen the silhouettes of their tracks in the data, felt her nose wrinkle involuntarily at the vague scent of their passing, perceived their scat on servers where they had loitered for a time. They lurked in the unlit spaces beneath concealing layers of encryption; behind shifting, dead-end walls of virtual networks leading nowhere. Networks that reconfigured themselves on regimented schedules to avoid mapping. A maze where all the walls and doorways moved, nothing where you left it. These self-disciplined wraiths emerged to strike before evaporating like mist in morning sunlight, leaving only empty air. The apex cadre of the breed vanishing before arrest teams knew they were there, leaving untraceable digital fragments to mark their fleeting presence.

She leaned back to sip her coffee, forcing her shoulders down, scanning the social media postings of several persons of interest, puzzled as always at what she saw. The comforting illusion of connection to the hive mind must stroke something buried very deep inside the human brain. Once available, adoption had been immediate and all but universal. People stood around now in docile little herds, heads bowed, faces lit from below with blue light as they absorbed information that was irrelevant to them, posting things no one cared about.

Ericka joined the Dark-Web Intelligence Unit, DIU for short, when it was formed—a dispersed group embedded in several FBI regional offices, virtually linked and centrally coordinated. When they unearthed a target, the DIU notified and briefed nearby field units or state police on the operation. If the target turned out to be in another country, they created a dossier allowing local police to home in. When it was time for a takedown, a DIU member would often accompany the arrest team, capturing and securing any precious data available on-scene. Many arrests brought them the prize of the target's colleagues from his own computers. They operated in the background behind public-facing teams like Darknet Enforcement.

Ericka looked at her watch, wondering where Tim was with dinner, glaring at his empty desk—unlike hers, which was cluttered and dirty. He was an accomplished analyst in his own right but deferred to her mastery, a brother in spirit if not in blood. Joining the FBI after years in the British GCHQ working counter-intelligence and military support, he was always first through the splintered door. Smiling to herself, Ericka shook her head.

All cops lived for the takedown and it was her uncontrolled response to one that had placed her in her current predicament, suspended from active fieldwork. She shook it off, sipping as she read the morning's intelligence briefings. No one could entirely hide their demons forever, and hers were much more active than most. Too active. Soon it would be time to put the FBI behind her.

It was coming back again. A change subtle at first but it

was there, like coming home from a long camping trip with skin oily and unwashed, clothes writhing. Except it was on the inside and she couldn't wash it off—thoughts like a lingering, bitter taste, coloring her perceptions. She was never going back down that hole again. She caught her reflection on the surface of a darkened monitor, lines of fatigue marring her features. To be expected since she made a point of ignoring almost every lifestyle choice cheerfully promoted by internet health mavens. There was no denying it though, the wear was showing.

The day's intelligence package arrived, chiming for attention, containing the usual collection: jihadi traffic, missing persons, reports of operations underway. She scanned the list—once for her, once for the FBI. Even now, twelve years later, it was her own search that drove her. Her police work was systematic and thorough; as clinical as she could make it, as it had to be to keep her sanity, achieving a success rate beyond any reproach. Her search for the three men who destroyed Patty, her sister, was different—a defining quest.

She glanced down. The final item on the morning's list was highlighted—very unusual—a video of a murder in progress, possibly a snuff film. The apparent origin of the video was somewhere in southern China but depicted a scene the originating analyst thought likely was in the United States. She clenched her teeth, pulling her sweater up around her shoulders, steeling herself. She never got used to it. After the obligatory warning, the instructions asked them to first work their sources and, failing success, scan the metadata against known profiles for entity resolution. This was fancy geek language for trying to use data fragments to identify the human behind the data, the fingers on the keyboard.

Ericka sat straight up as she ran the video. It was real—her recognition instant, seizing her attention, making her shake her head as goose bumps rose on her arms and neck. She stared at the screen, not comprehending. She ran the beginning again, her throat dry, struggling to contain herself. "That's not possible!" Her unintended shout echoed off the far wall. She watched a third time. She had no doubt it was her, the same girl, the same terrified look of abject horror burned into her memory. One she had seen on a dead face with her own eyes, all hope extinguished, welcoming the end, her naked body bloodied and tied.

That greatest of her professional failures was the culmination of months of incessant work, from the first hint of what he was planning, until she'd finally found enough to zero in on him. It was his sharing what first appeared to be nothing more than sick fantasies in a hidden chatroom that had put him in her sights. Soon she'd come to the icy realization that he was very different from his peers. He'd been the one talking logistics of how he might do it, rather than just his fantasies of enjoyment. Planning, not dreaming, down to the clear description of the girl he was watching. A haunting mental picture of an unsuspecting teen, blithely going about a child's business, unaware of the monster's unwavering gaze.

Ericka had driven herself through endless hours of searching, scrutinizing the data for the slightest detail about him. But she'd failed. The bastard had been good enough that, at first, she could only locate him within a ten-square-mile section near Boise, Idaho. She'd alerted local police and moved into position ready to strike at the first hint of his position.

Then he'd slipped. Bragging in the chatroom about the things he was stockpiling for his big day. He'd given away a little too much detail and she'd begun looking for anyone who had rented a rural property within an hour's drive. Too late. When the alert had come up about missing sixteen-year-old Rachel Sutherland, there'd been no doubt. She'd known from the area of her school and home, from the girl's smiling round face and long dark hair, that this was the one he had been stalking.

It was a frenzied search for the GPS tracks of rental cars that gave him up. The error of a man focused on other things, not considering the details of what he was doing, the real-time trail he was leaving. A utility van rented an hour before anyone last saw her. First in motion heading out of town for an hour and fifteen minutes. Then stationary for two hours on a property that looked on satellite maps like some sort of hobby farm, leased just a month before. He had forgotten to use an old vehicle that didn't call home. They'd missed saving her by minutes. Rachel's body had still been warm.

She watched the video again, face close to the screen, shivering hard, her hand trembling. "Christ, there is no way!"

"No way what?" Tim stood by the door, putting down the bag of burgers and fries before tossing his jacket over the back of his chair. "Bloody hell, are you all right? You look horrible." His eyes were wide as he looked at her.

"No, I'm not all right. Watch this!" She yanked the screen in his direction, pulling on his arm, then restarted the video while she stared at his face. He paled, his lips compressing into a thin line. "Recognize anything?" He watched for some time, leaning in, mouth open, shaking his head.

His dark eyes held troubled disbelief as he looked at her. "It looks exactly like her, but it can't be."

Her guts tightened with a stab of anger. He wasn't seeing it. "Look again. In the same room, wearing the same clothes, tied up the same way and bleeding from the same cuts. But do you see the difference?"

He reached for the mouse and rewound a few seconds, playing it again, the tendons in his free hand standing out as he gripped the table. He shook his head. "Even the bastard's arms look the same when they're in the picture. Same shirt. And yes, that's the same room."

"Yes, exactly. Staged exactly the same way, but this is different." She waited, teeth clenched for him to see it, testing her own perception. Recollections of another crime twelve years before flooded her mind. She saw her sister's face again.

He shook his head, pointing at the screen. "It's filmed from different angles and spliced together. Sometimes all we see are his hands, then it switches to wide angle. More than one camera."

She was sweating now, her skin crawling, reliving when they burst into the room. How she'd taken the dangling hand, limp to her touch, like a piece of meat. Rachel's vacant eyes open in a permanent grimace of fear, framed by features still softened with baby fat. Her life was gone, stolen by a monster—all the child's many futures lost. She'd run outside, bent over, gasping for air to hear the sharp reports of a rifle as the arrest team gunned down the suspect in the nearby forest. Almost two years ago now, but so vivid that to dwell on it was to relive it down to the remembered smell of that hellish room, the metallic scent of blood overpowering the miasma of incense.

Tim stood up, his shoulder muscles visibly tense. "Who the hell is shopping this now? He's been dead two years. We have all the video. He didn't live long enough to do anything with it. What the hell? Where did this come from?" He dropped back into a chair, his bulk making it creak in protest.

"It's not the same video." Now she was feeling sick, arriving at the only possible answer, the pain of an old wound torn open. She pressed the thoughts back down, struggling to focus.

He ran his fingers through his close-cropped hair. "Bullshit! It's exactly the same. Everything is the same!"

"No. It's close, just a slightly different perspective, and look at the fisheye effect on the edges. It's different, moving sometimes like it's handheld. I don't think it's even the same format."

"How the hell do you know that just by looking at it?"

"Because I see this in my sleep sometimes, that's how."

He shook his head, staring away at nothing. "He never broadcast it. He wasn't connected while he was filming. He never made it off the property."

"No, he didn't. Correct. Think it through."

She saw the light come on behind cold dark blue eyes, opening wide. "That can't be." His voice was a hoarse whisper as he slumped.

She gripped his wrist, crimson in the margins of her vision. "There was someone else there. We missed one. One of the bastards who did this got away. God, I need a drink."

2

The Scent of a Phantom

But it had never been one drink, always far too many drinks, and so now she slept and drank no more. They had worked well into the night before dragging themselves home for a few hours of sleep. Comfort came from tea now, thick black tea with a generous dollop of milk, so strong the first sips almost burned. A new addiction fostered by the owner of the pale green eyes scouring her thoughts over a steaming mug of the same brew. The eyes of the woman down one floor with whom she shared this morning ritual whenever her schedule allowed it, the formidable Mrs. Margaret Donnelly, Tim's aunt, dressed as always in the morning in a thick housecoat over a flannel nightgown.

They faced each other over the antique table, set with cream, sugar, toast and the old woman's own marmalade, the comforting scent of breakfast blended with the small, potted flowers near the window. The well of strength that had brought her back while she was suspended. The old woman had moved in below Ericka's top-floor condo, helping her fill the days and quickly becoming her confidante and counselor.

Mrs. Donnelly's eyes narrowed as she sipped, the rising sun's glow on the horizon in the window behind her. "So how long are you going to stay on then? I thought you'd decided?" Many found her thick Irish accent hard to decipher.

Ericka stared into her mug before glancing at the oiled oak sideboard. The woman could read minds. "I have, but I do have things to finish."

Mrs. Donnelly lowered her tea, exposing soft features, wrinkled and etched by a lifetime's joy and pain. "There's always a new last one. You weren't meant to do this. It's not in you anymore, girl."

"This is the one from Idaho again. Turns out there were two of them. It's not one I can walk away from."

"None of them are! Christ save me, but we've just finished getting all of the pieces of you stuck back together. There's only so much a person has in them, and you're pretty much all used up. I expect they're still keeping an eye on you."

There was no avoiding it, so Ericka met the probing stare. "They are watching me and I have to go and see that shrink again this week." A shiver accompanied the thought of her suspension while the investigation took its course. A dark time. Now the memories of the incident that spawned it seemed to belong to someone else, not hers at all, more like a recollection of horrifying scenes in a movie, things seen through someone else's eyes. Just the one time she had let it all go. Only her ten years of service and the silence of those close to her had saved her.

The disapproval was palpable. "You're not the only one this has happened to y'know. Listen to what people are telling you."

Ericka nodded, remembering some of the things Tim

had told her about his great-aunt's life in Northern Ireland. A family consumed in a struggle so vicious it would take generations to heal.

She leaned back as the old woman reached out, gripping her hand. "I'm not going back down that hole again. Once I find this one, I'm pulling the pin—finding a job as far away from this as I can. But I'm not giving up on Patty." Her face tingled as she felt her cheeks flush.

That brought a snort of laughter and a wry smile. "I wouldn't expect you to. We Irish know a thing or two about hanging on to our revenge. But you've paid a terrible price looking for yours."

"It not revenge. It's for Patty."

"No, love, she's long gone and she's never coming back. This is just for you." A sharp stab in the guts made her flinch as panic drove a surge of adrenaline. She opened her mouth to answer, but the words wouldn't come. The eyes were looking inside her again. "Did you see what I planted on the east wall of the garden?" Mrs. Donnelly always changed the subject to gardening when she saw Ericka starting to unravel again.

"No, it was dark when I got home." Their rooftop garden was a project the two of them had begun on Ericka's large deck while she was suspended, a distraction from her endless brooding. A rooftop oasis, a garden of shrubs and flowering plants, a harem of silent companions shielding a few chairs and a bench, open to the sky, blocking the sight of other buildings, muffling the urban rumble. A fleeing connection to a world buried now under layers of concrete and pipe. Those who knew her would have been shocked to see her with soil on her fingers, but the dirt Ericka feared was unseen, resisting all efforts to eliminate it.

"A few of those hanging pots planted with small, sweet strawberries. Just what you want with scones an' cream." Ericka pictured her description, squinting as she thought, wondering if the evening light would be enough. She looked up in time to catch Mrs. Donnelly hiding her smile, mission accomplished.

"Thank you." She studied the furrowed topography of the face across the table. "This will be the last one. I promise."

"Don't promise me, promise yourself! Better get shifted if you're going to be there by a respectable hour."

The dark form leaned forward, his face a frozen mask of concentration, the only light in the room spilling from five large screens arranged in a semi-circle around him. The walls were draped in gloom, other bits of furniture mere suggestions in darkness. Sound came from more than a dozen cooling fans in the servers arrayed behind the monitors, accompanied by a lower-pitched hiss as the air conditioning flooded the room with chilled air, offsetting the heat of overworked processors. The complete lack of any smell in the room was attributable to the high-efficiency filters cleaning the incoming air, augmented by oxygen tanks to keep his mental efficiency at its peak.

Satisfied with the scan, he reached to flip down the augmented reality visor perched on his head, projecting him a constant stream of data. He lifted his gloved hand, extending his fingers to toggle controls that weren't there. He paused again as if lost in thought before lifting the visor back up, an audible click confirming it had locked in place. His fingers floated over the keyboard as his head turned to look at the left-most screen. He paused again, eyes scanning line after line of routing information. He reached out and tapped his keyboard. Reliable assets took so long to develop but such a shocking lack of judgment was intolerable, letting go of a one-of-a-kind video. There was simply no choice in the matter—he needed to be dealt with.

Thousands of miles away, a text chimed for attention on Ba Lian Ming's mobile, telling him to open the embedded link in privacy. A member since his youth in the Lóng Zhànshì, or Dragon Warriors, he was now one of the ancient gang's enforcers, descended from so-called triads. The current organization traced its heritage from a secret society predating the People's Republic by hundreds of years. He nodded to his underlings seated around the low table, drained his glass of baijiu and stood up, glancing around the poorly lit room before moving. When a message came from this one it did not pay to wait. Not a member of the gang, he was a valued ally whose information was impeccably accurate and worth every bit of the exorbitant price they paid him. No one had any idea who was behind the steady stream of information he supplied, but experience had shown he was not to be trifled with.

He settled into the driver's seat of his Mercedes, slid on his glasses, checked his men had his back and tapped the link on his car's screen. His eyes scanned the poorly translated message. Certainly not a native speaker but understandable. *And so, Pàngzi Mah, my trusted accountant, what have you done that you have so irritated our formidable associate? So much so that he went to the trouble of detailing your sins line by line, irrefutable proof you have been hiding profits not yours, perhaps the only unforgivable act for which there was just one response?* Mah would not survive the night, nor his family if they failed to pay back the money plus a substantial interest penalty. Rules were there for a reason after all. He would need to be questioned first, but as the saying went: 'True gold does not fear the furnace.'

Maybe they could find out what brought about the message that triggered his demise. He deleted the link and gestured to the closest of his men, repressing a shudder, wondering if any of his own secrets were safe. He scanned the area behind his men one more time before pressing the button to roll down his window.

"There they are, behind the others. Hold me steady!" Tim's hands grasped Ericka's narrow waist, his grip like a vise, holding her trim physique steady. Her toes balanced on a lower shelf, she leaned forward, coughing at the dust as she dragged the three boxes across the shelf towards her. She handed them down to Tim who dumped them on the exhibit room's table. A knife appeared in his hand, and he sawed through the sealing tape, popping the boxes open as he did. They were alone in the musty-smelling room used to store evidence and exhibits from cases long closed. Like all such rooms, it was below ground level, a largely unused corner of the station, always with only one armored door controlling access. Endless rows of boxes haunted the room with the restless ghosts of a thousand crimes. Signing out the keys was always an ordeal.

He glanced back at her over a broad shoulder. Tim's physique was hard as if carved from wood, the kind that caused lingering stares in the gym, envious and interested both. "I think these are it." He glanced at the printout in his hand, peering for a moment at the boxes, then nodded to her. "Just these three." His voice echoed from bare cinderblock walls behind the table.

She sighed as she began rooting through the bagged exhibits, some still showing dark spots of dried blood through the clouded plastic of the bags. Leaning over the box closest to Tim, she scowled. "We did look in that gaming console, right? I don't remember imaging it." Gaming equipment was often a surprisingly good source of evidence about the people who used them.

"We did—nothing on it but a few messages from kids. This thing wasn't connected to his camera. He had that hardwired to his computer. Remember?"

"Grab it for me. I'm going to image it again." Tim shrugged and set it aside. "Anything else in there?"

He leaned over to peer in. "Just the controllers and a pair of busted VR goggles like you predicted." He lifted them out and handed them to her, one brow raised. "Didn't the locals clear this scene? How did you know they'd be here? I don't remember seeing them."

Ericka cocked an eyebrow at him then reached in, pulling an exhibit bag from the bottom of the box, dangling it at eye level, squinting against the dim lighting. The handwritten label read 'plastic fragments scattered on floor near gaming station.' She held the bags with the plastic shards and the goggles side by side. "Looks the same to me. Must have been broken since the last time the floor was swept and this guy was pretty meticulous if I remember right."

"So? How did you know?"

"Part of the second video was filmed using a VR protocol,

though processed in a way I've never seen before. I'm thinking these're what our phantom was wearing. Smashed them on his way out. Right under our noses."

He held the bag close to his face, squinting at the contents. "Looks like it has a camera built in. No logo on it though. Maybe some sort of knockoff?"

Ericka shrugged, focused on her theory. "Let's think this through. The camera on the tripod was connected to a stand-alone computer. I remember he had even gone as far as to take out the network card. No way to broadcast it. I think the new one was filmed using either those goggles or something like them, streamed out through the gaming box and recorded somewhere else."

"Sure, but how the hell did the second guy get out? We had the place buttoned up tight."

"We need another look, I'm thinking."

"Looking for what? Some sort of bolt-hole?"

"Maybe, or just a fresh look."

Tim gave her a small, mocking bow, shaking his head. "I'll get us sorted. Do we have to take this upstairs at this point?"

She had no desire to spend a day writing a briefing memo for suits on the top floor just yet. "Let's see what we find first."

"When do you want to go?"

"Now."

Tangled, dirty-looking brush from several summers past narrowed the overgrown driveway. Grown now so that they touched over the gravel road, the trees bare with winter's approach, gnarled branches sounding a rattlesnake's warning as they brushed together. The forlorn way up to the old house disappeared into a lifeless brown tunnel of dormant vegetation, oppressive, as if the land itself bore the pain of what had happened here. Tim undid the chains holding the gate shut and got back into the passenger side of their rented car. They'd flown out that morning on a commercial flight. He glanced sideways at Ericka's pale, drawn face.

"You okay?"

She wasn't and blurted it out. "What is it about these places? Like the crime alters it forever. Know what I mean?" She swallowed, her throat dry at the thought of seeing the place again. A place that would haunt her always, a reminder of the failure of being minutes late, the memory of state troopers thundering up this very driveway, trucks throwing plumes of dust as the FBI helicopter overtook them, roaring over the trees. Too late, the remembrance of the child's empty features a monument to her failure. If there had been another responsible for this horror, there could be no rest until she found him. The eyes of restless victims brooded on her every move, judging her. Her new career and life would have to wait and the irony was not lost on her. The gut-level compulsion that drove her to work these cases until solved created the wear and tear that was taking her apart. She just wasn't wired to let any of it go.

Tim's voice snapped her out of her recriminations. "Either that or you're nuts. Could be either."

She suppressed the urge to laugh, flipped him her middle finger and drove through the gate, dried twigs and gravel crunching under the tires. "You know damn well what I mean. It's been two years and they still haven't managed to sell this place."

"Maybe there isn't much demand for out-of-the-way

shitholes used to commit a child murder. And you should have better manners when you're counting on me not to rat you out for violating your fieldwork ban." He grinned at her with the genuine affection of a sibling.

The road curved to the left, entering a field, overgrown except where patches of early snow speckled the brown grasses. The house nested against the forest at the far end, well built, updated by the owner years before the killer rented it. Now, the paint was fading, flaking in places. The leaves and branches of the autumn before filled the gutters, as if the horrors inside had driven all life from the home, leaving it a dried husk. She tried to shake it and focus on why they were there. "What did the real estate guy say about the stuff?"

Tim stretched, glancing at his holster as they slowed in front of the porch. "Mostly he moaned about what a waste of money it was and how he was never going to sell this place. And that everything the state troopers left behind is boxed up in the barn."

"We'll look at that later. We've got to know how the second one got out. Got the keys?"

Their footsteps drummed on the wooden deck. Inside it was as she remembered except now there was a stale, musty odor. All the furniture was gone and the low sun projected bleak, window-shaped patterns on the oak floor. As they walked, dust swirled in the sunlight, marking their passing. Tim opened the creaking door to the basement and gazed at her, one eyebrow raised. She nodded, and they started down. The room was empty now, but her mind filled in the details, recreating the nightmare, forcing her eyes shut against the sudden rush of nausea.

Tim stared at the hallway to the outside cellar entrance.

"Front door, back door, and basement door, each had a trooper scoping for anything that moved."

"The victim was dead, the suspect was dead, not a lot of motive to do a detailed search of a torture chamber when there isn't going to be a trial." Ericka kicked at some of the panels below the wainscoting, listening for any hollow spaces. "Unless it's customary to build secret tunnels out here, we have to presume he went out a door." She stood where the killing table once rested, squeezing her eyes tight for a moment to clear the memory from her mind: the girl's dead eyes staring at the ceiling. She could swear the faint scent of incense still hung in the stale air. Smell could trigger the strongest memories and the house brought a twinge of nausea and guilt each time she sensed it.

Tim was staring at her with what she interpreted as a controlled, neutral expression. *He's watching for the pieces to start falling off again. Thanks, brother.* He shook his head. "No way. We missed this by minutes. He stayed inside long enough to film the whole thing. No way our phantom got out without being seen."

"Unless he changed into his SWAT outfit." Ericka scanned the room while Tim gave her a look, one eyebrow raised. "Let's go look in the barn."

The barn had no electricity, the only light creeping through open doors from the sun now sinking into the treetops. At the field's edge, the bleak forest contemplated its secrets, giving her a sense of foreboding and loss. She had to dig deep to shake it off and turned to the inside of the building. A small pile of boxes lay behind the stacks of furniture. Lying on the ground behind them was a satellite dish.

"What are you hoping for?"

"I'm hoping the satellite box is still here. Some of them have pretty decent-sized RAM and storage. Now that we're pretty sure phantom boy streamed it out through the gaming console, I want to see what's left for routing information." Ericka bent over to peer into the first box. "Here we go, right on the top." She snatched her prize up to catch the light, peering at the specs label. "Lots of memory. This will be worth looking at. If we can't figure out how he got out, we can try and follow the trail where he sent the video."

Tim stared up at a ceiling vent. "The only thing I can think of is some sort of bolt-hole around here where the second one could slide past the containment team."

Ericka pried the back off of the satellite box with a screwdriver, half listening. "Just to be sure, why don't you ask the local sheriff if they have any ground-penetrating radar rigs or something like it."

"Tunnels?"

"Or any spaces where someone could have hidden long enough to wait for his moment."

"Worth a try, but you know there's nothing."

She shrugged her answer, knowing he was right. "Let's load this stuff up and get out of here. I don't want to stay here after dark."

3

Threads of the Web

Tim walked into the forensics lab, sighed, and tossed the sheriff's report onto the table beside Ericka. The lab was one floor up from their work area with gleaming white walls, and dry, filtered, chemical-smelling air. LED lighting reflected off sterile workbenches, while retractable vent hoods hung from above. Worn stools and chairs were arranged haphazardly around the room. "Nothing. No space in there big enough to hide a white rabbit, no bottomless holes in the garden. We did the whole thing twice. What the hell's that?" He nodded at the small globe sitting in its exhibit bag next to the equipment they had taken from the house. The silvered orb, smaller than a golf ball, mounted on a square, black base.

"One of the smallest three-sixty VR cameras I've ever seen, though the final video was rendered as a flat image." Ericka glanced up from her screen. She wore a stained white lab coat, latex gloves lying next to her keyboard. "Never seen one before?"

He shook his head, bending over to peer at it. "Just the

kind nutters use to make Red Bull videos. You think our phantom used it?"

"I think he was watching both through it, then the goggles when he wanted POV."

His head snapped up to look at her. "So now you think he was never there?"

"It's beginning to look that way." Engulfed in the horror of the girl's body, she hadn't thought through the scene at the time. She idly turned the bag holding the camera as if doing so would reveal the identity of the watcher. She fancied her chances of figuring out where the signal went more than tracking a person's physical movements this far down the road. Rain washes away footprints and blood, but the internet is forever.

Tim furrowed his brow. "You think the killer himself was selling the show?"

She shook her empty coffee mug, sighing. "Remember the guy we took down had a closed circuit, just a camera and a stand-alone computer. Probably for his own use. I think the clean-up team missed the real broadcast link."

"No way! How?"

"Sure, they could. Look at this." Her fingertips rolled the ball of her mouse until she found the picture she wanted. "See it?"

On her screen was one of the crime-scene photos taken just after the coroner left, showing the tiny camera in the background. Tim leaned in, squinting wrinkles onto his rugged features.

"It's sitting on the bench to the side. The clean-up team of locals probably didn't recognize it. Can't blame them—we didn't notice it there. It looks more like an ornament than a camera. As I thought, it was piping wireless to the gaming console, which was wireless to the satellite box, which got it out to the target audience. The fact that the second video took this long to surface makes me think the audience might have been pretty small, maybe just one. There was never any indication there would be a broadcast in the initial evidence that led us there."

He shook his head. "How? We looked on the console and there was no trace of video in the buffer."

Ericka leaned back and stared at him. Discarded data remained and could be recovered until the device needed the space and overwrote it, so it was always the first place she checked. "No but there was a ton of VPN and encryption fragments, though not a kind I've ever seen before, but it's what they are. And there was a modified dark web browser on the satellite box. Run-of-the-mill pervert software."

"This guy was that techy?"

"And wealthy—this stuff isn't cheap. I had the state troopers look at his probate. Turns out he had a fair stack of crypto-coins in a brokerage that no one tried to source. He was a teacher's aide and the school board doesn't pay in crypto. Our phantom may have sent him the equipment." Ericka turned back to her computer, wondering what kind of target they were dealing with now, and what he might have been up to in the two years since.

"Why do you think that? Our guy had receipts for lots of the stuff."

"If I wanted in on something horrible like this, it's one of the ways I'd do it. Send him the equipment and a link. It self-executes and installs. When the show's over it mostly overwrites itself leaving just a few bits of junk data. If he'd had time, he might have destroyed the equipment, getting rid of any possible connection to the phantom."

Tim's face flushed as he stared towards the tiny window, the light of the setting sun streamed in, lighting up dust motes tumbling in the air. "So, we got the dog, but the master is still out there?"

"Looks that way to me."

"Enough left behind to profile him at all?"

Ericka sighed. This was going to take a while. "Not even close. Whatever he left on it to do the data-cleaning did nine overwrites and got almost everything. He's good."

"Now what?"

"We try to find out if he's done this before or since. Assume to start, he'll stay in profile. If we can find others, maybe the combined crime scenes will let us build something. You look through the cases for similar crimes; I'll root through the bits he left here."

"Do your magic," he said to the back of her head. She barely heard him, focused on the hunt, closing out everything else, concentration clearing her mind of brooding thoughts.

Magic would be a better way than the real one. Dark web investigations had few eureka moments—just a lot of detailed slogging. The whole purpose behind these networks was to hide who was using them; like hunting in a dark forest with nothing but a headlamp. No usernames, no profile pics. The name of the game was to leave nothing that leads to the surface web or real world. No IP address to follow, just a dark web browser and layers of encryption leaving a trail of fleeting breadcrumbs into the underbrush. It was not what these traces told you individually, but what the collection said together when you piled them up. Even a basic digital portrait was a starting point.

First, she would identify what kinds of software he was using, his brand of VPN, his choice of browser and their settings combined with his choice of encryption technology. Add to that any settings or digital fingerprints he left behind showing kinds of hardware he might have used. The dark web used the same architecture as the surface web, you just had to be able to distinguish the pathogens in the sea of data coursing through the day-to-day bloodstream of the global network.

Ericka pushed her mouse around its pad, glancing around her workstation for something to eat. She stood to stretch, noting the sun was almost down before beginning to pace. Peering towards the door to ensure she was alone, she stopped to root through Tim's desk and pirate a pair of granola bars from his bottom drawer. She munched on a bar without tasting it as she settled back into her chair.

It could be as little as recognizing a line of code from encryption software or VPN system. It might be embedded fragments of file names, or bits of routing data, even the font or screen settings of the device. Each meaningless on its own, but if you combined enough of them, it formed a fuzzy profile of sorts, like a cartoonish police artist's sketch of a previous generation. An impressionist's vision of what the subject might look like. If the same combination turned up in another place, it might be the same person and that was the starting point. If the same profile matched up with one on the clear web, the hunt became very focused. In the end, she needed to look into the mind, habits, and interests of the suspect; the digital trail was just the starting point.

Ericka sighed at her screen as the analyzer parsed the data fragments from the gaming console and satellite box, then smiled as the results appeared. Consistent on both and some on the camera too. An off-the-shelf browser the same as every other aspiring script kiddie on the web. Nothing on its own, every hairy-necked wannabe in his mother's basement had one. Standard VPN software set to bounce all signals through server farms in both China and Pakistan. Then something much more valuable: the encryption software was different. She leaned forward nodding, her brow furrowed as she scanned the lines of code. Either something commercial she had never seen before or something maybe he wrote himself, a distinct piece to look for.

The profile could be a match for any number of dark web denizens, but it narrowed the pool. The trick was to surface them, like an old-time naval battle. The captain of the destroyer—knowing the sub lurks below—lobs depth charges into the sea, trying to get it to move and reveal its location. Like the explosive spout of a surfacing whale, it would signal to the man on the harpoon that the quarry was in range. Most often, the technique was to work backward from the physical world. Guns had to move from van to van in a darkened parking lot. Trafficked illegals had to get to the new brothel. Money had to change hands. Then the man behind the keyboard or his lackey stood revealed.

She chewed her lip knowing perfectly well that was not going to work with this one. If he wanted part of the physical crime, he'd have been there. Whatever he wanted from this, he got it from the comfort of his chair. But if being there didn't interest him, why didn't he just watch videos? It wasn't like the internet was short on cruel, violent porn. Was he directing the guy on the ground minute by minute, or did he just get his kicks from seeing it in real time?

The FBI had several units of profilers, but Ericka had little use for them. People were different on the web, feeling free to do and say things they would never dare in the living world. Shrinks built profiles based on the study of psychology in the real world, the virtual was different. Free of culture's civilizing restraints, unimpeded by the cowardice that normally bid them hold their tongues, hidden behind a handle in the safety of their basement, and anything goes. The web substituted anonymity for restraint, and camouflage for courage. Looking at how people acted on the web said little about what they might look like on the surface.

Ericka chewed on a second bar, this one hard and dry. She had begged off morning tea that day, not keen on the lecture she'd receive for her exhausted appearance. She had sat for hours, muscles tense and stiff, her eyes sore and dry from endless concentration on her screen. No simple search was going to narrow it down here. His apparent disinterest in the real world would make it very difficult to get the rat to stick his head out the hole, if he had left tracks at all. If he wanted to watch something, the broadcasting computer at the crime scene had to send it somewhere, however encrypted and circuitous the data's eventual journey. That was her only shot.

Looking for her quarry's software profile alone would go nowhere. Time to release the hounds to do their work, or crawlers more accurately. Crawlers and spiderbots—software that scoured the internet making copies of whatever you told them to find. Commercial search engines used them to create a massive index of the web to speed up searching, the better to send customers a quick answer to their search with a heavy side of targeted advertising. Hackers used them to crawl the web, harvesting email addresses and seeking open personal information for spam attacks and identity theft.

Hers were different, creeping over the web's servers, copying every match for the profile fragments she fed it. Unlike commercial crawlers, hers kept their searches small and targeted to avoid tripping alarms. Using the digital equivalent of a rock-filled can suspended by a string between trees, some targets left traps alerting them to someone else's interest. Compounding that, much of the dark web was set to reconfigure itself at carefully prescribed intervals, so a successful crawl today did not permit access even a short time later. Like a ground search where you were given a new map every hour and everything had moved.

But that did not matter to Ericka. All she needed to know was whether someone with her phantom's profile had been there and not waste time trying to enter encrypted spaces. Footprints going in and out of the door were enough. She could kick the door down later if she needed.

As her program worked, it would place its hits on a map and every set of traces configured like her target would soon display, appearing random at first. Clusters would occur on servers where traffic was frequent. This would give her some hint of the locations of things of interest to him. Next, she would overlay the locations of carefully chosen similar offenses in the past three years and look for matches. Her last step would be to draw a geographic circle around each possible offense and search nearby servers. This time not just for tracks, but for social media and web traffic that might be her target getting sloppy. Anywhere she found both her cluster of traces and a crime could be a match. If the same hit also included social media or other personal traces at more than one location, she had a firm target.

The hounds bayed their find to the hunter and the chase was on. But sometimes the hounds tipped off the quarry, which took to its heels at the first sign of danger, going to ground, sometimes never to emerge again. Occasionally they returned with a fresh, new profile. Some days you eat the bear and some days the bear eats you.

She finished the coding, setting it for a slow methodical crawl that would not trip any software he might have watching his back. The hunt was on. She sat back and put her feet up, looking out the window into the dark. One last time, the hunt was on.

4

Disciples of a Wraith

The small box on his doorstep was plain, bearing no writing, no name, no addresses, neither his nor return. It had been a slow drive home from the airport, and before that a protracted day in the hangar hunching over his computer, updating and debugging the entertainment software of the gleaming airliner behind him. Mechanics swarmed over the jet, running the immense list of maintenance items needed to recertify the bird for flight in a three-day turnaround. In nine short hours, he would be back for another day.

He turned to look over his shoulder, scanning his neighbors' doors and windows before letting himself in. No one was there. Stepping inside, he toggled through his security video until he caught a flash of movement. A man in jeans with a hoodie pulled tight around his face, tossing the box onto his step just after lunch, disappearing out of view in seconds.

As he was unmarried with few friends, his colleagues accounted him a loner and a bit odd. Harmless enough they thought, but they were wrong. Despite his almost privileged upbringing and keen intellect, Richard Schmidt had a very unfortunate, compulsive attraction to children. One he barely contained. A secret he had told no one his entire thirty-seven years. One he preserved by having almost no physical contact with the world except for work and daily necessities. He was tall, strong-featured, now starting on a belly, his short dark hair standing up like a scrub brush. Glancing back at the door, he tossed his coat on a peg. His clothes stank of jet fuel and sweat but a shower would have to wait. His last few nights had been sleepless hours of guilt and fear, waiting for this to arrive.

He unlocked the heavy door to the stairs, slid the steel bolts shut behind him and walked down, sitting at his basement desk. He pressed the power button on his special computer, the one he had built himself from separately sourced components. It booted up from an encrypted thumb drive containing a clean copy of Linux, loading only his VPN credentials and a stripped, dark web browser. A computer which, by design, had no hard drive and a selected motherboard to ensure it was incapable of storing anything incriminating. It stored no data at all.

The terrible videos and recordings he acquired and savored, some he'd made himself on his two Thailand vacations, he stored in encrypted servers far away from any cop who cared about such things. These he watched, pleasuring himself to the sight of something he had rarely done or seen in the physical world. Each time he walked away from his computer sated but nauseous, leaving nothing that would tell a forensic examiner what he had done. Not a trace. In the desk drawer was a Glock 9mm pistol. If they ever did find him, he was never going to jail.

While his system booted, he cut open the box that the message had told him to expect, gingerly lifting out the VR headset and tiny thumb drive taped to the cardboard inside. He picked at his nails for a time before inserting the thumb drive into a slot. His eyes widened as multiple scripts ran, installing software and changing settings. In his eleven years as a software engineer, he had never seen anything like it. When it finished, he picked up the goggles, matte black and featureless, turning them over inches from his face. Sweating now, he pulled them on, the visor eclipsing all outside light, the earphones dimming the sounds of the furnace behind him. Swallowing hard, he touched the switch on the right side and sat back.

For several minutes, nothing happened. He pulled the goggles off confused, again holding them close to his face. Two green LEDs glowed to life. He tugged them back on, turning his head to look from side to side, grinning as he did. He was in a large virtual hall, Gothic stone arches flowing from the tops of columns on both sides, disappearing into the ceiling's gloom. Polished white marble covered the floor, gleaming as if wet in the dim, flickering light. Ahead of him on both sides, sputtering torches backlit the naked silhouette of an enormous, hugely muscled figure standing so close he had to look up towards the dark face. He swallowed hard, wishing he could take a step back from the giant. The only sound was the faint hiss of the torches.

"This is very nice! Do it yourself? I know gamers who'd kill for this kind of resolution in VR." His voice cracked despite his efforts, his fear obvious. "The torches are especially well done!" Despite knowing it was an illusion, he had to fight the trembling in his hands.

"I find it a suitable place to meet for the first time." The voice was deep, almost melodical, echoing from the walls. "I may have much more to show you later, depending on what we agree today."

Schmidt's tone was accusatory, his stomach knotted from days of fear. "Well, you have my undivided attention. That's a good gig, getting people to watch the stuff you're peddling and then threatening to light them up." Included with the invitation days before was a server schematic of every single place he had ever hidden his treasured videos. Clearly, they'd been mapped and copied so it would make no difference if he erased or moved them now.

The huge head tilted down, features shadowed, just the outline of the hairless scalp visible. "I threaten no one. And I gave you more of what you sought, some of which you would have never seen without me. Why do you question my motives? I saw what you wanted and gave it to you."

Schmidt gritted his teeth, but his voice was toneless and controlled. He needed answers but provoking this one could end him. "Sure, and then made it absolutely clear you know who I really am and pretty much everything I've done in the dark. Enough to put me away for decades. How much do you want?"

"I am not going to expose you. I merely wish you to know how thoroughly I have seen who you really are. How completely I understand your needs. I do not want your money, only to help you find your way. Guide you on the path you were born to through no fault of your own."

His shoulders lost some of their tension, relief flooding him, almost like the absolution of the confessional. In the real world, sweat trickled down his neck, making him writhe.

"Kind of like a perverted Robin Hood you mean? Steal from the rich to finance giving happiness to the pedos?"

"If you wish." The deep vibrato carried a hint of amusement. "Here we are not bound by the rules made by people who are not like us for a world that does not accept us, where we will never be welcomed. Here, there is no shame, no fear."

He adjusted the headset, taking a deep breath. "And what do you want in return?"

There was a moment's pause. "Merely your allegiance. I will help you down your path and supply you for your journey. You are not the first seeking fulfilment. I have helped many. One day, I may ask you to help me accomplish something in the physical world. In the meantime, merely enjoy becoming what you were meant to be. Accept it. Delight in the pleasures available to you. I will send you the same gifts as before and we will speak again soon."

The figure turned sideways for a moment and began walking away down the great hall fading into deepening gloom. The half-glimpsed profile was one of exaggerated beauty, the receding form rippled with toned, perfect muscles, skin gleaming as if oiled.

"Aren't you going to tell me who you are? A handle?" Schmidt called after the receding form, impressed to note the echo the VR environment added to the matrix.

Without slowing, the huge head turned and spoke over a hulking shoulder. "My name is Dantalion."

5

Footsteps of a Shadow

"Your crawler's got something." Tim perched on the edge of her table as she walked through the door. He looked disheveled, his eyes red and sore.

"Knew it would." She tossed her dripping coat at a hook on the wall while giving him a sour look. Rain pounded on the windows, pouring off the trees edging the parking lot. Tim's appearance was familiar to her. "Lots of hits?"

"Loads of server footprints—hundreds and hundreds— and no associated crimes. Perhaps our case was his first time out?"

"Could be but given how this bastard gets his kicks I'd rather not be sitting here waiting for him to set something else up if we can help it. Nothing at all?" Ericka leaned on her desk, peering over her glasses at the screen. Rolling her mouse ball she zoomed out from the map, shaking her head. "No big geographic clusters. Looks like we're tracking at least a couple of hundred guys with similar profiles. Good stuff they're using, touching pretty much every server available. Ones we'll never be able to get at."

"What search terms did you use for the crimes?"

She sighed, turning to look at him. "They were pretty tight: female victim, fourteen to thirty-five, sadism, sexual assault, confinement. Let's broaden them up a little and see what happens. I'll expand to include males and lose the age restrictions."

Tim shrugged and leaned back while she typed. "Maybe he does a clean profile every time he does something likely to light him up."

"I hope he's not that careful." She stared at her screen for several minutes, clenching her teeth. "And nothing anywhere in the country. Damn!" She pursed her lips, thinking. Guys like this usually avoid physically crossing borders where there'll be a record of their movement from customs or the airline. This one wants some kind of virtual presence, so operating in more than one country at a time isn't going to faze him. She expanded the geographical parameters to the whole globe.

"Right, there we go—four hits, including our case." Tim slipped off her table, pulling a chair up close to the desk next to her where she could smell sweat and some sort of horrible, drugstore perfume.

She glared at him in disgust. "You know what, maybe you need to shower off companion-of-the-week before coming to work in the morning. What would your Aunt Margaret say?"

He looked back expressionless, then grinned, laughing at the implied threat. "So I should. Sorry. I ended up closer to work than home last night."

She rolled her eyes, turning back to her computer. Ours, one in Croatia, one in India and one in Canada. She drew a circle around the Canadian hit, expanding the detail. After reading for a moment she turned to Tim. "That's an exact match for the software profile. More importantly, the bulk of the traffic is before the date of the offense. Almost nothing after. This is worth looking at." She clicked on the offense details, her eyebrows rising in surprise. "Okay, maybe this isn't him. A Catholic priest helping himself to his flock for a bit of enforced S&M wearing a devil mask. The victims are alive. It only picked it up on my search terms because he tied them up while he did it."

"What are the other two?"

Ericka read the summaries. "India is an apparent gang rape and Croatia is another priest, this time attending a convent without invitation. The summaries don't say anything about video or broadcasting, but we have the same pattern in the web traffic. Sporadic at first, then intense near the offense date, then nothing."

"A man of eclectic tastes if it's one guy. I'm not seeing an offender profile there at first glance."

Profiles are mostly based on what they like to do physically, not watch—sadists in particular she thought. "What if this is a serial guy?"

Tim looked at her, his brow knotted. "Serial what though? Funny way to conduct the business of being a predator. Omnivorous tastes but only likes to watch."

"No, no one's going to all this effort just to watch." If that's all he wanted, he would just look for videos and be dead safe. To watch in real time and maybe direct the action, he had to expose himself by communicating in advance and arranging for the right equipment to be on site. She thought for a moment, looking for any more behavioral commonalities.

Restrained victims, sadistic violence, but wide geographic dispersion. "The problem of finding a remote guy using this method is we're not seeing the whole picture. We're not seeing unsuccessful attempts he may have made and we're not seeing the successful crimes that aren't reported."

"Nor are we ever going to. Not following you?"

"So maybe we can see some of them. Basically, when we started this we were looking at a lot of footprints made by people wearing the same shoes as our guy. Just for the sake of argument, let's treat these four as if they were confirmed to be our target."

Tim nodded. "Go ahead."

"In each case we see not just a stack of footprints; we also see a chronological pattern of escalating web traffic with a sudden hard stop when the crime is over. Gimme a few minutes while I think how to search for that." He shrugged and leaned back to play with his phone, smirking at something he was reading. "While you're at that, tell her to spend a little more money on scent." He flipped her his middle finger without looking up. "Did you have any luck tracing down the source of the Idaho video?"

He shook his head, still gazing at his mobile. "The initial location of transmission was public Wi-Fi in a nightclub in Macao. From there it was shopped around a bit before our surveillance team picked it up. The club is a known gang place—we're not getting any help there."

Ericka pecked away at her console for some time, coding the search engine to scan for temporal clustering, with an escalating traffic pattern. A pattern she thought someone might produce in the lead-up to a crime planned from a distance, followed by an intense burst of traffic while it was underway. She scanned the lines of code one last time and executed, sending the search engine to probe the large group of possible hits from the original crawler results. She looked around, surprised she had not heard Tim leave.

6

Fragments of the Mind's Eye

The scanning software chimed for attention. Twenty-nine hits this time searching for temporal clustering with the same pattern as the first four. Pleased with the consistency, Ericka texted Tim. *Got something. Come back.*

Twenty minutes later he walked through the door eyebrows raised. "So?" She gestured with her chin at the screen. His brows rose in surprise and he turned to nod his congratulations. "Oh, very good—that's a pretty tight pattern. Think you can locate him?"

She shook her head, lips pressed together. "No way with just this. Way too well hidden. But it does give us a much broader pattern of what he's interested in." The man began to materialize from behind the data.

Tim leaned back to look at her. "But no more crime scene matches?"

"No, these ones could be attempts, crimes that didn't get reported or just something else he is devoting attention to that our search terms didn't catch. Doesn't get us the guy but makes me pretty sure it is actually a guy and not a random collection of things done by more than one person."

"Pretty busy boy and looks like he's active all over the world."

Ericka nodded, pleased her partner had spotted the same thing that had been needling her since she first looked at the data. "A really clever fellow, committing crimes through the dark web, would want to be careful to only commit one or two per country. Police everywhere are just like us, focus only on what's in their jurisdiction. No one will ever spot the pattern unless they do something like we did here. If you only worry about your own jurisdiction, everything he does looks like a one-off by a local." She nodded towards her screen.

"If it is a pattern, this is a good start, but it isn't going to convince anyone as it stands. There's still a chance this is just random."

"It isn't random!" Ericka's voice rose with irritation. She forced her shoulders to relax and took a deep breath.

"Cool off. It's not me wants convincing, but we're going to need more to take this any further, and you're going to need to dial down the heat. You're going to need to be ice-cold to get your hooks into this one."

She took another deep breath, letting it out as a long sigh, exasperated that he was right. "We need to get more intel from one of the four known crime scenes. Then get authorization for some real-time monitoring so we can get ahead of him." She looked at him, one eyebrow raised. "We can't get it from here."

"You can't get it from anywhere else. You're grounded, remember?"

"You're not. This guy's a killer. Can you live with another dead kid if we could've stopped it?"

Tim folded his arms and shook his head. "I know it's been a while since I mentioned it, maybe a minute or so, but didn't I suggest dialing down the angst a bit? No one is going to authorize international travel based on what we've got."

She knew he was right and sat back, sighing her exasperation. "You ever heard of this place in Canada? Whitecourt?"

"No, why?"

"I bet it's hunting season up there right now. You have any vacation left? You like venison?"

"I do like venison, and you're going to get sacked if we get caught."

She caught his eye. "The company shrink told me to take all my vacation. I'm just being a team player." Knowing this was her last one was very liberating. What the hell were they going to do to her?

Ericka caught Tim leaning in to stare at the GPS for the fourth time in the last thirty minutes. "Why don't you just keep still and ask me if we're there yet every five minutes like any other six-year-old?" She shoved him back into the passenger side of the rented SUV. As always, she drove, unable to stomach Tim's indifference to speed limits and road conditions.

"This is taking a lot longer than a hundred and thirty miles should." He sounded bored, leaning back before looking at the nav screen again. "I wonder if they've ever thought of marketing those as a marriage-saving device. It's like a woman who can read a map but doesn't mind getting shouted at when it's wrong."

Ericka refused to take the bait. "The church is on this side of town. I need to give it a look. Once we're done, we can head in. I'm sure there will be seedy bars and plenty of bored local talent just waiting for you to buy them a drink. An untouched harem who've never heard your black ops stories."

Early snow blanketed both sides of the divided highway through which spindly, leafless trees and thick brush protruded. Low, barbed wire fences leaned towards the road. The sky was a uniform grey, drizzling the occasional wet snowflake on the windshield, while the road gleamed where tire-polished ice reflected oncoming headlights. Almost alone on the road, they passed through rolling country already slumbering for the long winter.

The church was visible from the highway as they neared the edge of Whitecourt, its wooden steeple set back into a stand of meager trees. Ericka eased the car into the driveway, tires cutting grooves through untouched snow. Peeling white paint revealed bare weathered wood, framing boarded-up windows. Nailed planks held the main doors shut, while a tattered sign pointed potential worshipers to another church on the other side of town. They walked around the back to the priest's residence, forced to lift their feet in the deepening snow.

The flakes began falling in earnest, settling on Tim's toque, beard, and jacket. He looked at the forlorn structure with obvious distaste. "So, always nice to have a sniff around the scene, but what do you expect to see from the outside?"

Ericka smiled, pleased at what she was seeing, looking up under the eaves of the small house. "That's a good start. Recognize the brand?" Bolted to the siding was a filthy satellite dish, hanging precariously where the mounting screws had torn from rotting wood.

Tim shook his head. "Right, him and thousands of others, so?"

"Why would you bother with this rig, when the town has cable access?" She pointed at a nearby utility pole where an obvious line drooped past the ramshackle building.

"Good point. Are we breaking in or going into town to talk to the locals?"

She shivered in the cold, pulling up her parka's hood, knowing he would be game to do it. "I can't imagine there is anything left in there to look at. Here's the address." She held out her phone showing the location of the Whitecourt detachment of the Royal Canadian Mounted Police.

"Real FBI vacationing in my little town? And hunting season closed last week, by the way. What can I do for you?" The thick French-Canadian accent suited the gruff, heavy-set sergeant. He stood and leaned forward over his desk, extending a meaty, calloused hand to each of them, before gesturing towards the chairs. He smiled with what Ericka thought was genuine warmth, his eyes wrinkling as he did so, likely pleased at the distraction from his everyday routine. Sgt. Marc Thibault, NCO, in charge of the local detachment sat heavily, looking from one to the other. His large mustache and stubbly chin gave him a walrus-like appearance as he folded his hands in front of him on an oak desk that had seen many generations of use. The credenza behind him bore stacks of manila folders from a former time, the tiny laptop on one side of the desk a singular hint they were in the correct century. On the wall behind him, a pair of long service plaques bracketed a crooked picture of the Queen.

Ericka warmed her hands on the battered coffee mug she'd been offered and smiled back, feeling like she was beginning to thaw. "Well, this isn't an official visit, but there is actually something besides the balmy climate that brings us here." Thibault raised his eyebrows, still smiling. "We're curious about what happened at that little church on the east side of town. We stopped to have a look on the way in."

Thibault's heavy brows fell, darkening his features. The smile vanished. "Terrible business that. I been here eleven years and nothing like that ever happen before. Here, mostly it is oil workers come blow off steam and often they need a night in the bucket to cool off. Bit of drugs with the usual petty theft and break-ins. Nice quiet place other than that. If something serious happen, they send people from division in Edmonton. Like what happen here."

Ericka looked at Tim. "We may need to drop in there and pay our respects when we fly out." She turned back to the waiting officer. "We think your priest may have been connected to someone else we're looking for. Mostly we're hoping to have a look at anything he had on his computers."

Thibault pursed his lips, looking puzzled. "He didn't own any. This kind of thing is hardly unusual for Catholic priests. What really bring you here?"

Ericka nodded. The sergeant was no buffoon. Under the genial exterior, the quick mind honed by years of experience was obvious. "The summary we read made it sound a little more ritualistic than usual, but you're right." Ericka explained the profile traces. "Any gaming consoles?"

The sergeant pursed his lips. "Before I transfer here, I work on sex crimes near Vancouver. Now I keep an eye out all the time. And no, all he had was a phone and it was clean. One of the teenage boys have a game console. It was there when we arrest, but the boy say it was his and he took it with him. It never occur to me to send it to be analyzed."

"So, it was never imaged?" Tim asked.

The sergeant shook his head, shrugging, his expression now glum.

She hoped it was sitting in an exhibit locker somewhere. "Any way we can figure out what kind it was? Or get an image done if he still has it?"

Thibault drummed his fingers on his desk as he looked away. "Probably, the boy still have it. The other victims, the women, they move away, but the boy with the console, he still live here. We can ask the parents to have a look for us."

The sergeant put down the phone, sighing. "He did have it but, they sell it a few months after. They have pictures they took for the ad, which they send me in a minute."

The gaming console might not have belonged to the child. "They say why?"

"That poor boy. He say they are possessed and wouldn't use them anymore. He say when he put on the goggles, he see the devil or something. This boy have problems before. Probably why he was targeted. I think maybe I talk to the parents again about getting him some more help." His phone chimed, and he leaned over his desk to show them the photos.

Tim and Ericka exchanged looks. The game console and VR goggles were identical to theirs. Her face flushed and she bit her lower lip, trying to contain the heat boiling up, imagining herself in her garden to bring herself back to level. She imagined the smooth wood of the bench, the scent of growing things. *You're not getting away with this. I will find you.*

Ericka looked at him, eyes focused on his. "What about the satellite box to go with the dish?"

"Usually rented, but I look," the sergeant answered. He leaned over his laptop for a few minutes, pecking away at the stained keyboard with two thick index fingers. "No, I am wrong. It was seized and is still in exhibits at K Division." He read for a moment. "They never image it. No reason to think it was used in the offense."

"Where's the priest serving his sentence? Near here?" *What we have here is someone who has communicated with our phantom.* She knew it was unlikely he would talk, but sometimes what they wouldn't say told you something. The all-important evidence about the man behind the keyboard.

"No, he hanged himself in jail two months after he was sentenced. But he did give a statement. Maybe they show you." He scribbled a name on one of his cards and handed it to her. "She was lead investigator."

Ericka stood up, Tim following. "Thank you. You've been a huge help."

The sergeant nodded his welcome. "I will be very curious if you find anything. Around here, we don't see too much of this kind of thing. Thankfully."

Ericka had a sudden thought. "Any chance I can speak to the boy?"

Thibault shrugged. "I'll see what the parents say."

* * *

The untidy room had the thrown clothes, posters, and model cars of any young teenage boy, but the kid himself was exactly what she had feared. When he looked at her, eyes shrunken with age peered out from youthful features. A child's face with the gaze of someone who had seen too much, too soon, without maturity's mental discipline to help him cope. Ericka waited until she heard the mother close the door behind her, feeling the reluctant glare on her back. Windowpanes rattled, pelted with wind-driven snow.

The boy, Stuart, didn't wait for her to speak. "Why do I have to talk about it again? He's dead." He sat down hard on his bed, long hair flopping over his brow.

She pointed to the small desk by the window. "May I sit?" He shrugged, reluctant. She settled into the kid's chair, looking out the window as she spoke. "I don't want to talk about him."

Stuart's head popped up to look at her. "Mom said you did."

"Do you know who I am? What I do?"

He shrugged. "She said you were a cop from the States and you needed to know something about what happened. Why? He's dead—the police told me."

"I want to talk about what happened after."

"After?"

Ericka noted the stiffening of his shoulders. "The VR stuff. Why did you take it? It wasn't yours."

He gave her a quick, defiant glance. "The gaming console was mine. I took it over there when I would hang out—before it happened. Not like he was going to need his VR stuff in jail."

"Tell me what you saw when you put them on after." She

56

avoided eye contact, allowing him time to answer without the pressure of her gaze. When he didn't, she looked up.

His face was flushed red and his eyes were full of tears. He looked at the floor, shaking his head. "He'd find me."

Ericka took a deep breath to calm herself. "Who?"

Another shake of the head, then he turned on his side, lying down, facing away from her, like she wasn't really there if he didn't make eye contact. She decided to give him a few minutes. Hitting him with the question before he knew it was coming hadn't worked. An open sketch pad lay on the desk, a collection of charcoals and pastels. *The kid has a good eye,* she thought. She leafed through them and looked up to find him staring at her. She pointed to the pad and raised a brow. After a time, he nodded.

The second-to-last one was different. It had been torn out and crinkled up before being flattened and reinserted into the pad's coil. It didn't fit in the collection of cars and boy fantasies he'd drawn. The colors were lurid and the drawing simplistic, but it had enormous power, a gripping step into a half-remembered nightmare. A simple rendition of the head and one shoulder of a hulking figure, a partial silhouette against a smoldering red background. Simple, but the menace was palpable, fear expressed in every stroke.

She held it up and the boy winced as she did. "This?" He nodded, looking down before curling up again on his bed. Ericka laid the drawing down on the desk and took several pictures. "Thank you." She stared at his unmoving back for a few minutes before leaving, shutting the door behind her, burning fury at yet more carnage this bastard was leaving in his wake.

***

"That's quite a skinny trail you're following. Slow week down at Quantico?" Inspector Anna Kolisnyk, officer in charge of K division sex crimes, stared at them over her immaculate desk. K division held the RCMP's headquarters for the entire province of Alberta. Behind her, grey light flooded her fifth-floor office, the only color from the bricks lining the courtyard. It had stopped snowing but looked like it might start again any minute. "I'll have the satellite box looked at, but I'll need an official request to give you a copy of anything they find. Same with video of the statements he gave."

Ericka nodded, accepting the bureaucratic necessity after years of experience. Kolisnyk's hard blue eyes stared at her over reading glasses, her greying blond hair tied tight. Her broad shoulders gave Ericka an impression of very fit strength under her crisp, white uniform shirt. The inspector's desk and credenza held not a speck of dust, let alone files or reports. Her computer fed three screens set in an arc to one side of her. "As I mentioned, this visit is off the books, but we'll make an official request once we're back. Was there anything interesting in the statements from your viewpoint?"

"Interesting to the investigation no, but he spun quite the tale. He started off with the usual bullshit about how it really isn't his fault because he was abused when young. Then he starts in on how he thinks he might have been possessed. Said he needed to talk to an exorcist and the bishop about how a demon got into his head and made him want to do these terrible things."

Ericka's brows rose. That was puzzling. "No denial at all that he did it?" The story was not typical for this kind of offender. Mild mental illness didn't get them off the hook for sex crimes, so defense lawyers didn't usually bother with it.

Kolisnyk shrugged. "His DNA was recovered by rape kits from all victims so not much point going down that road."

"What's with the silly devil story then?" As Tim asked, his voice changed timbre and Ericka noticed he was looking at Kolisnyk's left hand which she was using to prop up her chin.

Kolisnyk looked back at Tim and Ericka fancied she saw a slight flicker of interest before she masked it. The inspector shrugged again, sitting up. "Probably spinning it for the bishop. It was quite the elaborate tale. Feeling like he couldn't resist, how evil was planted in him. He said the whole ritual and costume thing during the rapes was the demon's suggestion."

Ericka grinned at the inspector. "Ten years in the business and this is the first time someone has actually claimed the devil made him do it."

Kolisnyk smiled back. "Me too. Pedophile priests are dime a dozen here same as everywhere, but this was pretty elaborate. We'll send you the whole thing when your paperwork arrives. And anything on the satellite box. If this rig turns out to be what you think it is, we're going to have to start looking for it. It might not be the only time your target has paid us a visit."

Tim leaned forward. "So, you're seeing the same pattern we are?"

Kolisnyk nodded. "Possible pattern for sure. I assume you'll share anything that arises from our incident. The lawyers can figure out where to charge him. We may want to add our own if your target was directing the Whitecourt thing."

They all stood to shake hands. Ericka noticed Kolisnyk's

smile at Tim was warmer and the eye contact rather prolonged for a professional goodbye.

As the elevator door slid shut, she turned to Tim. "Don't! I'm sure this town has plenty of your usual type. We may need her."

He affected a wounded look. "What do you think now?"

"Now I'm dead sure we have a phantom. As soon as we get back, let's do an international assistance request for the other two hits as well. Then off to see the suits about getting a team together. Before this guy moves again."

7

Looking Glass

Ericka squirmed in an uncomfortable chair, waiting for her enforced monthly audience with the FBI's appointed psychiatrist, Dr. Claus Steiner. She closed her eyes, taking several deep breaths, trying to assert some self-control, remembering Mrs. Donnelly's admonition about her temper. Her desk suspension would continue until Steiner certified her ready to return to fieldwork.

She stared at her nails, forcing a calm façade onto her features, masking the fear these sessions always brought. Fear that she would let slip too much, making her lies apparent to his trained eye, that he would figure out what she was really after. Her inside name for Dr. Steiner was Piggy and he sat behind the battered desk with her file open in front of him, his laptop tilted so she could see nothing. The borrowed office was bleak, holding no personal effects. As always, she struggled with conflicting emotions, flashes of anger birthed by fear. All offset by the realization he really was some sort of well-intentioned Boy Scout. He wanted to help.

Steiner wore a tired department-store suit, which did not flatter his portly physique. His shirt and tie squeezed his neck so it bulged over his collar, leaving sweat stains on the worn material. "How are you today, Ericka?" His voice made her shoulders tense up, now on guard.

She forced a smile. "Thrilled as always to be here."

Piggy pursed his lips and self-consciously ran his hand over his chin, as if wiping something away. "We have a job to do. Please let me help you."

Deep breaths, a nod and Ericka gave him another smile. "Sorry. Go ahead."

He began, working from prepared notes asking the obligatory opening questions as to her health and well-being since the last session. Then he looked up, holding her gaze. "Today I would like to consider again the Spokane incident."

She raised her brows, staring up into his eyes. "Why do we keep going back to that?" The knot of dread tightened her stomach. She was going to have to remember again. She would have to let it back into her head.

Steiner gave her a practiced, sympathetic nod. "Quite frankly because of your reaction every time it's mentioned. Take a few moments to gather yourself. I know this is very difficult for you."

She closed her eyes and the memory burst from its cage.

One toxic nightmare among many. A preteen child held for the purpose of a live sex show, broadcast from a dark web node to anyone willing to pay the price of admission in one of the accepted forms of crypto-currency. In the days before it was to happen, she got wind of it, parsed the geo-profiles, narrowing the location to a twenty-six-block radius in Spokane. The DIU engaged local police and they waited.

When the final link arrived, she resolved the location down to a single building and she and Tim went in with the local SWAT team, opening door after door until they found the right one, identified from the hallway by the desolate sobbing. The hooded officer battered the door open and she lunged into a scene from a nightmare. A crying, naked child sitting on the edge of a bed, small feet dangling above the floor. Her face tracked with tears, eyes wide with dread as she stared at the newcomers. The target wore a beast mask and nothing else, bent over his video equipment, his penis partially erect in anticipation.

Steiner was staring at her with a neutral, careful expression. "What are you feeling?"

She could feel her face flushing, her breathing shallow. She shook her head.

A slight nod. "Take your time."

Her eyes squeezed shut, tears pressing to escape.

The sight of the child, and the effect was instant, like someone flipped off a switch in her head. Off not on, all the blazing heat gone, replaced with a cryonic focus unlike anything she had felt before. Two social workers rushed into the room with clothes and blankets, whisking the child away as soon as the SWAT member removed the cuffs. She turned to the suspect, told him to put his pants on, then read him his rights. She told the SWAT commander they would handle the suspect for interrogation.

Steiner handed her the box of Kleenexes from his desk. "There is nothing wrong with any feelings you have from that day. That poor child—and a suspect's life ended abruptly."

I can't go there. He's seeing too much already. She closed her eyes and reached for the solace of the garden, but it wasn't there. Back to the horror, living it again.

He cocked his head, his gaze intent. "Can you describe your feelings?"

Ericka shook her head again, forced gasps, the scene unfolding in her mind as it had so many times since the day it happened.

She and Tim led the suspect out of the room towards the stairs, his hands cuffed behind his back while asking where they were taking him, whining for his lawyer. She did not answer. The door to the stairwell swung open to the stench of stale urine and rodents, cement stairs lit by bare fluorescent lights. Perfect. She looked over her shoulder to ensure only Tim was behind her, placed her booted foot on his lower back and shoved hard. He tumbled down the steep flight of concrete steps, his bones breaking as he fell, screaming with each impact. The cries stopped at the bottom as he hit his head, leaving teeth clattering on the landing like thrown dice. Knowing the screams would attract the cover team in minutes, she lunged down the stairs, dragging him to his knees towards another flight. Tim darted forward, grabbing her from behind, pinning her arms to her sides, pulling her to the ground on top of him.

She felt Tim's iron grip, his whisper in her ear feral. "Christ, stop! You can survive this, but not if you throw him again."

Her expression blank, a cold emptiness inside her, she nodded then lifted her booted foot up to waist level as if to kick the suspect, her body almost acting on its own. Tim twisted his body under her, hauling her to one side.

He leaned forward to look in her eyes, his expression stunned. "I said enough!" Blood oozed from the suspect's left ear, pooling on the filthy concrete.

She opened her eyes back in the office, knowing her livid face gleamed with a sheen of sweat. The silence was uncomfortably long. "What are you trying to get at? What is the point of making me relive this again?"

Steiner's eyebrows went up. "I am not trying to get at anything. We are trying to assess if you are fit for field duty. Not everyone believes the Board's conclusion about whether you intended harm to a helpless suspect you know."

Ericka flushed with an instant blaze of defensive anger. "If you want to see helpless, do some victim services work with children. That's helpless."

He cocked an eyebrow. "I'm not concerned with him. I'm concerned with you. In our first sessions you showed a lot of repressed anger and then suddenly nothing. Long-term anger like that doesn't vanish, but sometimes people learn how to cloak themselves even against a trained clinician." He looked at her, waiting for her to answer.

She leaned back and stared at him. "That's interesting to know." He doesn't know the half of it.

He held up a hand. "Calm down. There is no need to be angry. I want you to close your eyes and do your best to describe not the memories, but simply the feelings they evoke."

She drew a shuddering breath and did as he asked. It was easier to hide with her eyes shut anyway. "I feel regret for a life lost, that he will never face justice for what he did, and resentment that I have to explain myself time and again. I didn't do anything wrong." In truth, it was fear she felt. Terror he would see through the lies, understand her contrived disguise, see her for who she feared she was. No, not who she was, it wasn't who she was; she had just let it go that one time. She hadn't meant to kill him. Or was that just what she had convinced herself? Seeing the child released something in her she couldn't control. Dread at the knowledge that she had lost all control, fear it could happen again, that maybe it would happen again when she finally found the three she'd searched for all these years.

His expression was studied neutrality. "No one is suggesting you did. Your partner corroborated your version of events. The investigation is over. And yet your defensiveness would indicate some significant feelings of guilt. Why?"

She repressed the laugh. *Maybe it's because I live immersed in a sea of guilt.* "Because no one has looked at me the same since. These ongoing sessions aren't helping me restore my credibility."

Another long pause before he settled into his chair. "Why are you here, Ericka?"

"Because I was ordered to attend." She regretted the

sarcasm. No need to keep giving him more evidence of her struggle with self-control.

Steiner's composure didn't waver. "I mean why the FBI. You graduated at the top of your class from MIT, got a stellar launch in industry, were very likely being groomed for one of the big chairs but suddenly you resign and turn up at Quantico. As soon as you were able, you disappeared into online work, seemingly content to plod away. It seems like two different people or a profound change of heart. What happened?"

Time to trot out the party line one more time. "I figured out there was more to a career and life than money and decided to try and do something good with my talents." In a twisted way, that was true.

Almost imperceptibly, his eyes narrowed. "And you have chosen to have no children, no partner, no serious relationships at all?"

He's trying to provoke a reaction. "I didn't know they were required by the Bureau. In fact, I'm quite sure they're not. Being alone is sometimes the only option for people who do what I do."

Steiner nodded at the truth of that. "Yes, sadly that's correct. I am not concerned with your personal lifestyle choices, only your fitness for duty. What you do with your off-duty hours matters to my assessment. You have no family since your sister's death and you take vacations alone in places you won't talk about. All of this looks to me very much like somebody who is running from something. People who are running are often angry and fearful; they make bad judgment calls. They make terrible field agents."

Time to shut this down. She raised her voice. "There is

nothing to diagnose. I am devoted to my career; I don't have many friends or family, that's true; and I've never met anyone I wanted to share my life with. Are you telling me any of those are indicative of mental illness or instability? You're going to want to fire or suspend half the Bureau."

Piggy gave a resigned shrug and a smile. He'd given up for the day. He looked down, scanning his papers before continuing. "Drinking these days, Ericka?"

"Gave it up. You've seen the pee test I'm sure."

He nodded. "How are you finding your workload?"

Ericka couldn't resist the eye roll this time. "Challenging as always."

Steiner tugged down the lid of his computer, his smile bland. "I think we'll call it a day. I'm sorry, but until we make some progress, until I have some insight, you are going to have to continue under the current restrictions."

Stopped in the stairwell, she wiped her face. Few believed her story of an escape attempt on the stairs, where she had lost her grip when he started to run, falling to the landing below. Tim backed her up. The suspect himself never left the prison hospital and never recovered enough to tell his version of events. Despite the doctor's best efforts, he died four weeks later. The conduct review decided, in a complete absence of evidence of intentional misconduct, that she was guilty of negligent conduct resulting in injury and suspended her for three months without pay.

When she did resume her duties, it was desk work. Her supervisor SAC Abara spoke to her only once about the incident. At his request, they went for a walk and sat near a fountain in the park, where he turned to her, brown eyes boring into hers. He looked around before speaking. No one was close. "You don't say nothing right now. Just listen and I'll talk. I don't believe one fucking word you and your tame Brit said about that arrest. Not one fucking word. I know damn well what happened, but facts don't matter none now. I don't think you meant that to happen or we wouldn't be here, but I can't trust you. Managing you is like trying to hold a rope on a goddamn tiger. Never know what it's gonna do. If you go off the deep end again, it's on my ass. Here's what's going to happen. You are on inside duty only until I say otherwise. Every month you are going to sit down with a company shrink, and if I see one word in his reports about you lighting up, your ass is out of here. Are we really goddamned clear?"

She found Tim sitting in her chair, his feet up, staring at the screens. He turned to look at her. "Got it all sorted and cleared for field duty again?" He looked at her face. "Or have you been given the sack?"

He stood and she dropped into her chair. "There are no words for how much I loathe these sessions."

His thick hand gripped her wrist. "Ericka, love, you're going to have to make peace with the shrink sessions and the brass or you're going to spend the rest of your days down here, sitting in front of screens and lighting up amateur-hour perverts for the flatfoots to catch."

She scowled at him. "Easy for you to say!"

Tim drew a deep breath, letting it out, staring at nothing. Minutes passed. "No, it really isn't."

She stared at him abruptly, flushing with guilt. Tim's loyalty was the only reason she still had what was left of her career. If he hadn't been willing to lie for her, the suits would have prosecuted her. Her eyes welled up and she turned away to rub them. "Thank you."

"You are the best at what you do, and I believe in you, love. And I've foolishly grown rather fond of you." He smiled his crooked smile, accenting the scars on his face, then his expression changed. "I've been where you are. Or hasn't my great-auntie told you?"

Ericka leaned forward, surprised. "No, she hasn't. Mister straitlaced analyst boy got into trouble?"

"I did and, in many ways, not dissimilar to how it happened to you. I'm never going to talk about it. Suffice to say Afghanistan is a horrible place and some of the people we were up against there were as horrible as they come. Something that drove me half mad, something I wasn't prepared for—no one can prepare for—and I snapped the way you did that day. It doesn't make me evil."

She raised an eyebrow, wondering. "Other than your aunt, you never speak of family."

Tim's stare took on a hard tone. "I had the kind of childhood you take great care to forget. I left for university as soon as I could, then joined GCHQ. I volunteered to go in-country with various special forces to do cyber-support and just came up against my limit. That was the end of it. You know the rest."

She looked at him seeing the haunted expression and the weary mass of sadness behind it. She took his hand, squeezing it tight, nodding her understanding. She would not be here either if it weren't for that same relative. It kind of made them family.

He leaned back grinning, his crisp shirt tightening around his broad chest as he put his hands behind his head. "Don't go soppy on me. Especially not now. This phantom of ours isn't going to be caught with you feeling sorry for yourself. If you can't push yourself past this, all you've done will be for nothing."

Ericka forced Piggy's image from her mind and tried to clear the angry fog from her thoughts. Nothing ever commanded her focus like the hunt and it was only the next pursuit that allowed her to repress her searing anger over the years. She closed her eyes, pressing them tight, trying to drain her awareness so she could focus. After a few minutes, her breathing slowed and the rage subsided, leaving her covered with goose bumps. She shivered, opening her eyes a crack.

Tim was staring at her. "You're back!"

She nodded, real warmth in the smile she gave him, and turned back to her screens. "I have to get my shit together and get him off my back."

"I'm never going to tell anyone what happened in Afghanistan. If you describe some things, you relive them and they dominate you. Even if you're only talking to yourself. That's what makes these sessions so hard for you."

Ericka turned to look at him. "You're an insightful guy for someone who looks like such a knuckle-dragger."

The corners of his mouth twitched into a smile. "Don't let yourself go down that hole again. Not ever. You'll never get out."

"I'm going to find this bastard."

"I know."

8

The Ninth Circle

He tightened the goggles and helmet so they eclipsed even the dim light from his bulwark of screens. His hands trembled with excitement and he had to force himself to breathe. He couldn't rush this, such a moment required a clear mind to savor what was to come. He spoke into the mic, pleased his voice betrayed nothing of his excitement. "Please proceed."

The crisp green lights set in the goggles glowed to life, and all three men wearing them turned towards the fourth who was naked, glistening with the sweat of terror, bound hands, feet, and neck to a makeshift frame. Heavy blocks of wood supported it from underneath, leaving his head at about chest level, his body sloping down towards the floor. Below the blocks the concrete-lined basin was full of water, appearing like a pool of ink. Several harsh LEDs shone from above, illuminating his quivering form from all angles. The light didn't reach as far as the walls or ceiling of the cavernous textile mill, empty for decades, but sounds echoing back described the floor as huge. Behind the men, a small globe sat on a tripod, glowing LEDs displaying its status.

The men's eyes were just visible through the goggles, their unblinking stares intent on the bound victim, heads cloaked in the traditional black hoods. They were naked to the waist, wearing thick, insulated gloves.

"Time to make your peace with God!" This from the one with the belly covered in thick black hair, almost as dense as fur. He stunk of sweat and his skin shone with the accumulation of body oils.

Straining against his bonds, the bound man's voice was shrill. "I have money, more than you know. Let me disappear and it's all yours." His voice cracked as he made the offer to his captors, eyes wide, tears lining his cheeks.

The belly grinned under his goggles. "I expect you do, Franco. If you take thirty pieces of silver every time you open your filthy mouth, it will add up." They snorted with laughter while the tall, bony man pulled a small cylinder from a duffel bag behind the lights, his physique an animated skeleton. "You took the oath. Treason has a price. Be a man about it!"

"It isn't true! I swear on my children's heads."

What kind of a fool was this one? Not even the courage for defiance? Did he think they were bluffing? Time to impress his situation upon him. Plant some despair, reap the fear. "Show him what is to come but careful not to damage him yet!"

"Liar!" Skeleton lunged forward, thrusting the cylinder towards Franco's exposed belly, pressing his thumb on the small lever on top. The snake-like hiss of escaping liquid nitrogen blended with high-pitched shrieks of pain as the freezing gas raised a bubbling line of blisters across his exposed abdomen. Franco's back arched against his bonds then slammed back down on the frame.

"Hell holds a special punishment for traitors." The third man spoke at last. Blade scars crisscrossed his shaved, muscular chest, trophies from his hard-earned skill with a knife. He moved to loom over the helpless form. "This can be slow, or this can be quick, but it is going to happen. In death, try to be the man you never were in life."

"Go to hell, motherfucker!"

Indeed. Traitors deserved something special, a bit of creativity. I will oblige him. He wondered if Franco had ever read Dante. A thrill coursed through him, raising goose bumps. Time to get serious. "He doesn't deserve to own the balls he's got. Please remedy that."

Skeleton stepped forward again, applying a sustained spray of nitrogen to Franco's genitals. This time the screaming and writhing ended with him biting clean through his own lip, so blood poured down his face and neck. His muscles and tendons stood in gaunt, quivering relief under the harsh light.

Blade Scars leaned close to his face. "Who helped you?"

The crying started, eyes bulging, pleading now through sputtering blood, dripping from his chin. "Please."

Blade Scars cocked his head as if listening, then turned to Skeleton lurking in the edge of the light, his movements perceived rather than seen. "Take one of his eyes!"

This time it was several minutes before the shrieking subsided. Skeleton scooped some water from below and poured it in Franco's open mouth, bringing him back to consciousness, coughing and sputtering. Blade Scars leaned in again, nodding his satisfaction at the ruined socket then stared into the remaining eye. "You know you aren't half man enough for this. Who helped you?"

Franco nodded, torn lips trembling, resigned now. "One question in return?"

Unexpected. What does he think a final smattering of courage will get him now? It might be entertaining. Bargaining when everything is already lost. "Agreed."

Blade Scars nodded. "You have my word. Your wife's brother, yes? It has to be family? No one else would trust you."

Franco nodded. "But no one else knew."

Oh, that was just a bit too easy. A bit more bargaining at least—all the better with the end near. Terror is most entertaining when someone has the fortitude to resist it, however briefly, whatever the futility. "Put him in!"

Blade Scars pulled back, nodding to the other two who kicked the supports out from under the frame, plunging Franco into the shallow, icy water flooding the pool beneath. Belly reached in and wedged a block of wood behind his head, propping his face just clear of the water, allowing him to breathe. Then he and Skeleton walked out of the light and wrestled a large tank marked 'liquid nitrogen' near to the edge, their muscles rippling against the weight.

The water splashed and churned as Franco struggled against his bonds. "You bastard. You swore."

Blade Scars squatted down on his ankles, his hidden smile crinkling his eyes. "What do you want to know?"

"Who gave me up? I'll see him in hell."

Blade Scars heard the instant response in his headphones, the voice eager. "Tell him. I want him to know."

"We didn't catch you. All this—" Blade Scars gestured to the equipment, then to his goggles "—was the price we agreed to pay to find out who betrayed us. He came to us. I have no idea who he is. But what he offered us was our traitor. When we agreed, there it was, right down to the money being signed for at the police station to it entering your 'secret' accounts minutes later. Your phone records, places where you stayed. And all he wanted in return was to watch while we took our justice in the manner he suggested. His name is Dantalion."

He nodded to the others. To hoarse screams echoing from unseen walls, they poured the clear liquid into the pool where it bubbled and foamed, forming a thick slush as the water froze. A roiling fog obscured the surface, covering his almost submerged face, filling the area to waist level. His breath catching, Franco fell silent for the last time. Dragging the tank around the pool, they emptied the rest into the other side. In a few minutes, the mist dissipated, the water freezing a solid white, framing the face in distorted agony, remaining eye wide, mouth agape.

He blew out a breath he didn't know he had been holding, smiling now. In the end, it had been all he hoped. Recorded from multiple angles, he could relive it again from the view of each participant. Live each moment. He shivered with excitement. Almost reluctantly, he pressed the kill switch and began cleaning his tracks.

The light on the goggles and small globe went out. Blade Scars nodded to his men as he strode towards the unseen doors at the far end of the room, pulling off his hood. "All that equipment goes in the incinerators. No traces."

"This is nice stuff." Skeleton looked at the goggles, his longing obvious.

Blade Scars wagged a finger at Skeleton. "We made this deal and we're keeping it. Besides how bad do you want to piss off a guy who knows every secret you ever tried to hide?

We may want to do business with him again. Burn it!" A few minutes later, the room was empty except for the still form peering up from entombing ice.

His smile was genuine as Ericka walked into his office. "Well, you can't be here for legal advice. You've never followed any I've given you since we met." He waved her to his worn client chair. Robert O'Brien was just finishing his thirty-first year as an attorney with the Department of Justice. His polished desk was made of real wood and the carpet showed little wear. Lawyers really did rule the world. No cop ever got such luxury. The Robert F. Kennedy building looked more like a bank than an office, columns in front with a stone façade.

Ericka knew from long experience with him what his answer to her request was going to be. She and O'Brien had many spirited debates over the years, and she had come to value his insight and strategic thinking. She stared, waiting for him to continue. He was pale, his blond hair thinning, his body stout from decades of sedentary overconsumption. She noted he was still buying bespoke suits. Vanity she thought, for a long-vanished physique, but none of this detracted from his work.

"I don't need legal advice. I need to see lawyers working for a living."

O'Brien nodded straight-faced as if taking her request seriously. "Go down the hall, turn left, second door on your right. The new guy sits there. If you're any good at this, you don't have to work at it. Just comes naturally. All the bad guys taking a vacation day, or are you?" His expression neutral, he stared at Ericka for some time then sighed. "You knew perfectly well before you got here you don't have enough. Did you miss me or is there something else you want?"

Ericka paused, smiling at him before speaking. "Maybe I just needed a glass of decent whiskey."

He grinned back, nodding towards his infamous filing cabinet. "You could have just said so and saved me reading your materials." He pushed the file folder away and leaned over to pull open his drawer, his belly bulging over the arm of his chair. He rooted through his drawer to the accompaniment of clinking bottles, pulling one out, brandishing it towards her. "Black Bush?"

She raised her brows in mock surprise. "You're drinking Irish these days?"

"Yes, I'm on a bit of a health kick right now. Bourbon is giving me a sour stomach. Have to ask the doc about that." He pulled a pair of glasses from another drawer, looked at them for a moment, pursing his lips before taking out two more. "Almost time to do dishes, but I wasn't expecting company. You still dry?" She nodded and he poured a single generous glass, sipping as he looked at her, nestling the drink on his lap.

He paused for a few minutes. "How've you been keeping?" One eyebrow rose.

Ericka smiled and shrugged. "Still have me locked in the basement and keeping me there until they get an all clear from the shrink."

He took a slow breath and blew it out in an exaggerated sigh. "I'm going to say it again. Watch your back. There's no such thing as a concluded internal for something like your incident. Just inactive for a while."

Her skin tingled as the goose bumps rose. "You heard something."

He shook his head. "Just a gut feeling. People know we're friends so I'm not going to hear anything directly. Mind yourself around company shrinks and for Christ's sake no using company assets for your private business. You know what I mean."

She did, but his warning made her frown. "I need them. You think I can't fool an audit trail?"

O'Brien rolled his eyes to the ceiling. "I'm saying for now, don't give them a reason to audit you. Bide your time."

She nodded, irritated by the truth of it. "Thanks. How about that?" Her investigative summary lay open on his desk.

He paused to stare at her for a few moments before answering. "Okay, let me say it so we're clear. You're nowhere close to being able to get any sort of judicially authorized surveillance or formal international assistance. This isn't national security stuff so we can't use any of that legislation. You knew that right?"

"So, you're not seeing it? I thought lawyers were supposed to be smart." Ericka cocked an eyebrow at him, smiling and leaning back into the comfortable chair.

He smiled at the taunt. "I see how you've strung this together just fine, but you're way short on evidence this is one guy. Sorry to bring up the E-word with such an experienced and talented cop, but that's where I'm stuck. I see the digital pattern you're on about, but not a consistent pattern of human behavior behind it." He paused for a more generous sip. "You've got a software profile that could be any one of a thousand guys but you don't know who any of them are, and you've got someone with that same profile very active at the same time as several different offenses widely geographically separated. And bearing almost no resemblance to each other.

You've got to have something on the guy, not just geeky breadcrumbs. Show me the guy."

She clenched her teeth, knowing he was right. Throughout her ten-year career, she had often listened to prosecutors moan they only got to put away the bottom-feeders, the idiots. The ones police catch, they complained were stupid, unlucky, or arrogant—or some combination of the three— but Ericka knew they were wrong. Some of their prey were highly intelligent and executed their crimes with great skill. The ones ending up in front of a judge in an orange jumpsuit were those whose compulsions got the better of them, leaving them an easy catch. Now she had a hard target, and he wasn't buying it. "What about the recovered hardware?"

O'Brien gestured with his palms. "Standard satellite internet equipment, a new three-sixty camera and a type of VR goggles you've never seen. Consistent with a single individual but not evidence of a single individual."

She could hear the edge in her voice as she spoke. "I'm sure the goggles are a custom job."

He was unfazed. "Yeah, that and three bucks will get you a coffee downstairs. If you find proof of a single order of multiple pairs of custom goggles, that's something. These could just be some place in China knocking off someone else's technology and deciding not to advertise what they've done with a label."

"I'm never getting that!"

"Right, so let's sum up what you do have and think of how to fill the holes. For the sake of argument, we assume the snuff film was your guy calling the shots even though you don't have direct evidence of that. And we say the devil priest is him too, though I'm not seeing the 'human' connection between rape and murder of a young woman and the violation and flogging of church ladies and an altar boy. I can't think of many predators I've run into whose tastes would run to both of those. That kind of pansexuality is unusual. If we take the Croatian and Indian ones as your guy, then we do see a weird pattern of tastes connected by sadism and control, but you don't have the hardware connection there and aren't going to get it."

Another generous swig. "This last one puts the lie to all the others. A bit of mafia housekeeping where a guy is frozen with liquid nitrogen, no hardware, but with the familiar spike in web traffic. How do we say that's connected?"

Ericka knew how weak it sounded as she said it, picturing the eye-rolling that would accompany any formal request. "Just the software profile in proximity and the chronological data spikes near and at the time."

"You have to admire professionals though, especially literate ones."

She had been waiting for him to spot it. "Maybe Dante is required reading for mafia guys. It was a pretty creative rendition of the ninth circle."

He nodded his agreement. "You're thinking a devil-acting priest and wannabe masters of the city of Dis is a connection? You have nothing like that on any others."

"I know, I get it—consistency with and proof of are two different things."

O'Brien flipped a few pages in the file. "Did the Mounties give you anything more on the priest?"

She knew where this was going. "A bit. Same cleverly wiped box but the data fragments left behind sound like they match what we have already. The devil story was pretty elaborate as it turns out. Says he was coaxed and encouraged, but it was something he never would have done on his own."

O'Brien looked up, appearing puzzled. "How did you get all that without a formal request? Since when do Mounties ignore protocol?"

She gave him a deadpan look. "I think Tim has developed a bit of a rapport with them."

He looked at the ceiling. "Bastard—what is it about him? Shall I tell you the biggest hurdle on this?" She nodded. "It's going to be getting someone interested in ponying up the resources for something everyone's going to see as someone else's problem. We in the justice industry are supposed to sort out bad guys afflicting the people paying us. And all you've got is a well-founded gut feeling that a string of offenses spread out all over the planet are the same guy. That's going to make it all the harder to get the suits upstairs to think this is their problem."

That was irritating and she didn't bother to keep it out of her tone. "And if I was going to commit these kinds of crimes, I would do it exactly the way he has for exactly that reason. Cops keep an eye on their own backyard. If he keeps hopping through jurisdictions, no one spots him or sees the serial aspect of what he's doing. One remote crime per jurisdiction and he's on his way. I'd have never spotted it if I hadn't seen a video that shouldn't exist of a crime scene I was at. And that's the bit that puzzles me—how that video got into circulation years after. No videos of the others have ever surfaced."

"Maybe just a fuckup on his part sharing it with someone not quite reliable enough. Maybe you should have a look and see if any known perverts have suddenly disappeared. Remember your Sun Tzu." Ericka groaned theatrically at the coming lecture but had more than once benefitted from the ancient master of conflict. She nodded, and he spoke after a pregnant pause. "'If you wait by the river long enough, the bodies of your enemies will float by.'"

Ericka made a mental note to set the crawlers looking for postings on any of the known pedos who had gone quiet. "I wonder if the mafia guy was that revenge happening? They're usually pretty careful to weed out the perverts."

"The leak of the video? But how would he get mafia guys to do his dirty work?"

Ericka made the response deadpan. "Make them an offer they can't refuse."

"You're dating yourself or at least your tastes." He was baiting her now.

"Everything I do these days dates me. So, what do I need before we can get a judge to sign the order and get some real-time monitoring here?"

"If you're right, this guy needs money to do what he's doing? Could you look into that?"

"Tim's doing that right now, but that would be a colossal fuckup on his part to catch him that way."

"Sometimes long shots are worth it. I think you're going to have to wait for the next one and be set up and ready this time to be there before the trail goes cold. Or are you still under travel limitations? I thought you were going to quit?"

She winced as the image of Dr. Steiner filled her mind. "I'm working on that. We'll find a work-around. And yes, the minute this guy is in the lockup, I'm throwing my badge in the river at the deepest spot I can find."

"I'm sure you will. Here's my advice: don't jump the gun. You may just get one shot at him. If he's half as good as you're thinking, he'll go to ground and you'll never see him again. Or only years later at best. God knows what he will be up to in the meantime. We can persuade people upstairs we need to act on this guy if we go loaded for bear, but we have to get it right the first time. The Bureau is eventually going to tell you to move along."

"I don't know that jumping the gun is a big risk with this guy. He's very calculating this one, and I feel like what he wants, he's got to have. I just can't figure out what he's getting from this. I see the common thread technically, but I can't picture the guy who gets his jollies from such an eclectic mix, some sort of pansexual sadist. I have no read on the man behind the machine."

"Be that as it may, you may still just get one shot at figuring out who he is. You can't do anything that would warn him. Sun Tzu time!"

She smiled at him, feeling genuine affection for the man. "Hit me."

O'Brien thumbed through his worn copy of *The Art of War* for a moment. "Here we go." He looked up, smiling. "'Let your plans be dark and impenetrable as night, and when you move, fall like a thunderbolt.'"

Tim stared at her hands as she walked in, bent under the weight of a laptop and two large document bags. "You went all that way and forgot the order on the judge's desk? And where's lunch? You've been gone all morning." He wore his characteristic crisp, long-sleeve shirt, buttoned high, pressed trousers worn a little too tight and black shoes buffed to a military shine.

Ericka shook her head, giving him a fond look, and tossed him his sub from one of the bags. "Was it your sense of humor got you kicked out of England? Canada wouldn't have you? I think we are on our own for a bit yet. Have you been working or lining up the weekend's entertainment on your phone?"

He smiled from under a cocked eyebrow. "Both if you must know, but I was mucking about with your engine while you were gone and found something you want to look at."

"Do tell?" She was half listening as she settled in, staring at her screens and brimming inbox.

"Our guy has to have a good cash flow to fund his hobby. None of the gear he is using is cheap and having cracked them I agree the VR goggles are customized. From what little we know, he must be paying various goons for minor dirty work too."

She typed as she spoke. "Everything we see this guy doing tells me he isn't interested in money."

Tim shook his head. "No, of course he isn't, but no business runs without a petty cash box."

She was skeptical anyone this clever was going to leave a money trail leading to his door, but mentally shrugged. He wouldn't be the first one finished by an amateur-hour mistake. The FBI had brought down a whole dark web empire because one of the owners was stupid enough to use the same handle on the surface web. She tore herself from her screen and pivoted to look at him. "Find anything?"

"Remember eighteen months ago when someone programed all those cash machines in Europe to simultaneously spit euros out all over the sidewalk?"

"Vaguely. The one that got in through the multi-bank cash machines? Nailed several of them at once?"

Tim nodded to her. "Right. Whoever was behind it had mules waiting on the sidewalk. They scooped the lot, converted them to cryptos and sent them off to a server, where they promptly disappeared. They left a lot of banks and insurance companies crying real tears."

Ericka played with her pen. "And I take it someone wearing the same shoes as our guy was active while all this money was spewing out on to the sidewalk?"

"Very, but interestingly not right down to the machines themselves. Lots of simultaneous traffic but no direct connections. And there were several other similar profiles equally active. The Europeans are quite sure it was a group but never put a finger on anyone calling the shots."

"That's not what I'd expect for him. Let me look." She rolled her chair sideways, bringing up Tim's work, gnawing at her pen until she could taste the plastic. "I'm seeing widely dispersed tracks all over, but nothing direct at any of the sites where cash machines went mad." She smiled looking over her shoulder at him and nodding. "This could be him. It's very careful. His tracks are everywhere but where the action is. He's doing something, but from somewhere nobody would have looked and leaving no trail."

Tim spoke around a mouthful of his sandwich. "He's a clever lad this one. If it's him. Same temporal clustering as the other ones, but not active anywhere near the actual crimes."

"I bet you he just supplied the software for a cut. What did the EU investigation turn up? That's a lot of people on the ground handling the loot who might blab."

Tim shook his head. "They caught four of them and one talked. All the investigation summary says was he was told when and where to be, scoop all he could, keep a third and convert the rest to cryptos, then send it on to a specified server. He said he had no idea who he was working for."

Ericka nodded, not at all surprised. "No, of course he wouldn't." *This is how I would do it,* Ericka thought. "It probably won't give us anything, but maybe we should get someone over there to re-interview him. Where is he now?"

"Staring at the grass from underneath. Died in his cell in Belgium. Suspicious circumstances with no one charged. I'm beginning to think our phantom or his mates might not be fond of loose ends."

"No, I'm sure he isn't." She chewed her pen, tasting the sour styrene flavor again, thinking this might be the first break they'd had. "I wonder if he thinks he got away clean with this? How much did they net?"

Tim bent over his tablet, his thick fingers fumbling to retrieve the report. "Not that much if they were sharing it. Just under four million euros. You think he'll be back at the well?"

"No reason not to if he thinks he is clean away. Did they try to trace the cryptos?"

"They did. It got fed through tumblers all over the place, then vanished."

Ericka nodded, expecting nothing else. Feeding illicit crypto-currency through a tumbler was the money-laundering equivalent of converting it into small bills and running it all through a casino. A tumbler was a dark web site that blended the funds from multiple sources then created a jumbled series of transactions, each unit of currency taking a different path. All converted from one currency to another, routed through servers in countries that would not provide help to an American investigation. You got about the same amount out, but they were not the same coins you put in. The same amount minus the bite the tumbler's owner took. The going rate was five percent for a partial cleaning and thirty percent to make a proper job of it. Police software could sometimes trace through a partial cleaning, so the pros paid the extra to be sure.

"Okay so this guy is maybe at least partly funding his bad habits through this scam. I wouldn't be surprised to find him running several small ones like it rather than attract serious attention with a bigger one." Ericka thought for a few minutes before breaking the silence again. "My gut tells me we're not going to surface this one the usual way. He's never going to allow a traceable coin to end up in his pocket or buy something stupid that flags him. I bet he steals it, stores it in a cold wallet someplace nowhere near him, then spends it on his escapades without the coins ever getting near him. I wonder if he ever comes up. I've always wondered if there was a kind of dark web critter that never surfaces, ever."

Tim shrugged, tossing his sandwich wrapper into the garbage. "He's got to live on something, never mind paying for the bag of tricks, hired help and gadgets we've seen so far."

"Well, he can use stolen money for toys and minions as long as he keeps a clear wall between himself and the dirty stuff. Other than that, all he has to have is enough to live on somewhere in the world. That isn't a tall order."

"No, I suppose it isn't." Tim shrugged and picked up his phone. "If that's true, he's either going to have to get really stupid or we're going to have to get very bloody lucky."

Ericka's stomach tightened with welling frustration. "We'll get him. Whatever he needs from this, he has to have it."

9

A Whiff of Brimstone

Her mobile chimed, displaying O'Brien's face with its characteristic grin, looking well pleased with himself as always. "Go ahead, Bob, make my day."

"Jayzus, do you do nothing at night but watch bad old movies? You're making me question your taste."

She leaned back in her chair away from her screens, pleased to hear from him. So far, the day had brought nothing but endless reading of this week's target profiles. "I'm sure you'd expect no more or less from me. What's up?"

"You having any luck with that dark web phantom you came to see me about?"

"Nothing solid right now. Why?"

"Well something I'm working on right now you should maybe know about."

"Do tell?"

O'Brien paused for a moment and she imagined he didn't want to give away too much on the phone. "We're running a wire on a group of bikers shifting the usual mix of guns and drugs. I was listening to some of the intercepts and reading transcripts so I could apply for an extended order. Some of the stuff made me think of your guy." He paused as if waiting for a reaction.

"You've got my undivided attention." Her mind raced with possible connections between her target and a group of drug-lord bikers.

"I think we should have a drink or I'll have one while you watch. I hate talking on the phone. Besides, you're one of the only pretty women I know who'll talk to me in person these days."

She laughed, rooting for car keys in her bag. "I'm on my way."

She lounged back in O'Brien's office chair, watching as he sipped his drink. "I thought you were off bourbon?"

"Who can stay away from a good shot of Eagle Rare?" He sat back and put his feet up on the corner of his desk. His skin was blotchy and his eyes had the watery look of too much alcohol combined with fatigue.

She shook her head while staring at him. "You really need to start taking care of yourself."

"Thanks, Mom, I know. Five more years and I am out of here." He smiled at her, appearing quite pleased at the thought.

If you have that long, she thought, *I should talk.* "So, do tell?"

"Let me give you the unofficial version first. If you think I'm on to something, you're going to need to go through formal channels to get into this. It's ATF. You know how they are. Territorial like a pack of wolves." She nodded and he continued after a generous swig from his glass. "The bit that got my attention was in the texts from one of the runners. Nothing to do with the main event for this one. Run-of-the-mill gun stuff the bikers want to use to protect their turf and have conversations with their competitors." He paused for another sip. "Did I tell you about these guys two years ago? Very heat-conscious. They somehow figured out we were listening and led the local police a serious chase."

She shook her head. "Not that I remember."

"Turned out the leak was a judge's secretary. She was tipping them off every time the cops came to get a warrant. But back to the runner. This fellow is one of these guys who hangs out with bikers but isn't one of them. Does contract work for them, gets a piece, but is expected to take the fall for the big guys if everything goes to shit. Nothing there that you care about." He pulled a small sheaf of papers from his file and pushed them across his desk. "You can't keep them, but if you think there is any chance this is related to your guy, I'll make the introductions." Intrigued, Ericka picked them up with an inquiring look at O'Brien. "Go ahead, I've got email to answer. The runner is a guy called Ramirez. He's listed there as T15 but we don't know who it is he is talking to. Some VoIP system we can't source."

She leaned back and began to read.

T15: "That other thing I was telling you about."

U/K: "Yeah, what about it?"

T15: "Keep it really fuckin' quiet. I don't want the big guys thinking I have loyalty issues. It's nothing they'd give a shit about anyway."

U/K: "This is the guy with all the shows? Stuff you said you can't get anywhere else?"

T15: "Yes and he'd fuckin' kill me too if he knew what I'd told you. And this guy knows every fuckin' thing you do. Believe me. Blow makes me stupid or I wouldn't have even told you."

U/K: "Any chance I could get in? I like the sound of this stuff. How did you find him?"

T15: "I didn't, he fuckin' found me. I was looking at some shit, hard-core stuff, and suddenly a message pops up and asks if I'd like to see more or maybe try the real thing sometime. I go along getting more and more stuff."

U/K: "Fuck—for free?"

T15: "Ya fuck, nothing's for free. More of a trade. I do things for him. Deliver things. Ship things for him. But that's it, no money."

U/K: "Sweet! How the hell is he going to know if I watch some of it with you?"

T15: "This fuckin' guy has some sort of voodoo going. He knows where I am and what I've done. I dunno how."

U/K: "Gimme a fucking break! How's he going to know I'm in your living room with you?"

T15: "It isn't like that. About a month after I started helping him with stuff, I got a present out of nowhere in an unmarked package. A serious pair of fuckin' VR goggles like you never seen. It's unreal. Sometimes he talks to me there too. That's really quite the fuckin' show."

Ericka's heart stumbled as her head snapped up to lock eyes with O'Brien. Her head nodded as her mind raced. "It could be, it really could be him. Just the way he'd snare a pawn and ensure loyalty."

He swiveled his chair back to face her, nodding. "I

wondered. Even if it isn't, you don't have any serious leads at this point until your guy does something else. Worth a try."

"If I could get my mitts on those goggles while they're live." Her eyes squinted as she ran through the code she might find. It might not lead to him, but it could lead to servers and places where he was active.

He leaned back a bit as she spoke, girding himself. "I was thinking more of an expanded wiretap order. We aren't ready to move on the bikers just yet. Years of work have gone into this."

Her voice was sharp, and she regretted the heat as she spoke. "This guy's a killer."

O'Brien tilted his head, cocking an eyebrow at her, unmoved, hide like a rhino. "Get in line, you should see the pile of bones these guys have made over the years. Go and talk to SAC Whatshisname, get your brass to back you. I'll talk to the ATF guys and see what they're willing to do."

She nodded to herself, not looking forward to the inevitable questions that would be asked when she approached her superiors for interagency cooperation. No help for it. "Thanks for this. This could give us a real shot at getting ahead of him."

O'Brien nodded. "My pleasure."

SAC James Abara, commanding officer of the DIU, glared back and forth between Ericka and Tim. They sat in their chairs waiting for the inevitable tirade. He leaned forward over his cluttered desk, his pristine white shirt sweat-stained from the day's stress. His tie remained snug around his neck, his top button always done up. She watched him fiddle with the huge gunmetal watch he wore on his left wrist, a sure sign he was agitated. Nicknamed Abs for his immaculate attention to his physique, he rubbed his stubbled chin before speaking, looking over at his desk picture of his wife and kids.

"So, before we get started on how this is going to go down, one of you going to tell me why I'm just hearing about this now? You've been on this target a while, you've engaged other agencies, and apparently one of you has been up to Canada for a little impromptu international assistance." His eyes narrowed as he watched her. "Can't have been you right? That would be like fieldwork."

"I only travel on vacation." She held her face expressionless, her tone neutral.

"Right. And when we're done with this, I want you to stick around for a few minutes so we can have a discussion. Now I want to know why I am just hearing about this? This is bullshit!" Both looked out the window behind Abs for a few minutes before Tim opened his mouth to speak.

Abs beat him to it. "You know what, Tim, maybe you can excuse us a bit. I think I need to have a little one-on-one with my section head here." Tim rose to leave, pulling the door shut behind him too forcefully. Abs turned to stare at Ericka who was peering back at him, defiant, feeling her cheeks flush. "This always seems to go a little easier if I do the talking so just sit tight a minute. You know damn well I coulda drummed your ass out of here five times over if I wanted. And still, you don't trust me enough to give me the least amount of information I need to do my job. You're down there in the basement working on something like this—" he pointed to Ericka's memo in front of him "—and I hear about it after an outside agency is already involved. That's just bullshit!" His dark face reddened as he spoke, jaw muscles clenching at his temples.

She looked down at the floor, not wanting him to read the dread in her eyes. Dread that he would reassign the case to someone who wasn't suspended pending review and under psychiatric evaluation. Guilt gnawed at her. Abs had always been more than fair to her. "You're right. I just didn't want to come to you before I could convince you it wasn't a goose chase. I also didn't want to have one of those dilettantes at International Operations grabbing this. They'll want it for profile, but they'll screw it up. This is serious dark web stuff. No one over there has a clue about how to do this kind of work."

"Okay, I get that, but you can't be burning through resources and not tell me anything about it. Look, I just don't know why you don't get it. I'm on your side. You do shit that makes me crazy, but you are the very best at what you do. But you have got to work with me. I've got to know what you're doing down there." He waited until she nodded, his expression softening. "And I read from Steiner's report he feels he's making little progress with you lately. Can you meet me in the middle and at least pretend to cooperate with the whole shrink thing?"

She failed to stifle the snort of laughter. She looked up, finding herself feeling almost bashful in the face of his open admiration. She nodded. "Deal."

"And this—" he looked down at her operations plan "—is brilliant. I got to fix it up a little, then I'll take it upstairs. Then we argue about who is going to pay for what. I know what that murdered girl in Idaho did to you, to everyone who was involved. If you're right and this guy had a piece of that, I promise you we will hunt him down no matter how long it takes. Some things just cry out for justice. This is one of them."

O'Brien sat at the head of the table in the ATF's Sacramento war room, bracing himself like he was about to referee a wrestling match. On one side were six ATF field agents all leaning in, sporting grim expressions. From the other side, Ericka, Tim, and Abara stared back. Supervisory Special Agent Manuel Vargas, ATF, rested his chin on balled fists and stared across the boardroom table. The scratched surface reflected the cheap fluorescent lighting with its characteristic, irritating flicker. His neck bulged over the top of his shirt and his body armor looked so tight, she wondered how he could breathe. Despite the cool of the room, beads of sweat stood out on his swarthy forehead.

Ericka could not read his face other than he was controlling his expression, but it was clear he resented the FBI intrusion into his carefully crafted investigation. She had not expected he would be pleased to have them parachuting into his case.

Vargas glared at O'Brien. "You know what we're dealing with here? Why are we doing this? We're talking about serious American military firepower here. Going to acquire and defend biker sales territory. People are getting killed and we're really close."

Ericka understood his determination to plug the pipe. "We understand. Your ops take operational priority."

"This your idea?" Vargas stared at Ericka, who nodded. He turned to look again at O'Brien. "And the DOJ is cool with

WITSEC on this? It isn't going to be cheap hiding anyone from these people. Never mind the guy you're looking at."

O'Brien smiled and folded his hands on his belly. "All signed and funded. He and his mother can go to ground as soon as they are done debriefing him."

"So, this Ramirez guy is not only a runner for Satan's Tribe, now it seems he is in on some sort of dark web cult?" Vargas cocked his head, looking back at Ericka, his raised eyebrows and controlled smirk telegraphing his skepticism.

"Something like that. We don't really know what our target's in on here." She cringed, painfully aware how much of her theory was based on unsupported inference and how little rested on actual evidence.

Vargas snorted. "I don't think you even really know if you got a controlling mind behind your internet goose chase."

O'Brien leaned in to interject. "We're satisfied there's enough evidence to warrant a proper investigation. This started with a real snuff film made on American soil. A teenage girl was slaughtered, not someone selling fake Viagra over the internet to people who were never going to get laid anyway. They're not there yet with enough to get any sort of order for interception on their own, but the FBI dossier on this is compelling in my view. You've already got the authority to listen to this target." Ericka said nothing, letting O'Brien's DOJ clout do the heavy lifting.

Vargas shot O'Brien a dirty look. "I got that, or you wouldn't be trying to parachute them"—he nodded at the other side of the table — "right in the middle of my investigation."

Abara glowered back at him, lowering his head as he leaned forward. He had hung his jacket over a chair and was sitting with his sleeves rolled up. "We're bringing more to the party than we're taking. All we want is this one guy out. If he sings, you're going to get a lot you didn't have before. We might get a line on our target. A bit of cooperation, one quick action, and we'll be out of your hair."

"If you don't blow it for us." This from the enormously muscled South Asian man hunching over the table next to Vargas. He had not introduced himself when they came in for the meeting, nor had the other ATF agents, but the nametag on his body armor read Vihaan.

O'Brien waded in again. "It's a little Hollywood I grant you, but any way it works out, this Ramirez guy is out of the picture. Even if it doesn't pan out for them, he's gone. No way he can blow it for you."

Vihaan was staring at Abs' bare forearm. "That a green beret tatty I'm looking at?" Abs nodded, looking at him. "Buncha pussies. I was a SEAL."

"Yeah, how's your wife and my kids?" Tim shot back.

Ericka waited for a few seconds before interjecting over the laughter. "Well now we have the obligatory big dick contest out of the way, are we going to play nice?"

Vargas nodded. "We can do business. It all turns on whether you can get him to 'deliver' or not."

"Leave it to me. Setting up like that, they must have a contingency plan." Ericka grinned at Vargas. "The guys running this show aren't dumb."

Ericka huddled with Tim and three of the ATF agents around a table set up in the darkened master bedroom of the small house rented for the purpose. Listening equipment lay piled on the tables, blue LEDs and three screens lighting the faces peering at them. All wore headphones, heads cocked. She smiled at Vihaan, as he grinned in anticipation, cracking his knuckles and flexing his bulging arms. Police of all stripes lived for the takedown.

Ericka glanced at Vargas, pulling off her headset. "This is pretty well run for a bunch of bikers." Buy three small cars, paint and decal them up for a pizza place, deliver without anyone batting an eyelid.

Vargas nodded. "It's not bad at all. The bikers bought the place after it went under. No one makes pizza now. The numbers on the cars and the door are fake, and the real number is word of mouth between the hypes. Blow and chiva to your door in minutes."

Typical biker organization. All the full-patch guys are two levels removed and only show up if the situation requires their armed attendance. Most of the drivers are users themselves, working for a cut. Ericka leaned around the equipment to look at them. "Did Ramirez ever drive?"

Vargas answered, "We think so, but ever since we've been on to him, he's run the pizza place in the old building where it used to be, inventory and cash flow. I wouldn't want his job. He's got to make up any losses and hypes are hardly a reliable workforce."

Vihaan grinned at Tim. "You guys hear what happened last night?" Tim shook his head. "Let me play it for you. His guys forgot the codes. Then this." He fiddled with his mouse. "Listen."

"Chief, I'm a little fucked up about what I'm supposed to be delivering?"

"Six Pepsi, breadsticks, and a small pepperoni. Like I told you."

"Yeah, I got that. I forget what they mean though?"

"You fucking idiot, you can't keep driving back every time you forget the codes."

"Well you won't let me write them down, right?"

"No shit I won't let you write our fucking codes down."

"I'm sorry, Chief."

"Are you fucked up?"

"Maybe a little, yeah."

"You fucking moron, one more time and I am going to ventilate your ass. A Pepsi is a gram of blow, breadsticks are cut, a small pepperoni is fucking gram of chiva. Now I've given the fucking code out over the phone. One more fucking time, I am telling you."

"Sorry, Chief."

"Fuck, go home after this and sleep it off before you screw us."

Ericka laughed as she hadn't in some time. "I don't think I would want his job. Ready to go?"

Vargas gave her the thumbs-up. "All in position now."

The smell of the old wood-fired oven, now cold, competed with the pungent odor of rats. No one was paying for air conditioning. The place was filthy, containing the one desk and several plastic bins on the floor that would be replenished by runners as needed. Ramirez was responsible for producing a certain profit margin. In his line of work, upper management had something of an unforgiving attitude to unproductive middle managers, and being given the sack was often painful, requiring rehab and physio. He looked at his watch then stared out the window. His phone rang.

"Rocky's. What can we bring you tonight?"

Ericka looked at Tim who grinned back, struggling to keep her voice level, controlling her breathing. "Hey sweetheart, how ya doing?" She could do a passable bimbo voice when she wanted to.

"All good here," Ramirez answered, the tension in his voice audible. "What would you like?"

"Two mediums, one ham and pineapple, one whatever meat lovers special you have. And you guys have mix? A couple of twenty-sixes of Coke would be a good start."

"Sorry?"

"Is the connection bad, sugar?" She gave Tim a dirty look as he snorted.

Ramirez's voice quivered as he spoke. "No, it's good."

"Did I get you right at closing time?"

"No, no I was just thinking we might be out of pineapple. I was just looking."

"Sure. Can I have those at 1121 Dartmoore Lane? And how much will that be?"

There was a long pause and Ericka imagined him making up prices then trying to add them in his head. "That'll be twenty-five bucks, fifty for everything." She could hear the tremor in his voice as he thought through what to do. She fought down the laughter threatening to erupt, avoiding eye contact with Tim.

"See you guys soon! Hurry, I'm starving." She flipped a switch on the monitoring equipment and pulled off the left side of her headset. "This will be good." She leaned in on the center monitoring screen as a line of code appeared and the machine began recording again.

"He's dialing. Wait for it." Her heart thumped against her

ribs and her cotton shirt clung to her skin. She looked up at Tim, his eyes pressed shut as he held his headphones tight against his head, concentrating, a faint smile on his face. As the call engaged, the noise of heavy breathing mixed with the sound of dialing. Ramirez was gulping his breaths. The call connected with a loud click.

"Yeah, what?"

"Boss?"

"What the fuck? Why are you calling me on this number?"

"Something's happened."

"It'd better fucking be important. What?"

"Someone ordered a pizza."

"Huh?"

"A real pizza. I'm worried we'll fucking be blown when we don't deliver."

"How the fuck did they get the number?"

"I don't know, she just called a minute ago. I got her number. Want me to call back and ask?"

"Fuck! Are you stupid? No, don't call her back and ask."

"What if she gets curious about why we didn't deliver? It could heat us up."

"Look, moron, it's simple. Take her a fucking pizza."

"We don't have any pizza."

"Fuck! I know we don't have any pizza. Go buy a fucking pizza and take it to her."

"Buy one?"

"There's still some boxes in the back from when the place was open, right?"

"Yeah?"

"Pick up a box, drive down to Luigi's, buy a fucking pizza,

put it in the box and take it to her. Fuck, do I have to think of every stupid thing around here?"

"What if she doesn't have cash and wants to use a credit card?"

"One more stupid question and I am coming down there and hit you so fucking hard your grandmother will get a nosebleed! Say the fucking machine is busted and comp her the fucking pizza! Idiot!"

"Right. I'll do that."

"And you call me on this phone again and I'm going to stuff it up your ass sideways. I just got this one set up. If I have to throw the chip in the river, I'm going to be really pissed."

"Sorry, Boss."

"Fuck—get on with it!"

10

Social Engineering

The takedown was over in seconds. The knock at the front door was almost timid. Ericka shouted at him. "C'mon in, sugar."

As Ramirez stepped into the dark living room, Vihaan loomed out of the shadows, plucking the boxes of pizza aside while Tim kicked his legs out from under him, taking him to the floor hard. It was over in seconds. Both looked at each other, seeming disappointed at being unable to show off their fighting skills.

Vihaan popped open a box and stuffed a piece of pizza in his face with obvious relish, chewing noisily. He grinned at Ramirez, his mouth full. "This is really good pizza, did you go to Luigi's? Your boss has good taste." Ramirez nodded without changing his mournful expression. He sat slouched in his chair, handcuffed and surrounded by several officers visible on the edges of the light. He bowed his head after staring at the blinking array of monitoring equipment.

"Everyone in your racket gets pinched. Why so sad, pal?" Vihaan asked solicitously.

The prisoner looked from face to face. "Aren't you going to give me my rights and my call?"

"No. No lawyering up for you, my friend. You're not under arrest." Ericka moved a chair in front of him, her elbows on her knees as she spoke. He was scared enough to bite, breathing hard and his pulse is going so fast it was visible on his neck.

"I'm not huh? You been listening to me on a wire. Why the fuck not?" Ramirez tilted his head towards the stacks of equipment as he spoke, his slouching posture conveying his resignation.

Ericka continued to lead. "We have a proposition for you."

"I'm not rolling. You forget who I work for?" His shoulders were rigid now as expected, steeling himself.

Time to try it on. "I'm very interested in who you're working for."

Ramirez all but rolled his eyes. "I said, I'm not ratting."

She shook her head, her eyes locked on his. "I don't think you've thought this through yet."

"What's to think about?"

Ericka stared at him. Time for him to sip the Kool-Aid. "If you don't want to talk to us that's fine; we're just going to let you go."

That set the hook good and deep. His head snapped up, eyes bulging in fear. "You're going to set me up. You know fucking well, they'll think I ratted on them."

Ericka gave him her best fake yet kindly smile. "Tough business you're in, it's true. I don't think their assumptions are my problem. You lie down with dogs, you get fleas. Nothing to do with us."

"My mother lives in Chico. They'll kill her."

"Now she'll have another reason to be proud of her son. We'll do our best to protect her." Ericka's intent gaze was devoid of emotion. He had to believe she would do it.

"You gonna use my mother to jack me?" His tone was biting now, and he spat as he talked.

"Not at all. We'll take her into witness protection at the first sign of trouble."

"You know these guys. They find people in protection all the time!" A siren wailed outside, passing on a nearby street.

Ericka nodded with fake sympathy. "That's true too. Always hard to build a perfect system. But it isn't those guys I want to know about. You've been two-timing them." Ramirez looked at the floor, drawing in a deep shuddering breath. He said nothing. She let the silence build for some time before speaking. "You told one of your guys about someone on the dark web. A fellow who may have supplied you with things that you want. Want to see the texts?"

Ramirez shook his head, shoulders tense, fists clenched. "I'm fucking dead already. No one can protect me from either of them, him especially."

"Don't be too sure. Maybe you want to hear me out on the deal I'm offering." Ericka looked at his trembling hands. Now he was scared enough to work with, more scared than at the retribution the bikers would exact. That said something. "Yes?"

Ramirez said nothing, so she leaned over and lifted his chin, her eyes boring into his. She saw no hope, just fear. A slow shiver, and a deep thrill began crawling up her spine. Not only was there a phantom but he engendered enough fear in his minions that this idiot would rather take his chances with one of the most brutal motorcycle gangs on the west coast.

Ericka shot a look at Tim who nodded back. "So, here's what we're offering. We don't give a shit about your little dial-a-dope operation. We want two things. First everything you know about the Tribe's guns. Who's the source and how they're moving them? Second, everything you can tell me about this guy on the dark web. What's he into? What's he had you do? Any plans you know about, but most importantly, you tell me where I can find whatever device you use to talk to him and help me secure it before anyone has a chance to wipe it."

"And I'm getting what for this?"

Ericka leaned closer to show him she had no fear of him. "WITSEC for you and your mother. Out of the country."

Ramirez lunged forward against his restraints, his face flushing red. She did not flinch. "You fucking bitch! Are you stupid? These guys don't give a shit about WITSEC. One of them doesn't even know what a country is. They'll find me no matter what you do."

She nodded once again, painting her features with fake sympathy. "True. It is a bit of a predicament you've gotten yourself into, it's true. Let's go through your options. We let you go, the bikers hear you got pinched without charges. They're grumpy with you. You go into WITSEC and give evidence against them, they find you and they're even grumpier. Probably mad at your mother too for giving birth to you. You tell us what you know about your dark web boss, and he finds you and kills you a second time for good measure, maybe has someone defile your body. That about sum it up? You're pretty dead all around, I'd say."

Ramirez glared at her, his face contorted with anger, twisted with bewilderment. "You are a serious fucking bitch."

Ericka grinned at him. "That was a really lucky guess."

"So why am I going to help you with anything? It sounds like no matter what I do I'm dead."

"Yes, I had the same thought."

He stared at her, his expression vacant, his eyes holding nothing but fear.

The Tribe's clubhouse was at the far end of a quiet street on the northern edge of town. The long driveway clear of brush and trees gave the occupants an unlimited view down to the chain-link fence separating the property from the street. Tonight, the party was in full swing. Metal guitar boomed out the open front door into the yard where rows of motorcycles sat in neat rows, parked with almost military precision. A runaround wannabe sat in a folding beach chair, smoking and keeping an eye up the street for trouble. The Tribe were new on the scene and very unpopular with the people they had displaced. Trading hits was a recognized part of the business. 'Spindles' McKay had drawn the short straw tonight. Named for his skinny legs, he was to keep watch and alert the patched members at the first hint of trouble.

Spindles slouched in his chair as the sound of women's laughter and squeals drowned out even the thrash guitar. He gritted his teeth and sipped his beer. He had sat there staring with envy as a dozen peelers from the Tribe's strip club arrived in a stretch limo sporting more after-market parts than a monster truck rally. They were reeling from drinks, having emptied the car's little fridge.

Spindles pulled a package of cigarettes from his rolled-up T-shirt sleeve, trying to shake himself out a new one before the last one went out, fumbling in his ridiculously tight jeans for his lighter. He could hear the sirens but took no note. When the approaching din made it clear he was hearing multiple police cars, he jumped to his feet and bounded up the front steps three at a time. He flung the screen door open, lunging inside, bruising his hand and staring around the smoke-filled living room. "Boss!"

"What the fuck?" Theodore 'Rattlesnake' Reid lurched to his feet from the ancient couch and lumbered towards him, shoving two of the spandex-clad women out of his way, spilling their drinks. Named for blinding speed with his fists, he was the club's sergeant at arms, responsible for both security and discipline. He grabbed Spindles by the shoulder, making him flinch, then shoved him out onto the cracked, concrete porch. "Trouble?"

Spindles nodded up the street. Racing towards them, a compact car led four police vehicles. It careened around the corner towards them, tires screeching, audible even at this distance.

"Jesus fucking Christ!" Rattlesnake thrust his head back through the door and roared, "Cops! Flush the shit now!" Spindles watched in fascination. Despite being loaded, the club members all followed the prescribed protocol for a raid. He turned to see Rattlesnake nodding to himself as he strode down the driveway to the front gate. He turned over his shoulder and snarled at Spindles. "Call the fucking lawyers! Tell them to head for the police station!" He straightened the leather vest sporting his colors and stood arms folded behind the gate in the center of the gravel driveway. Spindles made the call and ran to stand behind him.

Spindles stared as the lead police car raced towards the

cul-de-sac's end alongside the compact car, then veered towards it, forcing it into a parked truck with the heavy boom of folding metal followed by the tinkle of spreading bits of auto glass. Spindles gritted his teeth, seeing the familiar livery of a pizza delivery car, hearing his boss swearing to himself under his breath. "How fucking stupid do you have to be?"

Spindles gasped as the driver of the delivery vehicle squirmed out the shattered driver's window, twisting and falling to the pavement, blood visible on his white shirt. He stumbled towards the gate before ducking behind a parked car, reaching for the pistol shoved down the back of his pants. Rattlesnake let out an explosive breath as the man drew it, pointing it at the armored police crouching behind car doors. Several officers trained their rifles on the bleeding man. The fugitive shot first, setting off a fusillade of return fire. His body lurched as the rounds struck him, and he flopped to the ground, a marionette with its strings cut. The police advanced, keeping their weapons trained on the lifeless, bloody form. They went through the motions of cuffing him, one of the officers holding him turned to look at the officer in charge, shaking her head.

Spindles leaned to whisper in Rattlesnake's ear. "That looks like fucking Ramirez. He's one of ours."

Without turning his head or changing his expression, he hissed his response. "Shut your fucking mouth and go back in the house. Tell the others to stay inside and out of sight. Get one of our fucking lawyers down here and come back out with an ETA. Clear?"

"Got it," he whispered, and scurried off up the driveway.

The officer in charge, Lieutenant Mark Hughes of the

Sacramento PD, strolled over, stopped at the gate and nodded up to the leather-clad behemoth just as Spindles returned. "Mr. Reid, can I help you with something?"

"What the fuck is going on? A shootout right in front of my fucking house and you ask what I want? I want to fucking know what's going on?"

"Took him down dealing. Red-handed. When the cover team moved in, he took a shot at one of them and tried to get away. Stupid guy and a terrible shot. One of yours I think. That was a nice touch, reopening Rocky's as a dial-a-dope."

"Never seen that guy before and don't know what the fuck you're talking about."

"Why don't I come up to the house and we can talk about it?" Hughes grinned up at the huge biker.

"I'm looking but I don't see a fucking warrant in your hand."

"If I had one, we wouldn't be talking down here."

He looked down at Spindles who nodded and mouthed the word *fifteen*. "Enjoy the rest of your evening, Lieutenant Hughes. One of our lawyers will be here soon if you're feeling chatty. Try not to run up my tab too much."

"Have a nice evening, Mr. Reid." The officer was already walking back to the cluster of patrol cars to wait for the coroner's van.

Richard Schmidt had grown used to the virtual audience hall of his benefactor. He lounged back, sinking into his basement armchair, its smell familiar, the VR goggles his only visual and auditory input, sitting in two worlds at once, hard-pressed to tell where one ended and the other started. Grinning, he turned his head side to side, taking in the flawless, immersive graphics. The detail in each individual piece of stone made them indistinguishable from reality and the overall effect took his breath away. The sound was fully three-dimensional, the torches guttered and water bubbled in the fountain behind him. This took a lot of work, detailed, painstaking work. Perhaps his patron had started with a high-resolution scan of a real place.

At first it had puzzled him why anyone would spend the time and effort, but he had begun to suspect it was more about his host's enjoyment than for the amazement of guests. It might well be his benefactor lived in this world more than the physical one so took the time. He had arrived home from work to see the goggles blinking with three green LEDs, signaling an invitation to meet with his virtual master. Dinner could wait. He pulled on the headgear and tapped the power button.

The headphones fed his ears the creaking sound of a massive weight settling into a padded leather chair. He tilted his head until the video feed rotated, allowing Schmidt to see the source of the sound. As usual, the massive form was backlit with firelight from low and behind, leaving a flickering glow playing over the hulking silhouette, all features submerged in shadow. The shape leaned forward, making him grin again. The presentation was flawless, his familiar baritone resonating from the walls.

"I trust those last videos were to your liking?" The huge head cocked to one side, listening.

"Thank you. Where were they filmed?" A warm flush of guilty pleasure rose to his face as he remembered.

"Are you becoming interested in some more travel?" The tone carried a hint of amusement.

"Perhaps. I never thought I'd take the risk again. You're a bad influence."

No reaction to the irony. "You are just coming into your own now. You were not born to fit into their world. You must make your own here in this world that I can provide you or stay hidden in theirs."

Schmidt's guts tightened as he thought about it. "Everyone who travels for the real thing gets caught eventually. As long as I stay here and live by the right protocols, there's no chance of a knock on my door."

The great head shifted forward and came to rest on a huge fist, some of his facial features visible for the first time. High cheekbones protruded from the black, framing an aquiline nose. Unseen eyes lurked in the shadows of deep sockets and a heavy brow, full lips hinting at a cruel mouth. Schmidt flinched, leaning back. "Nor is there any risk if you make the journey in segments, remain for a time at each stopover while you switch identities and carry nothing with you but clothes. You just have to do it properly. I will help if you choose to go." The gaze of hidden eyes made him clench his jaw, his heartbeat uneven. Knowing it was just clever illusion did little to diminish its gut-level effect.

"I think I'd rather just indulge myself as I have for the time being."

Schmidt heard a short sigh from his master before he spoke. "You fail to reach your potential when you lack the imagination to visualize what you might be." The huge form leaned back in repose, a well-oiled mass of dark, defined muscle glistening red. "I wonder if there is something else you hunger for more than sexual gratification?"

Schmidt nodded as he spoke. "There were a lot of things I didn't know I wanted, until you showed up."

The voice carried a hint of a smile. "This world—" a large hand on a muscled wrist gestured "—can be whatever you want it to be. But sometimes it is not enough. Even then it can provide a cloak of concealment for, shall we say, careful interaction with the physical world."

Schmidt felt bold. "And do you ever interact with it?"

"The role I have chosen is to help those confined by the moral restraints of a world not theirs, one in which they exist but were not made for, first to visualize what they need for fulfillment, then to create that world. If the virtual is insufficient, I facilitate the harvesting of what my companions need, sometimes sharing their enjoyment."

"Harvest? An interesting choice of words."

"I loathe burying truth beneath semantics. Everything in the world that eats consumes the life of something else. Nature's way does not stop at the threshold of the virtual world, but who is the prey and who is the hunter can be altered."

"Each of us recreating the world in our own image?" Schmidt grinned.

The menacing form sat in repose, hands resting on the arms of his immense chair. "If you like, but it does not end there. Recreate yourself if you like. Here you are limited only at the point where your imagination fades. Look down!"

Schmidt did as his host asked. He started, muscles jumping, then barked a nervous laugh. The virtual body of his avatar was changing. First, a reasonable image of his real body, paunchy and relaxed, slouching in his chair. His legs expanded, grew oddly shaped muscles and sprouted thick hair, his feet twisting into cloven hoofs. Then the hair disappeared, his limbs contracted until they were smooth and lusciously curved, enormous breasts swelled to obscure his view. He cackled again. His final body mirrored Dantalion's: dark, immense rippling muscles, his genitals several times their real size.

Schmidt gasped as he spoke. "That's really quite the trick that you can do that in real time. Very impressive."

The acknowledging bow brought the smooth top of the great head out of shadow for a moment. "A small sample of what is possible with me."

"And you can combine this kind of visualization in real time with physical sensation? I could be shagging a goat in my basement, but see a porn star here?"

"Or the other way around, if such is your taste." The head tilted again, the rich timbre of the monster's voice carrying the hint of an unseen smile.

Schmidt snorted with laughter then paused, digesting what he had seen, before leaning forward to speak. "If you can do this—" he gestured, pointing with his chin "—why are you so curious about my work? You're generations ahead of anything that's ever been put in an aircraft. Even the military's through-hull visualizations aren't as good as this."

"As I have said, sometimes creating what we want requires some overlap with the physical world. The virtual world currently feeds only part of our array of senses. Sometimes that isn't enough. This is what my companions can do that interests me."

"Surely, there are easier ways to do this?"

The right hand came up, raising an index finger. "If that

is what you want, yes, but choosing what is easier is often merely concealment for cowardice."

"So, I take it you want something more?"

"This is about what you want. I facilitate your desires, your needs."

Schmidt knew he was being played. "How do you know what I want?"

"You are not a difficult man to understand. Your sexual urges are not permitted in the physical world, so you do not live the same life as your colleagues. You are different, isolated—they do not trust you. You have no wife, no children, none of the trappings of so-called normal. Your personnel file at the company shows they regard you as having limited future potential. Whether they act consciously or not, basic primate behavior demands ostracism for those perceived as different. You will end your career where you are, a useful widget. And you have no one. You are a society of one."

Schmidt sat, muscles rigid and teeth clenched, resenting the stark truth of the words, hating the speaker. "And what does someone so pathetic have to offer you?" He spat the words, glowering.

"Much, but I see you for what you can become, not as 'normal' society sees you. There is a great deal we can do together. In the purely physical realm, you must adapt and hide in the world as it is. What I offer is to use the tools of this dominion to remake the world with yourself at the center."

"I'm listening."

The avatar leaned forward as if to speak, then the upper half spun to one side so fast the legs were left facing Schmidt and the seamless illusion was lost until the software caught up to the abrupt move. The huge form disappeared into the shadows of the chair, as if he had evaporated. The voice came, disembodied and from all directions, echoing from the virtual stone. "We will speak again soon. Something requires my immediate attention."

The goggles powered down, leaving the LEDs on the outside blinking in sequence. Schmidt pulled them off, finding himself chilled and feeling out of breath as always. He sat for over an hour, chin on his open palm staring at the goggles, wondering.

11

A Wraith in Sunlight

Ericka crouched by the front door, scanning the street. Not the kind of neighborhood where a warrant would be an unusual event, but the presence of the FBI brought onlookers. Del Paso Heights was Ramirez's kind of neighborhood. No one on the darkened street but eyes everywhere. The houses were old, blinds drawn, the road littered with clapped-out cars. She hoped Abs would forgive the transgression of going in herself, but she couldn't leave this to anyone else.

"FBI! Search warrant!" The masked and armored agent waited a few seconds, not expecting a response, the rest of the squad covering him from behind, assault weapons poised at eye level. He lunged forward swinging the handheld battering ram hard, knocking the flimsy door off its hinges to clatter into the hall. No sound came from the dark interior, no movement. They had cut the power seconds before. The agents poured through the entrance, clearing the rooms, their gun-mounted flashlights splashing beams of light through unkempt spaces.

Tim stood on the threshold glancing along the street while

holding his earpiece tight, looking at Ericka. "Couple of minutes. The SWAT guys can't get into some of the rooms. Won't be long now."

She took a deep breath. "They're taking way too long. Light a fire under their asses. This's a serious shithole of a street. If someone tips him off, he'll only need seconds to brick everything up." She leaned to look into the darkened doorway, trying to visualize the scene, grinding her teeth at the enforced idleness. This was a whole new kind of torture.

"All clear!" came the sergeant's voice.

Tim darted in with Ericka hot on his heels. He had his pistol out, but Ericka carried just the equipment to secure the exhibits.

The sergeant's voice crackled again. "Downstairs. None of the lights work, but some kind of power is still on. Battery backup. Your guy is straight up so far."

The thump of Tim's footsteps resonated in her head as she followed him down, muscles strung like piano wire. Everything turned on getting to the equipment before their phantom got wind and erased his tracks, either a rapid overwrite of all the data or an encryption program. She didn't think he would risk either a commercial encryption program that might have a back door or expose something of his own making to police analysis. She was betting his failsafe was a generic program to overwrite all the data multiple times, leaving just random binary values to mark his passing, torrential rain over footprints in sand. It was what he had used in Idaho, but that took time. Time brought him risk.

Tim cursed as he tripped and brought something to the floor with the distinctive tinkle of broken glass. "Bloody hell, leave it, where are the computers?"

"Over here, on the table." An unknown female voice. "Man, this place stinks. What a fucking pig!"

Tim shouted over his shoulder to Ericka. "You were right, the computers are running, overwriting everything. Looks like something triggered it before we even got down here. Shit, same with the satellite box. We're screwed. He's here ahead of us."

Ericka yelled to the SWAT member standing near the wall. "Unhook the damned things! No over here, behind the table!" Two of the SWAT team members dove to where she pointed to tear wires from the stack of car batteries.

The lights still didn't go out and she felt like screaming. "Forget the power source. They have internal batteries. Use the ram! Smash them! Stop them running—whatever you have to do. We might get something off the disk fragments. What about the goggles?" There was no response except the sound of heavy breathing and the noise of things being thrown about.

Tim answered from the dark to her left. "Got them! Fuck! Same thing. They must be wireless to one of the boxes. Who's got the Faraday bags? Jesus, just throw it!" A SWAT member tossed them from across the room. Portable shielding for mobile devices to stop remote access. Tim cursed under his breath, shoving the goggles into the bag while reaching in to pry out the power source. Finding nothing he sealed the bag, then yanked the ram from the hands of the man holding it and smashed the contents.

Ericka held out her hands. "Throw it!" She peered into the bag, seeing no light from the LEDs. She wrapped the bagged fragments in a second Faraday and sat on the steps looking at Tim's silhouette. "We're just bringing back bags of bits.

Ramirez was right—we didn't even get close. Something set them off before we got down the stairs. How the hell did he know?"

Ericka perched on the stairs controlling hard, ragged breaths, her head low. How the hell indeed. *This one's different from all the others. Like nothing we've seen. He's thought eight moves ahead of us. He's got software we've never seen before mated to state-of-the-art hardware. Who the fuck is this guy?* She lifted her head up, chewing her lip and polishing her glasses. All this screwing around with the bikers might be for nothing.

Tim walked over and leaned on an old chair. "Any ideas?"

Ericka glanced up at him. "I don't know. The fact that he told Ramirez to wire the power around the fuse box and into backup meant it needed time for something to run after a breach. I've no idea what triggered it. Ramirez said he had no alarm or motion sensors. It could be triggered by a cell call in, but what tipped him off to do it, I've no idea. And cell's way too risky. We could follow that trail. He's way beyond something that amateur hour."

When Tim spoke, she could hear the weariness. "This one gives me a very nasty feeling. He's leaving a trail of bodies across the bloody planet, and we haven't any idea who or where he is."

She stood up, feeling sick. "Let's get the stuff back to the lab and leave SWAT to clean up." *Ericka girl,* she thought, *the reason you've cracked every single dark web baddy you've turned your attention to is that you're better than any of them. Not anymore. Not this one. He's something different.* She shivered despite the heat.

* * *

Ramirez bowed his head over folded arms, leaning on the table. His skin shone with sweat and he was unshaven. The borrowed clothes he wore were several sizes too big for him and he stunk. The light in the interrogation room was poor, outlining wrinkles and making the two men look more haggard than they were. "We've been through all this. We're done. I have nothing more to tell you."

"We're done when I tell you we're done." Vargas stood on the opposite side of the metal table, palms flat, leaning in to scowl at Ramirez. "I believe you about the guns. A guy shows up every month or so in a rented van like he's delivering groceries. You don't know him. Only the big guys talk to him. Got it. But the other guy, you're holding out on me."

Ericka spoke into her mic from her seat in the monitoring room down the hall, looking at Ramirez's image on the screen in front of her. Tim leaned over beside her, sipping his coffee and scribbling notes. "Get him to run through the deliveries again." She spoke to Vargas as she turned to Tim. "He's playing us."

Tim nodded. "He is but I don't know he's actually got that much to give us. Our target isn't stupid enough to tell idiots like this anything that could burn him."

In the interrogation room, Vargas sat down in the worn metal chair, leaning back and tilting his head. "What, you think this guy can still find you or something? You're dead remember?"

Ramirez looked resigned. "While I was working for him, this guy knew everywhere I went, what I bought, and who I talked to. Unless I want to spend my life on some fucking farm, picking cauliflower and shitting in a ditch with the rest of the wetbacks, he'll find me."

Vargas nodded. "True, you're never going on the internet again. Tough go for a fucking pervert like you. Why'd you help us then?"

Ramirez curled his lip in a snarl. "I shouldn't have."

"Well, you've done it now. Seems to me if you're right, your only hope for a brighter future is us taking him down." Vargas smiled but it didn't reach his eyes. "Or am I missing something?"

"I have no idea who he is, or where he is, or what his gig really is."

Vargas' tone was biting. "No names, emails, texts, nothing? That's what you're telling me."

"Calls himself Dantalion. That's the only name I know— his handle. I told you."

"You know what the name means?"

Ramirez rolled his eyes. "Some sort of fucking devil or something. I Googled it. He gets into your mind."

"And you were working for this guy? Some sort of dark web nut and you're running around doing his dirty work?" Vargas shook his head. "What some kids won't do to make their mamas proud."

"That was the deal at first. He'd let me watch videos he had. Really wild stuff. All he wanted was for me to take care of a few things for him. Send boxes to people. I don't even know what was in most of them. They'd arrive at my door and I was told not to get too curious about who else was helping him move stuff."

Vargas waved at him in a dismissive gesture. "Just a straight commercial transaction? FedEx for internet predators."

"Fuck you! He found me. I was watching girl movies—you know, where maybe the *chicas* were a little too young, and suddenly he starts talking to me. Just some sort of chat program pops up. He says if I do him some favors, he will help me out. More movies and he gave me some info on my competition. Told me who one of the rats was in town. That got me in good with the Tribe. He was ratting on them too."

Vargas leaned back, eyes narrowed. "Your 'pal' Carlos? That got him killed."

"He was no pal of mine. Fucking rat."

"Where did devil-boy get his information? Where did the equipment come from? Tell me again?"

Ramirez shrugged then reached for his water, taking several sips. "He told me to watch for a box. Said he was going to send me something he only gives to people he trusts. A little satellite dish, console to work it, and those wild fucking goggles. All I had to do was wire it up to bypass the fuse box and connect it to a couple old car batteries. Keep them on a charger. Then plug in the stick he sent with it into my computer and it set itself up. Then I burned the stick like he said."

"Go on."

"After that, every time he wanted to talk to me, the lights on it would flicker. Man, that was fucking something when they fired up. Like being in a video game except better than any I've seen. A huge devil church kinda place where he would sometimes look like some sort of demon, real as you are now. Except he didn't smell of shitty aftershave like you. Where the fuck are you buying that shit?"

Vargas grinned back. "Maybe you should be a fucking

comedian when we get you resettled. I hear they're always glad of a little entertainment in those Siberian fishing villages."

That drew a smirk from Ramirez. "His face was always shifting when he spoke; sometimes he would have different bodies, sometimes in a huge chair with a book sitting on the arm. Always wanted to know stuff about me. Why I wanted the stuff I do. Said it would help him make me better at what I wanted to be."

"Wow, a dark web life coach. Actualize your true potential. Bhangra clapping and drumming circles? Nice guy. Why are you so scared of him then?" Ericka and Tim both snorted with laughter as they listened.

"Because some of the stuff he showed me was people being killed. I mean really killed. Real people." Ericka and Tim exchanged a look.

"How do you know it's not all smoke and mirrors?"

Ramirez sneered his answer, glaring up at the camera. "I know. It ain't like I've never seen someone die before. It's a little different than in the movies. You know what I mean."

"And all this because he wanted you to be his delivery boy? Just like the bikers. Maybe that's all you're cut out for. Maybe we'll find you a real fucking pizza place to work at."

Ramirez lifted from his seat shouting, "Fuck you! I'm not just a runner. He watched out for me. Said all he wanted in return was loyalty."

Vargas reached over the table, almost casually shoving him back down. "Well isn't he an idiot then, trusting you. He'll be very impressed." Vargas looked up at the camera.

Ericka spoke again. "That's good for now, thanks. May need to have another go later." She turned to Tim. "So that's something we didn't have before. Man, this guy is careful."

Tim stared down at his notepad. "More than we had, but no closer to flushing him out than the day we started. The fact that he has outed several gangland rats means he has either busted into police computers or has one of his minions working inside somewhere. We'll need to look."

She smiled, putting her feet up on the monitoring desk. "Except now we know he exists. One guy. When we came into this, we weren't even sure of that."

"We don't know that. It could be several sharing an avatar and handle. Maybe that's why the inconsistent taste in victims."

Ericka cocked her head, indulging in her usual habit of gnawing on her pen. "True enough and good thought, but you know what I mean. The trail we're following isn't a bunch of unconnected events."

"Okay, sure. We've established there's a target. Now what?"

"Time for a little bit of lab work. As soon as the techs are done lifting the data off the bits you sent them, I'll see what we've got. Maybe look at the VR chipset and see if there is anything we can use."

"So, you know how he did it?" Tim perched on a stool, leaning over the lab bench where Ericka was working. He'd rushed to the forensics lab moments before, out of breath in response to her text. He blinked at the bright lights, staring at Ericka who was hunched over a bench wearing coveralls.

She sat up straight, pulling off the magnifying goggles. The imprints they left on her face made her look like a flushed, pink raccoon. Her lab coveralls were sticking to her skin and she was dying for a shower. "Simple overwriting software. That was easy. It was the triggering event that gave me trouble. The key was the multiple antennae in the goggles' network card. Minor physical mods, but a pretty clever trick on a little chip." She reached for her water bottle and drank most of it, enjoying the cool water soothing her parched throat. The lab's temperature and humidity were controlled, leaving it a very dry work environment. "It was us and the entry team that set it off." She relished his look of puzzled alarm.

"Don't mess with me. I'm having nightmares I set off something simple."

She nodded, teasing him. "Our phones."

"Phones?"

Ericka pointed to the equipment on the workbench. "He's done something new here, but we can be ready for it next time."

"You're killing me."

She smiled, deciding to let him off the hook. "Next time we get anywhere near his stuff, everything has to be powered off. We're going in naked." He cocked one eyebrow and waited for her to continue. "The goggles are constantly scanning Bluetooth, Wi-Fi, and cellular. Kind of like a multi-function Stingray. As soon as it detects two or more sources in proximity, it commences wiping on all components of the rig." A Stingray was a mobile tracking device used by police to capture cellular signals so they could intercept a target's traffic. Instead of the nearest cell towers, all mobiles within range hooked up to the police equipment.

Tim was staring across the bench at the wall. "So, any nearby grouping of phones not on airplane mode is presumed to be cops, and it fires up the failsafe?"

Ericka nodded, staring at the exhibits in front of her. "Yes, precisely. More complicated but that's the gist of it. Probably why he tells his goons to set up in a basement. That way any group of kids driving by heading for pizza doesn't shut it down. It's got a pretty tight range."

"Sounds like it will generate a lot of false alarms."

She shrugged her agreement. "I'm sure it does, but he likely prefers that to leaving his stuff exposed. It wouldn't take long to reload if it was a false alarm. Just need to send a link to the minion."

Tim's expression was thoughtful. "So next time, all we'll have to do is have an airplane-mode SWAT crew?"

"I don't know. I might not have found all the triggers yet. There were two others for sure." She had a grudging but mounting admiration for Dantalion's technical prowess. Very few companies or intelligence agencies in the world had code this advanced. A monster he was, but there was some real brilliance in the execution. She was accustomed to chasing easier prey; he was at least a peer, perhaps more. She squeezed her eyes shut.

Tim's voice jolted her back. "Other triggers?"

"If the goggles are left off the charger, this wiping protocol runs as soon as the batteries get down to thirty percent. If they're lifted off the charge cradle and no one puts the password in the attached device within one minute, the protocol runs on everything. If they lose contact with the connected devices for more than a minute, same thing. There may be more. All I've found is those, a copy of the software that did the wiping, and the rest is just random binary values. If there were more security protocols, they were overwritten with the rest."

"Jesus bloody Christ, that's thorough. Anything we can use in the overwriting software?"

She leaned on a fist as she answered. "Nope. It's just slightly modified freeware. Set to do nine overwrites on every bit of storage except itself. He's careful to go generic wherever he can."

"How did you figure out the tripwires then?"

"Bit of code on the chips and the way the card was configured. It stored some data on the machine it was linked to. Really very elegant. If he gets sick of being a dark web monster and overlord, he could patent and sell this as an anti-parent, anti-teacher, anti-boss, anti-cop add-on to every teenage boy in the world."

Tim was studying her features, looking thoughtful. "Time for a break. You more than me. Let's go get a burger and get ourselves sorted a bit."

She opened her mouth to say no, then saw the time on her phone—10:17 PM. Not getting anything else done tonight. She nodded and dragged herself up to the locker room where she peeled off the sterile coveralls and threw them in the overflowing hamper. As she did, the ripe smell made her think a shower was in order first. Towel around her neck, she caught a glimpse of herself in the mirror and smiled. Nothing like continuous nerves to keep you trim, combined with minimal food and no sleep.

Ericka rolled her eyes at Tim as they stood in the doorway scanning for a table. Rico's Eatery was full and the crowd was noisy, servers bustling between the kitchen and the bar, never stopping. Most of the crowd were kids, sitting at long communal tables, a full display of millennial chic underway. Second-hand clothes were the order of the day, faux lumberjack shirts, ironic toques, and tragic beards so bushy she wondered if they latched together like Velcro when they leaned in to speak to each other. Or maybe their piercings hooked together. How is it some portion of each generation conspires to be revolting to most of the generation before?

"The food's good, cheap, and we can make do." He gave her a look. "You're not old enough to pretend you're their mother. Give over."

She smiled, remembering the reaction some of her youthful hairstyles had attracted. "As soon as the smell of deep-fried anything hits me, I'm sold. There—" she nodded "—they're leaving." As she brushed past the long, garrulous tables, the smell of drugstore bodywash was momentarily overwhelming. They slid into the high chairs, leaning back while the server gave the worn surface a perfunctory wipe. Tim ordered from memory, fearing they wouldn't see her again for some time if they didn't. "And a Coke and a pint of Smithwick's if you still carry it," he added, glancing down and ogling her short skirt as she turned to leave.

"Very suave, very subtle." Ericka missed poking fun at him while she buried herself in lab work. That's what brothers were for.

"Force of habit. Not my type."

"Can I talk shop and get it out of my head?" Ericka pulled several napkins from the steel dispenser and wiped the table again before smiling at Tim.

"Why do you ask? You're going to do it no matter what I say. Just remember to pause when the waitress walks by or I won't be listening. Count of four or five should do it."

She gave him her best mocking eye roll. "I'm sure she appreciates the attention of old creeps like you. I can't figure out where to go next. We may have heated him up." As she reassembled the crushed bits of VR goggles, looking at their ability to record as well as display, it occurred to her it might have sent off some images before Tim smashed them.

Tim shrugged at the idea. "If he did, all he got was the Hollywood-looking SWAT guys coming down the steps into the basement. All faces were covered. Nothing we did in there tells him we're aware he exists."

She shook her head. "He's going to wonder why an FBI strike team is kicking in the door of a bog-ordinary drug dealer. The more I see of this guy's work, the jumpier I get. I'm getting leery of doing anything targeted with the crawlers now. He may well have tripwires all over anything he's doing. He's that good. If he becomes aware we're watching him, albeit in a very limited way, he may go to ground."

Tim eyed the server, then drank half the pint without a pause before answering. "That's better. I'm less concerned about the technology than the guy himself. Nothing about this guy adds up. Not the kind of guy you read about in the profiling manual and I can't think of what drives him. I still wonder if we're dealing with a cabal of some sort."

Ericka had been thinking the same thing. It was very rare to find a serial offender with no discernable taste in victims. "No real commonality at all. Real-time virtual participation seems to be as close as he personally gets to touching the physical world at all."

Tim sipped his beer, gazing down at the table, sighing. "And two classes of cohorts working with him. He has these idiots like Ramirez running his errands by feeding them some 'entertainment' not safely available anywhere else. The others must take a lot more work and risk on his part, like the mafia guys. He's got to find them first, groom them, get their trust, and then plan whatever he wants them to do."

"And every step of the way, he needs a fast way to bail without leaving tracks anyone else can follow. And having looked at this guy's work a bit now, I'm not convinced we've seen his whole bag of tricks." Ericka was actually very sure they hadn't.

Tim shook his head. "Forget the techy stuff for now. We aren't up to latching on to him that way and as you say we might send him to ground. The harder bit for him has got to be moron control. For the runners, he can pick the kind of guy he wants and keep the jobs simple. For the predators, he's stuck with what he finds. Remember in Idaho, we only got there as soon as we did because the on-site predator screwed up last minute with the vehicle. That's where he's vulnerable."

She leaned to one side, toying with her glass. Tim was right. Dantalion's biggest vulnerability was the same one that made online predators as easy to pick off as they were. They cannot control their impulses when they get close. The dick starts making all the decisions and dicks are lousy at strategy, kind of single-minded. "O'Brien has been lecturing me on Sun Tzu. Build your opponent a golden bridge to retreat across."

"Sorry?"

"It mainly means that an enemy facing defeat will fight all the more desperately if there is no way to retreat. Give him a way to escape and he will take it. You win with the least cost. But it also means, he retreats directly to ground you've chosen for him." Her mind raced through the possibilities. "Much as I'm loath to let him set up another one of his atrocities, maybe we can spook him into doing something stupid, like run across a bridge we've made?"

"You've lost me."

"Watch for the pattern. Disrupt it as it's happening. We know we can't follow his tracks to a location, but he doesn't know that. We might get him to panic. If he does, he might start trying to plant erase-and-overwrite programs without thinking it through. Follow where those came from."

Tim looked thoughtful as he reached for his beer. "Tricky bit is going to be approval. So far, our target has made very sure he spaces out the attacks. Idaho and Whitecourt were both on the continent, so I doubt his next venture will be close. To do what I think you are suggesting means disrupting foreign servers. You may even have to trigger an outage to be sure we disconnect him from the action on the ground. We do that without approval and you're going to have to squeeze into a little dress and heels at your age so you can flog burgers and beer here. You might look silly."

She smiled at the mental image. "We may briefly take a few servers offline, but most traffic should be rerouted around what we're doing. I think Abs will support this. I can persuade O'Brien to get us a Rule 41." Rule 41 allowed a judge to issue a warrant for police hacking irrespective of where in the world the data is located.

Tim nodded, waiting to speak as their food arrived. Their mouths watered at the smell of the thick burgers and double-fried chips. After a few huge bites, he leaned back. "I can start working on the material, but there's an angle to all this we're going to need to deal with before we go to a judge."

Ericka nibbled on a fry, resisting the urge to shovel them into her mouth. "The cosplay demon thing?"

"It isn't something we are going to be able to get one of the shrinks to profile, even with Ramirez's description. He isn't exactly what a judge is going to think is a reliable source either."

She cocked her head in mild annoyance. "Remember we didn't find Ramirez on our own. He fell into our lap. Did you read up on 'Dantalion'? This demon persona he likes to play at?"

"Yes, but not in any detail. Just Google."

"According to Crowley, this one has the ability to make people think his thoughts, see what he wants and do what he wants. Isn't that exactly what he's doing? It might tell us something about where he's going."

He cocked one eyebrow at her. "Maybe, but he could just be finding people keen to try what he is interested in and creating converts. Always easier to preach to the choir than the heathen. Either way, it's enough of a profile we can at least describe it well enough for a warrant, yes?"

She nodded. A faint shiver made her pull her sweater over her shoulders. The thrill of the hunt, to catch a demon and silence her own, and then perhaps some peace, for the first time in memory. She shook her head at his quizzical look.

"And you, Ericka love, how are you holding up? My aunt has been asking after you."

She glanced away, feeling Mrs. Donnelly's penetrating gaze, reacting to hide her thoughts as if the old woman were there. "I'm holding it together, but I have to get this one. You know why."

He nodded, holding her stare. "I do. But remember, no one

else can know. With this going on, they are going to watch you closer than ever before. They see you step outside the lines, and internal will be all over you, never mind the shrink."

Ericka recoiled from the table. "I know that!"

"Do you? This won't bring her back."

Irritated, she looked away, sipping her drink, on the verge of a cutting remark about amateur-hour shrinks. "Your aunt been telling tales out of school?"

Tim's stare fixed on her as he frowned. "If you think you're hiding what goes on in your head from anyone who knows you, think again. You've got a choice to make and neither outcome leads to a future full of puppies and sunshine."

She glanced up to meet his stare. "Let's get out of here."

"I'm not finished."

She glared at him, gritting her teeth at the lecture. "Say it then."

Tim hesitated so she scooped out the last of the fries from his plate. "We're supposed to be the good guys." He paused, his mouth open, clearly trying to get his words right. "You know I love you like a sister. Think long and hard about what you're planning. If you're nursing some sort of fantasy about taking them out, what happens after? Presuming you make it back in one piece, what next? You've talked about going back to industry and I have to say that sounds kind of appealing to me too, but..." he stopped again "...there are some things you can't walk back from. There might be no after. Yes?"

Ericka looked down at the table, chewing on the last of the food. "I'll make it work." She knew as she said it she had no idea if it was true.

12

Thunderbolt

Tim grinned at her from the door of the forensics lab. "So, a big breakthrough you say?"

She smiled back, lifting the goggles from her eyes, almost unable to slow her thoughts down enough to explain it. "The crawlers are picking him up again!"

"How?"

"Using the extra features on the Dantalion goggles. I physically reconstructed them and used them to broadcast in the lab then measured the network transmissions. They include a feature found on no other VR set I can find. They are comprehensively scanning the facial muscles and eyes of the wearer. Running that through a network creates a distinct signal at some points."

He thought for a moment. "So, he can see their expressions in real time? Pretty handy tool if you are trying to get inside someone's head. Or share a minion's enjoyment of their victim's pain and fear."

Ericka nodded. "And his need for that is what makes some of what he does trackable. He needs encrypted bandwidth that his software has to break up, bounce through the maze of VPNs, and reassembled for him to see, presumably in the form of some sort of avatar. They can see each other."

That was the price tag attached. With a unique technology comes a unique profile. She was no closer to finding his location, but now she had a better shot at isolating his traffic from other dark web denizens using much the same technology he did. Combined with the increased traffic near his intended victim, she had a very real shot of spotting him setting something up.

Tim gave her a slight bow. "When are you going to try?"

She gave him a salute of acknowledgment. "I am already. We've got to move really carefully. Too much focused attention and we could tip him off. He probably has tripwires. Trigger one of those and he'll be off like a hare and all we'll get is another flunky."

Tim held out his tablet. "We've got some intel on the ground. One of the local bosses is planning something of a demonstration about the price of working with the police. Another mob traitor. I think our guy has a thing for rats."

"How do we know?" They had to get this right.

"Our International Operations people are in touch with the locals who it turns out have more than one source inside the gangs. They are damn sure they are planning to ghost him soon. They just don't have any idea where except it's near Manila."

"We do. Have a look at this." She pointed to her screen. He stepped behind her chair and leaned forward, peering over her shoulder.

"What's this?"

"I geofenced the clusters for social media and started to narrow it to the gangbangers. Not hard. These guys aren't very careful, downright stupid talking in the clear like this, but they are all very interested about what's going on at a smelter this weekend. A rat barbecue, they're calling it."

Tim sounded amused. "Of course they are."

She shook her head. "The web chatter of the locals is pretty clear. Whatever is going to happen has their interest."

Geofencing software allowed her to monitor and record open social media in any physical area she specified. She drew lines around an area on the map in front of her and the program intercepted any data going in and out that met her search criteria. By searching the social media streams within, she isolated the feeds of the people she wanted and tightened the hunt by moving the virtual fences until they contained just the people she wanted in very confined areas.

Tim leaned back, sighing. "How tight have you got it?"

"Good enough. The patterns cluster outside Makati, near Manila. There's really only one building I can see that would suit. Out near some farms." The dilapidated smelter on the edge of the city was out of place. A grey, industrial sore like knee calluses and varicose veins under an expensive, sexy dress. The convergence could not be coincidence.

"How the bloody hell is he going to call the shots on something like this?"

Ericka shook her head, having already had the same thought. "He isn't. He does seem to have something for traitors, so I wouldn't be surprised if he fed them the rat's name and some suggestions about how to deal with him." She wondered if he would try something as creative as Dante.

Tim nodded. "Gangbangers are pretty hard on their rats. Their level of violence will have some real appeal to him."

"Good point. The more helpless the victim and the more they suffer, the more he's interested. These will always be no-holds-barred events."

Tim moved away and sank into his chair at his desk next to her station. "So, how's he going to watch?"

"There's enough converging traffic that's probably his that we can safely say this has his interest. Same pattern as before, likely talking to his guy on similar VR equipment. The data streams come from all over the place, almost perfectly random, but most of it is ending up on local service provider equipment."

Tim nodded, toying with his tablet. "Dantalion's got someone who's going to be there. Has to. He's going to have to be a bit more subtle about his equipment than usual. Not like he can have someone in the front row wearing his goggles and holding up his little three-sixty camera."

"Who knows what he's set up, but you're right, most likely someone wearing something hidden. None of the other gangbangers will thank someone for filming them at a gathering to off one of their own." Ericka considered and discarded the different ways this could work. "We need to let this progress as far as we can before the locals go in. They're going to want to wait a bit and see who gathers to watch anyway. It'll be an intelligence bonanza for them."

Tim stared at her. "Do a really tight geofence? See what we get from him?"

She shook her head. "That's why he always uses satellite connections close to the action. Worse thing for him is if we geofenced a complete stream before his routing breaks it up and starts bouncing it through VPNs. If we got that, it would tell us plenty."

"Some sort of Stingray then?"

Ericka sighed. None of the options were great. "That might get us something, but I doubt they have anything that sophisticated on the ground over there." She thought for a moment, visualizing the scene. A Stingray was a mobile cell capture device that could hoover all cell traffic in a tight radius so it didn't hook up to a real tower. "The local police have an asset who is going to be there. He's our best shot. We can try to wire him up to at least detect who's broadcasting. If he finds him, maybe we can get the device intact this time."

Tim put his feet up to stare at the ceiling. "The locals are going to worry letting this go too far. They've no idea where the bad guys are holding their asset. We might persuade them to let the bad guys transport him, but they're going to feel really, really silly if he gets whacked while they're standing in the parking lot. Apparently, the guy's family has vanished as well. Wife and two kids."

Ericka's shoulders slumped, and her stomach turned at the thought of frightened children held in fear of their lives. *Stay focused.* "They need to shut it down as soon as they think they have to. Getting the recording equipment would be a bonus but we don't need it. We have bigger fish to fry here if we can get any sort of trace on Dantalion."

All four of them sat in O'Brien's office, glancing at each other in turn, waiting for someone else to start the conversation. O'Brien turned to look at SAC Abara, opening his mouth then pausing a moment before speaking. "This is all good with you? I'm convinced they have it exactly right—" he nodded at Tim and Ericka who were listening from his office couch "—but it's going to take some doing to get a judge to sign off on this. What we call a Botox application." He smirked at Ericka, who wished he wasn't going where she knew he was going.

"Botox?" Abs' brow furrowed in bemusement. He turned to look at Ericka.

O'Brien sighed, straightening the papers on his desk. "Botox. It means you have to go see the doctor before the judge and get all your facial muscles deadened so you can make the application with a straight face. Ericka's specialty."

Abs scowled over his shoulder at Ericka who glared at O'Brien. Tim found something fascinating to look at in the parking lot. "You know, I'm not finding this very fucking funny. All of our asses are on the line. Crime on foreign soil, no idea where the target is and from what you tell me, unlikely he will do anything on US soil for some time, if ever. There won't be a second shot. This has to produce something."

Ericka gave O'Brien a dirty look for his flippancy, making a mental note to warn him of Abara's limited sense of humor when it came to procedure and rules. "Remember we have pretty good evidence this guy directed a murder of a sixteen-year-old victim on US soil. Wherever he strikes next, he's still the prime suspect for that. It isn't like we'd hesitate for a second to extradite him."

Abara nodded, mollified. "And with Ramirez, he's peddling kiddie porn at the very least." He turned to O'Brien. "You have all you need from us?"

O'Brien nodded, producing another chin as he did. "We'll get the order." He tapped the thick stack of paper in its folder.

Don't count on an extension if you don't get anything in the first round."

Tim answered, "If we don't get something solid on this, he's going to dive so deep we may never pick him up again. And given where this next one seems to be going down, we should expect International Operations to pick this up, maybe CIA too."

O'Brien pulled glasses from his desk drawer and poured for all except Ericka. "A toast for luck." He lifted his glass. "A successful hunt!"

Tim rested his hand on Ericka's shoulder. "The rest of the crew all set up?"

She nodded. "We'll have ten people in the ops room. Abs borrowed a couple of agents from Homeland. Not anyone I know, but they all look good on paper. When are you leaving?"

"Fifteen minutes. I'm on a military flight. The jammers will be on the plane. All we could get on short notice."

She nodded, gripping his heavy shoulders as she looked up into his eyes. "Still worried about the range?"

Tim shrugged, sighing. "Yes, but it's all we could get. No matter what happens, the local asset is just going to have to park his van as close to the door as possible. I've measured the distances for the outside on satellite, but I couldn't find anything about the internal structures."

"It'll be fine. The dish will be outside somewhere. As long as he gets the jammer within two hundred meters of the dish, it will work."

"Unless he's changed brands of dish or mucked with the frequencies." Tim looked at her, eyes wide and brows raised.

She'd worried through every angle already. "Nothing we can do about that. I doubt he'll switch on until the last minute so it isn't like we can scan for it first."

"Problem?" Abara stood in the doorway, leaning on the jam.

Ericka gestured Abs in, ready to throw cold water on him if necessary. "No, just going over things one last time before Tim leaves."

"Speaking of which," Tim said as he hoisted his bag, slinging it across his shoulders.

Abara slapped his back as he squeezed by in the doorway. "Good hunting!" He walked in and sat down in Tim's chair. "Got the jamming sorted out?"

Ericka swiveled to face him. "Best we can. This will get pretty sticky if that doesn't work. I need our target to think his equipment has failed and make a couple of tries at re-establishing the connection. That's our real shot at a location trace."

"How'd the testing go?"

Inside voice: *it could have gone better, but it'll probably work.* "Good. We're set up to monitor all local servers, Wi-Fi, cell signals and the satellite internet bands he's used in the past. He may try to hotspot his guy's phone as a way back in once we jam. In fact, that's my best guess how he's going to try. It's what I'd do. His guy will have placed the dish somewhere already. Then all he has to do is sync it to his guy's phone and whatever device they're going to use to video it. Remote-wipe the dish and just leave it abandoned in place."

Abara nodded but Ericka didn't think he was following. "Are the Philippine DEA playing ball?"

"Tim's been dealing with them, but they are all over the

plan as long they get their source and his family out. Bonus for them is getting to see who shows up to watch. It could be quite the intel coup. As soon as we're sure everything is lined up, Tim throws the jammer. Local SWAT is going to gas the place and make the bust, then it's up to us here. Tim will have a shot at getting the local equipment."

Abara played with his expensive watch. "And the monitoring so far?"

"Just as we expected. Some traffic into the area. Probably talking to his guy and what looks to me like some bandwidth testing in nearby servers. I'm sure he'll use the satellite stuff for the event video, so I think the server activity is some sort of backup." She sighed, running the plan through her head again as she had every few minutes since she thought of it, while at night dreaming of nightmare versions of how it would go wrong. She rubbed her scratchy eyes, wondering how they must look.

Abara smiled his approval. "The Homeland guys are very impressed with your plan. They're telling their boss we're doing something they never thought of. Talking about using it to hunt Jihadis. Congrats." He grinned. She smiled back, thinking he'd be a great boss if he just wasn't such a chickenshit procedure weenie. Doing things for the first time always means risk and it tore a chunk out of him every time she pushed the envelope.

"Thanks. We've done everything we can. We just need Dantalion to slip a bit, better still just a few minutes of panic and we'll have him."

He nodded. "With any luck, this time two days from now we'll be drinking O'Brien's scotch and you'll have this guy's head on your wall."

★ ★ ★

"Everyone set?" Ericka paced behind the monitors, trying hard not to hover. All ten stations formed a U with her own console in the middle. Against the walls, servers—each running several cooling fans—waited on standby. These were the best people they could muster. The room lights were dim, leaving the harsh light of the screens to illuminate each station's working area. Water bottles and half-eaten fast food littered the area around them, clothes rumpled from long stretches sitting. They had the ventilation running full tilt, but it was still warm. Each had an assigned task. Some were to shut down access to servers and force reroutes, trying to keep the data stream tight where they could read it. Others were to monitor any code seeking to re-establish the signal, with the rest trying to nail down anything they could about the source location or copy any of the software deployed.

Ericka nodded to herself, warmth spreading through her. *This is as good as we can do. With a bit of luck, it will end here.* She keyed her mic, checking her comms with Tim. "Tango Alpha, reading me? Turn on your video feed now." She stepped back to her own monitors and leaned over. "There we go, got it. Where are you?" On the screen, armored troops appeared, sitting facing each other in the back of a military truck. Hunched over, faces covered, each clutched the local variant of the redoubtable M4 rifle, butt on the floor, muzzle pointed up. Two of them cradled the heavier M240 machine gun. Gang work here was serious business.

"About three miles out in the country. Heading in." Tim's video feed vibrated as the truck rumbled down the road, plumes of mud curled up behind, the distance obscured by torrential rain.

"K, out for now." Ericka slid the channel selector and keyed her headset mic again. "International Ops, Tango Bravo, you there?"

"Here, asset on scene, live now, sending you the feed." Ericka recognized the clipped accent of SA Rosamie Tores, born in Manila, raised in the UK from a very young age and now the head of the local office.

Next to the window showing Tim's feed, a second one popped open on her left screen. She leaned in to squint at the video. The immense room was dark, large pieces of industrial equipment protruding from the shadows. Some daylight slanted in from a partially open roof, doing little to illuminate the floor. Fluorescent fixtures hung from the ceiling casting pools of light on the men milling below. Those outside were silhouettes. The ones she could see sported heavy ink on steroid-fueled muscles, the look favored by gangs and followers all over the world, idiots who learned how to be gangsters by watching the fake ones on TV.

Ericka keyed her mic again, scanning the team's screens. "Are you getting scene audio, Tango Bravo?"

"Yes, but not good quality and it's all in Tagalog. You speak, I can feed you?"

"I don't. What's going on?"

Tores' speech was pressured. "Nothing yet. They're just standing around. They're saying they've got him in the complex somewhere, just waiting for the iron to heat up a little more. Looks like almost twenty of them."

"Jesus Christ, are the kids and the wife there?" Ericka choked down a wave of nausea.

Tores paused before speaking. "We think so. No sign of them yet. The chopper's holding station close by. They can fill this place with tear gas on a minute's notice. Stand by—something happening now."

Ericka toggled to maximize the video feed from the agent and switched channels back to Tim. "Tango Alpha, looks like they're starting. You guys on your way in?"

He was barely audible this time and Ericka strained to make out his words. "Just coming around the parking lot. The main smelter's right in front of us." She could hear the thrill in Tim's voice, for once not wishing she could be in the field. Today, the real hunt would be here.

One of the FBI agents to her right turned, shouting, "Satellite signal just went hot! Enough bandwidth for high-res video. Just came on, working on encryption now." Sheila Clarke had been with the DIU for five years and was something of a protégé of hers. Fair-skinned, blond, and heavy, she suffered as they all did from too much time in dark rooms looking at screens. She was pale, her lips pressed together.

"Good, stay sharp, everyone. It's going to move pretty fast now!" Ericka scanned the row of backs, all focused, leaning into their equipment.

"It's starting. Shit, they've brought the kids out!" Tores emphasized each syllable, her voice laden with tension. The video feed showed a portly man, dressed like the others, standing on a pipe as he addressed the assembled throng of gangsters, exuding an air of pompous cruelty. To one side of him, a small woman clutched two children to her waist, her eyes wide with horror. On the other, two heavy thugs gripped the arms of a smaller man who stood with his hands zip-tied in front of him. "He's saying he still can't decide if he wants to make the kids watch or throw them in first." The thugs grappled with the smaller man who kicked his way loose for a moment before they regained control with a series of hard kidney punches. He dropped to his knees, vomiting, his head bowed. That would be the rat.

Rosamie's voice intruded on her fascinated horror. "SWAT are moving in now; they can't let this go any further." The boss waved to someone off camera and the great vat of molten iron began to move along its rails, shifting into position to pour. The mother pulled her children's heads in, stuffing them into her skirt, hiding their faces.

"Tango Alpha, ready? They're going to have to shut it down any second."

"We're outside the main doors, helo is inbound. I can hit the jammer any time." Tim's shaky video feed spun to show a military helicopter cresting coconut palms edging a nearby field, the downwash making the top fronds dance as it passed over, churning muddy puddles on the ground. "They're going to fire the gas any minute."

Ericka leaned over her screens to speak. "Start the jamming now please!" The jammer flooded the specified frequencies with a powerful signal, causing the target devices to lose their connection, set for satellite uplinks.

The agent looked back over her shoulder. "Done."

Clarke turned to look at her, nodding. "Satellite feed is dead. Jamming is working."

Ericka flushed with a wave of relief. They'd got that part right. The target should be blind now. "Thanks. Stay really frosty here!" *Okay, devil-boy, take the bait. You're missing all the action. Pop your head up for a look. It's just a glitch in the lousy local network, nothing to worry about and you're missing the show you worked so hard for.*

Chaos erupted in both video feeds. Gas canisters bounced through the open portion of the roof, causing the mob to dive for the two side doors, ending in shoving and kicking matches as the assembled thugs tried to clamber over each other. The SWAT troopers surged through the main door, rifles leveled, shouting and throwing gangsters to the floor. One fired a burst from a heavy machine gun into the air. The low-pitched, chugging report of the heavyweight gun got everyone's undivided attention. Most complied, diving to the ground. *Looks like they've seen this movie before and know they won't be told twice.* A man holding the informer made the mistake of lunging to grab the children who were huddling against their mother, faces still pressed against her, blocking out the mayhem. A SWAT member shot him twice in the face point-blank, spraying the mother with blood, brains, and bone fragments. Three more armored figures gripped the arms of the family and hustled them out the front door.

"Oh, nice shot!" said one of the monitors behind her as the local video feed went dark. The SWAT team took the local asset to the ground with the others. The staccato of several rapid shots echoed through the audio connection.

Ericka kept one eye on the monitoring stations as she spoke. "Tango Alpha, we've lost the inside video feed. What's going on?"

Several long seconds passed before Tim answered. "All good. Hostages are safe, got most of the baddies on the ground. SWAT are just chasing down the few who got through the door."

"Kids all right?"

"A bit messy but healthy, other than the tear gas. The wife looks like she's had some rough treatment. What's going on there?"

Ericka took a deep breath, some of the tension draining now the kids were safe. "Nothing yet. Hasn't taken the bait. See any of the transmission equipment?"

"Can't see a fucking thing." Tim's video feed showed him scanning the upper walls and rusting, partial roof. "Have to wait until the gas disperses."

"I've got something!" shouted one of the monitors, Maxwell, a pretty boy from Homeland Security Investigations, via some Ivy League school. "Encrypted signal through the local cell network, short pulses, it might be a reboot command. He's probably trying for whatever camera his guy was wearing."

He's bit, taken the hook. "Hear that, Tango Alpha? I think he's reacting."

"Similar, pulses on the satellite band. Looks like he's trying to re-establish his stream," Clarke reported from her station, voice high-pitched with tension. "Coming from multiple vectors at once. Can't resolve a location. Not sure if he has two video feeds or just another way to get the signal out."

Ericka sat down hard in her chair and swiveled to face her monitors, sporting a ferocious grin. "The cell is likely backup. He'll want the resolution of the satellite band." The hair stood up on her arms and she shivered, all her attention focused on the streams of code in front of her. "All right, game on!"

What she was seeing was puzzling and not what she expected. His smartest move was an immediate shutdown and go dark, then try to talk to his on-scene guy later to see what happened. *Someone this good has a disaster protocol for everything.* The one they'd run into in Ramirez's place had been exceptional. What her monitoring team were feeding her looked very like someone panicking as they tried to pipe back into the action, trying several things at once, becoming frantic. Not what she expected at all. Far more typical of a garden-variety pedophile losing his shit because, despite all his efforts, he wasn't getting it. *Maybe more than one guy using the Dantalion persona and environment and this one can't keep it together?*

Maxwell grinned at her over his shoulder, his smile full of perfect teeth. "Change of signal on the direct satellite feed. Steady stream. Might be something diagnostic. He's shooting lots of data at it."

The data was telling Ericka one thing; her instincts howled warning of the opposite. "Is it steady enough to have a go at the source?" *Way too easy; something's not right.*

"I think so, stand by please." Maxwell spun back to his screen, his posture flawless as always.

"Tango Alpha, we think he just tried a reboot and diagnostics for something on site. Any sign of his guy or any equipment on the ground?" Ericka waited, hearing nothing. "Tango Alpha?" She knew better than to ride him, but every second counted now.

The signal crackled with static, making Tim's voice sound more distant. "Nothing so far. They've got everyone hogtied in the parking lot. I've been by all of them. No one's carrying anything obvious. I was going to look in the main smelter to see if anyone threw anything in. Do you want me to look for the dish?"

Ericka weighed her options, nibbling her lower lip. Closing her eyes for a moment, she drew a deep shuddering breath.

Time to take a chance. "Shut off the jammer. If he keeps trying to hook up, we might get some solid trace data from here."

Tim's reply was immediate. "If he succeeds, he'll have no doubt how his gig ended! We don't know what he's got here for video. Could be several. One might be hidden and still running."

Ericka shook her head even though Tim couldn't see her. "He wouldn't be trying to fix the others if he did. A few more seconds and his automatic wiping protocols will engage, if they haven't already." She tried to picture her quarry, wondering at his next move.

"On my way." Tim's mic transmitted the sound of heavy, running footsteps on gravel, splashing through puddles, followed by a vehicle door flung open. A few choice curses. "Done! I'm going to go inside and look for anything his guy might have thrown away. Still no idea who his on-scene guy is."

Ericka switched channels. "Tango Bravo, any word on any of the locals taken down with video equipment?"

"Negative. They tend to do very thorough 'interrogations' once they have everyone back in cells. I'll query the local commander."

"Let me know." Ericka turned to her satellite station. "Anything?"

Clarke turned to make eye contact. "He shut down the second the local jamming stopped. Maybe he has some sort of anomaly-detection protocol running." She shrugged and turned back to her station. "The current trace ends somewhere near Beijing. Likely into a VPN portal there."

Ericka gritted her teeth, but it was what she expected. "See if you can find the input stream based on the earlier traffic."

Finding identical code streams on another server could negate the protection of a VPN. Once in the encrypted pipe, there was no way to see where the data stream was traveling much less capture and decode it. Sometimes you could find where data entered the VPN and where it exited. If you see a rat going into a hole and the same one coming out somewhere else, you don't care where it's been in between. Focus on the rat. Follow it to its den, look for its tracks. A long shot, but they had no other option.

Clarke's voice was tense with excitement. "Okay, that was almost too easy. I think the input stream came through Cairo where we had some earlier traffic we thought was him. The origin point is somewhere in Europe." Routing traffic through multiple VPNs was standard no-trace practice for any hacker worth the name. Better for the bad guy if he could situate entry and exit points in countries that wouldn't cooperate with each other later. Keep any traces out of reach so no one can put the puzzle together.

Maxwell's voice was rapid, clipped with tension and to her immense surprise, he was sweating. "The cell traffic is mostly in the clear. That's ballsy. The data pulses he tried to send are encrypted but coming from western Europe. I can't narrow it any further than that yet."

Ericka caught her breath. *This might just work.* "Anyone got anything on the larger stream, diagnostic or kill commands?"

Clarke shook her head without looking up. "Assuming that's what they were, the last verifiable routing was through Glasgow. He had to do all of these pretty quickly—no time to disperse the routing the way he usually does. He's somewhere in the British Islands I'm betting."

"Anyone have any data inconsistent with that theory?"

Ericka glanced from station to station. No one answered. Her instincts screamed again—*it can't be this easy. Not this guy.* She barked orders to the waiting monitors, staring unblinking from their stations. "Okay, concentrate the crawlers. No need for stealth now and geofence the UK and Ireland. Tango Alpha, any luck?"

Again, there was a long pause before Tim answered. "None of these guys had anything on them but standard burner phones. One of the local SWAT guys says he saw two of them throw things into the smelter before they got to them. Betting that's where our camera went."

"We weren't getting that lucky." She thought for a moment. "Find a satellite box?"

"We did. Wiping protocol ran long before we got to it. It has an after-market internal battery."

"And the dish itself?"

"Powered down but it's the same model as before. No onboard memory."

Ericka gritted her teeth. One more thing to try. "Power both up please, but load an image first. When it reboots and hooks up, it may shove any undelivered data in the satellite servers on to its destination and take something we can recognize with it. If we get lucky, we'll catch it as it tries to deliver."

Tim sighed before answering. "You're sure? Christ knows what else it will send."

"Worth a shot. What've we got to lose?"

"Switching on now."

Ericka looked up into the expectant faces of her team. "You know what to look for. We'll only get one shot. If we're right, it will pop into the clear somewhere near the UK and deliver. It may only be a few packets."

The only sound in the room was the whir of computer cooling fans, and the subdued patter of muted keyboard strokes. Minutes passed. Ericka calmed herself with the thought they had at least shut him down before he added another body to his count. She pressed her eyes shut, drawing a slow breath.

Maxwell's shout broke the silence. "Got it I think! Not the UK. Popped out in Dublin and routed to a private server. Locating now."

Ericka lunged forward, leaning over his right shoulder, clutching the back of his chair so tight her nails pierced the cheap vinyl. Then it displayed. Trinity College. Christ we've got him. She turned to Abara who was standing at the back of the room, his thick arms folded in front of him. "We need the local liaison to get the Irish police out there and lock this down. Even if he's gone, we'll have security video, maybe some DNA."

Ten minutes later Abara strode back into the monitoring room, his mobile glued to his ear. He made eye contact with Ericka and nodded, saying something inaudible into the phone. Lifting it away from his head, he spoke to the room. "Irish police will be on scene any minute." He smiled and raised his hands in applause as the team cheered and slapped each other's hands, high fiving. They relaxed, turning their chairs inwards towards Ericka, smiling and chatting. Several minutes passed. Ericka looked at Abara, eyebrows raised in query. Still listening to his mobile, he shook his head.

"What the fuck?" Clarke was staring at her monitor, shoulders hunched. "I just lost my outside connection?"

"Me too," another said. "No outside port. They're all plugged up."

Maxwell shook his head as he pecked at his keyboard. "Seriously? A denial of service attack is the best this guy has got?" He looked at her, shaking his head. "This is the overlord of the dark web you've been chasing?" A denial of service attack was perhaps the oldest and crudest form of cyber-attack, relying on nothing more than the sheer volume of incoming traffic to overwhelm the target and deny them the use of their own equipment.

Ericka glared back at him, irritated. "Seriously, we're going to get into a big dick contest now about who has the baddest bad guys? Try and find the source."

"Jesus, I'm frozen out of my machine!" Clarke was staring at her station, brow furrowed.

"What the fuck? Me too!"

Maxwell was staring at her, the light still not on. "How can a DOS attack freeze inside terminals?"

A cold shiver ran through Ericka's body, her muscles tensing, skin crawling. "It can't. Shit!" She spun towards the terminals, watching in cold horror as blank green screens appeared in sequence on the monitoring stations, unresponsive now to commands. She stared at the towers under the tables and over towards her lab servers lining the wall. Her chest tight, short of breath, she dropped to her knees and pressed her ear against the tower. The hard drive was reading at full speed, clicking like a mad Geiger counter. She shoved herself to her feet, diving towards the servers, pressing her ear tight. Same thing. She opened her mouth and drew breath to shout when the fire alarm sounded, plunging the room into emergency lighting, freezing everyone. She grabbed Abara's wrist and shouted, cringing as reality dawned. "The bastard followed us back."

"What?" Abara cupped one ear, but Maxwell had heard.

"It's just a DOS attack. Amateur hour as it gets. We have to get to the muster point."

Ericka leaned over to her team to shout, panic flooding her like ice water. "There's no fire. He did it. It's a cover! He followed our trace. He's here, in our servers! Christ knows what he's getting."

"Fuck me dead!" Abara's eyes bulged as he stared at her slack-jawed, then at the frozen monitoring equipment.

She shouted again to the team. "We're compromised. He's followed our stream back; he's here. The bastard's in here right now. The DOS and the fire alarm are just a fucking smoke screen. Pull the power, disconnect everything!"

Abara shouted at the team. "Listen up, all of you! Cyber war protocol. Physical isolation! Pull the cables on the routers and the network connections. Start in here, then in the server stacks. Everyone move your asses!"

The team scrambled, pulling cables, kicking out plugs and in the end using fire axes on their network equipment. When they finished, the room was silent. None of the machines showed the usual signs of digital life. Broken bits of black plastic covered the floor and one of the routers sputtered, spitting white sparks where it had been chopped open. The lab and the server farm were dead. This branch of the FBI was back in the 1950s.

Ericka slumped into her chair, shaking her head, nauseous like she was going to throw up. Her skin was clammy, hands trembling. She looked up at Abara with tortured eyes shaking her head, before burying it in her hands. *How the fuck did he do that? To move this fast, he must have had these countermeasures in place before he even started out. Ripped through our firewalls, along our network and into the data like none of our security was even there.* She groaned without lifting her head. *Decoyed us following obvious bullshit reboot commands, then suckered by an amateur-hour DOS attack. They're going to take this away from me. How the hell did he do this? Who the fuck is this guy?*

13

The Folly of Darius

"I can't have any surprises tomorrow." Abara's eyes bored into hers. "Homeland and CIA are both doing their own assessments. No one's faulting anyone right now, but if our brass doesn't hear it from us first, they're going to ask themselves if we're the best people to continue this. You gettin' me?"

Ericka nodded, opening her valise to look at her unnecessary notes scribbled in the small hours of the night before. Unnecessary as endless repetition had burned the details into her brain through sleepless nights. Nights spent in futile pursuit of sleep as she rolled and turned, sheets sticking to her, the details playing out time and again, like a horrible song heard on the car stereo and now stuck in her head. It was shocking and humiliating. She couldn't bear to look in the mirror or meet Mrs. Donnelly's gaze. Dantalion had outclassed her, plain and simple. And now he'd had a good look around inside. This wasn't ending any time soon.

She inhaled and lifted her head, looking around the table. The small boardroom overlooked the sports field behind the main complex from the fourth floor, the vivid colors seeming unnaturally bright to her fatigued eyes. Seated around the table were Abara, Tim, O'Brien, and Clarke. All sported bags under bloodshot eyes and clutched coffee cups like they contained some kind of life-saving elixir. Their eyes reflected their thoughts.

She knew she looked exhausted and worn, like she had been run over and scraped off the road with a very thin spatula. The old expression of her dad's almost made her smile. The very look she had tried to plaster and paint over in the bathroom mirror an hour earlier. The others were much the same—Tim in particular, hurt painted on his craggy face, overlaid with the fatigue of two trans-Pacific flights in a week.

Ericka forced herself to speak, projecting a confidence she no longer possessed. "There's no way to spin this that doesn't sound stupid, so I'm just going to say it straight up. We were completely outmaneuvered. He was playing us from the moment we started. However he pulled this off, he had it all set up in advance."

O'Brien's expression was grim. "You mean countermeasures in place for any time he got compromised, or ready for us in particular to this operation? Were you the target?" At least he wasn't complaining about having to convince a judge they were dealing with a real suspect.

Ericka sighed. *Go with your gut. We can't let him take us down again. Not like this.* "From everything I've looked at so far I've concluded he knew we were onto him well in advance of the operation and was set up to counterattack the minute we popped our heads up."

"Based on what?" Abara was aghast, red eyes and open

mouth displaying his horror. The Boy Scout type of agent was always flabbergasted when the good guys didn't win.

Ericka looked down, unable to meet his gaze. "I think he used our own code to penetrate our defenses. He somehow copied the parts of our own tools we had been using to look for him. I believe analyzing our own code got him in, at least initially, then likely some form of worm. We also have to consider the possibility he has a mole in here somewhere. Our audit trails are clean so far, but it's the first thing Homeland and the CIA are going to ask."

"Start from the beginning. Translating from geek as you go." O'Brien's half-smile was genuine, but fear and concern haunted his eyes. Ericka could see he was worried. *And he should be. We all should be. The best we could do, and he took us down like opening-act amateurs at a pro-wrestling match.*

"I'll start with Dublin. It was just a very clever relay point. A lightly secured server in the main stack, belonging to the physics department. He installed an encrypted share on it and set up shop. Getting through the university's security wouldn't have posed any issue to this guy. Most importantly, he was never physically there. These findings are preliminary, but I'm quite confident they are correct."

Clarke's large blue eyes stared at the table in front of her, her chin resting on her fist. "It didn't look like a relay to me while we were live. All the probable Dantalion traffic was emanating from that server. Are you sure he wasn't on the campus somewhere piping into the university's network?"

Ericka shook her head, looking down, still not wanting to make eye contact. "I couldn't find any trace of that. My theory is he had some sort of semi-autonomous AI set up in there. All the Dantalion traffic we were watching was sent by that AI while he was using some other method to instruct it. He may run several at once, making lots of Dantalion-looking traffic just to muck things up. It also accounts for his speed. I think all he is doing is sitting somewhere else, watching and picking up the communication and video streams he wants. The program itself can do all sorts of rapid, clumsy stuff like trying to reboot local equipment without placing him in jeopardy of a trace. Some sort of limited-memory AI, like the kind used in cars, so not that big and cumbersome that using it will attract immediate attention. If I was him with that kind of software, I would keep several handy but move them on a regular schedule."

Abara was leaning back, arms folded in front of him. "Did you find any actual evidence of this?"

Ericka met his stare now. Abara had to know what they were facing. "No, the whole server was wiped. Nine overwrites by the time the locals got there. I'm inferring from what I can see. On the university's network logs, there is all sorts of traffic coming out of this server but almost nothing going in. I think that means the traffic was being generated in the server itself by a program running there. What little did go in came from a network account of a nonexistent student, which was also wiped almost out of existence. So, no actual code I can say for sure is an AI or similar, but no other way I can think of that could produce what I can see."

"Has anyone ever seen any kind of AI deployed like this before?" Abara said.

"Not that I've heard of, but it would be worth looking at. Maybe pick up a lead?" Ericka made a mental note to do a search and ask the hive mind of her profession—a small, specialized group of investigators spread out over several agencies.

Tim looked up from his pad now filled with doodles. "So, he sets up well in advance. Anywhere in the world he can find unsecured or lightly secured space with proper processing and network speed. The computing capacity of university data modelling makes them a prime location for him. They run semi-autonomously doing the heavy lifting of whatever he's up to. He gives them general instruction as the event progresses, but mostly busies himself with overall strategy and enjoying his show?"

Ericka glanced over at Tim nodding. "It's the only way I can see he did this, based on the evidence we have."

"How would he get something as big as an AI into a server without triggering some sort of alarm?" O'Brien looked from Ericka to Tim, then to Clarke. "I thought those things were huge?"

Ericka shrugged. "Most are, but not all. Getting them in is not as hard as it might seem. His don't need to be that big. If you tried to do it all at once, likely security software would pick up on it. If you set these things up way in advance and just leave them there until you need them, that's much easier. You slowly increase your encrypted share and send little tiny bits of your code over a long period of time. Make sure you don't use a lot of processing power assembling it. Restrict your reconstruction to off-peak hours. Russian and Chinese hackers have been doing that for years. The scary part is deploying an AI for hacking, never mind from where. AIs aren't dangerous because they're going to take over the world, but several used like this could do the work of thousands of human hackers working together all at once. If he's figured out a way to do it, it's a game-changer."

No one said anything for a few moments before Abara broke the silence. "If it's any consolation, the Irish police forensics unit concur with your theory. Homeland and CIA are doing their own assessment and we'll hear from them tomorrow. Okay, the big question, how the hell did he get in here and what did we lose?"

Ericka's stomach twisted as she spoke. "I don't know exactly how he got in. Back to that in a minute. As to what he got, everything. Absolutely everything. Copied my tools and my intel files on him. He knows exactly what we know about him and precisely how we found it. Again, just an early assessment but it doesn't look like he was interested in anything else, just this unit, what tools we have and our progress looking for him. In case I'm wrong, we've also had to see to the security of all police informants. I don't think he got in there, but they're a favorite target of his so we can't take chances."

"Christ! What the hell are we going to do about that?" Abara's fists opened and clenched tight on the table in front of him. "And I'm not looking forward to fessing up to the other agencies on how bad we got hit. Tell you that for nothing."

Ericka sighed. "Already under way, but nothing so far."

"Any sign of him since?" O'Brien asked.

Clarke answered, "Nothing. Dead quiet, not a trace. Like he never existed."

Ericka took a moment to suppress the cold anger and keep it out of her voice. "And we aren't going to any time soon. Now he's got our tracking tools, it's the simplest thing in the world for him to come up with something we can't see. And perfect his countermeasures. Next time we'll be starting from scratch based on nothing more than knowing his general MO. I was counting on an element of surprise that it turns out we didn't have. Now we're on the defensive."

Tim shrugged. "It's not like he's going to stop. And we did head him off on this one. That could have been four more bodies to add to his count, two of them children. That's got to count for something."

"It does, but small consolation to the next victims if it takes us a couple of years to pick up his trail again." Ericka regretted the anger in her voice. Tim's eyebrows shot up. She shook her head in apology and gripped Tim's forearm. "Not directed at you."

Abara held up his hand to intervene, looking at each of them in turn. "Before we start thinking about moving forward, we have to deal with how he got in here. Pressure's going to be heavy to let Homeland or the CIA pick this up. They think they're better than us at this. They aren't, but if we show up tomorrow without any idea about how we got taken down, I'm going to have a hard time convincing anyone we should stay lead on this."

Ericka choked down the stab of anger and humiliation, but she knew Abara was right. This bastard had bested them, hands down. She let out another sigh. "I don't know the precise mechanism, but in general terms I have a pretty good idea. He's thought out everything before he even lifts a finger. He had countermeasures ready for anyone who latched on to him. I think he knew someone was on his ass long before this op. He may not have known who or where. If he found my crawlers and copied them, he might have been able to figure out something of the security he was facing. Some of the stuff my crawlers gathered may have brought back the bits for one of his hacking tools without me knowing it. As I said, likely some new form of worm with multiple AIs running to exploit the breach."

O'Brien held up his hand to slow her down, shaking his head. "In dumb lawyer English please."

Ericka smiled and nodded to him. "When we latched directly on to one of his streams pulling data in, we might have unknowingly pulled in the last pieces of some sort of ultra-sophisticated Trojan that kicked open the door under cover of that stupid DOS attack. How our heuristic scanning missed the assembly process and the execution, I have no idea." Heuristic scanning security software constantly searched for anomalies that shouldn't be in the normal traffic, trying to find commands or evidence of replication. Theirs was very sophisticated and placed suspicious data into immediate quarantine.

"You still think this is one guy?" O'Brien's face was a picture of studied neutrality, which she interpreted as skepticism.

Ericka threw up her hands, frustrated with her lack of answers. "I do. That's my gut anyway. What he did appears to be a novel application of existing stuff, modified with some real genius in how he deploys the components. He's going to know the best of breed in his colleagues, maybe he pays other people to be code monkeys for him. Build him components he configures into what he wants. Maybe they trade for something he has. I don't know, but every instinct says this is one person.

Tim's hand rose to stroke his beard. "But what kind of person? Who?"

Ericka stared out the window as it sunk in exactly what

they were facing. "An evil psychopath who is, unfortunately for us, probably the best hacker we've ever seen. The VR technology is cutting edge, nothing like it on the market that we can find. He's either building it himself or having some small manufacturer do it very quietly as a special order."

O'Brien turned to Abara. "What does behavioral science think?"

Abara shrugged. "They don't agree amongst themselves. The predatory sexual and violent tastes sure don't add up to one person of a kind they've seen before."

"In fairness to them, none of the usual indicators they use are available in an online environment." In truth, Ericka had no time for profilers. "Add to that he could be anywhere in the world, and the usual shit about how his mommy wouldn't let him have a puppy when he was little so he turned out nasty isn't really that helpful to us."

O'Brien, it seemed, had more faith in them than she did. "Sure, but can they say anything—male, female, old, young, anything?"

Ericka gave him a pointed look. O'Brien didn't deal with them that much. "Don't need them for that. These predators, they're all male, with female tagalongs being the exception. Age-wise he could be some sort of wonder-boy prodigy or an older man with a ton of experience. I tend to think the latter. He's very, very strategic and that's a quality more common in older men. Beyond that, we are where we always were."

"You've got all the technical stuff written up for me?" Abara asked.

"Sent it to you just before I got here. You'll be wanting me to present it."

"No, except for me this one is directors only for the Bureau. I'll muddle my way through. You're busy anyway." Abara gave her a look that made her groan inwardly. She could tell from the looks she was getting that people thought she was coming unglued.

"Do you want me to pop in before it starts and switch on your laptop for you?" Baiting him was probably a bad idea, but Ericka wanted him to know how irritated she was.

Abara gave her a probing look. "Look, smartass, we'll be very lucky to stay as lead agency after this. There will be people there who're going to badmouth you for their own purposes. You don't do well with that at the best of times. Leave this with me."

She had let her mouth and passions get the better of her more than once at high-level meetings. She nodded, looking down at the table then sideways at Tim who avoided her gaze.

"I must say I'm surprised you kept this appointment." Steiner looked puzzled, but his eyes shone like he was pleased to see her. He had been reading a book open on his lap when Ericka strode in, no jacket, obviously expecting her to miss her appointment. He stood to reshelve it, reaching for his jacket before sighing and dropping into his seat.

Ericka nodded, breaking eye contact. "I was reminded this morning by my supervisor. You've heard?"

He leaned back, not writing or typing this time. His laptop was closed. "No one in the building has spoken about anything else since it happened. You look like you haven't slept in days."

Her features tightened at the stab of humiliation. "Glad

to know I'm the talk of the town for a different reason this time."

A tiny smile crinkled Steiner's eyes for a moment. "I'm pleased you can joke about it." He paused for a few seconds. "I think this time, in light of recent events, we will do something different. Today, I will do most of the talking."

The vinyl creaked under her as she leaned back. "Aren't you supposed to ask me how I feel?"

"I could see that as you walked in. Guilt and humiliation are not going to serve you well at a time like this."

Ericka sunk further into the chair, staring at him, realizing she was squinting at him with sore, bloodshot eyes. She bit back a sarcastic crack about what kind of training do shrinks need to come to such clever observations. He actually did want to help, and she didn't need to keep her guard up if he was doing the talking. "I'm listening."

"You have never been willing to be completely open about whatever it is you feel is such a burden, and now is not the time. Obviously, your sister's death weighs on you, only exacerbated by the work you do. Attributing exact causation to each source is not relevant now, only relieving the emotional weight so you can function. No one can last long at this level. You are not letting Patricia down every time an investigation is unsuccessful or you are unable to locate a suspect in time to prevent a crime." Ericka opened her mouth to protest but he cut her off with a sharp wave of his upraised hand. "No, don't respond. I want you to think and I don't want to feel responsible if I don't write down what you say."

So, what is he getting at? Ericka wondered just how much he'd guessed. "So, now you're on my side?"

His jaw clenched then released with what she thought was frustration. "I have always been on your side, Ericka. I have a job to do, the one the FBI pays me to do, but I do it because I want to help. Specifically, the people who work here who suffer the most from dealing with society's worst."

She believed him but had no doubt if she went anywhere near coming clean, she would be finished. "So read my mind." She softened the sarcasm with a smile. "What am I doing wrong?"

The corners of Steiner's mouth twitched up in response. "It isn't about wrong, Ericka. It's about insight. So, here's how I see it. You feel your sister's death was due to your failure. Then you miss saving that poor girl in Idaho, possibly by under an hour. Then you suffer the trauma of accusations and guilt when a vile suspect dies on your watch. Plus, all of your other investigations. The load is unbearable."

Oh, so very close. *Careful, no reaction—he'll spot it.* "Go on."

"Ultimately the emotional dissonance, the mental toxin, is between what you think the universe requires of you and what is humanly possible. Now you are faced with an opponent who may be as talented as you are or better, and he doesn't have to obey the rules. You may not be able to stop him before he strikes again. You are eaten by fear of failure and on the verge of truly cracking." Steiner paused, looking at her without expression. "Today, take this one thing with you. Much you cannot change, but the irrational guilt you can and must."

She forced a smile, nodding her thanks, not believing a word. If only he knew. She was all Patty had in the world. Who else was responsible for her sister if not her? She was supposed to be on that trip; she should have been there. And Piggy, if you had been in that stairwell, you wouldn't be calling the guilt irrational. But he had it right about cracking. She had to find a way to end this.

Steiner paused speaking to stare at her for some moments. "I will simply write today up as insufficient time to base recommendations and leave it at that. Good hunting. We are all behind you. We will do only these short sessions until this is over so you don't feel you must watch your back as you usually do. Discipline your thinking to avoid the past. All your focus must be forward-looking. This is not forgetting Patricia or dishonoring her memory. She has passed and is beyond your power to help. Nothing you do benefits her now. There is no redemption for the past in future success. None. Seeking it will cloud your judgment. Free yourself of that and succeed."

Ericka turned away to hide the tears jetting from eyes squeezed shut. Her abdominal muscles were tight like she had been punched and she had to force herself to breathe. Minutes passed before she looked up, her mouth dry, knowing her face was flushed. She stood and gripped his hand, their eyes locking for a moment before she turned to walk out the door, dry and empty inside, very tired now.

Schmidt stared at the flawless avatar, awestruck again at the almost cinematic quality. Was this the urge he couldn't seem to fight, the offer of a world every bit as real as his own, but so much better? Why would anyone like him want to stay in the real one when this world offered them what they so badly needed? It had been some weeks since his last visit to his patron's cleverly crafted world and he had wondered if that had been the last time.

He was surprised at his reaction to the blinking lights inviting him to return. At first, he couldn't describe the feeling even to himself or think of why. Then he realized what it was. It was hope, hope for a way out of his hated existence, hope for a time where he could call the shots and live without the constraints of society. Whoever this guy was, he had changed everything. No more hiding in his basement jerking off and feeling like some sort of scum, waiting for the cops to come to the door, or worse to his work. He wasn't alone; there were others like him. Some had done things he had never dared dream of, things he could do one day. He belonged—a community to end the isolation—and it made him happy. The terrible loneliness of the outcast was gone. In this reality, it didn't exist.

"I trust you have been well in my absence." The same rich timbre to the voice but now the facial features were far less buried in shadow. They were so lifelike, beautiful. The voice was a bit out of sync but that could be transmission lag. The visuals were at least as good as the schlockier end of the Hollywood CGI spectrum. He wondered if the features were his real face, relishing the trust implicit if it was. Trust implied belonging.

"I was getting a little worried something nasty had happened."

The smile was sinister. "No, something I had to deal with. My apologies, but it took rather longer than I expected. One of my followers was less careful than he should have been. Nothing for you to be concerned about. I was very pleasantly surprised to find some unexpected talent in a place

I did not think to find it. I intend to look into the matter further."

Schmidt wondered if he meant cops or some sort of rival. "If I am understanding you, I don't think they will find your 'looking into' them very pleasant."

A bark of laughter rang through the virtual hall. "No, I do not expect they will." The huge figure leaned forward, eyes wide with an expectant expression, verging on eagerness. "I studied those schematics you sent. Thank you, my friend. They are exactly what I was looking for. That is all I need to know about the internal data structures for now. On the largest one, the one with two decks, I see it has a camera high up on the vertical stabilizer, yes?"

Schmidt thought for a few seconds. "Correct. It displays on two screens in the cockpit for use in taxiing at the airport. Shows them what's around the aircraft that they can't see from their seats. Why?"

"Are there others on that aircraft?"

"Depends what the airline orders. It's like a fancy car. You can buy as many expensive options as you like. They build you all the airplane you can afford."

The smile was broad, the teeth perfect if rather feral, amused now. "Where would I find a record of who had ordered which 'options'?"

Schmidt wondered where this was going. "The manufacturer would be the easiest source but that won't tell you about any mods the airline installs afterwards. We use ground-guide cameras quite a bit for a lot of airlines. They use them on routes where the airports are less sophisticated. Bad for business if they run over a father of six, slaving near a baggage cart. I'm sure you heard."

"I did. Is there any way you might provide me with a list?"

Cold bastard. No reaction at all. "Yes. It'll take a bit of time to compile without risking questions, but I can certainly do it. May I ask why?"

Another smile of tolerant amusement, a father telling an excited child to wait for Christmas. "I think I would rather that be a surprise. You will enjoy it, I assure you." The face emerged out of the chair's shadow. "Look forward to a new link in the coming days. One of your brethren has been busy. He and you are much alike."

Schmidt smiled, his skin tingling and face flushed with anticipation. "Thank you. Expect the list to be ready in two or three weeks. A question?"

The perfect hands rose, palms facing towards him in a gesture of welcome. "Please, my friend."

"Whatever it is you're planning with what I'm gathering for you. Do you intend me to be a part of it?"

"It is my hope you will be front and center in it. Something we shall do together. You have suffered with a need to release your anger for a long time. No more after this. Just be patient."

He had begun to guess at his master's intentions. Now, Schmidt wasn't as sure. "I'm intrigued."

Another savage grin. "As am I. We will speak soon." The avatar collapsed into a noxious-looking black cloud making a hissing sound, then drifting and dissipating in the space near the great chair.

"Love that exit," Schmidt said to no one as he pulled off his headset.

Far away in a room lit only by the glittering ambient light of the city below, a pair of hands lifted off a larger, more sophisticated headset, palms damp with excitement, placing it next to the backlit keyboard. He peeled the motion sensors from his arms and chest, and finally pulled off the gloves that mapped his hand movements. He sighed, contented. This was going to work out very well indeed. But first to make sure someone he first thought a mere irritant didn't become a problem. A worthy opponent was always worth the time it took.

"I'm sorry. This isn't what you're going to want to hear." Abara sat forward with his elbows on the boardroom table. He'd called Ericka's team to the meeting room next to his office. "First off, given the attack on this facility, we agree with Homeland and CIA that this is now primarily a terrorism investigation."

Ericka groaned knowing what that meant, reaching for her coffee and taking several gulps before putting it down to form another sticky ring on the worn table. Tim and Clarke shared a look, while Abara glared from one to the other, looking agitated at their reaction. "Why don't you hear me out first and do the bitching later?"

"Sorry, Chief, go ahead." Ericka knew Abs would have done the best he could. He was no mean negotiator.

Abara peered at her for a moment before continuing. "Lots of stuffed suits at this one, including our director, brass from Homeland and CIA both. The good news is Homeland concurs with our findings. The CIA wouldn't share theirs, but they weren't fighting us. That pretty boy from Homeland with the two-hundred-dollar haircut. What's his name?"

"Maxwell," the other three answered in unison.

Abara nodded, grinning. "Right. His analysis was exactly

the same as ours: that the target probably picked us up while we were watching him. They can't figure out how he got through either, but they aren't disagreeing with us. They concede their security wouldn't have fared any better. And that is what has everyone crapping themselves. If the FBI and Homeland can't keep him out, who the hell can? The only safe ones are those with no outside connections, like some of the military places, hardened for cyber-war. The only parts of our system we can call secure are the ones with some clear blue sky between our machines and the web." He paused to look at each of them. "Anyone or any group with Dantalion's capabilities operating in the international environment is a terrorist threat. The kind of guy who can open hydro dams and mess with air traffic control."

"Yes, no two ways about that." Ericka reached for her mug again, not disagreeing so far. "But he has to temper himself to some degree. If he oversteps, he'll attract the interest of people who aren't interested in him now. He can't hide if everyone in the world is looking for him instead of just us."

Abara nodded and continued. "So here's how it's going to be. We're the lead on the domestic terrorism aspect of this, but given how he operates, International Operations is going to take the biggest part of it. Homeland is going to stay purely on the international aspect; CIA isn't saying what they're going to do."

"That's because they have no idea what the hell to do." In Ericka's view the CIA hid a lot of incompetence behind a veil of ultra-secrecy.

Abara shook his head. "Not arguing with you, but it doesn't get us anywhere. This is the way it will be going forward."

Ericka chewed her lip, willing herself not to say it, and

then did. "How are we going to make any progress on this, babysitting those idiots at Langley?"

Abara gestured with his hands to Ericka. "A good question. What are we going to do? No one is going to question our jurisdiction to investigate the domestic crimes, and no one is going to turn down our help on the international aspect."

It was the question Ericka had been considering herself, dreading someone else would ask it. "We haven't picked up anything we're sure is him since we got hit. I'm cautious about being too aggressive with scans or searches in case we light ourselves up again. If he got from our servers what I think he did, we're almost going to need to start from scratch. First thing we need is an outside, stand-alone facility, so if we do get hit again, he doesn't get the whole farm this time."

Abara pursed his lips, glancing between team members. "Okay and then?"

"Then we have to scour all the police databases we can get our hands on, using our existing crawlers to search backwards through any older data we can. Find someplace where he has struck in the past. See if we can pick up a trail from before he knew we were onto him. Some undisturbed tracks. Anything. It's a long shot, but whatever he does next, we're not going to get ahead of him so we need to be on site the minute it happens before the locals mess it up."

Tim nodded, turning to Abara. "Any of the geniuses at Homeland or CIA have any insight into the guy himself?"

"Nope. CIA thinks it's a group; Homeland concurs with us that the behavior is more consistent with the focus of a single individual, though they are dubious any one person could do this without some assistance."

Ericka stared at Abara, wondering. "What do you see as our role in this?"

Abara leaned forward, waving at all of them. "I see the three of you making this pretty much a full-time job until we run this bastard down. Pull in whoever you need. I agree we need an outside facility to limit the damage if it goes wrong. I'll see the director about the money. Clarke and Tim, I want you to carry that. Ericka, we need to talk about your role. That's it for now."

Clarke and Tim got up to leave, but Ericka stayed, not moving. Might as well get it over with. She had seen the look in Abara's eyes when he walked in. Prolonged eye contact, an almost imperceptible shake of his head. She'd known it was coming since she let fly at one of the people from internal investigations looking into the security breach.

He waited until the door closed and the sound of footsteps had faded before he spoke. "Ericka, what the fuck were you thinking yesterday? You know what I'm talking about."

She looked down, twiddling her mug in both hands. "I'm sure it's pretty apparent I wasn't thinking at all. If you look really carefully at the evidence."

"No shit! This isn't funny. If you can't hold it together enough not to lose your shit when dealing with other agencies questioning your actions, then I have to ask myself what the hell I'm going to do with you." She nodded—hard to argue with that. She'd had the same thought. "I know what happened kicked the shit out of you, it would have flattened anyone, but if you aren't up to seeing this through then I have to know now."

"I just need a bit of time to clear my head. Get my energy back." Ericka knew what was coming. No point resisting it—just go with it and make the best of the situation. She could use the time to give the whole plan a quiet thinking-through.

"Damn straight you do. You're going out the door for some vacation. The question is, are you coming back?" His expression softened as he looked at her. "You're the best we have. I need you back, but you have to be ice-cold and focused. Take a couple of weeks. The others will get everything set up. I want to see you back here a few days from now. The real Ericka. Back here."

No, you don't want the real Ericka, you mean the one you think you know. She nodded and stood up. "Thanks, I'll talk to you soon."

Abara couldn't contain his surprise. "Well, I gotta say this is unexpected!"

"You know me. I'm a team player." She left the room to the sound of Abara's booming laugh.

14

A Wraith Revealed

The day started with tea and then into the rooftop garden, glancing at Mrs. Donnelly's wide back as the old woman tamped soil into a new pot, radiating a mother's disapproval. Certainly, the closest thing she'd had to a mother for twenty years. Her own so long gone she could hardly remember a face, a fading memory of indifference. This was different, a soothing presence that both allowed her to breathe and was sometimes too connected. The price she paid was she couldn't hide. It began when they stopped for a second pot of tea. Ericka wiped soil from her hands, chard now planted in the trays lining one wall of her deck.

The eyes were scanning her thoughts again, the old woman sighing as Ericka watched her choose her words. "Y'know nothing's as hard as disappointing yourself. And that's what's stopping you getting past all this. If you can't forgive yourself for Patty and let it go, you condemn yourself to a life chasing these horrible people instead of the ones you really want."

They'd had this conversation before. "Didn't you once tell me you knew about revenge?"

There was a slight hardening of Mrs. Donnelly's expression. "I did and I do. When I said it you were almost whole again. Now look at the state of you! Our Tim's worried you're going off the rails. He has to be caught yes, but it doesn't have to be you."

"It does, actually."

The old lady's eyebrows rose in skepticism. "Why?"

Just say it. It sounds terribly arrogant, but it's true. "Because no one else can."

"I wonder if you mean, no one else thinks they need to."

Ericka walked here almost every day, down the path by the river, then along home through the park. The trail got plenty of sun and had an expansive view of the river, an artery of life through urban sterility. From there, she could choose several paths home through wandering chip trails lined with the massive trunks of old trees.

It was the stopping and starting that made her first notice the car, just as the trail veered away from the river to run along the edge of the road before crossing into the park. It was a new-looking, sleek design, a make she didn't recognize, all black with a pointy nose and no front grill, likely an electric, with smoked-glass windows, opaque in the low-angle light of evening. It lurched to a stop, then hard acceleration before repeating the cycle, lost maybe. She turned back to the riverside, stopping for a moment to look at a mother tending ducklings congregated in an eddy behind a partly submerged tree.

Ericka crossed the road, leaving the crosswalk for the softer trails of the forested park, jumping at the distinctive sound of metal crunching right behind her. She spun to see the black car rebound from one of the metal bollards marking the start of the trail, leaving it bent over at an angle. She turned to walk back, seeing it surge to life with a squeal of tires, hurtling down the road away from her. She stood doing a double take as it continued to accelerate at an unbelievable rate showing no signs of braking. *Jesus, moron, watch where you're going.*

It braked hard, the ABS chirping as it struggled for traction, lurching forward and stopping just past the next intersection, not quite two hundred yards away. *So drunk he can't see straight.* She fumbled for her mobile to get a picture, but she had powered it off. Before her cell booted up, the car squealed its tires and disappeared around the next bend in the road, hidden by the overhanging trees. Nothing like someone standing with a pointed mobile to put the fear of God and police into a jackass.

A dark-haired young woman wearing running gear stood on the other side of the road, staring in the direction it had gone, her mobile glued to her ear. Gesturing with her free arm, her voice was high-pitched with excitement. "It nearly hit me. I think he's drunk..." a pause "...no I didn't get his license. It was a black car and I think it nailed one of those metal things at the trail entrance."

Satisfied, Ericka turned and followed the familiar trail through the mature groves of trees, their boughs sporting the bright greens of spring, not yet the deeper-hued leaves of full summer. Joggers passed her from behind, bounding along, holding a pace that was part of the privilege of youth. Ericka kept the fitness level expected of agents. Running on a treadmill in a room full of sweaty, red-faced people, while kid music pounded from the club's sound system was an experience the joys of which were lost on her. She vastly preferred the serenity of a martial arts dojo. She passed the small pond, seeing the usual collection of denizens lying on the benches, smoking and staring off into their own thoughts.

As Ericka was about to leave the park, instinct made her stop. Before leaving the cover of the trees, she scanned her surroundings, head cocked, trying to identify what had twigged her attention. She was conscious of nothing in her field of vision. Her mind was telling her something wasn't right, but with no awareness of what. She leaned around the rough trunk of an oak and glanced up the road to the north. There it was. The same dark car, the passenger door caved in and side mirror hanging from wires, the windows appearing black as the evening sky darkened. She stepped back behind a tree, placing it between her and the road.

Hers was a business where it was easy to make enemies from a pool of violent and angry people. Added up, her exploits over the years filled a prison cell block of her own. It was hard not to be a bit paranoid sometimes and this was odd. There were at least a dozen paths in and out of the park and the same idiot car was parked looking at the entrance closest to the route she had to take to get home. She bent for another look only to see the car start forward for a few car lengths before lurching to another abrupt stop. Maybe this was more than it first appeared.

Paranoid or not, it didn't pay to take chances in her kind of work. Ericka yanked her phone from her jacket and held the power button. She lifted it up, impatient at the time it was taking. The device was on but not hooking up to the network. She fumbled with the screen for a few moments while it chirped for attention. There was one unread text from her service provider, *We have cancelled your account as you requested. We're sorry to see you go. Please take a moment to give us your comments via the attached link and help us improve our service.*

What the fuck? She wondered if it was some jerk with a childish prank or just a mistake by the idiots in the billing department. Then it dawned on her how much effort it would take to acquire the information to fake an account cancellation. An unfelt chill coursed through her, followed by goose bumps despite the warmth of the evening. This was just a bit too much of a coincidence.

She glanced at her phone again. No data, but it was on the cell network—just without an account. Seeing no other option, she dialed 911 hoping it would still make an emergency call. It rang once, then: "911, what's the nature of your emergency?" Relief flooded through her, bringing a sigh while she leaned around the tree to take another look. The car was creeping along just above walking speed, moving away from her. "I'm an FBI agent, Ericka Blackwood, and I think I am being followed. Please dispatch a patrol car and forward this information onto the watch commander at FBI headquarters."

"Your location please?"

"I'm at a street entrance to the park at…" The phone clicked then beeped as the loss of signal abruptly cut off the conversation. She lifted the phone to her face and peered at the screen over her glasses. Now it showed no signal. Okay, that was way too many coincidences. She spun and ran back into the park until she came to where several of the forest paths converged. Her teeth clenched, pausing for thought, she took one to the left that would bring her out about half a mile behind where she last saw the car.

She lurched to a halt, almost hitting the yellow bollard marking the edge of the crosswalk. She swore under her breath. "Fuck!" To her left, approaching from the direction she had last seen it, the car crept along the edges of the parked vehicles. She ducked back into the cover of the trees. She looked at her phone again before it dawned on her. Shit, someone's hacked my phone; they're tracking me using the location data. Every time she tried to call, they were getting some sort of read on her, but probably not precise enough to pinpoint where she was, just enough to guess at where she would emerge. She tried to swallow, her throat dry, as it dawned on her at last who might have sent the car. What if he'd gotten her personnel file or just enough to use her phone data to see where she spent her time in the evenings? She'd done that all the time to see where suspects were hanging their hats.

She backtracked through the edge of the forest to get a better look, careful to keep behind bushes, wondering if direct confrontation was the best option. She was unarmed but no slouch at hand-to-hand combat, courtesy of her extensive training with Tim. As the car passed between two parked SUVs, she saw it from less than forty feet away but still couldn't see how many people were in it.

She dialed 911 again, holding the screen in front of her face. The call didn't connect, but the small symbol for the cellular network appeared for a few seconds. Emergency services could get an approximate location following the transmission direction from the known location of towers. Time to shut it down and wait for the troops to figure out where she was. She tore the back cover from the phone and pried the battery out, sliding the parts into her pocket.

Ericka left the trail and crept through the underbrush, wincing as roots and twigs dug into her knees, trying to avoid giving away her position. She looked up periodically to orient herself from the glow on the horizon, picking her way towards the road. By lying on her belly and peering from under the branches of a large bush, she caught a glimpse of a paved surface and a parked car. Her face tingled with excitement while her hands trembled from adrenaline. *Okay, think it through. They know I'm in here, but they have no idea where I am now. They're expecting me to come out from one of the trails and they don't seem inclined to come in after me. They don't know if I'm armed so probably they're worried they'd be sitting ducks silhouetted in this light.* She slithered forward, stifling a gasp of pain as she put her weight on something sharp.

Staying low, Ericka moved out onto the strip of grass between the bushes and the road. The light was dim now, the sun a glow behind the trees. The parked cars gave her some cover. Holding her throbbing hand, she peered around the fender of a parked truck. There it was, heading away from her towards the first trail entrance, still creeping along and lurching to a stop, probably to peer between cars. Time to chance it.

She raced across the street and into a driveway on the other side. The house's brick wall gave her cover. No sirens yet, they must still be working the tower data. *How goddamned hard is it?* For a few seconds, she considered putting the battery back in her phone to try 911 again but worried her pursuers would lock on first. *Let's make that work for me.* She popped the battery back in and tossed the phone across the road into the park bushes.

The house was dark, no one home. Maybe she could trigger an alarm and get the security company to respond. She spun around at the sound of chirping tires coming from the street as the car stopped in front of the driveway no more than a hundred feet away. All of its lights were off, presenting an ominous silhouette against the last of the light. It backed up and disappeared for a few moments then drove past the mouth of the driveway, lurching to a stop every few car lengths. She shook her head, not understanding. *It's like they're still able to track me.* She stuffed herself into a rosebush, gasping at the thorns as the car backed up past the driveway again, this time at speed, before the sound of hard braking announced it had stopped again. They seemed to know she was across the road somewhere, but not exactly where.

Ericka lunged out of the bushes and strode further up the driveway when she heard the sound, a quiet mechanical whirring, a small electric motor. She glanced up, seeing a small security camera, tucked under the eaves, tracking her as she walked. It dawned on her like a backhand across the face and she froze, her chest tight, her breathing shallow. Someone was watching her. She looked up again. *You motherfucker!* She knew beyond any doubt she was staring up into the eyes of her adversary. Flipping the camera her middle finger, she dove around the corner of the house, holding her back flush to the wall, sure she was out of the camera's view. High and up to her left, the same whirring sound. She spun to look up—another fucking camera. She squeezed her eyes shut and took a deep breath. This was going to get ugly.

She dashed across the backyard, pulling herself over the

brick wall just as headlights lit the garden behind her. The car was creeping up the driveway. She dropped from the wall, wincing as she landed, staring at the back of another large house, this one with lights on. She ran to the back door and pounded on it, standing on her tiptoes to peer through the small inset window. A child appeared holding a stuffed lion, staring at her with large eyes for a moment before turning to run further into the house shouting as she went. A wide-eyed young woman, no more than eighteen, appeared in the hallway. A big sister or babysitter.

The kid held up her phone to take Ericka's picture. "I'm calling the police. You better get out of here!"

Ericka bellowed her response. "Call 911 now and tell them an FBI agent requires immediate assistance."

"Yeah sure you are. I'm not letting you in. I'm not stupid!" The kid turned her back, holding the phone up to her ear.

Ericka craned her neck to look up straight into the unblinking eye of a security camera, a small black globe fitted close to the porchlight. "Shit," she muttered to herself. She weighed her options. *Stay here and wait for the local police to respond to the kid's 911 call or try and find a place without a camera looking down at me. If he sends the car here, I'm boxed in and unarmed. The noise could well attract other civilians, neighbors or others in the house and there could be shooting.* From a distance came the sound of tires made by a car cornering at high speed. It was decision time. She reached into her jacket as if fiddling with an unseen shoulder holster she wasn't wearing, then looked up again, mouthing the words 'kiss my ass.'

Ericka shoved herself away from the house, sideways across the manicured yard, coming to another wall. She pulled herself over and paused before dropping to the ground. No lights on in this one. Probably a camera somewhere out of sight. *Just have to stay ahead of his guys for a few more minutes. He can't know exactly what these cameras can see, at best a street address from where an IP address is located. Unless these places all have cameras and he's hacked the lot, he's guessing.* She decided she was better off out in the street. With these long, dark driveways she likely couldn't see much of the street from security cams. He might not be able to pick her up again.

She ran across the yard and loped down the driveway, scanning above for obvious security equipment. Nothing she could see. She came to a stop behind the wrought-iron gates, pressing her back against the concrete pillar anchoring them. The street was empty and silent, no headlight tracks from either direction. Without warning the gates pivoted open, shoving her against the rough bushes growing beside them. Someone was coming home. Headlights appeared in the street and lit her up as the vehicle turned into the driveway. It stopped right in front of her no more than a few feet away, the damaged door within arm's reach of her face. *It's them— the gate must have an app.* Pushing against the metal, she managed to scramble up the wall using the top of the gates for purchase. In the moment before she dropped over the wall, she glanced over her shoulder. The dark windows obscured the interior. They were just sitting there watching her.

Ericka pivoted her legs over the top and pushed herself off onto the street side, landing hard. She gasped in pain, stifling a scream as something sharp and metallic tore through the skin of her right calf and deep into the muscle underneath. She fell on her side, tearing the pointed end of the iron shrub fencing out of the wound, causing blood to spurt onto the neatly cut grass. Groaning, she dragged herself to her feet, limping towards parked vehicles as the dark car backed out of the driveway. The sound of multiple sirens now carried on the cool evening air. The car turned and drove away from her. She nodded, grimacing in pain. *Got yourself all turned around, asshole—you've pointed your goons the wrong way.* She gasped as she tried easing her full weight onto the injured leg. It hurt but she could move.

She looked across the street. Another wall covering the end of a lane with a thick hedge growing right behind it. If she could get over them, through into the lane behind, she should be no more than a block or two from the back of her complex. She would be home and have some firepower. *Where the fuck are those patrol guys?* As if in answer, three police cruisers passed the end of the street, engines roaring, lights on but sirens off. The sound faded and another chill flooded her. The kid's 911 should have brought them right up this street. She gritted her teeth against the agony, hyperventilating, eyes squeezed shut. *He's probably hacked the dispatch and routed them away, fed the car terminals the wrong address. I'm on my own for a bit yet,* she thought. *Best to try for home.* She blew out several hard breaths, fighting hard to suppress the pain.

She stepped out from behind the parked van and hobbled across the pavement. The car stopped hard, the reverse lights snapping on, followed by full acceleration towards her. She escaped by diving through the gap between parked cars on the other side of the road. She crawled up on the grass to the sound of snapping plastic and folding metal as the dark car scraped the sides of the two vehicles she had disappeared between. The parked cars hopped towards her, almost hitting her. Her attackers screeched to a halt unseen, the car concealed from her view.

Gasping, Ericka limped towards the wall, hauling herself up, unable to suppress a cry as her torn leg rasped over the coarse surface. As she dragged her injured leg over, the car pulled off the street at a driveway, crossed the sidewalk, then moved towards her. Its tires ripped at the grass below the wall, doors grinding along it, its roof striking her foot. She screamed, feeling her right fibula snap. The force of impact tipped her over the wall into the hedge where she slid to the ground, rolling out in the close of a dead-end lane. She shoved herself to her feet only to drop to the ground, grinding her teeth against the blinding pain. She tumbled back to the ground, struggling to stay conscious. One leg was clearly broken and the other oozed blood, soaking her leg and pooling in her shoe before dribbling onto the pavement.

She pushed herself into a sitting position, back against the wall, fighting nausea. No sounds came from beyond the wall. *They've lost me again. It won't last long—he's seen me in so many places, he'll figure out where I disappeared to and send his guys.* She weighed her options. The sirens came back on in the distance, then stopped. They must have made it to the girl's house. *They'll fan out from there. I hope they brought a dog.* She steeled herself to wait.

She shifted her weight, feeling her broken leg, gasping when her probing fingers found it. She was staying put, like it or not. She was looking at her other leg and trying to apply pressure to stop the bleeding when the headlights played over her hand and the fabric of her pants. No more than two hundred yards away, the car turned into the lane and stopped, flicking on its high beams, flooding the concrete walls around her with light, leaving her blinking in the sudden glare. No way out. She tried to stand, thinking to climb back over the wall, but her hands wouldn't reach the top from this side. She sank to the ground again, her legs giving way under her.

Ericka forced her eyes open as she slid into a sitting position, a surge of anger tightening her guts. *It can't end now, not like this. This bastard has to pay for what he's done—they all do.* The deep bark of a dog boomed over the wall from not very far away, but not close enough. It would wait for the officers following it, standing impatiently over the blood trail she had left. This would be over long before they got here. She waited, staring into the headlights, waiting for the sound of car doors opening. Instead, the tires squealed as the dark form raced towards her, reducing the distance to the wall, accelerating hard. She closed her eyes, accepting death, determined to die without fear, then opened them to stare her killers in the eyes.

As she did, the car's nose dipped hard to the loud, chirping squeal of anti-lock brakes. The car shimmied in the confined lane as its computer fought the tires for every ounce of traction, coming to rest almost touching her chest, her legs pushed to the side. She was pinned. Panic gripped her as she fought to suck in breath, her vision dark. She tried to see over the hood while above came the scuffing sound of shoes on the top of the wall, followed by an explosive exhalation.

The sharp reports of rapid pistol fire from above echoed from the concrete walls around her, followed by glass fragments raining on her head. Tim and several uniformed officers dropped from the top on either side of the car. "Grab the bumper, pull it off her!" It took several tries but the four of them pulled the front of the car back enough so that Tim was able to drag her out to the side where she drew a shuddering breath to the accompaniment of shooting pains in her ribs. He left her for a moment to run to the driver's side where the windshield sported several bullet holes. He tore open the door while two of the officers crouched behind aiming their pistols into the interior.

Tim straightened, his expression slack, taking a step back as he saw what she already knew. "What the bloody hell?" The driver's seat was empty. There was no one in the car.

15

Off-Grid

Ericka lifted her head at the sound, unconsciously sliding her hand over the worn blanket to where her holstered pistol lay within easy reach. Likely just Tim and Clarke coming with groceries, but recent events brooked no other response than complete vigilance. Her leg throbbed as she lifted herself to peer out the front window over the porch. Rain dripped from the roof, onto the railing, and from there to the aged, sun-bleached deck planks. This place had seen much better days, but for what they needed now, it was perfect. The cabin was set near the base of the hills surrounding the south end of the Tillamook valley in Oregon.

A place selected for having no connection to her or anyone she knew, literally air-gapped from her life. Seized by the FBI years before from a California gangster, the Bureau kept it for the same reasons he did: it made a perfect safe house. They'd brought her here after several days in a military hospital where she chafed to be on the move, doctors warning that she would be six weeks healing.

Originally built by off-grid hippies in the seventies, it had its own water, septic system, canned propane for cooking and now, paid for by its last owner, a very expensive solar array and battery system. It had no connection to the outside world, nestled so close to the surrounding trees it was barely visible on Google Maps. As long as no one forgot the rule about no phones within five miles, it was a place entirely in the physical world with no digital presence.

Ericka recognized the sound that had jarred her from her nap, penetrating the lulling ambience of rain on the metal roof and dripping water from the eaves. To the sound of a vehicle tire splashing through a deep puddle, the old Land Rover appeared between the trees lining the driveway, pulling up in front of the porch. This was the other part of the off-grid protocol: no modern cars whose array of computers might decide to call home looking for software updates. The Portland office kept several old vehicles as part of maintaining this place.

Tim and Clarke got out, pulling up hoods against the rain, then waving to her before going to the back to root for gear and groceries. They came through the front door dripping wet, kicking off shoes before walking over to the dining table to dump several bags of groceries. Tim opened the back door, leaning out to scan the leafy wall of the nearby forest before returning to the kitchen. He maintained a high state of vigilance even in normal circumstances; now he never seemed to stop scanning and evaluating.

Clarke pulled off her raincoat and hooked it on a peg by the door before dropping into the blood-red leather armchair across from Ericka, eyeing it with disdain. "What is it about gangbangers? None of them have any taste. How's the leg?"

Ericka smiled, sharing Clarke's opinion. "It fucking hurts."

"How's the other one?"

"It fucking hurts too."

Tim pulled a chair from the table and dragged it over. "Oh, quit moaning, it's barely going to leave a scar worth bragging about. You're going soft."

She cocked a cynical eyebrow in his direction. "Tell us again about wrestling polar bears on ice floes before breakfast when training with the British army. I never get tired of hearing about that shit."

He grinned, handing her a vial of pills and a bottle of water. "If you like, but if you're going to be nasty to me, I'm going to ration you."

She gave him a smile before taking two, toasting him and taking a generous sip to down the painkillers. "What did you tell your Aunt Margaret?"

Tim winced, his expression communicating all Ericka needed to know. "Not much, and she was ready to throttle me for the little I did. Seems to think I'm supposed to follow you around and keep you out of trouble. You'll get yours next time you see her."

Ericka blanched at the thought, turning to look at Clarke. "So, tell me?"

Clarke nodded, taking a deep breath. "Well first, I don't have any doubt it was Dantalion. He's changed his transit profile, and his routing, but it has his dirty fingerprints all over it. Once he figured out where you lived, he or someone working for him hacked every security camera and internet-connected device along your route home. We think he may have taken your personnel file out of the main company servers while we were chopping up our equipment. Once he was in, he had the run of the place for a few minutes. Looks like he made the most of it."

Ericka blanched at the thought of what he might have from that file. "And the car? To listen to the people who make those things, these cars with self-driving capability are supposed to be unhackable?"

Clarke's smile was cynical, rolling her eyes. "First time I've had to do forensics on that part of a car. He's a clever boy. Those things don't have the bandwidth to allow someone to look through the cameras and drive the thing in real time. He found another way."

Ericka nodded, of course he did, a diabolically clever bastard. "He wasn't doing a very good job of driving it. When I first spotted the thing, I thought the driver was three sheets to the wind."

Clarke chuckled as she spoke. "Yeah, I see that from the GPS—he was all over the place. Like he didn't know exactly where you were and was trying to drive it on about a three- to five-second delay."

That sounded about right when she thought about it. "So how did he do it?"

Clarke waited a few seconds for dramatic effect, then continued. "The combination of the car's regular diagnostic bandwidth plus the infotainment system's bandwidth running both cellular and through all the home Wi-Fi he could hook up to. It was hit and miss for him."

Ericka shook her head, brows furrowing. "Those aren't supposed to be cross-connected in the car I thought."

Clarke nodded. "Correct, but this one and probably a lot of others had been modified at the factory to allow it. The electronic guts of these things come from a factory in

Guangdong province in southern China. He must have a guy there who inserted his mods into it. He did this long before you pissed him off, so he must have some other plans for them. I hate to think."

Ericka sighed, tentacles everywhere. "Bastard. So how many of these Franken-cars are rolling around out there?"

"No idea. The company is doing a recall for what they're telling everyone is a battery issue so they can check. It's easy to fix once you know what to look for."

"And my phone?" Ericka glanced to Tim, but he was staring out the window.

Clarke looked almost embarrassed as she spoke. "He used the company remote admin function. Probably got the creds during the attack as well, though we don't know for sure. He might have gotten them another time. He was switching the services on and off as he liked while you were walking along the river with your phone powered down."

Ericka mentally kicked herself for the oversight. "Fucker! And the 911 dispatch?"

"He didn't get them at all. He was spoofing your phone and sending the dispatchers bullshit location data. Even sent them a text from you telling them to disregard your first call. They didn't but this all slowed the response time. For a while there, the location data said you had made it home, so they went there. The 911 call from the babysitter in the house was what saved you. It got them in the right area and dogs are hard to hack."

Tim put his feet on the expensive coffee table, giving her a reproving look. "You should have run back into the park. No cameras in there."

Ericka glared at him, leaning forward to respond, making

her ribs twinge. "Says the armchair quarterback on Monday morning. I thought if I did that, they would come in after me on foot before help could arrive. I hadn't figured out who it was before I crossed the street." Her tone was sharper than she intended.

He nodded, conceding the point, his eyes worried. "He very nearly got you."

Ericka sighed, turning to stare out the window while she took another sip of water, enjoying the chill. "No, he did get me. He just chose not to kill me." Ever since she had woken up after surgery, she had racked her brain for an answer. All that effort for what? He had to expose himself to some degree to try for her and gave them pretty convincing evidence how far his network penetration had gone. Just scaring her didn't seem like it was worth the risk unless he was so overconfident now that he was underestimating them.

"You mean because you're not dead?" Clarke stared at her, shaking her head. "I don't think his intent is clear at all. You were up against a wall; the car's collision avoidance stopped just before the car hit you."

Ericka didn't believe it. If he just wanted her dead, there were far easier ways to have done it, like pay someone to shoot her in the Starbucks parking lot. "He could have shut that automatic braking off. I'm sure he wasn't surprised when it engaged."

Clarke nodded with a slight shrug, conceding the point. "True. He actually had it shut off for most of the time he was driving it. He was having a hell of a time keeping the thing going in a straight line. Near as I can tell, he switched it back on while it was stopped in the alley facing you."

Ericka stared at Clarke for several moments before

speaking. "Right, it was the only way he could take a run towards me to scare the shit out of me and be sure of not killing me."

"Nonsense," Tim interjected, "those cars are designed to stop way before it did on collision avoidance. It was an inch or two from killing you. Either way, the fact is this target has taken a very personal interest in you. His actual intent changes nothing."

There was no arguing with that. Ericka felt her ribs under the blanket. "If he just wanted to kill me, he didn't need all the fancy hacking and toying with me. This was a demonstration."

Tim shook his head. "Demonstration for what? Like beating us down in our own headquarters wasn't demonstration enough? It isn't like the FBI is going to back down because a bad guy poses a threat to an agent. He knows that."

Ericka nodded—no arguing that. "Maybe he just enjoyed scaring me. He might be taking the fact that we latched on to him a bit personally. But this was clearly a demonstration to us, perhaps just to me, of what he's capable of."

"He may well be thinking it's personal, but either way you're here for a bit."

She shrugged her response to Tim. It was going to take time to think up a way to get the investigation restarted anyway. The enforced inactivity was the hardest part of this for her. She didn't fear him; she was gritting her teeth waiting to resume pursuit. "Have they figured out where they're going to put me? Those internal security guys have no taste either."

Clarke laughed. "You're here for a bit yet, but eventually one of the witness hiding places by the Marine base. It's on the top floor so you get a little deck. They're busy gutting it of anything invented after 1975 and then reinstalling secure stuff. Usual bulletproof glass and armored doors."

"I don't think he'll have another go at me. As you say, it isn't like the investigation stops if he succeeds. He's made his point."

Tim's tone and smile telegraphed he was about to tease her. "And no more flashy little Audi—that's going into storage for a bit. They've got you an old fully analogue Landcruiser they're stuffing with Kevlar. As Clarke says, you are moving back to the seventies. Better think about your wardrobe perhaps."

"Internet will be hard-wired in and then gapped. I've created a new identity for you to use from home." Clarke shrugged at her in sympathy. "It won't be too bad. Best we could do. Maybe no working from home for a while."

She was just going to have to live with it. "So, Tim, any word from Abs about what my role is going to be in this?"

He nodded. "He thinks you should continue as planned. Heightened security protocols, but he says criminals don't get to decide who investigates them by making it personal. Said your fieldwork ban is over 'til we catch him."

Ericka dropped her shoulders a notch and took a deep, relieved breath. She had faith in Abs but worried the weenies upstairs would take her out. "Homeland or CIA have any bright ideas they're willing to share?"

Clarke sipped tea from her growler, putting her feet up next to Tim's. "Nope, they're still wandering around all bug-eyed at how far he got into our network. Theirs run on the same system. Everyone's busy hardening up."

Tim grinned, raising his eyebrows in mock astonishment. "Behavioral science has concluded he's taken something of a personal interest in you. Might be you have something of a groupie. I hope they didn't stay up all night working that out."

Ericka giggled at the thought. "I'm sure they did, but let's think about that for a moment from our perspective. Does this create an opportunity? So far, he's been pretty untouchable technically. What would possess him to telegraph an interest, even if this was supposed to kill me?"

Clarke grinned at her. "Possessed? Clever choice of words."

"Maybe our lord of the dark web is spooked a bit?" Ericka shifted her legs over the side of the couch, grimacing at the sudden jolts of pain from both legs.

"Maybe he wants you to join him on the dark side? Little does he know!"

Tim's flippancy irritated her from time to time. "Maybe you should let me sleep. The pain meds are kicking in now."

Clarke stood up and kicked the leg of Tim's chair. "C'mon, smartass. Drive me back to Portland—I have to get back to work. Ericka needs her sleep."

Tim glanced at her, brows raised, and she nodded to reassure him. "I'm fine. See you back here around dinner? Buy some sushi while you're there."

Ericka settled back into the worn, comfortable couch, snugging the blanket around her legs, checking again her gun was at hand. She didn't for a moment think he would have another try for her here but took odd comfort knowing its cold metal was inches away. And why indeed the interest in her? It wasn't like she had found him through any great flash of technical genius. It was him or one of his idiots who let that video go that got them started. Dantalion had her investigation file so he knew that. He may have enjoyed the way they tried to set him up in the Philippines. They'd gotten pretty close. Perhaps the attention was feeding his ego. Her eyes grew heavy as she succumbed to the numbing calm of opiates. *We have to figure out him, not his technology—that's where he'll slip.*

Ericka awoke with a start, the room dark, not knowing where she was at first. She was nestled on the same couch, but it was night and the sound of Tim's deep, regular breathing carried from a nearby bedroom. The rain had stopped, and moonlight frosted the tree trunks in pale light. She slept like the dead for hours, not waking even when Tim returned. She settled back into her nest, instinctively thinking to check her mobile, before realizing again the nearest one was miles away. It was an odd feeling in her business, living without technology, disconnected from the world that had been hers for all her adult life. At first, she found it disquieting, like something was wrong, a subdued kind of panic that things were going on and she wasn't part of it.

Most people spent their time on the clear web, the world of shopping and news websites. A place of selfies, social media, likes, friends and followers, a digital community replacing the less convenient and barely mourned physical world. Below that, the dark web, truly a realm of shadows. Ignoring laws binding the physical realm, it lay concealed from the world above, a new frontier ruled only by its own lawless code, one little different from that governing the jungle.

Perhaps the social media thing was some deep-rooted need for the safety and comfort of a tribe's acceptance, even an ephemeral one that would last for days at most before dissolving and reforming around the next one. While the social good it did in many instances was significant, it was an odd and very sudden evolution in human social behavior. This single-generation move to the virtual environment was seamless, belying its immense scale. Change on the scale of the time thousands of years ago when people had left their forest tribes and formed into agricultural communities, only to later abandon them for urban life. Each time the social matrix reforms, and now it was happening again, unperceived by those participating in it. As society evolves, the criminal element, the predators within, adapt with it, some more successfully than others. That was what she was dealing with here: a supremely effective adaptation by a psychopathic predator to a new and unexplored environment.

Ericka sat up, her broken leg twinging. She spun her legs down onto the floor and reached for her water, gulping hard. That was how they were going to have to do this. She wiped the sheen from her forehead with the hem of her T-shirt. *We're trying to hunt a tiger in a dark jungle with spears, so all the advantages are his. Behind this offensive array, a near-invincible wall of digital fangs and teeth that might spring from the dark, is a human being as weak and fallible as all the rest. We need to bait the tiger out in the open. We could follow tracks through the jungle forever and never catch sight of it, finding only the remains of its kills long after the feeding was over. But how?* She sighed and flopped back onto her pillows.

"You all right?" Tim was a light sleeper.

"Fine thanks, don't get up. Just getting a little restless."

She craned her neck to peer out the window, the setting moon now just touching the treetops. *We're never going to flush him out. We're going to have to find something he wants so much he'll stick his head out of his den for a taste, all on his own.* Until then, she would have to steel herself to watching a trail of carnage and endure being able to do nothing. As with so many things in her life, back to the wisdom of times long gone.

She often reflected that of all the things she had learned at university, there was very little she applied on a daily basis with the exception of philosophy. Taking and enjoying several courses had earned her the playful derision of her highly technical clique but had given her something she had pursued ever since. They gave her the one thing no other area of study ever had or could. It didn't give her knowledge; it taught her how to think.

Aristotle for logic, Zen to quiet her mind, but now the task before her would take stoicism. The thinking of Zeno, founded in Athens twenty-three hundred years ago, and refined by Seneca and Marcus Aurelius. From it came strength, patience, and forbearance to endure as long as was necessary. A resolve of courage, the kind that cannot be touched by fear.

She smiled to herself as she drifted off again. Why was it the mind came up with things and woke you up in the middle of the night so you would remember them? She would have him. Then she would have the others she'd pursued so long. Which one of the philosophers had said it? The difference between justice and revenge is just a matter of perspective. They were right. That and the matter of weighing the consequences.

And with that, she fell asleep.

16

The Faithful

He called himself Abdul-Qader Ghazali now but was born to a different name and a different time. That was before taking up arms and service with a man who ran a significant portion of Balochistan province's gigantic drug trade, before he came into his own and carved out a portion for himself. Straddling the porous border between Pakistan and Afghanistan, their lucrative pipeline of opium out of Afghanistan had made them all wealthy men. Money to finance their cause, for arms and supplies. Ghazali was what Western intelligence services labeled a Jihadi, a man dedicated to his group's vision of sovereignty, based on their interpretation of Sharia, and imposed through violence if needed. Western ways must be expunged, with a return to traditional values enforced at the end of a gun.

Today was an unusual day for which he had traveled to Quetta, Balochistan's largest city and conveniently close to the border, to his old haunt at the university. For a generous gift to a student there, a distant cousin, he would use the university's internet connection with a borrowed set of credentials, specifically manufactured for him. He sat in the creaking chair, looking over his shoulder again to ensure the door to the small office was secure. Ghazali glanced around at the untidy shelves, piled with books and papers, the place filling him with contempt for its owner. The lair of an infidel. He turned to the laptop on the desk, inserting a thumb drive before pulling the goggles over his eyes and ears, eclipsing his vision and shutting out the incessant roar of distant traffic. Blinking lights at the far left of his field of vision assured him the device was powering up and programing itself. He settled in to wait.

In another part of the world, the seated man saw the beckoning signal on the farthest right of his five screens and smiled. Ghazali at last. He watched for a moment as the authentication code ran, confirming a secure link. He glanced to the left, to another screen, leaning in to gaze at several flickering graphs that would indicate someone might be taking an interest in him. Satisfied, he keyed in a sequence, activating software hidden on a compromised server far from him, commanding it to commence its task of routing the signal through as many different nodes and VPNs as it could, while maintaining enough bandwidth for signal clarity. He tugged on the sleeves and gloves, laden with sensors that would feed movements to his avatar before pulling on his own, much larger sensory helmet.

Ghazali started as the screen powered on, formless black replaced with the grand interior of a traditional madrasa, an institution of Islamic learning. Intricate blue-colored tiles decorated ornate arches favored by master architects of centuries past. Beautiful but something that until now he had seen only in books and pictures. His upbringing had been rather more harsh and did not include sipping tea with philosophers surrounded by the soothing murmur of fountains. The tinkling of water came from just behind him, and he could almost feel the breeze's cooling touch on his neck. This was truly a kind of magic, denying him the ability to tell which world he was truly in, his senses duped.

He found himself seated on the floor across a low table from an enormous man who wore the traditional garb of a border tribesman, an arch's shadow obscuring his features. A teapot and two cups rested on the table, also accurate to the period of the illusion. The detail was precise, the magic complete.

He turned to look around him, impressed by the seamless imagery. "You have outdone yourself. This is certainly much more pleasant than the cave from last time. Wise to choose this setting rather than a mosque. I have my doubts that you count yourself amongst the faithful."

The half-hidden smile was warm through the heavy beard, the rich baritone friendly and engaging. "I intend no offense. Merely your comfort. It has been some time since we have spoken."

Ghazali didn't want any gifts from this one, however ephemeral. "No need to go to such trouble. Ours is a business arrangement."

"It pleases me to see to my guest's comfort. What would you prefer next time—a hareem, perhaps a traditional slave market? You seem to have a preference for the institutions of the past."

Time to warn him where the boundaries of courtesy lay. "Careful, Janaa Saghir! I will not be mocked!"

The giant leaned back. "I do not mock. I provide for the

needs of my friends and allies. The question was genuine."
He gestured around him. "Here we are limited only by
imagination."

None of this made sense to Ghazali. "And yet you always
bargain for what you wish from the real world. You are not
satisfied with just money. Why, when you can dwell in this
world you have created?"

The giant nodded, conceding the point. "I do value some
things far more than mere money. Like you. And I have a
request today. But first, the information I provided was of
some value to you?"

There was no denying that was true. Ghazali and his men
had no other source even close. "Yes it was, very. If we had
not known the Americans were watching us, that meeting
would have ended for me in a ball of fire from the sky. As it
was, they created just a crater and a cadre of new martyrs.
I wish I knew how you obtained it. It is a source of infinite
value to me."

Another nod accompanied a smile. "And you may rest
assured, I will continue to look to your interests. You need to
search your men's belongings. Someone has a phone they are
leaving on. No phones except in towns. I fear one day I will
not be in time with my warning."

Ghazali nodded, gritting his teeth and scowling to himself,
wondering who it was. "I thank you. I wonder if we have a
traitor or a fool?"

A dismissive shrug of immense shoulders stirred coarsely
woven cloth. "Both must be dealt with in the same manner.
Today I am interested in Rajm. I hear the practice has begun
again in areas your chieftains control?"

Ghazali's head snapped up, shifting the goggles on his head, reminding him where he really was. "You want to watch a stoning?"

"I do."

"And how will you watch?"

"Destroy the thumb drive you used today. The next one will come with some additional equipment that must be thoroughly destroyed afterwards. Can I trust you with this?"

But you will not make mere entertainment out of such a solemn matter. "You can. You are smiling. Why?"

The figure shrugged. "I look forward to our continued, profitable venture, and I have had some recent success, which pleases me. Are you familiar with the term for a kind of experiment called a 'proof of concept'?"

Ghazali bit his lip to quell his irritation. "Do not mistake me for a fool. I was a student here for several years. I am a man of learning and scholarship."

"Quite so. I meant no insult. We shall speak again soon."

Ghazali jumped as the screen inside the goggles went black. He pulled them off, looking at them for a few moments, his lips pursed in thought before stuffing them in his bag. He pulled the thumb drive from the computer, mentally noting to toss it into a fire tonight. One never made enemies without a reason and he would not want this one as an enemy. A man who could hack information from the American intelligence network and give it to them, could also do the opposite if he chose. He shivered at the thought of the power such an ability gave him.

The sound struck Ericka as she walked through the door: a dropped pot, followed by a stream of Gaelic, cursing if the tone was anything to go by. Tim had dropped her home moments before and would be back in thirty minutes. There to pick up clothes and essentials for her enforced exile, she limped down the hallway in her walking cast to the kitchen, looking out through the glass doors to see Mrs. Donnelly bent picking up bits of broken ceramic. She leaned out the door, saying nothing, but smiling at the old woman, irrationally happy to see her despite the certainty of a scolding.

"Well, there you are then. Where've you been? You and Tim both, gone without a word where you are. I suppose it's too much to hope for that you've finally found a boyfriend and run off for a holiday somewhere?" The thick eyebrows rose as she waited for the answer.

"Just work, sorry." Another frequent bit of advice, to find herself a man and make some babies. She often wondered whether the old woman knew of her habit of short-term relationships with somewhat younger men. Probably not, or she'd have never heard the end of it.

Mrs. Donnelly stared at her in horror, mouth hanging open. "Jayzus, what've you done to your leg?"

Now she was for it. "Bit of a car accident. I'm fine. I'm just back to pack some clothes, then I'll be gone for a bit."

The old woman's eyes narrowed, clearly having none of it. "What kind of an accident? You can't even take a bit of time to let that heal?"

"Can't. Tim's taking care of me."

Mrs. Donnelly shook her head in exasperation and turned back to her gardening, muttering over her shoulder. "That'd be something to see."

Ericka tossed clothes into two suitcases, followed by half the contents of her bathroom. Then she added the very few family photos she had: her parents just before the crash that killed them, and finally the collage of her younger sister. She held it, a blend of smiling faces beginning with them together, one a toddler, the other a baby, until the one from the beach twelve years ago, just before she died. She laid this one on top of piled clothes and placed a thick sweater on top to protect it. But not before touching the beaming smile of the eternally young Patricia. She wiped away the tears on her sleeve and closed the suitcase, trying to take a deep breath against the welling pain and found she couldn't.

She texted Tim. *Got a lot to carry. Can you come up when you get here? Door is open.*

Will do, came the response a few minutes later.

Ericka glanced outside at the large rooftop deck. Mrs. Donnelly was manhandling what looked like a sapling apple tree into a large pot. Wincing as the extra weight made her leg throb, Ericka limped out on to her deck, carrying a bucket of water. She pulled up a chair and set to work watering and pruning dead leaves and stems, leaving them in a pile. Engrossed in her task, she started at Tim's voice behind her. "Just the two in the bedroom, or is there more?"

Ericka turned to see him leaning against the sliding door. "I'll just check the fridge, then we're ready to go." She stood, wincing as she turned, looking up at Mrs. Donnelly, but she was not looking back. She stared above and behind Ericka, eyes bugged wide, mouth open. A loud humming sound filled the air and she spun to look just as Tim took her to the ground. He stood astride her while she lay on her back looking up, shielding her body from the small, dark mass hovering over his head. He dragged his pistol from under his jacket, but as he brought it up to fire a small object dropped from the drone, which was holding position no more than ten feet over his head. He ducked, and it bounced off his back, landing on the deck tiles next to her head.

Mrs. Donnelly roared, red-faced, her finger stabbing the air towards it. "Jayzus, Tim, shoot the bloody thing!"

The humming pitch of the rotors increased, and the small aircraft darted out of sight behind the eaves and over the roof. He stood, weapon skyward, waiting for it to return but it was gone.

Ericka rolled on her side to look at its payload, starting as she recognized it, her heart racing. "Christ! Tim, look!"

He spun, pointing his weapon down before lifting the muzzle up again. His eyes were wide as he looked at her. "Bloody hell, is it?"

She nodded, afraid to touch it until forensics had looked at it, but there was no mistaking it. Clear plastic stretched over the black mass. There, sealed in a plastic bag sat a pair of VR goggles, and there was no mistaking who sent them.

17

Evocation

"Got it?" Ericka asked, her voice muffled by the plastic face shield. She held the edge of the bag with tweezers while the technician used a large syringe to draw out the bulk of the air. Ericka struggled to hold her gloved hands steady. She blinked to clear her vision in the lab's harsh light, glancing up at the young man whose tense features displayed his focus. He nodded, his eyes unblinking. Rock-steady hands held the tip inside the bag, pulling out the contents as the bag collapsed. Breath misted the plastic in front of his face as he controlled his respiration, keeping the slightest tremor from his hands. This sample had to be pure to have any chance of succeeding. In a single smooth motion, he withdrew the syringe, capping it before straightening up.

The package rested inside an enclosed vent hood. Ericka was taking no chances they contained a nasty surprise. Reaching farther inside the containment area, hands clad in built-in gloves, the technician slid the sample into a container, sealing it against the outside air for safe removal. She looked at him again. "Purge?"

He nodded. "Yes please."

Ericka pressed the red switch mounted on the top of the unit, activating the exhaust system above. The powerful fans roared to life, emptying the small chamber of any potential contaminants. She would take no chances with this one, not anymore. She snapped the venting unit off. "Okay, go ahead." Her gaze never left the goggles while he opened the access hatch on the end of the isolation unit and pulled out his case.

"I'll walk it right down. We'll be on it straight away." He flipped up his visor, nodding to her, before pivoting to stride into the lab airlock. She had told them to analyze the trapped air sample for any pollen or other biologicals that might betray where the bag had last been open to the air. Equally important before anyone handled the device in the open, they would test for any biological or chemical agents. They had grossly underestimated him one time too many already.

She turned to look at Tim and the second technician, both clad from head to toe in white 'bunny' suits, gloved, masked, and peering at her as they stood back against gleaming white walls. She gestured with her chin to the young woman, lead technician Biyu Ho, who stepped forward. "Hold the edge while I cut the bottom seam to get them out." Ericka wanted to avoid cutting any flat surface that might destroy any chance they had of a fingerprint. Not like Dantalion had sealed the bag himself but any clue as to the origin of this thing or where it might have been on its way to her could give them a starting point. The operation took over five minutes as they leaned from their stools, peering into the containment unit.

Ericka snapped the tweezers she had been using into their case. "Okay, got it? Biyu nodded as she placed the bag into a second, identical case and pressed the seals shut. She ran the purge again, removed the case, and Ericka watched as she hurried down the hall to begin examining her prize.

Tim nodded to one of the lab computers, flipping up his face mask. "They've processed the MRI. Shall we?"

Ericka nodded, pulling off her visor and peeling off the latex gloves. The lab's dry chemical-scented air filled her nostrils. "Is there a report?" Tim handed it to her and she dropped onto a stool, popping on her reading glasses, while he craned his neck to read over her shoulder. She read for a moment before stiffening and looking back at him. "See this? It says there's what looks like a note inside."

Tim smiled, always fond of irony, his lab suit rustling as he stood straight. "The dark web overlord uses paper."

Ericka grinned back. "We are going to want to fish that out as soon as they confirm no toxins or bio-agents." She leaned back to continue reading out loud. "No liquids or suspicious solids, very tiny memory and just the components you'd expect. Looks like another custom job based on commercial components. I wonder if we can pull the note out far enough to read it inside the containment unit?"

He shook his head. "Don't mess with it. They haven't swabbed the outside yet."

She glared at him in mock disapproval. "Yes, I'm sure Dantalion licked it or rubbed it on his skin before he put it in the bag. Probably got his DNA all over it."

Tim raised an eyebrow as he returned her stare. "Whoever packaged it for him might have got something on it. You can't be serious?"

Ericka shook her head. "I'm not, but I really want to read it. Psychos always screw up when they think they're so clever that they start taunting the investigators."

"Maybe he's writing to threaten you."

"Good. If he is, it would mean we got a lot closer to him than we thought."

Tim tilted his head back as he often did when thinking. "Perhaps. If this is some sort of chest-beating ego display, that tells us plenty. We know it's one person. If it was a group, they'd have never taken this risk."

"That's true." Ericka scrolled through the layers of MRI imagery. "It looks very similar to the bits of one we got in Sacramento. Almost nowhere on it to store data. We're not going to get much off it afterwards."

Tim looked genuinely surprised. "Afterwards what? They're never going to let you activate it."

She spun to stare at him, stunned, verging on shocked. It never occurred to her that they wouldn't switch them on. "Of course we're going to run it. What's the downside? If we learn nothing, then we're no worse off."

Tim gave her a skeptical look, raising his hands, palms forward. "We're going to have to convince them we can contain whatever comes down the pipe. Our past performance on keeping him on his side of the drawbridge isn't reassuring."

She sighed her exasperation. "So, we'll use an air-gapped computer with all the networking stuff yanked out. If I was our suspect doing this, I'd have put just enough code in these things to call a transit point and do all the processing remotely where I could see everything was wiped long before anyone could get to it."

Tim's short laugh was humorless. "You think the brass are going to let an agent, who this guy just tried to kill, chat with him and see how his day is going?"

"He didn't drop it on anyone else's deck. He dropped it on mine. What if he won't talk to anyone else? Think what we could lose."

Tim looked away, shrugging. "That's true. Not to throw a wrench in the works but I still think you're going to have to come up with some pretty compelling sort of ops plan before you get to meet our Dantalion."

"It will be the best ops plan on their desks by virtue of being the only one they've got. Their only other option is to sit on their hands and wait for him to strike again, hoping we find out about it at all."

Ericka waited while Abara settled into his chair at the head of the boardroom table, having arrived late from a directors' meeting. He was dressed as always for such meetings, in a tailored suit sporting expensive accents. He ran his hand over thinning, close-cropped hair ensuring none were out of place. Ericka, Tim, Clarke, and Biyu Ho, who had completed the lab testing, waited for him. Ericka made a point of never dressing up for internal meetings. Biyu wore a well-worn lab coat and sat perched on the edge of her chair, her valise open in front of her. Outside the window, the sports field was empty and hard wind-driven rain spattered the boardroom windows while the trees below gyrated in the gale.

Ericka broke the silence. "Are they going to authorize it?"

Abara shook his head. "Decided not to ask them yet. We need the lab results if I'm going to convince them we have no other option. Did we get anything at all?" He turned to Biyu, eyebrows raised.

Biyu's voice caught as she looked down at her notes. Even

in lab wear, she was strikingly pretty, dark-eyed with jet-black hair tied up. "We did, but nothing that is going to help I'm afraid. No pathogens or toxins on any of the materials, no explosives in the structure. The note is laser-printed in standard Arial twelve on nondescript paper and the edges were hand-cut with scissors. As I mentioned last meeting, we did recover DNA from the outside of the bag and two kinds of pollen from the air inside. The results don't tell us much. The DNA is from an unknown Asian male and the pollen comes from plants common throughout China and the rest of Southeast Asia. The plants are both seasonal so likely the exhibit was bagged in the last two months. The bag is generic packaging material, available anywhere in the world. The goggles themselves look like they were handled by someone wearing gloves, which left traces of latex on the outside. As with the previous ones, these goggles are modified from commercially available models and contain some customized circuitry. They are fitted with real-time facial mapping, which could allow the person on the other end to construct an avatar that would display the wearer's facial expressions. That's all we have."

Tim smirked at her. "So, we've narrowed it down to an unknown male somewhere in China or Southeast Asia? That simplifies things."

Biyu cocked an eyebrow at him. "A little something to add to all the excellent fieldwork."

Tim flinched in mock pain, smiling at her. "Every pair of goggles so far has been different? You've looked at all of them?"

Biyu nodded, her face expressionless. "Correct, I suspect he buys small numbers of various kinds and has them modified at any one of a thousand small electronics shops in Asia. It would make most sense from his perspective to use a different shop each time. Many of them operate under the radar and could arrange for direct shipping that wouldn't leave a trace. Any coding could be added later."

Abara nodded his thanks to Biyu and turned to Tim. "What about the drone?"

"We got a report from local police that someone saw one drop into the river about three miles from Ericka's place. It took some time for the divers to find it and the current dragged it along the bottom so we just got bits. It is a widely available model, unmodified and bearing an Amazon logo sticker, but it wasn't theirs. We didn't recover the chips or memory, so we have no idea which type of controller was being used or from how far. The device itself can be piloted either visually or in VR using the onboard camera. If it had a web-enabled connection, Dantalion himself might have been flying it. It could have been bought in any one of a thousand places anywhere in the world. We just don't know."

"No numbers on it?" Clarke asked.

Tim shook his head. "They're easy to take off, but we didn't find the bit where they would have been mounted anyway. We've sent the manufacturer everything we have, hoping they can at least narrow down where they shipped it."

Abara folded his hands on his waist, looking at Ericka. "And the note? Maybe read it out again."

Ericka ran her fingers over her tablet, then began reading, holding her voice even with some effort. "Ericka, I request the honor of a meeting. I find myself a great admirer of your work. I trust you are recovered now from your walk home. Follow the instructions on the back and we will meet. Be patient, my response may not be immediate. This invitation expires in four days."

They had all heard it several times. There were two more days to go. Abara glanced from one to the other, palms up. "Any progress on how we might record this?"

Clarke looked to Ericka to Biyu and back. "He's going to have onboard encryption to stop us watching his signal. We can obviously duplicate the stream and try and decrypt it later, but that's probably all we can do for the visuals. If we put anything on her face to record the VR screens, the goggles could pick it. As Biyu said, it looks like it can do real-time face mapping. Audio is easier—we can just clip a microphone in Ericka's ear to listen to him."

Abara rested his chin on his fists and stared at Ericka, saying nothing, before sitting back. "I can't think of a good reason not to do this. I want to but I just can't. My gut says it's a real risk, but nothing I can articulate. I don't think we've ever done anything like this before."

Ericka drew a deep breath before answering. "That's not a valid reason to avoid giving this a try. None of the technology to do what this guy does even existed five or ten years ago. Everything about this target and how we're chasing him hasn't been done before. Past practice is of little relevance. There's no checklist to follow."

Tim nodded his agreement. "If it's properly set up, there's no risk to data or assets and no way Ericka can come to harm. There's a tiny chance we'll get some tracking data or a new software profile and a better chance he'll say something stupid. The only reason to not do it is we are giving the bastard something he wants, for very little possibility of return."

Biyu raised her hand to interject. "I know I'm not really

qualified on operational matters, but if he's spending his time obsessing about Ericka, he isn't out there running his normal gig. He can't just want to look at her, he wants to say something to her."

Ericka nodded at Biyu. "That's what I think too. He's given us a shit-kicking; made it clear he could have killed me if he wanted to and now he's set up this virtual meeting. That's a lot of time and energy spent diverted from what he usually does for no apparent gain. So, he must be getting something out of this. We've never had any real grasp of what makes this guy tick. Even if it turns out to be a manic rant about his greatness and power, even that would tell us something we don't know. It may be more than that. No one's ever latched on to this guy before. Maybe we've rattled him."

Abara sighed, looking down at his hands. "Okay, so Homeland will try to acquire location data, we'll get an audio feed in real time and other than that, we wait to see what he has to say? Anything else?" He was shaking his head.

Ericka nodded, holding up a finger. "The investigation is at a standstill if we don't. We'll just be sitting here waiting for him to strike again and hope we pick it up before he kills someone else. We probably can't. When he got our files, it told him how we tracked him. Our best hope at getting in front of his next strike now is talking to him."

Abara's voice was almost a bark. "I don't like it!"

Ericka gave him a quizzical look and raised her voice as she responded. "No one likes it. We're playing his game, but if we don't try, what the hell are we going to say to the family of this bastard's next victim?"

Abara slumped in his chair. "You're right. Let's do it. I'll get the authorization from upstairs."

★ ★ ★

It was cool and dark in the back room of the Dantalion field office Tim and Clarke had set up in a long-unused building in the nearby Marine Corps barracks. There were no windows, the floor was industrial linoleum, the walls grey, painted concrete. It was as technically and physically secure as they could make it. For the operation, they had a dedicated computer, fresh out of the box and never used for any other purpose, installed with a basic operating system and browser, and connected through a commercial internet account.

She ran through her mental checklist. The computer would duplicate and save all data from the transmission stream, though none of them thought they would be able to decrypt it later. Ericka expected the goggles themselves contained the encryption key somewhere and that it would be overwritten as soon as communication ended. She had the team from Homeland set up to try and source the transmission, holding out little hope they would be able to trace it beyond the first of several nodes. Short of blind luck or a staggering screw-up from Dantalion, this was all about her and what she could get from him. She expected the only reliable recording would come from the small, hard-wired microphone in her left ear, which should capture the target's speech. The throat mic she wore would record what she said.

She sat in the high-backed chair with the goggles on her lap, closing her eyes for a few seconds to steady her thoughts. She could hear the whirring of device cooling fans and the faint, rhythmic thump of a distant military helicopter, accompanied by the dusty odor of electronic equipment. She glanced over to Tim and Clarke seated to her side behind monitors, wearing headsets and eyeing her apprehensively. Both sweated, staining their clothes despite the cool of the room. Ericka nodded and they turned to their equipment.

Clarke gave her a thumbs-up. "All set, you can switch on any time. Homeland says they're ready."

Ericka looked at Tim. "How's my mic?"

"All good."

"Okay, let's pair it and get going." Ericka powered the device on with an audible click and three green LEDs lit up, blinked twice, and began to flash in a linear sequence. "Have you got it?"

Clarke nodded, not looking up. "Pairing now with a device calling itself 'Ericka.' Okay, complete."

Ericka rolled her eyes—*cheeky bastard*—looking back at them before settling in her chair, glancing at Tim who leaned into his terminal. He peered around his screen to look at their router, which had begun to blink showing it was transmitting. "Okay, it's calling home. Get ready." She forced her shoulders down from where they were hunching, and took long, slow breaths, feeling her heart race as it drummed against her ribs. *All up to you now.* Her hands left sticky patches of sweat on the arms of her chair and she squirmed against the tickling rivulet of moisture dribbling down her back. She clenched her teeth, focusing on the dark wall in front of her, angry with herself for the fear. She should be able to do better than this. There was no way for him to strike at her here.

Dantalion should fear her, but she knew he didn't. If nothing else, this exercise telegraphed his complete confidence and mastery of the technology, though it could be a display of narcissistic bravado. She realized it wasn't fear of him but of not being able to stop him. That despite her best efforts, he would continue his rampage. The fear was confronting a foe she knew was better than she was, a squire facing a fully trained, battle-hardened knight who fought without rules, unhindered by moral restraints of any kind. Taking him head-on in cyberspace was not going to work.

The router beeped twice. Tim's head snapped in her direction. He nodded and gave her a thumbs-up. The goggles chirped for attention, the three lights now a solid green. It was time. She pulled on the headset, blotting out her vision and cutting her off from all the sounds in the room. Her world was dark and silent, her sensory isolation complete, alone with whatever was coming.

18

Dantalion

At first, she could make out just a faint hissing sound, then her eyes began to perceive the dim gloom of a vast hall built of immense stone blocks. The sound came from guttering torches lining the walls, set at regular intervals in between arches, covering blackened hallways that led away into nothing. The detail was staggering, the illusion complete, a visual environment exceeding reality. She glanced down, surprised to see her body accurately displayed, wearing clothes very similar to those she had worn the night of the car attack. She was both irritated and impressed. She lifted her head, the goggles tracking her head's position, the display delayed by a fraction of a second. Too many relays to project this in real time. He wasn't taking any chances.

Her avatar sat across from an immense stone chair, empty and partly in shadow, in the illusion no more than six feet away. She gripped the fake leather arms of her own seat to remind herself of where she really was, the feel of vinyl reassuring. *Hold on to the tactile to override the visual if need be.*

She spoke, projecting her words, ensuring her voice radiated confidence, but cultivating an element of contempt. "Yes, very nice dungeon. Are we going to talk or am I supposed to sit here and admire the view?" Her voice echoed back from the virtual stone walls. A few seconds passed—transmission delay or was he being dramatic?

The voice came from all angles, engulfing her, not loud but a compelling, almost warm baritone, the cadence like a skilled priest giving a sermon, building anticipation with each word. "Welcome, Ericka, I knew you would come." A slight echo reverberated from the walls.

That was fucking irritating. "Obviously, we weren't going to pass up a transmission stream. Why don't you switch off the video game and tell me what you want to say. I've seen better graphics. These don't impress me." That wasn't true. These were the best she'd ever seen in VR, but provoking a bit of anger might get him talking. Looked like he'd spent some time in the gaming industry. She made a mental note.

Another delay that she interpreted as transmission lag. When it came, the voice sounded amused and continued with the same deep timbre, rich with hubris coming now from behind her. "Do help yourself to the transmission data. Following it is beyond you. Perhaps next time, I will create an environment more to your liking. This is one of my favorites."

She started, the hair on her neck standing up. Turning to look behind her, she saw nothing but the empty hall receding into shadow. She spun back to the throne; a male figure of stunning beauty now occupied the chair. Tall, appearing seven or eight feet, an enormous naked frame clad in smooth, rippling muscle, dark-skinned and hairless. The skin gleamed as if oiled, reflecting the flickering red light of the torches.

Hidden in shadow, she could make out deep-set eyes gleaming under a tall forehead, high, sculpted cheekbones, and a heavy jaw. Full lips curled upward in a cruel smirk. Clothed just in darkness, his genitals were disproportionately large. He lounged, leaning to one side, his left elbow on the arm of his seat. Her heart began to pound and sweat ran from under the VR set. The presentation was intimidating, and she gripped her seat again to anchor herself.

Forcing herself to ignore the display, she gave a derisive snort. "Don't flatter yourself."

"In a place limited only by imagination, flattery is not a relevant concept, but perhaps this will assist in making you feel more at ease." His hand gesticulated toward her body, a magician's theatrical wave.

Ericka noted the same transmission delay again, but the motion-capture of the gesture was flawless, the voice synched to his lip movements. She looked down to see her body change shape, a decade stripped away, her waist narrowed, her thighs slimmed, and her breasts lifted and jutted further from her chest, her body as it had been in her twenties. He'd prepared that in advance—no way to program the morph in real time, or could he? Straight to sexual imagery for some form of assumed dominance. Disgusted as she was, she was stunned at the technology. She controlled her reaction to leave out any hint of how immensely clever she thought this was. "Are we here so you can show me you've mastered 3D gamer technology, or do you have something more impressive in store."

"You were not impressed before today? The FBI's scourge of the dark web taken down, digitally ravished, repeatedly and at length in your own lab, then toyed with on the streets?

You are a hard woman to impress, Ericka. Is that why you have stayed single all these years? Admire yourself too much for any competition?" He leaned back leaving only dark pools under his heavy brows, but the smile broadened, his full lips parting.

Enough with feeding his ego and letting him play at being a dark lord. "Toyed with? You couldn't even get the code right to drive straight? More like a twelve-year-old joyriding in Mom's minivan. I am not here to play games. What do you want?"

His upper body straightened. Now she could see his pupils, the motion capture catching even the blinking as his eyes narrowed. That seemed to annoy him a bit, like he had a show all worked out and didn't want to be taken off script before he got it all done. "Why simply to meet my nemesis of course." The tone betrayed no irritation, but it might be filtered by the augmentation giving him the rich vibrato of a club singer's voice. "You were the first to notice I existed, even if you did rather clumsily announce your interest. I must admit, I was less impressed once I read your investigative file and saw it was the error of one of my disciples that tipped you off. Still, it did not take you long to isolate some of my interests and begin to track me. Your crawler looking for spatialized chronological clustering was very impressive, I must say."

"Or to figure out who was behind the car with you hacking security systems along the way. Any script kiddie could have done that." That was complete nonsense, but narcissists can't stand belittling. See how he took that. She needed to keep him off balance, see if he slipped at all.

He tilted his head, dipping his chin. "I am sure you have

determined by now how I did that. I do enjoy doing things you security experts have told everyone cannot be done. Mostly I wanted you to know how badly I wanted to impress you. To be sure you would come here with your attention undivided." A slight grin displayed exaggerated canines.

"Now you have met me. So?" The voice augmentation was going to make it very difficult to isolate any regional accent. From what she could hear, he sounded either American or Canadian.

"Now I wish to know more. While your investigation was not as much entertainment as I had hoped, your personnel file made for some very interesting reading. I could not put it down. We are much more alike than I would have thought."

A bright flare of anger. "We're nothing alike!" Ericka growled her words without intending to, then took a deep breath, regaining her control. "Just what the hell do you think makes me anything like a sadistic murderer?"

The feigned expression of shock was flawless. "A murderer? I have never killed anyone. I just assist my followers fulfill themselves in ways they could not manage otherwise."

"You helped that murdering pedophile in Idaho rape and kill a child."

The immense head turned once. "No, I did not. I gave him the means to do something he had always wanted to do. Actually, I must admit to some surprise he had the resolve to go through with it. I enable and watch. I have never killed nor ordered anyone to kill."

Ericka fought down the anger so she wouldn't shout. "And yet an innocent child was tortured to death. You will answer for that. You also seem to have made something of a specialty in outing mob rats. You know perfectly well what happens once gang bosses have that information. Some of the ways they've died seem a little too creative for low-brow gangbangers. Suggestions of yours?"

The massive shoulders shrugged dismissively, affecting boredom. "As I said, I help people down the path of their choice, but I have never killed." He paused for another smirk, one eyebrow raised. "And I have never had a handcuffed prisoner I was escorting fall down a flight of stairs and somehow manage to give himself a fatal brain injury and multiple fractures. A fortuitous bit of bad luck if fairly improbable, it seems to me."

Her breath exploded out of her as her stomach muscles spasmed. *The fucker has the internal investigation reports and probably my psych assessments. Christ, he could publish them whenever he feels like it. That would bring me to a very abrupt end around here if the press got ahold of that.* Her mouth went dry, knowing Abara and others were listening at headquarters.

Ericka leaned forward, her chin on her fist. She had to keep trying to get him to spit out as much as she could. "So, tell me what's with the demon cosplay? Why all the theatrics?"

"I like theatrics—they amuse me—and it is hardly cosplay."

"Oh, so you think you're a real demon?"

He leaned forward, both palms up. "A lapsed Catholic girl like yourself should know one when she sees one. After all, what is a demon? I will tell you, shall I? It is a non-corporeal malignant entity. So, who deserves the title if not me? In the realm I inhabit, Dantalion is as real as anything else."

She almost laughed. *He's right, got me there. And the bastard does have my personnel file—he isn't lying about that.* "So, you've been on Google and found yourself a secret identity. Now what? What do you want?"

"A great many things. I am still assessing the possibilities. The line between the physical world and the virtual is blurring. This new world holds almost unlimited opportunity for a creative thinker."

She wasn't letting him get away with that. "And yet all the things I've seen do nothing but inflict pain and suffering, sometimes on other criminals, sometimes on helpless innocents. That is hardly creative. Garden-variety sadistic pervert."

He displayed no visible reaction to the taunt. "Perhaps not, but as I have often pointed out to my followers, the laws of nature do not lose jurisdiction at the threshold of cyberspace. We bring with us all our wants and desires, and there are still predators and prey as there always have been. All that is gone are our self-imposed limitations."

"They're not gone if you have the character to retain them."

"Ah but character is not enough to retain them." He steepled his fingers over his navel and slid lower in his seat, smiling again, like he was enjoying the conversation, the company of a respected colleague and rival. "You know as well as anyone the complete lack of restraint many feel in the virtual world. For them it is very freeing. We both know it, but I am going to say it. So-called civilized behavior is a cultural construct we have built to keep peace amongst us. We are not what we once were as a species. Do you know what the leading cause of death in hunter-gatherer societies was?"

"Do educate me, please."

"Male-on-male violence. A terrible lack of manners could earn you a caved-in skull. A lesser version of this constraint has existed ever since. We are always subconsciously aware of the potential for physical violence or hostility when we are in close physical proximity to others. Hidden deep within our minds is the instinct to evade anger from those around us if only to avoid retaliation for what we have said or done. We restrain our behavior and words. Fear keeps us in line. The basest of motivators. Step out of the physical world, into our world, and that fear vanishes. Our self-imposed shackles cease to exist."

"You mean those of narcissists and sociopaths."

She saw another tiny shake of his head. "It is a little more widespread than that. Now people will say anything, attack each other without fear of reprisal, knowing full well there will be no retaliation, no consequences. At the very worst, they abandon their online persona and create another, reappearing in society with none the wiser. Have you not watched people? They express disagreement with vicious verbal attacks, troll each other endlessly, feeling no remorse. Give them a place where the only law is the law of beasts, and they instantly revert to the jungle.

Ericka decided to keep him going—no telling what he'd say if he continued his rant. "If you're right, why do most still behave in a civilized manner?"

He gave a derisive snort. "Don't be naïve. Culture and civilization have laid only a very thin veneer over what walked out of the forests so many eons ago. We have not fundamentally changed our nature at all. Now we have a generation most of whom are content to live their lives in this realm. Basic physical needs must still be met, but social, economic, and even sexual gratification come in endless varieties without so much as stepping out the door. As our species explores this new frontier and decides how they will use it, I will be there leading those who feel the least constrained, free to explore beyond the boundaries imposed by society. To help those I select as they find the boundary and balance between the digital and the physical."

"All hail the prophet!" *Keep him talking. A bit more of this, and we may actually get enough to give us a profile.*

"The distinction between online and physical society is fading into oblivion. The mind only perceives the world through human senses, what the eyes see, what the ears hear, what we taste, smell, and touch. The so-called reality each of us creates in our heads is a mere interpretation of those senses. Those are the only connections one has with the world as it exists. When those same senses are fed through a device like the one you're wearing now, you interact with a reality that does not exist in the physical world. You create a new one, but one unfettered by physical limitations, laws, or cultural mores. Your mind expands into the new reality. One that contains only what you want it to contain. Finally, the forbidden fruit of Genesis—people now create the universe they want to live in, bringing from the old one only what they wish. Self-gratification on an unheard-of scale. Fulfilment through hedonism, which can be nurtured and shared. I take down the barriers of fear and release the person imprisoned inside."

Ericka steeled herself so the goggles would not display her emotions through her avatar, trying to dampen the loathing. All this and nothing underneath but the narcissistic self-stimulation of an out-of-control ego, hiding behind the twisted wants of others. "So here you are the dark prophet of the coming digital society and all you want to do is watch and masturbate while others do your dirty work, too much the coward to join in. A very petty use of this great power you seem to think you possess. I wonder who is hiding behind such a hulking avatar?"

He sat up, his lips curling back in a snarl, opening his mouth and drawing breath to speak before subsiding back into the shadows. *Got him,* she thought watching him glower from the darkness. It was several moments before he spoke again. "It may be that you are not aware of some of the things I have done. You asked what I want. A fair question and the answer is that I have not decided yet. I have many plans in motion."

There we go, he's on the defensive, acting like he has to explain himself. Need to keep him talking. His calm returned as he appeared to realize she had baited him. He stopped speaking, giving the now familiar half-smile. "Ericka, I do enjoy your company, but our time is now short and there is something I need to speak to you about before we are finished. You may want to disconnect any listening device allowing your colleagues to hear us. This next matter is very personal, and I would hate to think I had exposed your secrets."

Her stomach tightened as she wondered what else he knew. "Personal? How can anything you have to say to me be personal?"

"Please yourself. As you have realized by now, I have your personnel records and I must say I was very intrigued. Not by what they reveal, but far more by the questions they raise. You know they do not trust you, why everything you do there is so carefully controlled. They question your judgment because they do not perceive what motivates you. They do not understand you. Why you left where you were and joined the FBI in the first place. They also realize your value to them, an asset with capabilities possessed by no others, but they fear what you will do unrestrained. But I do know, and I understand. Can we talk about Patricia? Let's be clear what we are talking about. Look up."

The air above his head shimmered for a moment before the two images resolved into clarity. A grainy scan of Patricia's obituary and a cropped police report detailing the suicide of a grad student. Hate welled up in her like bubbling, black tar, a red haze filling her vision. She squeezed her eyes tight. How the fuck did he know? He had her. "Stop!" she shouted, pulling the mic out of her ear, flinging it to her side.

His eyes glinted from the dark orbits of the brooding skull. "But I would like to talk. About your lengthy and repeated trips to parts of the world that should hold no interest for you. Because it looks to me like you are searching for something. Year after year you return, never wavering. So, I wondered what it is, and it did not take me very long to find it. As I said, we are not so very different at all. I will not spoil your secret; I think I would very much like to help you with it. It is what I do."

She spat the words, Patty's image gutting her, violated that he was using it. "You bastard, take down those pictures!"

"As you wish." She watched as Patty's image faded, her throat tight, making it hard to breathe and her gaze dropped to his wide, staring eyes as he leaned forward, his expression eager, almost hungry. "So, I see my conclusion was correct. Now I see my way forward in this. What if I could find them for you? Tell you where they are now. What would you give, Ericka? How badly do you want them? Think on it and we will speak again." He vanished in a violent explosion of black smoke that billowed towards her, blotting out her vision. And stayed dark. She pulled off the VR set, gasping, throwing them skidding along the floor in front of her, before leaning over, fighting the urge to throw up, unaware of her surroundings.

She rested her elbows on her knees, drops of sweat spattering and pooling on the concrete floor between her feet, her breath coming in shallow gasps. She straightened her back, pulling herself upright before she could bring herself to look at Tim and Clarke. They sat motionless, speechless, staring back at her with wide eyes. Tim pushed himself away from his station and stood, then walked over to her.

He gripped her elbow lifting her up before grasping each shoulder in his calloused hands. Staring into his face, her eyes tracking the long vertical scar before returning to his eyes. He tightened his grip before speaking. "Let's go outside. You need some air."

As they walked, he held her elbow, steadying her while she glanced over her shoulder. Clarke bent to pick up the goggles, scanning the floor presumably for the FBI mic she had torn off. Ericka raised her hand to her ear where the device had been taped, causing a twinge and returning with a smear of blood. "It's worse than we thought."

Tim raised a finger to his lips, shaking his head, gesturing with his chin towards the door. "Deep breaths, just get your heart rate down a bit and gather yourself." As they reached the door, Clarke caught up, handing her a bottle of water chilled and perspiring in the humidity. She held the bottle to her forehead as Tim shoved open the outer door, allowing the brilliant late-morning sun to pour over them. She and Tim sat on a bench along the side of the building, a relic of its days as barracks, probably Cold War vintage.

Clarke stood a few feet away, speaking on her mobile, presumably to Abara. "She looks a little shook up so we're just outside getting some air. I'm going to retrieve the goggles and get them back to the lab. No, we haven't debriefed why the mic failed." Clarke glanced in Ericka's direction. "We'll get started on voice analysis. How did Homeland do with the trace?" Clarke shook her head as the others leaned in to listen. "Yeah, we didn't expect they would, but we can go through the data anyway. Might get lucky." She slid her mobile into a pocket, smiled at Ericka, and walked back inside.

Tim looked at her, waiting until a marine helicopter had passed over, its heavy rotors vibrating the bench and drowning out all other sound before it crossed the base perimeter and disappeared to the south. "Think it through very carefully before you talk. I know enough to guess what that last bit was about, but you'll want to think this through more than once before you give a statement."

She nodded, twitching, sweaty and dirty, but not the kind that can be washed off. "The bastard has my personnel file and probably my shrink reports." She cringed again, the possibilities of what he could do with them running through her head. It would be very hard to continue her own search with this evil bastard watching and interfering.

"Jesus bloody Christ!" Tim turned away, tugging at his short beard. "The last thing on our recording is you yelling stop and then to take pictures down. Just your memory of what he said from that point on." He looked at her, both eyebrows raised, nodding.

She nodded back, looking down. "That rattled my cage. Not what I expected at all. He really puts some effort into his avatar. At least as good as the best gamers—the graphics were really something."

"That tells us something. There may not be many people in industry who could do that kind of VR work."

She nodded. "Worth following up. Let's go get the debriefing over with. Then I need some time to think." This could change everything.

19

Ericka

She was suffocating, couldn't draw breath, unable to move her hands to push herself up. Ericka sat bolt upright. The pillow that had been covering her head went flying to the side, knocking the lamp to the floor; soaking sheets constricted her arms. She had writhed herself into a homemade straitjacket. Yanking her arms free, she sat with her knees up, dabbing her forehead with the corner of the sheet, trying to find a part of it dry enough to mop up the perspiration. She glanced over at the clock, seeing it tick over to 1:00 AM, thinking with dread certainty that was the end of sleep for the night, three nights in a row jolted awake and gasping for air by the same vivid dreams. She had to find a way to rest, she was cracking as it was.

She snapped open the vial of sleeping pills, downing one with a gulp of lukewarm water from her bedside glass. They were misnamed—not sleep at all, more a kind of chemical unconsciousness. Rest of a sort, but the price was dreams of startling clarity that lingered, the taste of their experience a bitter flavor in her mind.

She wanted to hate him for bringing back these dreams, but it was nonsense. They had periodically returned to haunt her for the last twelve years, a searing burden from long before his intrusion into her mind. Sometimes they would subside while she was away searching, and other times when work refocused her thoughts in hot pursuit of a suspect—never for very long though and always bringing back the same horror undiminished by years. When they returned, sleep was a rare privilege earned through pharmaceuticals or absolute exhaustion. She drew a sharp breath as pain lanced up her leg. Free from the walking boot, it would not bear any twisting. She pulled her other pillows into a pile and lay back propped up.

How the hell had that bastard put it together? Her psych assessments would have told him about the loss of Patty and how she died, but putting the rest together was a serious feat of digital sleuthing. The thought made her throat go dry. Somehow, he knew her. He had not just read about her; he knew her. She spoke little even to close friends about where she took her so-called vacations and why. Except for Mrs. Donnelly, it was a part of her she kept buried, far from the revealing light of day.

Tim had put most of it together, but he was her closest friend, a brother. He covered for her when she lost her shit that one time, and now he'd made sure the brass was at least wondering what had happened in the final moments of her encounter with Dantalion. They knew he had taunted her with images of her dead sister, but nothing beyond that. If they did, if they had any inkling where she was going and why, her career at the Bureau would come to an instant stop like driving into a brick wall.

The horrible thing was the dreams were the only time she could see Patty's face now. Twelve long years and now she couldn't form a mental picture while awake, not without looking at a picture. But now, even in her nightmares, her sister's features often blended with the face of that dead child in Idaho. Calling for help that would never come, dead faces accusing her of something she couldn't have stopped, a festering mental wound that eluded healing. And now this monster with his demon persona, mocking her for her lack of ability to find him, scorning her for failure, reinforcing all she dreaded about herself.

Alone so long, and now the memories were fading, corrupted by the horrors of her calling, poisoned by a career where vile human behavior was an everyday part of life. It was time to get out, before she lost her mind, but not before she put this monster beyond doing any more harm. Then time to find a new life, like the one lost to the limits of memory, more felt than remembered, her family succumbing to the final death when all recollection fades from the minds of the living, leaving her alone, even in her mind. Mrs. Donnelly had tried to tell her so many times. She nodded off again.

She was sixteen at the time of their parents' funeral, Patty fourteen. She stood once again huddled against her sister, sharing an umbrella against the sheets of wind-driven rain. Two closed caskets poised over fresh graves, a droning priest the legacy of her parents' faith. The truck that had broadsided their car denied her a last glimpse of their faces. Behind them, faceless adults, members of her parents' faculties, formed a cordon seen as if painted by an impressionist.

Patty stepped forward, stooping for a handful of sodden earth, letting it fall on the caskets from her muddy hand. She turned to face Ericka, her features now indistinct, like a watercolor spoiled by rain. Patty ran, pushing her way through the assembled adults who parted to let her through before closing ranks behind her. Ericka ran to follow but no one would move. She pressed her way between them, unable to move, as if fighting quicksand. When she staggered through Patty was gone, the empty graveyard giving no sign of her passing. Motion caught her eye near the cemetery's lone tree. Rooted to the spot, she watched with paralyzed horror the dark shape of a car driving away without haste. Patty was gone.

Ericka turned in her sleep, moaning as she tore at her pillows, Morpheus dragging her with the remorseless power of chemistry. Ericka bit her lip, muscles bunched with tension as she rolled on her side, dragging grasping sheets with her. The glow of streetlights outlined the curtains against the wall, deep gloom accenting pitch-black. She sighed, pulling the pillow over her face to shut out the light for a moment then gave up. The clock showed 3:04 AM.

She dropped into the desk chair and pried open the laptop, stuffing in her secure memory stick. This was a familiar sleepless ritual, poring over her files, racking her brains for the next step. She looked at her files and remembered, details of a night she would never forget. The pivotal point in her young life twelve years before. The phone call—Patty was in hospital, on a Mexican vacation, calling for her sister. A vacation they were to go on together before Ericka cancelled last minute to work, a friend taking her place. She remembered nothing of the flight from California.

Her memories began with the hospital room, Patty's swollen eyes, staring down, avoiding contact, her sister clutching her tight, shaking her with hard, racking sobs. "Why? Why did they do that?" She was broken inside, never to heal. When she slept at last, Ericka slipped from the room to speak with the waiting doctors.

Ericka toggled to the sparse notes from the Mexican investigation. Early in the investigation they had begun to piece it together before they stopped trying. The three men had targeted Patty, likely they thought at one of the resort town's many nightclubs. Invited by one of them to another party, they had spiked her drink with something that had left her half conscious and giggling as she left with the man, tall, in his early twenties and well dressed.

When she was dumped from a car at 3:30 AM across the street from an all-night gas station, she was only just conscious. Medical examination showed she had been repeatedly raped and savagely beaten. It was hours before the drugs wore off and a day of surgery to repair her torn body before the Mexican police could talk to her. Missing hours at a location she couldn't identify, by men she couldn't remember. An eternity of suffering, as they held her down, a pillow over her head, smothering her while they punished her, first terrorizing her mind and then by complete, prolonged dominance of her helpless body, dreamlike memories of the lust of monsters.

Her body would recover in time, but her mind lay shattered, her spirit gone. In later years, Ericka would come to regard that as the night Patty died. The consulate kept her updated while she sat by Patty's bed. They methodically pieced together what they could, interviewing partygoers, finding the high-end apartment where it had happened, her blood still on the sheets, her attackers long gone. Everyone in town knew them, wealthy young men from somewhere in Central or South America, sneering arrogance and flashy cars. Always together, spending family money on clubbing and women. Gone across the southern border before the police even knew their names, vanishing in an instant. Well connected to serious drug money the police speculated, new identities and the code of silence, no one to extradite even if the countries who might harbor them would hand them over. In such places, those who governed and those who were the government were often not the same people. She stared at the same pictures Dantalion had so gleefully shown her.

Ericka leaned back in her chair, making it creak, reliving the time as she always did. Bringing Patty home to Boston, she had been powerless as her sister, lifelong companion, and last remaining family faded from the world. As her body healed, her mind withdrew. She wouldn't talk, ate little, and stared off into a distance seen only by her. She refused to go outside, leaving Ericka to care for her as best she could, returning home only to explain to her employers and arrange a leave of absence. When she could cajole Patty into a slow walk through the park, Ericka fought surges of anger as her sister flinched in fear at any man who came near, clutching her arm. No amount of therapy, talking or simply holding her seemed to help. Ericka worked as she could from Patty's apartment, despair welling as the light in her sister's eyes continued to fade. Patty had always struggled with depression, leaving her without a fraction of the strength to return to the surface and resume her life.

The end came while Ericka was on an infrequent trip back to her San Jose condo, this time to put it up for sale, and move the last of her things back to Boston. She tried to time the trips home to when Patty appeared to be stable, spending the least number of nights away, but it was time enough. When Patty failed to answer the phone, she knew. Her stomach in knots she dialed again and again and again. After scrambling to get on a flight, she arrived in the piercing dawn of a cloudless sky. She unlocked the door and walked down the hall, finding her where she knew she would, in bed and at peace. The pink glow of the rising sun cast a compelling illusion of life on her still features, her final expression like contented sleep, the covers tucked under her chin as she lay on her side. She had hoarded her meds in secret away from Ericka's watchful eye, written a note, and gone to bed one final time. The note lay on the bed next to her, the pen on the floor.

Ericka, thank you for taking care of me. You knew this was coming and I'm so sorry for the pain. Please forgive me. It's time for you to get back to your own life now. I always thought we would grow old together, but fate had different plans for us. There is no other way for me to end this pain. I know you don't believe, but I do. I can feel myself drifting away now. Time to go. See you on the other side.

The blackness that had consumed her was her faithful companion ever since. Held at bay by sheer power of will, sometimes forgotten for a time, only to bubble up like effluent from a cracked sewer pipe, poisoning her spirit with her sister's torment. It changed everything. She returned for a time to California and Integrated Security Systems, brutal hours a needed distraction from the ever-present memories of Patty's final weeks and days.

She drove the Mexican police without respite, refusing to accept the bastards were gone beyond the reach of theirs or American justice. Obsession is mortal enemy to reason. The trail went cold in the warrens of South America's biggest cities. Two of the men were scions of wealthy drug cartels, families with the resources to hide them from the world, buy them new identities, and set them up where they would never draw attention. The American consulate went as far as to speculate local police had been told continuing the investigation would be unhealthy for them.

Years ago, the internet was very different, social media a mixed blessing just emerging, real cyber-sleuthing still more science fiction than a standard police tool. But Ericka could see what soon would be possible as she ground through endless hours. She could see what the law enforcement community was building and foresaw what they might one day be capable of. To the shock and dismay of the ISS executive, their prized star announced she was leaving to take up a career with the FBI. No amount of promises or piles of money shown to her made any difference. She left without regrets, remembering now the fierce determination welling in her.

Ericka had never given up, never let the driving anger fade, using the tools as time permitted, but she had never found them. Armed just with passport photos and the names they had used before, a copy of the scant Mexican file, her pursuit was relentless. She assuaged the hunger by ridding the world of as many like them as she could. Refocusing on new targets, bringing them down one by one. Until that day in Spokane when the frightened eyes of a captive child held the same anguished desolation she had seen before in a Boston hospital room. Patty's eyes had held that look. Bubbling pitch welled up through her mind, blotting out restraint and logic. Now, no one at the Bureau had ever looked at her the same way again, the lid on her future welded down tight forever, but she didn't care.

Dantalion was right about the solo trips to the south. Vacations in the sense they salved the hurt, a feeling she was close to them, hope supplanting despair as she strolled through endless towns in Central and South America. Her Spanish and Portuguese were flawless. Dressed as a local, her olive complexion and dark hair cloaked her in anonymity. Her concealed video cameras recorded all around her as she pretended to interest herself in market stalls and food. She took long, slow walks through high-end neighborhoods, her gaze averted from people and homes, never raising the suspicions of ever-vigilant security. But she had found nothing. Gone from the world like they never existed.

Despite the intense curiosity of her colleagues, she told no one where she was going or what she did on these vacations. Office rumor had it she traveled to exotic locations to sate herself in the company of men years her junior, compensation for her perpetually single lifestyle. She said nothing to dispel the gossip, smiling to herself remembering the times when it had been true. A long sigh brought her back, maybe she would sleep again. She flopped into bed, drawing the damp covers to her chin.

★ ★ ★

They were back in their favorite bar just off the MIT campus where they went to school together. Teasing Patty about getting into grad school when she attended just enough classes to avoid academic probation, her fondness for marijuana excessive. Free from the confines of boarding school, Patty experimented with great enthusiasm, Ericka far less so. They lived together in a state of tolerant bemusement. Ericka was leaving for Silicon Valley, enticed away to California, groomed by company recruiters.

Faceless wraiths swirled around them, chatter diluted into white noise by music she couldn't hear. Ericka scanned the moving figures but could see nothing to justify the danger she sensed, a kind of ambient menace.

They stood up to leave, Ericka cringing with anticipated dread. She couldn't walk fast enough to keep up with Patty, watching as her sister wandered through the open elevator doors, a baffled smile on her face as she turned. The doors began to close, but Ericka couldn't move. She opened her mouth to scream a warning, three hulking shadows on the back wall of the elevator projected by men who weren't there. The door shut. Ericka shoved open the door to the stairs, running down, bursting into the parking lot two floors down. She waited as the elevator arrived, the doors painfully slow to open, excruciating. There was no one there.

"Fuck—enough!" She sat up. The red glow of sunrise bathed her room, warm light seeping past the curtains. The poison drained from her mind despite the lack of sleep. That would have to wait. She looked around the sparse furniture, her home until she could return to her condo. She relaxed her shoulders, taking several deep breaths, feeling at peace. She'd lost a fight, taken some serious lumps, but she was still there. Time to regroup and get ready for the next one, analyze the errors, and rearm.

She smiled at her reflection in the dresser mirror, pleased to see her own face again. The next battle she fought would be on very different ground, and it would end very differently.

20

Wrath of God

Ericka hunched forward, scanning the lines of code parsed from Homeland's attempts to track their target while she was talking to him. The recorded conversation itself remained a meaningless block of encryption, defying all attempts to crack it. The lab analysis of the audio recording gave them nothing, no background sounds, no detectable accent. Linguistics gave a high probability the speech pattern was educated, growing up in western North America, which gave them nothing about his current location. She leaned back, gnawing her pen and staring out the small windows into the night sky.

They worked from their self-contained project rooms tucked in the same dingy building. The goggles themselves yielded nothing, just enough computing power to encrypt the transmission key beyond the reach of any algorithm they had. Except for one chip that did not seem to function with the rest, holding a small amount of lightly encrypted data that yielded to Tim's efforts after several hours.

"Got it!" he had yelled loud enough that she and Clarke jumped, followed by a disgusted, "Jesus Christ!"

Hours of effort produced a short line of text. *I hope I'm not keeping you up nights, Ericka.*

"Fucker!" Ericka shook her head, walking back to her chair. She pulled up Homeland's report on the data stream and profile markers, reading it for the fourth time. They were right. He had changed how he operated, but he should be trackable in the final segment of the transmission, perhaps in the last few servers to final destination. Upstream, he was using something new they couldn't track at all. There was no reason he couldn't use his fancy system all the way to the endpoint. Ericka suspected he was well pleased if people knew it was him, smug behind his technology that they could get no closer.

She sighed and peered over her monitors at Tim's and Clarke's tired faces lit from below in unflattering blue light. "Unless one of you is about to make the big breakthrough, we should knock off for the night." Both had spent the day combing intelligence reports and staring at incident records, hoping to find something that had the familiar scent of their quarry.

Clarke leaned back and shook her head, while Tim stared at his screen for a few moments before glancing up. "Something that might be worth following up if you think Dantalion might have a taste for Jihadis. Mossad filed something odd they picked up between someone in Pakistan and a suspected financier in Saudi."

Ericka perked up. "I'm sure Jihadis are right up his alley. What?"

Tim leaned into his screen, staring with bloodshot eyes.

"Unknown entity in the Pakistan border areas telling a financial benefactor about a pending execution of someone they both don't like, a stoning. Said to be for the crime of sodomy."

"And? So?"

Tim's eyes locked with Ericka's. "He's telling him, he thinks it might be broadcast and says he will ask if his patron too may watch."

Ericka bolted upright, causing her chair to squeak. "How the hell can they transmit anything from the tribal areas? That would be an engraved invitation to a drone strike."

Tim nodded. "Clearly, yet here it is. And a drone strike is why Mossad handed it over."

Ericka thought through the possibilities. "Did they get a location on the source?"

"They did, and the transmission gave the name of the village near where it's going to happen. No time though, just the day."

Clarke leaned over to look, her eyes wide. "They must have figured out which satellite network they hooked up to?"

"They did." Tim smiled, leaning back.

Ericka nodded, her stare intense. Almost anything was worth a shot. "We can shut him out easily then. It isn't like he has a lot of fail-over options in that part of the world. We have to talk to the military, no drone strike on this one. Maybe if local authorities can shut it down, we can get the equipment intact."

Tim shook his head, looking pained. "That's a lot to ask. People could get killed trying to get us another pile of stuff we can't decrypt. Thinking about it, they weren't going to drone strike this anyway. Half the village will show up to watch. Far too many civilians. If they can track the Jihadis as they run, they can fry them later."

Clarke looked at them, brow knotted. "Someone's about to be murdered. How could we not tell them?"

Ericka nodded. "Quite so. Let's have a look. If this is him, maybe it's time he made some enemies."

Clarke leaned forward, her eyes squinted against exhaustion. "Sure as hell that's him."

Ericka nodded, biting her lower lip as they stared at the code analysis from the satellite uplink. Her heart pounded against her ribs, all thoughts of sleep forgotten. "Looks like he tested it just after the comms Mossad picked up. Not much bandwidth, he's going to have to settle for just straight video on this one. Cocky bastard—he must know we might find this."

Clarke leaned back, brushing her lank hair from her forehead, staring at Ericka from red-rimmed eyes. "Maybe it's bait for something like we fell for? Looks easy to follow until he inserts parts of a worm or something into the data stream. It isn't like we'll fall for that one again, but we may not be the only people he's fishing for."

Ericka squeezed her eyes shut, wincing at the remembered humiliation. "Either way, we're not biting. If we can't get at him directly, let's squeeze his friends. He must have given them something in exchange for this show he wants. The only thing it can be is intel he's hacked from somewhere. What else could he have that they're interested in? Maybe we make sure they know who led us to their stoning."

Clarke's brow furrowed. "But he didn't lead us to them. It was Mossad. Just luck. What do you have in mind?"

Ericka shrugged and smiled. "What if his tame Jihadis thought he did?"

His breath shuddered with excitement as he readied the equipment, a twinge of annoyance he was only able to watch, not direct. Goose bumps rose on his neck and he slid a fingertip over one of his screens to raise the room temperature. Almost time. This would be something new. A unique death, one that moved at a pace allowing it to be savored, weighted with biblical gravitas, all the more thrilling that much of a community would participate. Did they enjoy the fear as he did or view it as just another duty, to act as the resolute hand of a vengeful God? He knew that feeling, but of course believed only in himself. The stoning was a ritual he had long coveted and now, at last, would have for himself.

A screen flashed to life as the feed began, flooding the area with sunset colors. He pulled the goggles into place and switched to VR mode, a bit disappointed with the visual clarity, but pleased with the sound. The footsteps of those around the cameraman on the coarse gravel and the nickering of the horses behind him brought him into the crowd as if he were there. They stood in a semicircle around the terrified man, buried to his neck, tears streaming down his face as he pleaded with those around him.

Ghazali stood to one side in solemn conversation with a man who must be the presiding mullah, mountain crags in the distance behind him lit with the vivid hues of the dying sun. It would be soon now. He tried to steady his breathing, to calm himself. His eyes were shut when the first shots rang through his headphones. Sudden chaos as the man with the camera ran, his initial task forgotten. Then a series of blurred images as the camera feed pelted through a sequence of rocks and bushes, then a brief glimpse of a horse. Riding at a gallop now, the man turned to look behind him. Helicopters were landing in the village. American helicopters!

He sat back, switching the VR feed to display on a monitor and pulling the headset to perch on his forehead. The scene continued to unfold, but his attention was elsewhere. This might just be terrible luck, but he hadn't come this far by being sloppy. There was a chance this was not luck at all. One of Ghazali's fools might have been careless but there was another possibility. He brought up his communications routing, making copies of transient data from several servers before it was overwritten, setting his algorithms to parse for what he feared.

The answer was instant. Someone was tracking him. Running a finger along the lines of code on his screen, he jumped with the shock of recognition and a jolt of anger. He ran the analyzer again but there was no mistake. Bitter rage welled up, tempered by grudging admiration. *Very good, Ericka, if this is indeed you. I hid this against all the tools you had, but you've adapted. Very clever girl!* Then the rage again, now tinged with fear. She shouldn't have been able to do this.

He glanced at the live feed. The camera was motionless, lying in the gravel, the light dim, discarded and forgotten. The horsemen were nowhere to be seen, but not so very far away that the camera didn't pick up the white flash of the arriving missiles. The sound arrived a few seconds later. He nodded to himself. Idiots. Hellfire missiles. America's weapon of choice against jihadis, perfectly named.

He turned back to his main screen, leaning back and steepling his fingers, wondering how close she was. It was going to be necessary to accelerate his plans. *And you, Ericka, need a change of career before you really make a nuisance of yourself.* He smiled and reached for his goggles, all anger forgotten. How could he stay angry with such a worthy adversary?

Ghazali's voice shook, his body trembling. "You fool! You led them right to us." He sat in the same university office as before, his body contorted as he tried to shift his weight to avoid the lancing pain of his injuries. His right arm was broken in several places resting in a makeshift cast while several wounds on his abdomen dribbled blood from between crude stitches. His left eye was swollen shut under a patch, but he glared into the goggles at the bearded, turbaned visage in front of him, this time seated on cushions, the wall of a tent in the shadows behind him.

The avatar scowled back, his voice booming through the headset, making Ghazali wince, jarring his already aching skull. "I told you there was either a traitor or a fool in your midst, perhaps there was more than one. Do not seek to blame me for your own shortcomings."

He hissed his retort. "When the army arrived supported by American commandos, at first I thought it mere bad luck. I was shocked at the ease of our escape given their numbers. When the missiles came out of the evening sky as we were squeezed together in a canyon, I knew. They had simply let us run to a place where we were easier to kill all at once. All but eleven of my men are dead, including one of my sons. Their bodies lie in burned pieces on the stones. I live only because I was riding ahead. This is my just punishment for letting an infidel treat holy law as mere entertainment. One day you will pay for this!"

The huge figure leaned forward, his face distorted with rage. "Think of who you speak to! You would not fare well with me as your enemy."

He bellowed back. "I find I am not doing very well as your friend!"

"Do not point a finger at me because you let them herd you into a trap like sheep!"

"Yes, there is truth to that, and I will bear the memory until I stand before Allah. But they knew we were there because of you! I sent one of my men back to talk to the villagers after the army left. Shall I tell you what the American advisors told them? They found us because the FBI was following you!" Ghazali was shouting now, spitting with rage. "They knew of the stoning and they were waiting for us. They told the villagers they followed you to us through the satellites. You are a dangerous fool thinking yourself invisible to the Americans. I pray to Allah they find you so I can see your face as you are dragged off to prison." He tore off the headset, flinging it to the ground where it shattered into a chaos of fragments held together with wires.

The blue glow lit his face, the only movement a throbbing artery in his neck. He took several slow, deep breaths before peeling off his sleeves and gloves, disconnecting the wires feeding motion sensors, laying his sensory helmet gently in its cradle. He sighed, stroking his chin for a moment before sitting back, irritated by his loss of face, the damage to his reputation.

The bodies on the ground half a world away never impinged on his thoughts. Yes, time now to move with all possible speed. She might be closer than he'd suspected.

Schmidt pulled his headset on, enjoying his patron's latest efforts. Adrenaline surged through him, raising a sheen accompanied by the tingle of goose bumps. This was a new one. He sat on a marble deck. Driven as if by a crisp wind, wisps of powdered snow crossed the stone around his bare feet, parting like flowing water to go around them. There was no railing and his stomach lurched as he peered down the mountainside below. Endless slopes of granite and glacial ice stretched out until they vanished into the boiling cloud layer miles below, a sea of white cotton reflecting painfully crisp blue tones. Hazy in the distance, other ice-capped peaks protruded through the cloud layer. Above, the sky was much darker than usual, as if seen from the window of a jet at high altitude. The keening of the wind and hiss of blown snow and ice completed the illusion.

Movement to the right caught his attention and he turned to look. There was a slight lag, and it took a second for the vista to turn with him. The familiar giant figure stood naked as always, his jet-black skin shining with the cobalt tones of the sky and reflected glare from the ice. Hands behind his back, he stared into the void below before turning and walking closer. He lowered himself onto the edge, his feet dangling over the precipice, turning to gesture to Schmidt whose avatar obeyed, lowering him so they sat together, their shoulders almost rubbing. The figure looked at him over a left shoulder muscled like a weightlifter.

The rich tones of his voice did not echo here, making him seem far less imposing, an impression reinforced by the slight smile. "Welcome, my friend. I trust given what we are planning you are not fearful of heights?" He spoke with his usual tone of mocking amusement.

Schmidt stared out into the distance. "This is really quite something. I used to think you must have a games design background. Seeing this I am thinking Hollywood-grade CGI, accented with bits of real video. A lot of what I see below looks like Everest filmed in IMAX?"

"Who I once was is unimportant. Who I am now is all that matters. And yes, blending the virtual and the physical is what I do. It is time for the barrier between them to come down." The huge figure paused for a moment as if thinking. "Have you thought on our last discussion?"

Schmidt nodded, wincing as he remembered. "You were right. Even if they can't quite articulate it, my employers suspect what I really am. It is only a matter of time before they squeeze me out."

"No one can fail to see how different you are. So, you have come to a decision then?"

The deep-set eyes bored into Schmidt's, different in this illusion, now the irises threw back the red and orange tones of the sunlight. A very nice touch. "I'm in. Making the decision was very freeing. Like you said it would be."

Now there was an edge to his deep-timbred voice. "How are you progressing on the hardware?"

"I've installed it in four so far. No one but another engineer would even notice it was non-stock. Even then, there is no reason to be suspicious. The software you sent can be added at any time; it will only take a few minutes and can be done remotely or from any seat."

The smile was broad, baring his teeth, the expression sheer ferocity. Whatever he was using for facial capture was exceptional. "That was not required. What do you have in mind, my friend?"

"I want to be there." He was never going back now anyway.

"Then so you shall. Would it pose you any difficulty if we advanced the schedule somewhat?"

"None at all, but the longer we wait, the more of them I can install and the more choices we'll have."

"We will speak again soon." Another smile as his form became translucent, fading to nothing in a matter of seconds. The marble ledge disappeared and he was falling, his chest tight as he held his breath, then the rock and ice rushing by faded and he was in darkness again. Schmidt peeled off the headset, seeing his basement wall, and took several shuddering breaths before shaking his head, unable to repress a smile.

He spoke to an empty room. "How did the bastard know I'm afraid of heights?"

What the hell is making that noise? Ericka lifted her head from the arm of the couch, wincing at a stiff neck. The others had gone for the night. She'd stayed, planning on an extra hour but succumbed to the dubious charms of the old couch and fell into a deep sleep. Her sweater was draped over her and she fumbled in it for her phone to silence the noise. It was silent, 4:30 AM. The noise came again, not in the room, a soft but persistent chiming, coming from the lab. Light came just from the streetlights outside, but it was enough to limp over to the doorway ajar a hand's breadth. Rubbing sleep from her eyes she pushed it open, seeing green LEDs in the windowless room. She snapped on the lights, staring across the room, eyes tearing at the sudden brightness. On the table, the goggles blinked from inside their exhibit bag. They chimed again. He was calling. How the hell did he switch them on and reprogram them?

She pulled on exhibit gloves and drew the headset from the bag, staring at them. *This is going to be a mistake, not the first, not the last.* She had to know. What if this was a warning of something to come? Ericka sat down and tugged them on, cutting off all light and sound, all black stillness now, and waited.

21

Thirty Pieces of Silver

No throne room this time, just darkness. She sat waiting, anticipating something like a jump scare from a bad horror movie. After a time, she began to wonder if the goggles had activated, then the sound of rushing air, an immense breath drawn. The sigh that followed accompanied the appearance of the massive figure, seated as before, but dimly lit, allowing her to see a partial silhouette. She could see the head, shoulders, and torso, the throne and lower body hints in shadow. His eyes were mere pinpricks of light, glinting from beneath heavy brows. He nodded, a half-smile spreading over his features.

"So now I hope we can speak in private?" The same engaging baritone as before. "You will not have to playact for your audience this time."

Poke him back. "I can't say I was expecting to hear from you. Are you calling to turn yourself in?"

The smile spread further. "I believe I made you a promise I intend to keep. I have news and I knew you would not want to wait."

The adrenaline coursed through her. That could only mean

one thing. She waited for a few moments in silence, then spoke. "You have my undivided attention." Get him talking, egg him on.

"Thank you. Before I show you, permit me to say how much I admire your perseverance and to say you were not all that far off the mark three years ago in Panama City."

Ericka's stomach tightened as she remembered the trip. "Far off what mark?" Make him say it. The more he talks the better.

The massive head tilted. "Surely you are not going to deny the obvious, especially after all the effort I have gone to?"

Her tone was mocking, provoking him, time to try and rattle him a bit. "Got some extra time on your hands you didn't expect? Miss out on a little entertainment with your Jihadi friends?"

Now a full grin, polished canines in the dim glow. "More than made up for by the pleasure of your company. And I thoroughly enjoyed the wit. That was your idea? Telling the villagers I led you to them? Deception and manipulation. Men blown to bits with fire from the night sky. And you contend we do not share the same tastes! Well done, Ericka!"

She winced. He was poking an open wound. She clenched her teeth, just holding on to her anger, struggling to keep her tone level. "You think raping and torturing helpless people and war against an armed enemy are the same?"

He paused, letting her dangle, his eyes picking up orange and red flecks of color, like someone sitting next to a fire. "It is true we deal with the hunger differently. I am more broad-minded. But don't try to deny it exists. You have not been chasing these men all these years to arrest them."

She paused before speaking, seeing red in the margins of

her vision, willing the anger back down. The last time, he had gotten way under her skin. Not again. "You said you have something to say."

Another deep sigh stirred the bulging shoulders. "As you wish. Look." He pointed above and to the right with his chin. The dark space shimmered for a few seconds. And there they were, pictures of their smirking faces, the old passport photos, as young as they must have been at the time before they vanished from the world. All three young men were darkly handsome, in their twenties, their arrogance and sneering entitlement on display even in a still picture. The same photographs she had stared at with such loathing for so many years, probably taken from the same police file from where she had requested them.

She looked down to find him leaning forward, chin on an immense fist, waiting. "Friends of yours?" She knew he could be recording her responses. *Give him nothing.* This could just be him looking to take her out.

"Let's not dwell on the past. Let's see them as they are today." The same flickering effect and three new pictures materialized. There was no doubting it was them. One of the pictures was grainy, perhaps distilled from a security video, but it was clear enough. Two were balding, one had a beard, the features of all three now sporting the lines and wrinkles of over a decade's further living. The same cruel pride she had always seen in their faces: Frederico Martinez, Antonio Rojas, and Enrique Hernández. Names permanently etched in her mind. Ten years using all her skill and resources and nothing. This bastard found them in a matter of weeks.

She held on to it for a few seconds, but couldn't stop the question exploding out of her. "Where?"

Another shrug of the massive shoulders, tilting his head to one side. "It may be that I have access to things you do not. Organizations like the cartels need people to keep track of their money. Trusted people. People who sometimes have to dole out the money to pay for new lives, new names, sometimes even new faces. People with long memories. Such people sometimes make mistakes leaving them open to persuasion. Once I had the new names and cities, the rest was all too simple."

No point pretending now. Her reaction wasn't telling him anything new. Now she knew for sure her quarry were still alive, the longing was unbearable, there was no way to hold back. "Tell me where!"

He leaned back, steepling his fingers as he had before. "Where indeed? Shall we bargain a bit, talk price? I think the traditional one in the circumstances. I want your soul." He was smiling again. "I need an act that shows me you accept how alike we really are."

He can't be serious; he's just toying with me. "You think I am going to join you? Go to hell!"

He rolled his eyes, pursing his lips, his expression comical. "Look around you. No, I do not want you to join me. We are too alike—we would just squabble, get under each other's feet." He nodded, then paused as if searching for words. "Divine retribution is a myth made up by priests to explain unanswered prayers. If you want your revenge, you are going to have to take it yourself."

"It's not about revenge, it's about justice." The lie sounded silly as she said it. There was only one kind of justice for what had happened. The only question was whether she could restrain herself from taking it. Certainly not and still stay with the FBI. She might not live through the attempt. Perhaps he really did just want her off his trail.

His eyes widened, his tone openly sneering. "Oh, do please spare me. What does justice accomplish? An arrest, a prosecution? Does that unrape a woman or bring the dead back to life? Will it please Patricia's ghost? You are being ridiculous. You know perfectly well your only peace will come from vengeance."

Under her skin again. She felt like throwing up, tasting bile at the back of her throat. A stiletto sliding unseen between armor plates, felt just as the blade's icy kiss penetrated the skin. The monster was in her head. "Fuck you!" She needed time to think but if she broke the transmission, he might never offer again.

"My price is not so dear that you should balk. One thing I ask. Leave the FBI. Nothing more. And I will give them to you. I might even have some creative suggestions for you. As I said, your soul, after a fashion."

That was unexpected. The amusement in his voice conveyed his delight. He had her. His gloating at her hesitation was palpable. Got to keep him talking. "You think if I quit, they won't find you? Even if I did leave, someone will do it. You can't do this forever."

He shook his head as if he were speaking to an idiot. "Of course not. I do not want to do this forever. It grows tedious already and I have much more interesting plans. Perhaps revenge of my own to take."

For what? They had to know more about the man to get close to him. "Why then?"

"It pains me to see you wasted there. Barely tolerated by people without your ability. You are not like them." *That's a fact,* Ericka thought as he continued. "This is what you want for yourself? A life chasing deviant cretins across the internet? Picking the low-hanging fruit from trees dangling with idiots? You are destined for better things. And you can have the life you deserve. If I understand you, and I think I do, Ericka, you probably only joined the FBI in the first place thinking it your best chance of finding those men. If I give you them now, what reason do you have to stay?"

She was speechless, her head bent down, shaking. She wondered if the tracking sensors in the goggles could make out tears. The bastard had tapped something very deep and genuine in her. All technical wizardry aside, this was his real genius. He could hack minds too. "And if I don't, you'll out me for my *travels*?"

"Perish the thought. I would very much like you to succeed. I am all for richly deserved vengeance. Nothing is quite so cathartic even when tasted second-hand, redressing wrongs I didn't suffer. If I wanted to stop you, I would have just squashed you against that wall. There are so very few with our abilities, our vision. Remember after years of rivalry and civil war Caesar wept when Pompey was murdered. I would feel the same way."

She spat her words. *What the fuck did he really want?* "I'm not working with you. You're a fucking monster."

His short laugh was a cross between a giggle and a snarl. Any jackal would have been proud. "Well true, there is that, but I am not asking you to. Just do this one thing that shows me you accept certain similarities in us and that will be enough. The offer stands, but not forever. Resign and go back where you should be. Resume the life you were meant to have. Keep the goggles so we can talk again."

He was gone. She reached up and pulled the headset off, clutching it in her lap, her mind flooded with panic. He knew her deepest secrets and she still didn't even know his name, let alone where to find him. What if they couldn't take him alive? Would the information she so desperately needed die with him? Her mind swirled, a confusion of contradictory thoughts. *This is exactly what that bastard wants.*

Placing the VR rig back in the exhibit bag, she staggered out of the offices and down to the washroom—old and done entirely in worn, white tile. Pre-dawn light glowed through the frosted window. She splashed cold water on her face, gasping, trying to feel clean, but the filth was under her skin. The faded mirror reflected puffy, red eyes staring out of gaunt features. She forced several rapid breaths struggling to order her thoughts, then wet a paper towel holding it against each eye in turn as she staggered back.

Tim was there bent over the coffee maker. He looked up. His usual cheerful smile faded as he looked at her, his eyes going wide. "Bloody hell, what happened to you?"

She dropped into the worn couch. "Poor choice of words." She nodded towards the lab door. "Guess who just called?"

He stood for a moment, his mouth open. "And you answered? What were you fucking thinking? I thought those things were useless now?"

Yes, my friend, better if they were. "Looks like we missed something."

"What did he want?"

Ericka couldn't tell him everything. If it went wrong, it would take him down with her. "Same as last time. Boasting of his might and reach. Taunting me about my lack of success and how he could find them." She looked down between her knees avoiding eye contact.

He stared pointedly at her. "Ericka." He waited for her to lift her head. "Does he know something more about you and your 'mission'?"

She looked down again nodding, knowing he understood more than he acknowledged, but bringing him in any further was just too dangerous. "And he let go a few things he didn't the last time." She glanced up. "It sounds like he's planning something big. He also said he doesn't plan on doing the same things he's been doing much longer. Oh, and he congratulated us on the Jihadi thing. Seemed to think it was quite funny."

"Jesus, Ericka. If the brass finds out."

Her voice dropped to a whisper. "Fuck, I know."

"What now?"

Ericka needed time to process and get some help from someone knowing his offer wouldn't compromise. "All his boasting has got me thinking. Mostly because it's true. He really is in a class of his own."

"So? What do you make of that?"

They had to draw him out somehow. It was that simple. "We've said this before. He didn't spring up from nowhere. Talent like this doesn't appear out of nothing. He's not some script kiddie who had a big idea while playing games in his basement suite. Someone's got to know him. Industry scours the colleges for guys like him. He started somewhere. Maybe we've been coming at this all wrong. We've been fighting on his battlefield since we started, and he's kicked the shit out of us. We need a different approach."

★ ★ ★

Ericka was startled to see how old he looked now. He must be sixty-five. Chris Fowler was no longer the CEO of ISS but had accepted an emeritus position at Caltech and still haunted his old labs, now a consultant. His head shaved as a dignified alternative to a comb-over, he sported a close-cropped goatee. Looking into his eyes there was no mistaking it was him. They were the same icy blue, mildly cross-eyed, making his gaze all the more disconcerting, which he knew. He stood up and leaned over his desk, grasping her outstretched hand in both of his, his smile warm and open. Gone now were the power suits. He dressed like most academics, his loose-fitting khakis and shirt both wrinkled and worn. The office shelves were covered with reference material, dusty stacks of paper, and various bits of computer hardware—clutter the hallmark of his razor-sharp thinking.

His pleasure at seeing her brought a surge of longing for the life she had abandoned. "Look at this, the girl-wonder all grown up, even dressing like a cop. It's so good to see you. I think it has been seven years. Are you limping? Please sit." He lowered himself into his creaking chair and leaned back.

She smiled back, overwhelmed at how happy seeing her old mentor made her. "You're looking well. Thanks for seeing me so quickly."

He shook his head as if she'd said something silly. "I was hoping you had finally come to your senses and were coming to ask for your old job back? After all this time." The half-smile was genuine. "As you know I'm not bossing it anymore, but your reputation precedes you with my successor."

"That may happen if I want it to or not. But not today." And would happen—she had to hang on to that vision.

An eyebrow rose as he leaned forward. "Do tell?"

Ericka took a deep breath. One of the foundations of their successful working relationship had always been pitiless honesty. No reason to change that now. "I'm repeatedly getting the shit kicked out of me by a target. He's able to hit and vanish no matter what we do. I think he's got some sort of mobile AIs he prepositions to hide himself and do the heavy lifting. He strikes all over the planet, rarely engaging more than once in the same jurisdiction. Lately he's taken to taunting me directly, having hacked my personnel file, shrink reports, and discipline record. We're not even close."

Fowler stared at her for a few moments, his face now a mask. "Shrink reports? Discipline? What the fuck is going on over there?"

She clenched the arms of the chair, unable to meet his gaze, humiliated, fearing to admit the depth of troubles facing her dying career. "It has to be in strict confidence."

He nodded. "Of course. Don't be stupid."

In painful detail, she recounted the investigation, retreating further back for context for her personal problems and ending with Dantalion's offer. "And there you have it. If he keeps this up long enough, he will slip or one of his idiot followers will, but a lot of people could be hurt or dead before that happens. Especially as it sounds like he's planning to accelerate whatever schemes he has."

"Christ, what a monster." His brows knotted over the glacial eyes as he peered at her, his clenched jaw and tight fists conveying what he would not say. "But what do you think I can do that you can't? No one I know of has gone as far down your chosen path as you have. I couldn't have done the things you've already tried. You deep-state spooks know more about the hacker community than anyone else."

That made her laugh. "Because I don't think he's from that community. We have sources all over the dark web. Not a word about this guy until we picked up his trail, not even a word since. He can't be part of the Russian or Chinese groups. They work as teams so they'd never let this bastard do the things he's done if for no other reason than it's bad for business and he'd heat them up."

He nodded his agreement. "What are you thinking?"

"He's got unusual skills for a hacker. The stealthing software sure, but he has AIs, absolutely cutting-edge VR technology, a command of graphics verging on cinematic, and quite an array of followers doing his running for him. That's just the toys. He seems to be able to get into people's heads in a way I've never seen before. Like one of these charismatic preacher guys who convince their flock to poison themselves because passing aliens are going to take them away. He's offering them something they can't resist."

Fowler nodded, squinting his eyes as he stared out the window as he did when thinking. "That's a lot for one person. Either he's a very busy boy or he's contracting out."

"He's almost certainly using his network to get things done. We've seen that in the physical side. People are making things like the customized VR gear, delivering them, maybe even doing some basic graphics work for him. I just don't know, but I need to zero in on him, not the gadgets."

Fowler stared at the floor, his brow furrowed. "And you haven't been able to trace any of this down?"

"No and it isn't that surprising. Someone with his global reach can do that. It isn't like the Chinese police are going to go factory to factory for us looking for a guy who builds things in his spare time based on specs he gets from someone he doesn't know."

Fowler chuckled. "No, I suppose not. You can't be thinking he's here in Silicon Valley? No one here has the time this would take without someone noticing."

Ericka leaned forward, elbows on her knees. "No, but I think he might have been once. I think he really got going three or four years ago, so he would have had to disappear somewhere in the four-to-six-year range."

"Why didn't you try that first instead of trying to get the jump on him?"

"It took half the investigation to figure out we were really dealing with a single entity. The depth of his capabilities we just found out about recently." When she saw his left eyebrow go up, she winced inside, knowing he thought otherwise.

"It's funny how we keep making the same mistakes as we go through life." She drew a deep breath. *Here we go.* Fowler continued. "For you it's that classic mistake all the smartest people seem to make. You think you're the only one. You thought you could take him head on and win. He was better."

This wasn't the first of his lectures on this point she had endured. "Touché."

"I think Socrates said it best. 'Intelligent people learn from everything and everyone, average people from their experiences, stupid people already know all the answers.' But I think you've already come to the conclusion that you need a different strategy?"

"Yes, our investigation turned up absolutely no surface contact for this guy. None of the usual ways they surface. The pedos have to come up to touch, the guys in it for money want to spend it, the guys selling something have to move product. He has his hand in all kinds of pies, but never breaks the surface. That's what makes him different and it's got to be the key to finding him."

Fowler stroked his goatee, staring at her before nodding. "I think if you can't find anywhere he has come up, maybe you look for where he went down in the first place. Even if he has no real-world contact, something I think unlikely, he did at one point."

Her chest went tight, as he articulated what she had already been thinking. "Which means I'm not looking for him in the present, I need to look for him in the past. The question is how?"

Fowler smiled, giving her the approving nod of the wise sage. "As you say, he didn't spring to life suddenly with all these abilities. He learned them somewhere and he would have to experiment along the way. Do the feds still run programs stealing and archiving the whole internet these days?"

"Yes, including some newer stuff no one knows about." These systems allowed the NSA to collect and store vast streams of internet data, which could be parsed through later for evidence using any search criteria required.

"And is it retained?"

It was the world's worst-kept secret. "Not all of it, but some."

"What if you went back through it from years ago, looking for this Dantalion when he maybe wasn't as good as he is now. Look for innocuous things where he might have tested his technology without drawing attention to himself by doing something illegal. It won't still be on internet servers anywhere, but your spooks might have at least some of it if they have been archiving it all like everyone thinks they do.

Go even farther back to see if anyone was trying out early versions of his technology from the surface web."

She bolted to her feet, unable to sit still, adrenaline coursing through her body so much her voice quivered. "Find anything that looks like his early experiments, follow him backwards in time using some sort of single-entity resolution search, then crawl back up the hole he first dove in. That should produce a very short list of real people and he might well be one of them."

Single-entity resolution was software able to draw connections between seemingly disparate fragments of data and suggest which ones might originate from the same individual. Find him while he was trying his hand from the dark web and resolve that to any real person who might be him before he went under. Then work the list. With enough computing power, it might even give them a location if he'd stayed in one place long enough.

"You know one of the greatest disappointments of my career was losing you to the FBI. Do you know why? Because of all the people I trained and mentored over the decades, you were the only one I knew who would have exceeded me, has exceeded me."

She smiled, fighting tears. "But I needed you to figure this out."

"Nonsense—you'd already realized the hide-bound thinking that had prevented you from succeeding. That is a product of the environment you work in. You can't always follow a goddamned checklist. You had this half thought through when you walked in. I just gave you a prod."

"Thank you."

"Thank me by catching this fucker. And then by quitting

and coming back. We can still work together. You were never meant for the kind of work you're doing."

That was a fact. This career had dragged her in as a compulsion, not a calling. They clasped hands. "I just might take you up on that. When I'm done."

Their eyes remained locked as his narrowed. "Done? Patty has been gone a long time. From how you've described her, it would be the last thing she would want that you sacrifice any more of your life trying to avenge her."

"Avenge?"

"Spare me the bimbo act, it doesn't become you. Your Dantalion called that one right. Just because he's evil doesn't mean he's stupid. You always liked the stoics, a quote from Marcus Aurelius: 'Your mind will take on the character of your most frequent thoughts: souls are tinted by thoughts.' Ericka, it's time to let her go before this truly defines all you are."

"I don't know if I can." The bald-faced lie all but caught in her throat. She had no intention of trying. There was no way back up the path she'd chosen.

He sighed before making eye contact again. "Careful, Ericka. I fear you may find yourself at that terrible moment when we realize the person we believe we are is just an 'elaborate lie we have told ourselves.' Sometimes that lie preserves sanity, but it remains a lie."

"You are looking much calmer. I wish I could take credit for my good advice being the reason, but I know better." Steiner sipped his tea while holding eye contact, the paper cup in a gloved hand. They sat together on the park bench, alone for some distance, the trees around them sporting the lush canopy of early summer despite the chill of the day. All formality lost now, they met here at Ericka's request. For most of the scheduled session they sat watching a group of children who were enjoying the eternally fascinating activity of throwing stones into water.

Ericka sighed, nodding. "This is certainly more pleasant knowing I can talk without having to worry the internal investigation team is poring over every word you write."

He looked away, his expression tightening a bit. "I do what I am required to do, but as I think I have told you, providing managers with the information they need is not what gets me out of bed in the morning." He turned back to her, eyes shining. "Is it true, you have actually spoken to him? To Dantalion?"

Ericka nodded, setting her coffee on the bench between them. "At least to the persona he wants me to see. It was quite the show. The behavioral shrinks all concur that he is some sort of sadist and dangerously delusional narcissist. For all the help giving him a label does. I could have told them that before we switched on."

Steiner nodded with a nervous smile. "And is the rumor true that he appears to have taken your personnel file and my reports?"

Her eyes locked on to his, looking for the slightest hint. "Yes, it seems so. Anything you put in them I should worry about?"

He didn't flinch but reddened. "Yes, quite frankly, and I would expect him to use them to toy with you if he hasn't already." He studied her for a few moments. "Something has changed. The Ericka I know should be in the middle of tearing out my throat right now and yet you are as calm as I have ever seen you."

If only you knew. Ericka wondered if he had heard the recorded audio from the first call and was playing cute. Studying his face, she saw no hint of guile and decided as a contractor he wouldn't have direct access to current investigational materials anyway. "Perhaps all of your hard work has finally paid off."

He laughed out loud, the first time she had ever heard him do so, a surprisingly rich and charming sound. "Ericka, you and I both know all I am able to do is draw inferences and make educated guesses in my reports. I have no magic. The only effect I am able to have on someone as intelligent as you is to invite self-awareness, provide you questions to ask yourself. Whether you answer them honestly and act on those answers is up to you."

She took another sip to hide her hesitation. "Thank you for that. I will when the time is right. When this one is over and I have left the organization. That last part in confidence please."

Steiner slumped, not trying to hide his disappointment. "I suppose I shouldn't be surprised."

She was touched he seemed to care, gripping his forearm. "I'm better now I see my way forward." At least not an outright lie, just not all of the truth. "Thank you for today. Therapy at its best."

His mouth was open, looking like he wanted to say something. Ericka nodded, smiling. Steiner hesitated again before speaking. "A thought if I may on your target? I'm sure my colleagues in the behavioral unit have given you their views on him, but in any event, an observation. As you look for the man, rather than the technology he uses, don't hang up on the means, but understand his goal."

There was far more to him than she'd thought. "Yes?"

"Remember this eclectic mix of victims and crimes doesn't represent his need per se. They are all a means to the same end. This is not about sexual gratification, or a desire to cause pain and death. He wants fear. Just fear. To generate terror, he subjects the victims to what he thinks they fear the most, hence the lack of a more typical pattern of criminal acts. Look for a man who savors fear in others above all else."

Yes, that's exactly what he does. "What does he look like?"

"You'll know him. He will surround himself with weak people he can dominate and scare. Remember the priest. It wasn't the victims that enthralled your suspect. It was the fear and self-loathing of the priest as he was compelled to do Dantalion's bidding. He will tolerate no rivals, attacking anyone he thinks may challenge him."

She was surprised at the insight. She really had underestimated Steiner. *But first I have to turn up some suspects.* Ericka nodded her thanks, leaning to squeeze his shoulder before turning to walk away.

He held on to her arm. "One more thing." She nodded, curious. "There are things that have been obvious to me that I have never articulated or included in my reports." His eyes were locked on hers. "Anger of the kind burning in you is very dangerous. You know what I'm talking about without me saying it. The stoics you are so fond of called anger a type of insanity and they were right. No mind that angry makes rational decisions, it operates only to feed uncontrolled want. Your mind has rolled the fury at many things and hurts into one overwhelming desire. If you think you can make rational decisions in the face of that, you're kidding yourself. Don't follow your heart. It will lie to you and lead you astray."

Ericka nodded as he let her hand go, pressing his words from her mind, before they took root, before they made her think about what they meant.

22

A Hall of Mirrors

O'Brien stood in the doorway to the forensics lab, leaning on the doorjamb, his visitor tag crooked around his neck. He nodded towards the copy of the judge's order pinned to their bulletin board, hanging amidst the clutter of long-forgotten memos and policies. "That took some doing to get and the NSA is going to be pissed at me for some time. I hope this works. They hate admitting how much data they have squirrelled away, especially to judges." A week earlier he had obtained an order allowing the FBI to search any retained data up to seven years back, seeking to identify their suspect.

Ericka smiled over her shoulder, enjoying needling the stocky lawyer. "Well if you can hold off patting yourself on the back for a few minutes, you should come over and look." She leaned back, gesturing towards the screen. O'Brien pulled on the obligatory white coat then lumbered over, holding the back of her chair while he leaned in. Clarke and Tim reclined in their chairs, sharing a look.

"What am I looking at?"

Ericka pointed her pen at the screen. "We started from data traces from last year we now know for sure are Dantalion then went back in the earlier data looking for more hits and found several. Things he was up to we didn't know about at all. It looks like he was up and running a bit earlier than we thought. On the theory his software would have evolved over time, we used fuzzy searching and entity-resolution software for any traffic sharing some of the attributes of his known work. That produced a fair number of hits—most of whom aren't him or we aren't sure are him. Following?"

He nodded, squinting as he leaned closer. "So far so good."

Ericka glanced at Tim and Clarke who were pretending attention. "We continued the process working backwards into data the NSA hoovered from the surface web. Mostly commercial stuff but not all. This gave us a list of twenty-nine people or companies resolved to an evolutionary similarity to data traces like Dantalion is running now. It doesn't give us him, but it gives us people and outfits that might be able to do things like he does. Leads worth following up."

O'Brien pulled over a chair and sat down. "Death by jargon. And?"

Ericka glanced back at him: *welcome to my world.* "We focus on the North American and European stuff. As best we can tell from voice analysis, he is from here. Hackers from India, China, or Russia, might be able to pull some of this off, but our most probable targets are out of Silicon Valley and other North American tech centers. That's where we focus now."

O'Brien glanced at his watch, then around the table. "Figure out where he is from and hope it leads to where he is now? What's next?"

Ericka nodded to where Tim and Clarke were sitting. "Now we have to get out and do some traditional police work. Do some interviews. We have several field agents and local police doing some of the preliminary legwork. We may need some warrants if cooperation is limited."

"Don't count on getting them if you don't have something pretty solid. I'm never going to convince a judge that this—" O'Brien nodded at the screen "—amounts to probable cause without something more, some kind of corroboration."

Ericka nodded, having already come to the same conclusion. "The list isn't as long as it looks. Some of these hits are various national security agencies trying to do what he does but not doing them as well. Another bit looks like a Chinese hacker group doing something similar with GPS stealthing. Others are not the match the search software thinks they are when we look at the code itself. But we have seven solid leads, all connected in some way to security software, VR gaming or AI. None connected to all three categories but that's not surprising. We have four who have both gaming and AI in their background, two dead and two still working in the industry. First thing we'll do is make sure the dead ones are really dead. We'll need to get some DNA from medical samples or something, but we may need to exhume. It seems too obvious for him, but I'm not leaving anything to chance at this stage."

"What does your gut say?" O'Brien glanced over to Clarke and Tim as he asked.

Clarke leaned forward. "We all have our own theories. Tim and I think we came up dry and should run it again with different parameters."

Ericka interjected. "I think the most likely candidate is one of the dead guys, but given how he died, I'm afraid he really is dead."

"Do tell?"

She leaned over her keyboard, and tapped her screen. A picture of a coifed, late-thirties pretty boy appeared sporting a very commercial smile. "Clyde Bromwich. First, from all accounts a serious asshole. He bounces through several gaming companies, brilliant gaming-engine designer but no one can stand working with him. He partners up with another guy on our list." The picture changed. "And they go out on their own. This guy, Frank London, does some pathbreaking work using AI in gaming, real machine learning. He's alive and now has a different company in Silicon Valley making some sort of investment software for brokers. He too is heartily disliked by almost everyone. It must have been a real treat to work for them."

Tim grinned at O'Brien. "This bit is where it gets fun."

Ericka glared at him for interrupting. "Their partnership went very well initially but ended very badly. They have a fist fight that Bromwich wins, then go tearing down the coast road north, Bromwich in his Ferrari, London in his Porsche. The police reports say people who see it can't tell if they're racing or if the Porsche is chasing the Ferrari. They touch wheels and end up plowing over an embankment and bursting into a ball of fire. Bromwich is killed and London is badly injured but crawls free and passes out before his car burns. Turns out Bromwich has been stealing company money and shagging London's lovely wife, Claire. London goes down for dangerous driving, but because he's so badly injured and it isn't clear he caused the accident, he gets off with a kiss. Now several surgeries later, he's up and about, sets up a new company, marries a different woman and settles into mundane family life with young twins."

O'Brien pursed his lips, looking at Ericka. "I get why you like the sound of Bromwich. You really do have to check, but that sounds like he's fairly dead to me. London though?"

Ericka shrugged. "He doesn't fit the demonic dark lord profile. From what people tell us, he's a changed man. Even found Jesus after the accident. He does fit the profile in terms of ability and the code profile from the NSA data is a fairly strong match. I suspect much of Dantalion's abilities are from something new in AI. Maybe our target worked for him?"

O'Brien shrugged. "So why interview him?"

Ericka gave him a look like he was being thick. "Because he may know the names of people with similar expertise. In this industry, everyone knows the competition. I also want to nose around a bit and find out where he was at the times we know Dantalion was active. That could eliminate him without having to get a warrant to get into his computers. Or make you embarrass yourself with the judge trying."

O'Brien cocked his head, his habit when thinking. "It all sounds like a good start. Who's going out to talk to him?"

Ericka had trouble keeping the smile off her face. She was having difficulty sitting still. "Tim and I. Time for a trip to California. Abs has let me out of my cage for the duration of chasing this target. Clarke is going to run the parameters again and see if anyone else turns up. We're also going to see if we can find any video of London around the time of Dantalion's escapades. Try for matches using facial recognition software."

"Sounds like a plan and you know where to find me."

O'Brien squeezed Ericka's shoulder, a fatherly gesture, nodded to Tim and Clarke, and lumbered out, heading for the front desk.

"He's not doing badly for himself, is he?" Tim stared around the beautifully appointed reception area of London Financial Solutions. The entire area was done in glass and silver, even the chairs exuding wealth, the lighting and layout the obvious result of a designer's touch. The receptionist was stunning, professionally coifed and wearing a suit more expensive than any three in Ericka's wardrobe combined. Her hair was a deep auburn, skin flawless, makeup applied by an expert. She rolled her eyes at Tim's rapt attention and clumsy attempts to chat her up. When the receptionist turned her head to answer the phone, Ericka elbowed him in the ribs, hard. He gave her a hurt look and busied himself with his notes.

Even her voice was perfect, well-pitched and crisp. "Mr. London will see you now. This way." They followed her down the hall to where she gestured them into a small but expensively furnished boardroom. Natural light flooded the room from above, casting shadows below the gleaming table. The chairs were padded with supple leather and the sideboard sported water in a cut-crystal decanter with matching glasses. At the table's head sat a man who stood to greet them, moving as if in some pain. His neutral expression gave neither welcome nor hostility. He was tall and gangly, thin arms protruding from a short-sleeved golf shirt. His thinning hair was colored, his beard close-shaved, leaving him looking rather older than his forty-five years.

"Agent Blackwood, Agent O'Connell, please sit. Has Estelle offered you a beverage?"

Ericka nodded as they settled into lavish, high-backed chairs. "Yes, thank you. We appreciate your taking the time to speak with us today."

London nodded, still not smiling. "I'm very curious. It isn't every day the FBI comes calling. Before we start, my lawyers asked me to confirm that no one in this company is under investigation for any offenses?"

Ericka clenched her teeth. Fucking lawyers, they secretly ruled the world. "Correct, we're here looking for information regarding something unrelated to this company. More about your competitors if anything."

That drew a smile from London. "Good, if you want to arrest any of them, please do so with my blessing. Do I get to know what it's about?"

Ericka shook her head. "Sorry, suffice to say we're looking for someone who possesses a skill set that I imagine very few have. One similar to your own. We're hoping you might be able to give us some names."

London's shoulders were tense, and he paled. "Go on, what skills? You've already seized the remaining employment records of our old company, I hear."

Ericka nodded, concentrating on London's face for cues as to his thoughts. "We have. The skill set related to AI applications and machine learning. Network-based, able to optimize its function by managing secure networks and multiple input feeds at once."

London barked a short laugh, but appeared to have to concentrate to hold eye contact with her. "That's me and my company. Just what you'd need to build something that can comb an enormous number of inputs and help predict the market for brokers?"

Tim spoke, allowing her to better observe. "Yes, any other company doing this kind of work?"

London turned to Tim. "Not many and no one is as advanced as us. If this kind of capability is being used to commit crimes, why am I not a suspect? Or am I?" His gaze was intense now, unblinking.

Ericka decided on a half-truth to keep him speaking. "Because you weren't in the right places or times to have done what we're investigating."

London's expression tightened and his shoulders became tense, his face and body telegraphing he was closing up. "It's very hard for me to help if I don't know what you're investigating. On that very broad description you've given me there are hundreds of people employed by companies in the area. Several companies and all their key employees. Can you give me anything?"

Tim leaned over the table. "Someone who could create a complex, highly detailed, interactive VR environment and mask the broadcast location using AI to run a series of VPNs, encryption, and masking decoy traffic."

London reddened, looking for a moment like he was trying to compose himself. "No one I know. Anyone who could pull that off would be a very rich fellow very quickly. He'd be on the front of *Wired* magazine and you could find him there."

Ericka held her expression neutral now. Nothing about what they had said should have made him nervous, but he was playing with his fingers, swallowing too much, too lousy a liar to be their guy. "What about things in development that the popular press may not have picked up yet?"

He looked at his intertwined fingers and seemed to catch himself, folding them in front of him like he was concentrating on his demeanor. "No, and I wouldn't. That sounds like advanced gaming tech. I don't know anyone doing that kind of work."

Bad cop time, Tim interjected. "Not anymore, more your old friend Bromwich's cup of tea?"

London's jaw worked, now clearly agitated. "All right, enough games. What do you want?"

"Would Bromwich have been capable of that kind of work?" Ericka watched his face rather than listening to his answer. That's where she would get the information they needed.

"That thieving bastard couldn't code his way out of a supermarket checkout. And he's been in the ground for years. Best place for him. Now I know what he's up to."

He's pretending to be angry, but he isn't. He should be. Ericka ran through the possibilities. Why does he need to fake it? "From what we know he did a lot of work in the area. Is our information incorrect?"

"Everything I had to say about him I said to police years ago. Go read the state trooper's file." London leaned back in his chair. "I'm afraid we're done here today. We're happy to cooperate with law enforcement about any current investigations, but all future questions are to go through our lawyers. A warrant will be needed if you want any of this company's records. Are we clear? Please see yourselves out." He stood up, almost knocking his chair over, and walked to the door, disappearing down the hall.

★ ★ ★

Tim slammed the passenger door shut and pulled on his belt. "That went well. An asshole, but he's not our guy. Why the feigned anger?"

Ericka pushed the start button and switched on the air conditioning. Silicon Valley was hot even this time of year. "No, I never thought he was. I just wanted to get a sniff and see if he had any idea. At least until we're sure Bromwich is actually in the ground. We should have that later today." Tim had arranged for O'Brien to petition for exhumation for the purposes of a DNA sample to be matched against old medical samples taken while Bromwich was alive. He was interred in a family crypt, making the process rather less messy than usual.

Tim leaned back flipping through his messages. "So, I don't think this guy has internet dark lord in him either, but he wasn't happy to see us and was acting evasive for no reason I can think of. No way anyone could pull off all the Dantalion stuff from inside a company and no one gets wind of it."

Ericka put the car in gear, glancing over to the front door of the building where a security guard stood watching them. She waved to him, smiling. "I'm damn sure he has some idea who we could be looking for. Just my gut. And there aren't too many reasons for him to be cagey. One of his employees or someone he's scared of."

"In fairness, he doesn't know anything about what our boy has done. If we'd told him, he may well have a different attitude."

"Either way, he holds the cards. No reason to get all nervous-looking and fidgety. Just tell us he has no idea and keep a straight face." Ericka glanced over at the car's nav screen. "Now we've been turfed out the door, we'll be early to speak to the former Mrs. London."

* * *

Ericka held her badge up to the security camera and one half of the heavy wood double door swung open revealing the beautiful face of Claire Cole, formerly Mrs. London. Large green eyes, high cheekbones and full, slightly upcurved lips, surrounded by pale blond hair, applied color keeping any sign of age at bay. Mid-thirties, exercise gear displaying a perfect figure, full breasts perched on her chest where only youth or a skilled surgeon could keep them.

Stepping between Claire and Tim, she smiled, holding up her FBI identification. "Agents Blackwood and O'Connell, I hope our office called ahead. Can we speak?"

"They called a few hours ago but wouldn't tell me what you wanted. Please." She gestured down the entryway and closed the door behind them.

Ericka lied smoothly. "My apologies. Our office staff aren't always familiar with all aspects of every investigation."

The green marble floors echoed their footsteps as Claire gestured them into a room on the left, a small study. Like the hallway, immaculately appointed, the furniture expensive and the art all signed originals. Landed on her feet after her tragic loss, Ericka thought. Didn't end up shacked up with a truck driver, working at Taco Bell while the kids are at school. She and Tim sat on a perfect couch while their hostess settled into the chair behind the desk.

"So, how can I help?" She looked at Ericka, ignoring Tim.

Ericka decided to start easy. "We're hoping you can tell us about people who may have been associated with your former husband Mr. London and the late Mr. Bromwich."

Claire's face clouded over. "Which people? That was not a

happy time for me. Clyde's been dead for years and I never talk to my ex."

Ericka held up her mobile. "Mind if I record?" Claire shook her head. "We don't know names of who we want. We need to know about anyone you can remember who may have worked closely with them, technical people, particularly in AI or VR technology?"

Claire's brow furrowed. "Why don't you just get company records?"

Ericka nodded—not completely vapid then. "We did. They're incomplete and don't tell us who the key people were in Clyde's or Frank's view. Who did they talk about?"

"You're looking for pillow talk from my husband and lover both you mean?" Her tone was challenging.

Ericka stared into wary eyes. "Exactly, not to put too fine a point on it. The kind of observations that don't get written down in a personnel file."

Claire smiled without a hint of friendliness. "Arm candy for one and a conquest to be used by the other. Not exactly at my best I'm afraid. Look, let's not play cute for my feelings. Frank was a fucking monster, controlling, abusive, the nastiest temper I've ever seen. I was fucking Clyde half out of revenge, half because I thought I might need to run and I needed a friend. Then it turns out Clyde was syphoning money from the company and the rest you know from police reports. When Frank found out, spying on us from our computers, he went fucking crazy, said he'd be back for me and took off after Clyde. You know how it ended. What kind of crimes are you investigating anyway?"

Tim entered the conversation. "A very sophisticated internet predator."

Claire's expression was genuine surprise. "Seriously? So, I'm assuming you have reason to believe your suspect may have something to do with their company?"

Tim nodded. "We're hoping."

She looked up as if trying to remember. "All the ones I met at office parties were coding geeks, look like they were still living in their mothers' basements and playing video games when they weren't at work. I didn't know much about any of them other than Clyde and Frank both thought they were all basically disposable drones."

Ericka knew the kind of crowd well. "No one weird?"

Claire laughed, this time with real humor. "They were all weird, including Frank and Clyde. But Frank was more than that, he was a fucking psycho. Entitled like no one I've ever met. When he didn't get something he thought was his by right, he went nuts. Wanted to make someone hurt for it. Always made sure someone did and enjoyed doing it. Something dark and evil deep inside him I didn't see until it was too late. I don't mean just a bad temper or too-tightly wound. He was charming when he wanted to be, the slickest liar I ever met, fucking around on me from the minute we got back from our honeymoon. I even found out later he had frozen a semen sample without telling me. The doctor at the cryo place said he wanted to be in a position to father children by paid surrogate. Why, I have no idea."

Tim shook his head. "When we met him today, I'd have never guessed."

Claire's eyebrows shot up and she stiffened. "You met him? That's new Frank and it's almost like he's a different person from the old one."

Ericka nodded. "Tell me."

Claire paled as she spoke, licking her lips. "When he pulled himself out of that wreck, they thought he might never walk again. I've never seen that kind of anger. You could look at Frank's face, into Frank's eyes, but Frank wasn't home anymore. Then he went down to that hospital near Cancun, spent months there, but checked himself out before they were done treating him. Filed for divorce from his bed. When he got back, he was walking, the scars were healing, and all the anger was gone. I said to my mother, if I'd known, I'd have sent him to Mexico for a fucking personality transplant years before. He comes back, settles down, drives a boring Mercedes and becomes this tedious husband and father."

"Interesting—" Ericka leaned back "—but we know it isn't him. The guy we are looking for isn't operating out of Silicon Valley. When Frank came up in our search as a person of interest, we were able to eliminate him almost instantly."

Claire shrugged. "Can't help you then. This place is full of talented geeks, but not the kind of creep you're looking for."

"Is that the DNA from the exhumation?" Ericka eyed the report Clarke was reading.

Clarke nodded and took her feet down from the desk. "It is and this one's a dead end. That's Bromwich in the ground where he's supposed to be."

Ericka had been expecting that. "Damn. It would have been too easy. No one does the old fake death routine anymore."

Tim stared at Clarke. "Tell her about the other thing."

Ericka looked at Clarke, one eyebrow raised. "Other thing?"

Clarke turned her chair to face Ericka. "It might just be

a software glitch, but here it is. We used several pictures to see if facial recognition could pick London out of security video, trying to see if we could find him here when we know Dantalion was active."

"Right?"

Clarke's gaze became intense. "It glitched. We used a really good pre-accident picture and the current one from the company annual report. Taken maybe eight to ten years apart. Using the later one, there are all sorts of matches. Gas stations, malls, church. During the thing in the Philippines, he was asleep in a cabin at a church retreat."

"Well, that's that then." Ericka looked from one to the other, waiting for them to make their point.

Clarke's voice rose in pitch. "When we used the older photo, we get none of the same matches to local video. So, we tried another old photo same thing. Then a third. Nothing."

Ericka's mouth went dry, her heart thumping almost erratically in her chest, making her sit up straight. "You compared the old and the new London pics?"

Clarke nodded, her mouth curling into a smile. "We did. The software says they're not the same guy. Then we used different software. Same thing. There's something really weird here."

Ericka let her breath go in a loud sigh. "So, wait a second, maybe the accident just rearranged his face a little?"

Tim shook his head. "It didn't. We checked and then filtered just to be sure. As far as the software is able to tell, these pictures are of different men."

Ericka took a deep breath, thinking. "We need to get London's DNA from before the accident. We need to get a warrant and get that semen sample if it still exists. And then get a castoff sample from him now. If these are different guys, we may have something. The software trace to them was pretty compelling."

Tim waited in a nearby clothing store pretending to look at shirts until London turned the corner on his way out of the mall. He walked over to the coffee shop, checking the target was gone before leaning into the garbage can, a plastic bag over his hand. He picked up the paper cup London had tossed there, reversing the bag and placing it inside his jacket. With any luck a good sample.

He slouched in his car watching as London left the parking lot before driving on. The cryo facility was on the edge of town. When he arrived, he strode up to the front desk, smiling at the receptionist as he showed her his badge, then handed her the warrant. She held her chin as she stared at the document wide-eyed before calling the manager.

Minutes later a determined-looking middle-aged woman emerged from the back of the office, taking a few minutes to scan the document. "May I have few minutes to speak with our counsel?"

Tim nodded, lifting the small cooler onto the counter. "Of course. Ready whenever you are." Minutes later, he left heading for the local forensics lab, texting Ericka: *Got it. I'll walk both samples through and make sure it's top of the queue. We'll know soon.*

23

On Laughter-Silvered Wings

Schmidt was dripping from the noon sun as he walked under the enormous wing of the French Airways A380, soon to depart Mexico City for Paris carrying five hundred and twenty-eight passengers. He looked up at the gleaming hull, checking the tail numbers once again, reassuring himself. It was the same aircraft he had worked on, his employer subcontracted through KNR Industries to update the in-flight entertainment and passenger communications systems. Now the immense aircraft had enough bandwidth to allow streaming data to passengers while in transit, and a little something extra he had installed during scheduled maintenance. Something that looked identical to an original Airbus component.

Back in the sun he walked to the ground-level door, lifting his pass to the half-asleep security guard before tapping the door with it, letting himself into the relative cool of the air-conditioned maintenance hall. There he peeled off his coveralls and checked his appearance reflected in the smoked glass of the window. On the pretense of a final inspection of new wiring in the cargo bay, he had made sure the modified component was still fitted and operating as they would need, and that the input from the weight sensor could be manipulated remotely.

Now there was time to enjoy a well-earned drink at the first bar he could find before the boarding call to a flight that would be the culmination of many months of work. If all went as planned, he and his patron would accomplish something industry experts and legions of talking heads had sworn could not be done. His old life behind him now, he wouldn't miss it. He wondered again where his new one would take him.

He took a deep breath, relaxing his shoulders before pulling on his motion-capture gear for what would be his finest, most glorious hour. Extra screens now rested atop the usual array so the video feed, when it came, would fill his entire field of vision behind his augmented-reality goggles. Another deep breath as he scanned a side screen, ensuring his assets were where they needed to be, tracking them through their phones, occasionally using their mobiles to listen to what they were doing. Then he scanned the hacked airport security cameras, watching as the lounge filled with people waiting to board.

He spotted an attractive woman standing next to her husband as they waited to board. She took his hand, smiling at him, causing a surge of rage to bubble through him. *See how much you think of him once his pants are filled with shit and he is whimpering with fear.*

★★★

Schmidt stood in the narrow aisle, waiting as those ahead of him stuffed luggage into the overhead bins. He carried one small bag containing a very small laptop, VR goggles, and several small wireless video cameras. Customized VR goggles that both displayed augmented reality on the inside and filmed wherever he looked. He would see outside, inside, and have flight data fed directly to him.

On the flight deck of the giant airliner—the world's largest—Captain Jules Durant and First Officer Lara Marchand ran through the extensive checklist, bringing the great craft to life. Multiple screens gave them readouts on the immensely complex systems required to keep their bird in the air and on course. They had crewed together many times before and were confident in each other. Marchand contacted clearance delivery and received permission to pull away from the gantry. The huge plane shuddered as a tractor pushed on the nosewheel, moving it to where they would start the engines. She watched on the recently fitted camera mounted in front of the nose wheel as the crew detached the coupling, freeing them for taxi.

Marchand keyed the mic. "Mexico ground, this French Airways heavy one-seven-nine, request engine startup and taxi for the active."

A few seconds, then an accented response. "Roger, one-seven-nine, squawk two-nine-seven-one and respond when ready to taxi. Active runway is zero-five left." The transponder code, or squawk code, enhanced radar tracking and transmitted data to air traffic about the flight, aircraft type, altitude, and heading. The engines rumbled to life, the comforting vibration felt now through their seats.

She transmitted again. "Mexico ground, one-seven-nine is ready for taxi."

"One-seven-nine, taxi via delta for zero five left, following British Airways triple seven. You're number five. Contact tower when ready for takeoff."

Marchand tapped the mic again. "One-seven-nine is number five." Eyebrows raised at Durant, he nodded and she toggled the intercom to make the obligatory announcement no one could hear. Minutes later, the gleaming aircraft rumbled down the runway, rotating and lifting into the air, laden with a full load of fuel for its transatlantic flight.

Schmidt's large frame did not fit into a standard airline seat and this one was no different. Glancing at his watch, he got up and walked back to the washrooms, waving people past him in the line to ensure he got the precise one he needed. Once inside, he used his key to pop off a small piece of trim and drew the small oxygen canister from inside, placed there by him during the refit. He stuffed it under his loose-fitting shirt, flushed the toilet and walked back to his seat after taking his bag from the overhead bin.

Settling in, he tightened his belt, powered his machine on, and hooked up to the in-flight system, pleased to note the signal strength and bandwidth. The file sent to him by his patron sat on the desktop marked as family photos. He looked around him, smiling to himself before double-clicking on the file. While the scripts ran, he powered up his VR goggles, leaving them ready on his lap. Loading software while in flight was usually blocked except when wheel sensors registered the plane's weight from being on the ground. He had modified that function and was pleased to see all was working as planned. His hand trembled as he fingered the oxygen canister under his sweater, reassuring himself it was there. He looked out the window, seeing nothing but open ocean below. It would not be long now.

The first indication of trouble on the flight deck was a slight loss of electrical power on the circuits containing the in-flight entertainment systems. Marchand noticed it but seeing nothing critical didn't bring it to Durant's attention. They were cruising at thirty-seven thousand feet over the crystal Caribbean waters in near-perfect conditions. Multiple alarms sounded at once: engine fires, fuel pressure, cabin depressurization, all vying for attention while several of the cockpit screens flickered and lost resolution.

Marchand unbuckled and stood to look at each of the engines in turn, seeing no sign of fire. She turned to Durant who had the emergency checklist out, sliding his finger down the card as he read. His lips were moving but she couldn't hear him. Comms were out too. She shook her head while tapping her headset. He pointed out the window where she had been looking and then to the alarms indicating all four engines were on fire. She shook her head and gave him a thumbs-up. It was an instrument problem.

Her ears popped, searing panic as she realized the pressure alarm was real, confirmed as the flickering instruments showed emergency oxygen deployment in the passenger cabin. She reached for her oxygen mask when the nose of the giant aircraft launched skyward taking her to the floor, leaving her to try and push herself back up against multiple Gs. Then it tilted forward towards the brilliant ocean, throwing her hard against the cockpit ceiling. As the nose rose again, her unconscious form flopped down landing half in the left seat, her legs on the floor. Despite his years of experience, Captain Durant made a cardinal error. He looked to see if his copilot was alive before securing his own oxygen mask. He turned back to the controls, pulling on the stick, trying to level out. Nothing. He grabbed for the throttles and his hand missed. He tried again, his vision going dark at the edges, and then he was unconscious.

Schmidt sat buckled tight in his seat surveying the carnage around him, his oxygen mask strapped over his face, the bottle cold against his belly. Around him lay the unconscious forms of several passengers who had not been belted in, bleeding and still. Many of the overhead bins had burst open, flinging luggage up and down like missiles as the plane alternated between hard climb and descent like an enormous roller coaster. Very few had managed to get the overhead masks on and the three he could see wearing them were slumped in their chairs. The smell of blood, shit, and vomit filled the air. He typed into his laptop. *All unconscious, need a few minutes of level flight to finish set up. Go ahead and bring the air pressure back up. May lose some as it is.*

The response was almost instant. *Please signal when ready and secure.*

Schmidt got up to place the cameras, setting them where he had calculated would give the broadest view of the main cabin. As he buckled himself back in, his ears popped as pressure returned to the cabin. He held his nose to clear his ears and secured his goggles. He flipped on voice communication and pulled the mic near his lips. "Ready!" His stomach lurched as the nose of the plane again pointed down.

Ericka tapped the screen of her phone and held it to her ear. "Agent Blackwood here."

"Ericka, it's Maxwell from Homeland. Have you heard?"

"Heard what?"

There was noise in the background, several animated voices. "Hijacking in progress, French Airways A380 out of Mexico City. All contact lost, transponder off, cruising slowly at five thousand feet near Jamaica. Turns circles every so often. Over five hundred passengers on board."

"Jesus!" Ericka wondered what kind of help they needed.

Maxwell sounded out of breath as he spoke. "Wait 'til you hear the rest. All comms are down, all telemetry shut off except some automated stuff, but the entertainment system is still transmitting both ways via satellite. Multiple, high-volume encrypted streams."

"Oh, fuck!" Ericka's full-body chill and shiver were instant. It was him. She had no doubt in her mind. A sudden thought flashed into her mind. The car. Using the entertainment system to move enough data to drive it, cross-linking the systems. It was just a proof of concept. Jesus fucking Christ. This is what he meant. This would have to be handled very carefully. "Who's calling the shots?"

"The French. French Airways, their bird and it's over international waters. Close enough to Florida—we're scrambling two F-15s out of Tyndall in case it heads that way."

Ericka's mouth was dry. This was supposed to be impossible. "How is he getting his data stream to the plane? Must be commercial satellites?"

"We're on that. We should be able to shut down the stream."

Ericka winced at the jolt of panic. "If it is Dantalion, he'll have thought of that." *Think it through: what will his fail-over be? He always has one. Way too complex a system to guess at, he must have someone in the industry even to place the equipment. Maybe he was on board? Going out in a blaze of glory?*

She could hear a voice in the background. "Is that Blackwood?"

Then Maxwell. "Yes, ma'am."

The other voice again. "Get her on encrypted vid-phone if she's in secure facilities!"

"I'm in the lab. Give me a second." Ericka ran through two doors on her way to their shared office. Both Tim and Clarke were sitting peering at their screens. "Heads up! Homeland says we have a likely hijacking in progress. Might be our guy." She quickly explained as she dropped into her chair and swiveled to face her bank of monitors. Both swore to themselves as they pulled their chairs in behind her. A few keystrokes and Maxwell's face appeared, behind him leaning over his shoulder was Director Andrea Riley, head of Homeland's National Cyber Security Division. Her face was etched with worry, accentuated by the grim determination of her expression.

"Who's behind you?" Riley asked.

"My team, both part of this since the start."

Riley nodded. "You've been on this guy's tail longer than anyone. We've examined the code and based on our own investigation we think it highly probable it's him. You're the only person we know of who's ever communicated with him. I'm going to need your behavioral assessment as well as your technical backup."

Ericka glanced back at Tim as she spoke. "Of course. Maxwell, please send us the data stream so we can help analyze. Director, is the aircraft still turning circles?"

"Yes, still at about five thousand feet."

"Any word at all from it?"

Riley shook her head. "Right at the start someone in the cockpit keyed the mic for a few seconds. All they could hear were alarms, which I'm told were fire, fuel, and depressurization. Then someone shut off the transponder and all telemetry. Nothing now except a data stream bouncing between several sets of satellites."

Ericka thought for a few seconds. "Can we tell if the alarms were genuine or something he might have fed the onboard computers?"

"No way to tell, but ground observations from ship traffic report no fire and no apparent problems with airworthiness. It's right above a cruise ship so we're getting continuous reports."

Ericka's mind raced. That was probably no accident. He'd want an audience if this was his big thing. He wasn't sitting in the shadows anymore. He'd stepped into the light and that was going to change how he reacted. "If he's somehow disabled the crew, he may just be waiting for everyone on board to wake up."

A shout in the background and Riley stood and turned. "Are you hearing this? The fighters are alongside now. Give them the feed!" She gestured to someone out of view.

The fighter pilot's voice penetrated the crackling static. "Crew alive and gesturing out the cockpit windows. Some passengers visible in cabin windows. Aircraft appears intact and airworthy. Moving in closer." A few moments of static followed. "I can see the crew. Looks like they're holding up radio equipment."

Riley turned back to the monitor. "Assessment, Agent Blackwood?"

"He's likely waiting for his audience to settle in before he starts whatever he's planning." Ericka bit her lip. If he was planning to just kill them, he'd have brought it down by now and done it somewhere he would be sure there were cameras rolling. "It's all about control and fear with this guy. Killing is incidental to him. He won't hesitate to do it, but it's not his focus."

Riley nodded, grim-faced. "That's how our behavioral people are calling it too. But there are over five hundred people on that plane, ninety-one Americans. If he has full control, he could fly it into a ground target."

Ericka's tone conveyed her certainty. "He won't do that. It's been done. His ego won't let him simply duplicate someone else's hit. He knows it will be shot down long before it gets near any populated areas." *So, what's he planning? What's in this for him?* The remote control of an airliner had never been done or even really demonstrated as possible. "He always works through a proxy. He may well have someone on board. Has someone gone through the manifest?"

"Doing that now." That was Maxwell.

The fighter pilot's voice interrupted. "Target is turning east and descending. Crew gesturing they do not have control."

***

The aircraft leveled and began to descend, the sound of the engines diminished as they were throttled back. Around him, people were sobbing, families huddled, the flight attendants administering first aid. Someone screamed as they were helped up, grinding the ends of broken bones. Schmidt turned to look out the window, then yanked his goggles back on, engaging the interface. This pair were built into heavy glasses, not as obtrusive as the others in his home.

He typed into his keyboard. *You should have full control. Cockpit is isolated from flight controls. Expect them to re-establish communications shortly.*

The familiar baritone filled the earbuds. "Counting on it and thank you, my friend. Enjoy!"

The outside view projected onto the inside of his headset. He was getting the feed from an outside camera mounted on the tail of the aircraft, one normally used by the pilots when taxiing on the ground. The brilliant blue of the Caribbean filled his view, Haiti just appearing on the horizon. This was working beautifully.

Someone behind Riley shouted to her. She stood up straight, pivoting away from the monitor. "They're ready to try and cut the data stream."

Ericka sat back. "Maxwell, what are they talking about?"

"The French External Security Directorate. They've isolated which satellite services he's using and are ready to shut them down. They're hoping if they shut him out, the crew will regain control."

No, bad idea but they don't know this guy, Ericka thought. "Director Riley, ask them to think carefully about that. He will have thought of that and have something ready. If the plane is in no immediate danger, they should wait."

Riley's face appeared back on the monitor. "Not our call, it's a French plane, but I will pass on the recommendation."

Captain Durant twisted the last two wires together and nodded to his copilot. One of the radios lay on the floor of the cockpit, now hooked up to an alternate power source. It had taken them four tries before it showed any signs of life. "Try it now!"

Marchand keyed the mic. "Mayday, mayday, mayday, this is French Airways heavy one-seven-three, over." She repeated the call.

"One-seven-three, this is Port-au-Prince ATC. Go ahead."

Marchand blew out a sigh of relief, nursing her broken wrist. "Jesus, it worked. We have lost all access to flight controls. We had multiple alarms and, we think, controlled depressurization while at altitude. The aircraft appears to be intact and is being maneuvered remotely. Please tell these American fighters we are trying to re-establish control. We are currently descending, throttles are idling. Looks like we are on course to pass west of Haiti, over."

"Roger, one-seven-three, we are clearing airspace ahead of you. Messages relayed to French and American authorities."

The brilliant light of sea and sky reflected from the mirrored lenses of the goggles, his eyes visible behind them, his smile broad. He wore sensor gloves allowing him to toggle virtual controls in the A380 cockpit projected in front of him, in reality touching just air. His right hand gripped a physical control column mounted to the arm of his chair, his left on a throttle assembly. It had worked as well as he could have hoped. For a moment, he switched to the view from Schmidt's glasses, then the cameras, noting the relative calm now, his audience looking frightened and bewildered. Some sported injuries, bandages, and slings. Perfect.

He flipped back to external view then tilted the control stick to the right, noting the aircraft beginning to roll to the right on about a one-second delay. He brought it back to level, checking the altitude now at three thousand feet. He would hold the gentle gliding descent until five hundred feet above sea level. At that point, the real entertainment would begin. First, he waited for them to try the only ploy they could, grinning in anticipation.

"Thirty seconds 'til they try and cut it!" Maxwell held one side of his headphones tight to his head against the din of the Homeland ready room. "Fighters backing off now."

Ericka keyed her mic. "This is a mistake. We have nothing ready if he does something nuts except to shoot it down."

Riley tilted her head as she listened. "Agreed. Not our call. We may just end up picking up the pieces."

Someone in the background at Homeland shouted. "That's it—they've cut the link. Jesus, I hope that works."

Marchand was looking at Durant as his eyes bugged wide.

The four GP7000 turbofans roared to life, causing the nose of the huge craft to pitch up before something, either an autopilot system or whoever was flying, compensated late, bringing pitch back to level. The cockpit screens remained blank and a hopeful try of the flight controls proved useless. She glanced at the airspeed indicator, but it was dark. In level flight at this altitude it would not be long before full throttle caused a structural failure, likely the wings tearing free.

"One-seven-three, any effect?" The tower at Port-au-Prince was now relaying communications straight from French authorities. "We have turned off the entire satellite feed. Have you re-established control?"

"Negative. Controls unresponsive. The engines appear to have gone to full throttle, level at what appears to be about three thousand feet."

One of the fighter pilots cut in. "Targeting computer shows you at two eight hundred feet, now passing through four hundred knots. What's the max on that thing?"

Marchand answered, eyes blinking against stinging sweat. "Point-nine-six Mach, six hundred and forty knots but I'm sure no one ever held the throttle open with a fully loaded one at this altitude. Call out the numbers."

"Roger that."

Ericka turned to Tim, leaving her mic off. "What does that mean?"

"Airliners have enormous thrust they don't usually use except to climb to cruising altitude with a full fuel load. At that altitude in level flight, it will tear the wings off in a few minutes."

Very clever. Whatever malware he's gotten in there, as soon as he loses control, it defaults to full throttle, leaving us minutes to decide what to do. Ericka keyed her mic. "Director Riley!"

"Here." She was off camera, Ericka could see only the back of Maxwell's head as he looked at the room's main monitors.

Ericka wondered if the French authorities could hear her. "They need to give him back control. He'll kill them all before he gives it back to the crew. He must have some sort of default algorithm installed to force us to give him back the plane."

A moment's static then one of the fighter pilots. "Four seventy-five knots."

Ericka tried to keep her voice level. "Director, have no doubt he will kill them. If they give him back control, there's some chance they'll live. It's zero on the current course of action."

"Five hundred two-five knots."

"One-seven-three, starting to pick up some serious vibration." Marchand's voice was clipped, higher-pitched than before, someone fighting panic.

Riley spoke into her headset, her voice raised, apparently speaking to her French counterpart. "Yes, our assessment is he will allow it to crash before relinquishing control." She paused. "We suspect he has installed a default program, which is running now."

"Five-six-five knots."

★★★

In the cabin, Schmidt tightened his belt to the point it was painful. The roar of the engines was unbelievable, now felt as much as heard, as the vibration made all the seats and fittings rattle. A low groaning sound announced the metal was reaching its limits, soon to fail, bringing the end. Around him, some prayed, others clutched each other, tears streaming, their sobbing drowned by the noise of the engines. In front of him, a mother pulled her two children tight. He typed. *I don't think they are going to blink.* No answer. The entire link must be jammed. So be it. He looked around him, waiting to see where the light pierced through first, then it would be over in seconds. He started at the noise. Sounded like something starting to tear.

"Six-two-five knots."

Riley broke the tense silence. "They're doing it. The French have switched the satellite feeds back on." Ericka could hear her talking to someone else now. "If it turns towards anywhere populated, we can bring it down."

He blinked at the brightness of the light as his monitors came back on, showing him the video feed from outside the aircraft. He glanced at his airspeed indicator, six hundred and twenty-nine knots. They had left it very late as he expected they would. He pulled the throttles back and lifted the nose to bleed off speed. As the velocity came down, he banked the aircraft to the south, keeping offshore from Haiti and the Dominican Republic. No fun getting shot down now after all this effort, now down to five hundred feet.

Smiling broadly, he toggled viewpoints so he had only the outside video feed from the tail camera, overlaid with just the airspeed and altimeter. Like he was flying the huge plane sitting on the top of the fuselage. He opened a small window in the lower right of his view, showing the view from inside the cabin. Always best to be able to gauge your audience throughout your performance. Feedback was so important.

"Tighten your belt, my friend, it is time. You can transmit both video and sound from the cabin. Plenty of bandwidth."

The typed message from Schmidt responded. *Ready when you are.*

Now at three hundred knots, down to two hundred and fifty feet, he threw the aircraft into a steep, left bank, pulling back hard on the stick, generating several Gs and causing the trailing fighters to shoot past him and into his field of view, pulling up hard to avoid a collision.

A short, barked laugh. "Pay attention, gentlemen," he said to no one.

"Shit, that was close. Break off and let's get behind him, three miles back."

Ericka listened as Riley gave the fighters their orders. "Captain. Pull back and keep a weapons lock on that ship. You are authorized to activate weapons, but fire only on my command."

"Roger that, going weapons hot."

"Where the hell is he going?" Clarke looked from Tim to Ericka.

She shook her head. "He isn't going anywhere. He just

wants to toy with five hundred captive people and everyone watching, all at once."

Schmidt had always loved flying. Not the one step above livestock in a cattle car experience most airlines delivered, but real flying. He flew gliders as a hobby, full aerobatic freedom, with nothing but the hiss of air passing over the wings. A bird of prey searching for thermals, twisting and turning until feeling the lift of rising air beneath. The ecstasy of full freedom. This was very different. Screams filled the cabin as the plane plowed through maneuvers its designers had never imagined. Screams unlike the thrilled shrieks of people riding a roller coaster, but rather the terrified wails of people knowing death's hungry stare was fixed on their children, his icy grip on their shoulders. The structure groaned as metal flexed, popping as materials neared their structural limits.

Outside, the water appeared mere feet off each wingtip as the turns became progressively tighter. The cabin filled with the stench of vomit again. He gripped the arms of his chair, tendons protruding on the backs of his hands. Leveling from a tight left turn, the airliner twisted to a high-angle right bank, causing overhead bins to burst open, bombarding the passengers below. A father to his right covered his infant's body with his own, taking a small suitcase to the back of his head before slumping over. The child's mother screamed as she shook him while he bled on the wailing child.

"Christ, he's got it so close to the deck, he's leaving a visible wake in the drink. I keep losing tone. Switching to guns." The fighters had followed the great bird past Puerto Rico, twisting and turning as it went, climbing and banking at gigantic angles usually reserved for military aircraft and stunt planes. Over uninhabited jungle tracts, so close to cliffs and hills that palm trees twisted in the plane's wake as if in a hurricane. Now it was right down on the deck turning figure eights in the waters between the British and US Virgin Islands.

The pilot switched on the F-15's M61 20mm cannon, seeing the projected gunsights appear on his heads-up display. It fired six thousand rounds a minute and would blow the gleaming airliner into confetti if needed. Sweat trickled down his back as he fought down the thought of sending hundreds of civilians, many children, crashing into the water in a gigantic, tumbling fireball. His target banked hard again, and he made a wide, sweeping turn to stay on its tail, his wingman flying tight, gasping as the airliner's wing dipped to within feet of the gentle waves.

And now for the grand finale. Could he get it down, flying with delayed controls, on a runway just maybe long enough for this aircraft? He brought up the full control panel and began ditching much of the fuel. With this much on board, it would buckle the landing gear on touchdown and end up an inferno thousands of feet long. That would be inelegant, not the fitting testament to the glory of his accomplishment. He turned down the audio feed from the passenger cabin. Exhilarating as the screams were, he needed full concentration now.

His heart raced as he turned for a long final approach into St. Maarten, famous throughout the world for its proximity to the beach. Those so inclined could sit in the fine coral sand while approaching aircraft passed mere feet over their heads. It took serious piloting skills to put a medium-sized airliner right on the numbers. As far as he knew, no one had ever landed this type of plane there before. The runway was a mere seventy-five hundred feet long and the A380 needed an absolute minimum of seven thousand to land. That it needed ninety-five hundred feet to take off again was French Airways' problem. Presuming there was anything left of it.

Flying right off the deck now the waves were an indigo blur, a sudden mass of white ahead, a cruise ship. *Here's some good fun.* He waited until the last possible second before pulling the nose up, clearing the ship's stacks by mere feet before jamming the massive craft back down near the beckoning sea. Flipping to the rear view, he laughed as the fighters took the long way around rather than try to duplicate his feat.

Far below the normal glide path, he began to prepare for landing. He brought up the pre-landing checklist so it overlaid part of his view and began to run through it. The water flashed beneath him, the engines nacelles skimming mere feet over the surface. Soon the runway would come into view. A flush of adrenaline and a deep sigh, as glorious as he knew it would be, a god-like feeling of absolute control. He hoped the fighter jocks behind him were duly impressed.

"We're starting to see civilian marine craft in some numbers. If you want it brought down with a minimum of ground casualties, it has to be soon." The pilot kept his finger off the red trigger, his voice echoing through Homeland's ready room.

"Blackwood? You heard that. They're clearing the airport, but he could put it into the town last minute if he wanted." Riley stared into the camera, her eyes boring into Ericka's. "Assessment?" The combined shrieks and screams of the passengers echoed through Homeland's ready room. In the background, agents watching the video feed from the passenger cabin gasped before turning away.

Ericka gritted her teeth, trying to ignore the noise. The bastard had left them only one option. "I doubt he is trying to crash it at this stage, but they're rolling the dice as to whether he has the skill to do it." He probably does—he wouldn't have chosen this big a display if he thought there was a chance he was going to publicly fuck it up. His narcissist's ego was the passengers' best chance of survival. "Our best probability of saving lives is still to let him land it."

Riley nodded. "Not our call anyway, but the French know we've got the only inside line on this guy and his capabilities. I'm not going to give the order to shoot unless the French ask me to."

His heart pounded against his ribs, muscles tense, sweating hard under his headset, feeling more alive than he could ever remember, his grin making facial muscles ache. He had cleared several yachts by as little as he dared, knowing his wake would blow them over into a broach. He relaxed his grip on the stick, taking a deep breath, trying to anticipate last-minute movements of the great jet. He kept his speed up, loving the sensation of the rippling sea sliding below, but he was much too fast for landing. Just a few more minutes.

In the airliner's cockpit, the pilots exchanged stares. The airport beacon was visible, but they were screaming low over the water far too fast to do anything but crash. Both reached over the center console and grasped the other's hand, turning their gaze towards the fast-approaching threshold.

"He's coming in way too hot," the pilot of the lead F-15 kept his voice level, fighting a rising panic. "At this speed he'll skid right down the runway and off the end. No telling what he'll take out on the ground. Am I clear to fire?" Only static, no answer.

Ericka bowed her head, eyes closed, trying to blot out the terrified wails from the cabin audio feed. All those people riding in terror, their lives at the whim of this monster. Many more on the ground could follow if they'd got it wrong. Nothing to do but wait. The bastard had outmaneuvered them again.

On a long final approach now, he pulled the throttles to idle and lowered the flaps, knowing they were never designed to be deployed at this speed. Anticipating the resulting pitch-up, he pushed the nose down, using the flaps as speed brakes, scanning the airspeed indicator as the huge jet began to slow. No structural failures. He smiled knowing he would be leaving a full wake in the water behind him from the lift vortex. Airspeed down now, one hundred and ninety-five knots—just a little below the glide path, flying from his virtual seat on top and near the tail.

Between him and runway ten at Princess Juliana International Airport, were a mere few miles of shallow water, a beach filled with sunbathers, and a road. He calculated all his movements with the one-second delay his link was giving him. If he touched down a little early so be it. A thousand times in his simulator and the real thing at last. As every flight instructor told every new student, you can learn to take off in an afternoon, learning to land properly takes a lifetime of practice. He would get it right the first time. Landing gear down and showing green.

Bright specks on the beach marked the towels and umbrellas of people below the flight path. He didn't have the resolution to see them, but he imagined people scrambling out of the way as it became clear to them the airborne behemoth was headed for and not over them. Going to be a lot of bathing suits in the laundry tonight. He pulled the nose up a few degrees of pitch as the great plane slowed, twisting his control column to apply slight left rudder. Right down the center line.

Crossing the beach with feet to spare, the rear wheels slammed down on the center of the access road, squashing a small car flat in a gout of flame, the jet's wake turbulence blasting beachgoers off their feet to tumble across the sand, limbs flailing. Three of the six tires on the starboard side blew out with the force of impact, causing the jet to veer to the right. He compensated with the rudder before lowering the nose, applying full brakes and reversing thrust on the two inboard engines. From his vantage point, he couldn't see below but expected the brakes and tires would burst into flame at some point on the runway. The plane was slowing but the end of the runway was approaching faster than he expected. Nothing to do now but to ride it out. He held his breath as the seconds ticked past, a thousand more feet of runway to go. The two F-15s swooped low over him before turning hard to the northwest, likely heading for the US Virgin Islands.

The nose dipped down hard, the angle unexpected. The front landing gear must have buckled. He applied rudder to keep it centered but it was going too slow to straighten it out now. As the last of the speed bled off, the jet slid to the left off the runway, crossing the access road and a small traffic circle before coming to rest with its nose in the water of Simpson Bay Lagoon. Done.

He watched for a few minutes before smoke began to billow from underneath and several emergency exit ramps deployed from the sides. Time to go. He sent the command to wipe, then encrypt the plane's computers. Satisfied they were running, he disconnected and set several waiting algorithms to clean his traces across the networks he had used, in some cases encrypting entire servers, taking localized parts of the internet briefly offline.

He toggled his mic, alerting his man on the ground. "Be ready, Schmidt, will be out shortly."

"Understood."

Schmidt peered into the dark chaos of the cabin. For a few minutes during the landing, he had resigned himself to the end.

The plane shook when the landing gear went down followed by the impact of touchdown so hard he bit his tongue. Then came the shrill pitch of overloaded brakes echoing through the airframe and a rumbling crash like a dumping wave as the nosewheel sheared off. And now, silence.

Smoke obscured the entire length of the upper deck, the floor lighting disappearing into the gloom. Screams of passengers competed with shouted commands of the flight crew to move to the exits. Pure chaos, undiminished by the standard safety briefings delivered at the start of each flight. He crouched down, coughing, stuffing his small laptop into his shirt, his other gear into trouser pockets. He joined the shoving line in the left aisle sliding down into the warm water of the lagoon. He splashed ashore, pushing through the milling crowd and scanned the beach for the boat.

There it was, a white cigarette boat with a mermaid on the bow, its nose nudging the beach with the action of the tiny waves. An enormous African man stood behind the wheel, dressed as a local, his muscles bulging through a tight shirt. He sported mirrored sunglasses under a dark baseball cap. Schmidt suspected he was looking at the model for his patron's avatar. The man nodded as he approached, gesturing him aboard and then below. A few minutes passed before police arrived and ordered the boats full of onlookers to back away from the crash site. Feigning obedience, he nodded and started the engine, crossing the lagoon before heading north out to sea towards the British Virgin Islands some ninety miles away. Behind them the jetliner continued to burn.

★★★

Riley relayed the news from French authorities. "Looks like they got everyone out. Some injuries, but no dead passengers. The only casualties seem to be in the car it hit on landing. Both F-15s made it, though one was seconds from flaming out."

Ericka took a deep breath. *All those people. What the hell is next? Nothing probably, he'll go to ground now for some time. If we don't catch him now, it may be years before we have another chance.* She looked at the video feed of the burning plane—not going to be anything left in there. "Director Riley, has anyone spoken to the French authorities about anything they got on the satellite feed?"

Maxwell answered, "We're on it. Let you know what we get. Jesus, we've got to shut this guy down. A guy who can do this can shut off cooling systems at nuclear plants and fire other people's weapons." *Or give any number of people those same abilities if he wants.* The thought made her stomach turn over.

They were two hours out of the British Virgin Islands in the Cessna. Fitted with long-range tanks, it would easily make the six hundred miles to a remote strip in Venezuela where they would refuel before continuing on. His all but silent companion had said little about their final destination, his bulk filling the small cockpit so that Schmidt had to lean against the door to make room. He scanned the rudimentary instruments seeing all was well, then began to doze, lulled by the drone of the single engine.

He didn't see it coming, the ham-sized fist that pounded the side of his head into the window, then repeated the assault, again and again. He barely knew it when the same hand reached over and opened the door, before unbuckling his harness. As he tumbled through the air in the last few seconds of his life, he regained enough sense for a final thought. *Your idiot forgot to take the laptop.*

24

Doppelganger

Tim glanced up from the two DNA reports looking at Ericka, eyes wide. "How did you know?"

"Just a gut feeling. What does it say?" She had no idea how she'd known, but Frank London was not who he was pretending to be.

"The fellow who froze a semen sample and the one who drank from the coffee cup I picked up are not the same person." Tim paused for his usual dramatic effect looking from Ericka to Clarke with a triumphant smile. "They are, however, related. Half-brothers—probably same father, different mothers."

Ericka took a few moments to process, her gaze focused into the distance. "He must have swapped identities so he could disappear. Doesn't tell us why or where though. I think it's time we brought the current Mr. London in for a more serious chat. We've got him on impersonation and fraud for sure."

Clarke's delivery was pure deadpan. "I bet he's going to be a bit more scared of his brother than us." The others snorted with laughter.

Ericka leaned forward, her chin on her hands. "Let's see what we can get before the meeting tomorrow. From what I'm hearing, Homeland, the CIA, and the French have come up completely dry so far. They are going to treat our Dantalion as a serious terrorist threat from here on. See if we can stay relevant to this." She tried but failed to push the images of the three men from her mind, her teeth sore from clenching. Dantalion had them.

Arrested leaving church, London was sitting wearing a dark suit, his skin oily, glaring at Ericka across the interview room table. The bottle of water in front of him was untouched. He leaned on the surface of the old table. "I told you, I'm not speaking with you until my lawyer gets here." He lifted his head to glance at Tim who stood behind her, arms folded. "Why don't you get bad cop here to go and get the paperwork ready. Fraud, he said when he arrested me." He glared at Ericka, his eyes flashing with real anger. "Right in front of the whole congregation. Just the kind of games I should have expected from you people."

Ericka smiled, her tone like they were disagreeing in a discussion about gardening. "If you want to wait to talk that suits me. I'll talk. You just listen for a few minutes. Your DNA shows you are not Frank London, but rather a close relative. We don't have any birth records for a brother of Mr. London, so we assume you were born outside the country.

He shrugged. "Tell it to my lawyer."

"I will, her and a jury both. We do know you appeared here about seven years ago, months after Mr. London's accident and took the heat for him. Then after finding God, you ran around telling everyone you were him and using his reputation here to raise funds for a new company, which you have run ever since. A very profitable company that I think was likely based on work done by the real Mr. London before he went abroad. Now you have a lovely young wife, lovely young children, and wealth to buy your way into a community where you have no business being.

"I said, I'm not talking."

Ericka nodded. *He's bluffing, all bravado now.* "So don't. I'll talk. Whatever happens with any criminal charges we bring against you, that life is over with a letter and a DNA report going to your board, the IRS, anyone else I can think of. How is your lawyer going to help you with that?"

He blanched, jaw muscles bulging, not meeting her gaze. Ericka studied his face. *He's not even that smart. He's had an hour and he hasn't thought it through yet.*

"I want to speak to my wife."

"In good time." *So, the wife is the brains.* Ericka pushed his phone across the table to him. "Now you've had a moment to think clearly about the situation, do you want to perhaps tell your lawyer to turn around and go golfing instead?"

His eyes were wide. "You think you can blackmail me?"

Ericka gave him a bland smile, *just watch me.* "No, extortion is illegal. I was hoping you'd see it as in your interests to cooperate all on your own."

"Cooperate with what?"

Enough with the coddling, time to scare him. She leaned over the table, their faces not a foot apart, her voice filled with ice, eyes narrowed. "I don't have time for games. Our search team is back from your house and your computers are being hooked up to ours. I have a real suspicion the analysts are going to find what I want and lead us to your brother. If they do, talking to you no longer interests me and I'll just hand you over to local police to deal with and be on my way."

"You're not scaring me enough yet. Try harder. The alternative is a lot scarier."

Ericka fought to keep a straight face. *I'll bet. Not like Dantalion is going to trust this idiot with the keys to his door either. A different angle maybe.* "Let's start with the basics then. We know the London family background. New England, Ivy League schools. Who was your mother? Some cocktail waitress Daddy knocked up? Too dreadfully inconvenient to have you around embarrassing Mommy, Daddy, and poor Frank."

His face reddened, got him. "Dad stayed in touch enough to see I was educated, I knew who my brother was, never knew my birth mother."

Ericka shuffled through her papers for dramatic effect, all of which she had pulled from a recycling bin before the interview to use as props. What she needed, she had committed to memory. "While poor Mr. London was recovering in Cancun, someone named Alexander Dunlevy flew down there several times, and visited the hospital lots. Does he ring any bells?" An explosive sigh from him this time. "From what I can tell he was adopted by a Canadian family, but they moved to Oregon when he was five. A young man of that name got a driver's license in Oregon twelve years later. Looks a lot like you. Do we have to continue this bullshit?"

Dunlevy wouldn't make eye contact, looking down. "She wouldn't get an abortion, so she was shipped off to Mexico. Yes, that's me." It was over.

Tim looked up at the mirrored glass, knowing Clarke was already working. "So, if you're busy being Frank, where is Alexander and how did you arrange for your old self to disappear?"

"My old self was 'killed' in an accident in Costa Rica a few years ago. Local burial, death certificate duly filed."

"Your brother's handiwork?" Ericka waited for him to answer, then seeing he would not, continued. "So, brother Frank's hurt, lying in a bed at a private clinic down south and one day you get the call to start being him?"

"I'm wondering what's in this for me?" Dunlevy leaned back.

Time to give the knife a twist so he knew it was lodged deep in his guts. "If I was you, I'd be more worried about who's going to protect my family, if your dear half-brother thinks you've ratted him out. I'd think about asking for them to go into witness protection until we have our target under wraps."

Dunlevy closed his eyes and slumped forward, looking resigned. "We'd had contact over the years. He'd helped me out when I needed it. I was managing a bank branch. Our father was dead and managed to die broke. It was like I won the lottery. What would you do?"

Ericka's stomach lurched. *Here we go.* "Did he say why?"

Dunlevy waited some time before sighing. "He was lying in bed all busted up, said this was where his lifestyle got him and he wanted to start over, disappear completely."

Tim snorted. "And you believed him?"

Dunlevy's eyes flashed as he turned to answer Tim. "No, I didn't believe him. Man, there is something really fucking wrong with that guy, someone you know if you rubbed him the wrong way, he'd kill you as soon as look at you. When I asked about his wife, it was like he was possessed. Never seen rage like that. Said she'd been screwing his business partner who was fucking lucky he was dead already. I'm surprised she's still alive." He paused.

Ericka leaned forward, her hands folded in front of her. "Don't keep us in suspense."

"He handled everything—the divorce, the new startup, moved most of his cash offshore, and there was lot of it. All I had to do was sign everything and learn to be him. Lucky we look so much alike. Anyone who thought I looked a bit different assumed the crash rearranged my face a bit. And yes, my company's product is something he already had half-built. I hired people to take it from there."

"So how does he talk to you now?" Ericka knew he wouldn't answer.

Dunlevy was covered in goose bumps. "Look, what I just told you, you'd have figured out on your own. Anything further and nothing will keep my family alive. He has a thing about traitors. The one thing he won't forgive."

Tim leaned over the table to glare at Dunlevy. "You know we're investigating him for multiple murders, sexual assaults and now terrorism, right? You get that?"

Dunlevy met his stare. "Better them than me."

"How sure are you?" Homeland Director Riley's image was one of several on her screen, including CIA, and FBI brass. Abara, Tim and Clarke crowded behind her terminal.

Ericka answered for the FBI. "Very confident. London's a perfect profile hit on the skills and from what we can tell from interviews, a pretty clear match for personality. None of which tells us anything about where he is."

Riley's eyebrows arched up. "We're not as confident. Our team has been going through the passenger list and video from the hijacking and we think we may have actually caught an image of the suspect." She turned to gesture Maxwell forward.

Maxwell shuffled his notes for a moment before beginning. "There was a guy on the flight who worked on the hijacked aircraft last maintenance cycle, Richard Schmidt. He went to some lengths to be on that flight for no good reason we can see. It looks like the broadcast sound and video were his doing. Unaccounted for after the crash. Then it turns out, there are no bodies in the plane, so we start looking. No trace of him on St. Maarten. Then we found this." Maxwell showed a still of two men entering a doorway. One was a paunchy white male. With him was an enormous black male, whose bulk towered over his companion. "This is from an airport camera at the British Virgin Islands. The smaller male is Schmidt and the larger one is unknown. Witnesses say they boarded a small aircraft and took off a few hours after the hijacking. The tower swears there was a flight plan, but all trace of it has vanished from the relevant databases." He lifted his gaze for a meaningful look. "Big surprise. Then, last night a fishing boat pulled Schmidt's body out of the Atlantic two hours towards Venezuela."

Ericka sighed before speaking. "As usual, all the loose ends wrapped up."

Maxwell was grinning. "I saved the best for last. He had a small laptop under his shirt, tucked into his pants. He hit the water at terminal velocity, but it's mostly intact and we're getting some data from it. No sign of the plane or the other male."

Ericka shook her head. They had it wrong, but they were very much going to need whatever was on that laptop. "You think the big guy is Dantalion? No way. If he was coming to the scene, it wouldn't be to clean up loose ends. Way too much risk for nothing. He doesn't take personal risks. This other male is obviously one of his guys, but it's not him. Got any background on Schmidt?" Her mind wasn't on the conversation. Her heart was thumping against her ribs and she felt warm. That laptop changed everything.

Maxwell stared at her, expressionless for a moment before continuing. "Software engineer, works for a company that does contract work on airliner refits. No record, no family. His IP has shown up in pervert chatrooms a few times, but nothing concrete. In his basement he had the obligatory VR gear, but it's all wiped and fully encrypted like all the other ones you've recovered. On the other guy, we drew a total blank. Likely South American, serious 'roider, no facial recognition but the video we have is pretty lousy." Another pause. "Why are you so sure it isn't him?"

Ericka made sure her tone carried her conviction. "It's just not his gig. He's never shown up on-scene before and particularly not to do his own dirty work."

Riley cut in. "We're going to continue with it as a possibility."

"Agreed," Abara said before Ericka could respond. "There's no point duplicating effort anyway. We'll proceed with London as our primary suspect. Can we have whatever you get from the laptop?"

Riley nodded. "Of course, we'll send it to you as we

recover it. Are we all agreed, his most likely location is South America?"

As all nodded agreement, Tim whispered in Ericka's ear, "That narrows it down a bit!" On the screen, Maxwell shared a look with his boss.

Ericka leaned to whisper a response to Tim. "It doesn't matter. If that fucking laptop has anything at all on it, there is a way." This was the break that could change everything. A computer dropped into the ocean out of an airplane couldn't run wiping protocols, couldn't encrypt itself. The way to pierce through Dantalion's all but invincible technology were the deviants and idiots he had to rely on. That's where all his failures came from. She had to see what was on that computer.

Claire was pallid, features drawn, etched with fear. She sat on the couch clutching her husband's hand like a lifeline. He was dressed for the golf game they had dragged him away from, flushed red, mopping his forehead as Ericka outlined their reason for the return visit. Their living room was like something from a home décor magazine, the same as the rest of the house. Brandt Cole seemed to Ericka more angry than fearful.

Claire's voice caught as she spoke. "So, the new God-fearing Frank isn't him and that fucking lunatic is out there somewhere, you have no idea where? How the hell sure are you?"

Tim answered. "Absolutely sure. DNA confirmed."

Cole leaned towards Ericka over the gleaming marble coffee table, eyes narrowed. "Are we safe? Can you keep us safe?"

No point trying to bullshit him. Ericka stared straight into Cole's eyes as she spoke. "No, not here. You're sitting ducks. We'll need to relocate you to be sure. All of you, off-grid until we take him down."

"Jesus!" Cole pulled Claire onto his shoulder, tears streaming down her face. "Why hasn't he done anything before now? He's had years."

That was a question Ericka had been asking herself for two days. "Hard to say. Perhaps because that would telegraph for sure old Frank was still creeping around somewhere. Now he'll know we're onto him, and he has no reason to restrain himself."

"We've disconnected everything in this house from the grid. We'll need to take all your devices to look for any intrusion." Tim nodded at their phones on the table. "And to make sure he can't use them to track you."

Ericka pointed at the two laptops. "How old are these?"

Claire shrugged. "The top one is about six months old, the other one maybe a year older than that."

Tim gestured towards the house's vast interior. "Any others? We need every device in the house."

Cole shook his head. "No, that's it. We got rid of the older ones not too long ago."

Claire's brow furrowed. "No, there's a really old one down in the basement. I haven't used it in years. I keep meaning to get rid of it."

Ericka's heart skipped a beat and her neck tingled as all the hairs stood up. "When did you buy it?"

Claire stared at her. "Seven, maybe eight years ago. It's ancient."

Ericka squeezed her eyes shut. Maybe, just maybe. She

looked at Tim. His eyes were wide, she could see him fighting to keep the grin off his face. "Do you mind if we take that one too?"

And there it was. Calm determination replaced tension as Ericka scanned the data. Someone uninvited had been in Claire's old computer. Gotten in, loaded several different kinds of malware allowing remote access and then hoovered whatever he liked until the machine was powered off and thrown in a storage bin. That must have been a bit of an 'oh shit' moment for him when it went dark, leaving an unfortunate collection of data waiting for someone to find it. But time had done much of his work for him already. While a computer does not delete data beyond the reach of forensics, it does overwrite it over time. Old data lay waiting for someone to find it until the computer needed the space for something new. On an older, smaller-capacity machine like this one, portions of what interested her were now lost forever.

The three of them each worked from their own copy of the hard drive, searching through fragments of data, reassembling evidence of contact with servers, looking for anything pointing to who was controlling the malware. The first intrusion had taken place while he must have still been lying in his hospital bed. Script-kiddie tools sending data to servers on Mexico's Yucatán Peninsula. He would have seen, as she did, that the worms had little time to make a decent start on Bromwich before Claire had taken up with Cole. She keeps the clasp on her bra well-oiled does that one. In very short order, he'd picked up the tools of his new trade.

Later software was far more sophisticated, modified to leave no tracks, now masking not only his location but all traces that might identify the type of machine or what he had installed on it. His quick mastery of dark web technology was evident from the rapidly decreasing signs he left, gone below without so much as a ripple on the surface to mark his passing.

Tim leaned back from his screen and turned to Ericka. "I wonder if that's what set him off. Always an evil, narcissistic bastard. Then he finds his partner is stealing his money and shagging his pretty wife. Then he has the accident while he's probably trying to kill Bromwich. While he's still lying in his hospital bed, she's out prospecting in the country clubs and scores big."

Clarke nodded her agreement. "Pretty classic. He probably comes out of the box with serious psychopathy, an angry, entitled guy, someone who from all accounts goes off on a short fuse when he doesn't get his way, whose first reaction is to attack and inflict a whipping. He has a close brush with death and all the barriers come down. Everyone's betrayed him and everything he's suffered is everyone else's fault. The world has fucked him over, so he feels entitled to retaliate without any moral restraints. Anything goes and over time, he wants to press that button harder and harder. Now everyone knows he's pulled off something no one else has come close to. He's going to want more. Bad luck for the world this psycho is also the most gifted hacker anyone has seen."

Tim looked at Ericka. "And that leads to what he wants from you, I think. He knows he's in a class all his own. The fact he's beaten people he thinks inferior to him isn't enough now. He wants the admiration of his peers and I reckon you're the only one he sees in that category. He doesn't know you're just riding my coattails." He grinned at her.

Ericka had already reached the same conclusion. She had told Tim and Clarke about just a part of her second meeting, and they didn't know the half of it. Taking Dantalion's proffered gift would be the ultimate acknowledgment that he was capable of things she couldn't do. His price, ultimate proof he was beyond the reach of the very best law enforcement could throw at him.

He must just be reveling in the dilemma he's thrown me. If I keep on his trail, I may never find them on my own. Or I can betray all his victims, my people, Patty's memory and walk away. As he had alluded, Caesar measured his own greatness by the prowess of his enemies. Little glory came from conquering weak opponents but having the powerful kneel before him was as irresistible to London as to all other demagogues.

Ericka shook her head, changing the subject. "I don't buy this triggered stuff. These guys are mostly born this way. You don't go from being a run-of-the-mill asshole to a sadistic psycho because your wife and business partner are fucking around on you. He was like this before; he just repressed it."

Clarke folded her arms leaning back. "That ignores the effect of the physical trauma."

"Neither theory helps us find him now. If you're right, I'll buy dinner after we take him down. Either of you got anything?" Ericka looked at them, waiting.

Clarke shrugged. "A few bits, nothing that's going to have us knocking on his door any time soon."

"Same here," Tim said. "Bits that might be partial information about data-routing, but no way to assemble them."

"Let's keep going. When we get whatever Homeland can pull off Schmidt's computer, we'll have a shot."

"What do you have in mind?" Clarke asked.

She leaned back before answering. After the hijacking it had been very easy for Abara to get permission to run ISS beta software on the most serious hardware available. "We're going to feed the contents of both into one of the big Summit computers and load them with the very latest entity resolution software around. Something my old mentor has in development. Then we're going to add in everything our crawlers gathered since we got on this guy's tail. This Schmidt guy never had a chance to wipe his machine on his way down to the ocean. Every scrap of data we have from any device. Claire's too. Especially hers. That's our best shot. See if it can reconstruct a virtual of the routing data and figure out where he is."

Tim wasn't listening. He was staring at the lab counter where the goggles were again blinking and chiming in their bag. "I reckon that's for you. Do you want me to take a message?"

"Ericka my friend, I trust you are well?" His smile was solicitous.

She bristled at that, a reminder she was only alive because he had permitted it. She stared at the same massive figure, sitting as last time on his unadorned throne in a cavernous stone hall. "What do you want?" She could feel the body heat from both Tim and Clarke as they leaned in, trying to hear past the headset's earphones.

Brilliant facial mapping again—he's managing to look hurt. "What, no congratulations? No curiosity how I did something you and everyone else who should know better said could not be done? Or my brilliant landing? That took some doing you know!"

"That car you hit had a family of three in it, an eight-month-old baby."

Another, now familiar, dismissive shrug. "If local police cannot be bothered to get people out of the way, I fail to see why I should be blamed for that. My intentions were obvious."

Always someone else's fault, can't accept responsibility for anything. "Poor Mr. Schmidt. Does anyone who works for you live long enough to collect a pension?"

That drew a cackle. "It is true, I am rather demanding."

"What do you want?"

He sighed with another theatrical shrug. "Well, I was hoping to hear you had found another way to make a living, but if we must talk business, I have a message for your masters I hope you will deliver for me."

"I'm listening."

"I am taking something of a sabbatical. I have done what I set out to do and I want to take some time to smell the brimstone. Consider what I would like to do next. I want to communicate to them the potential consequences of continuing to pursue me. You can, of course, give them some examples of the kind of destruction I could cause. Use your imagination. I am sure you will agree, my escapade of a few weeks ago was a model of restraint." He slid down in his seat, as he had before, smiling, exuding menace. "You have seen the capabilities of some of my tools. I have others you have not seen. If I am pursued further, it is my intention to release them simultaneously as freeware, into the wild, to anyone who wants them. Hackers, thieves, Jihadis, every petty dictator, warlord or drug dealer will be able to both evade authorities and counterattack at will. Some of those people, I fear, may lack my sense of benevolence and restraint." Another smile, canines visible this time.

Sure you will, hand out everything that makes you special to every halfwit wannabe in the world. Ericka didn't believe him, but the risk was immense. "We will find you. It's just a matter of time."

"Please do, Ericka. I will leave your thirty pieces of silver on the counter." He bowed his head in a slight nod, lifting his index finger to his right temple.

Telling me to think about it. He knows I'm not alone. "Don't bother. Keep them." She wasn't giving the bastard the satisfaction of thinking there was any chance.

He tilted his head, smiling with the tiniest shake of his head. Then he was gone leaving only darkness, no theatrics this time.

It wasn't entirely what she'd hoped for, but luck had broken their way. In his flight away, the unfortunate Mr. Schmidt had given them exactly what they were missing. None of the Dantalion security protocols had run for the simple reason that the small laptop had run low on power some time after he left the hijacked aircraft, but not to the critical point that would trigger wiping. Schmidt had pulled the battery, likely to avoid the machine scanning for Wi-Fi and leaving a local trace. In his excitement, he'd prevented the protocols from running. A stolen speedboat and an ancient Cessna gave him no opportunities to recharge. Ericka could see software set to encrypt and wipe the instant of the machine's next start-up. Impact with the ocean and the salt water had destroyed much of the data, but there was enough. This was going to work.

The Summit was one of the most powerful computers the American government had at its disposal. Climate modelling had taken an enforced break, the prospect of the world's criminals and the country's enemies having all his capabilities all at once too terrifying to do anything else. Now its full capability, more than two hundred petaflops focused on every known trace of Dantalion-produced data using a piece of software months from being ready for beta testing. The most advanced single-entity resolution searching ever produced. Scour every possible combination of every fragment of data millions of times a second, seeking combinations that might resolve to a location. Hundreds of thousands of seemingly random fragments. Reassembling them to fit the criteria she stipulated and refined. It searched for any commonalities, like a thousand-part, multi-dimensional Venn diagram, trying to build a whole out of unrelated fragments no human would connect. Nothing like this had ever been tried before. With the old data from Claire's laptop, the recent stuff from Schmidt, their own investigation and the NSA's years of data, there was a real shot.

Time was running out. He could be readying himself to move, destroying all traces of evidence as he did. Perhaps he was gone already. Money moved where he wanted it, under the knife of a cosmetic surgeon where implants would change the shape of his face. Start again on the surface if he wanted. It didn't bear thinking about.

Her terminal chimed, bringing her half out of a fitful sleep. Her neck cramping, Ericka shoved herself upright on the old couch, staring at her phone—3:12 AM. Tim snored from one of the army cots set up in the hallway outside their offices. Clarke presumably farther down in the other one. It took her several moments to realize where she was. She groaned at the lost sleep, one of many false alarms. The array had a bad habit of finding hopeful combinations in the small hours of the morning. She dragged herself to her feet, staggering over to the interface. There wasn't time to waste waiting until morning. Every minute the Summit stalled waiting for instructions, the farther away he might be. The chair creaked under her and she heard Tim stir and swear to himself.

Rubbing her eyes, she stared at the three re-combinations it was proposing. Three locations for her to feed into mapping software. As she loaded the first into the program, she was already thinking of how to code the new parameters for the next one. First one resolved to a location that only made sense if he was in three places at once. *That one doesn't tell me anything.* She pasted the second one into the blinking window.

Her scream echoed from the bare walls of the old barracks. Tim leapt to his feet, Clarke almost tripping over his cot as she lunged into the room, skidding to a halt behind her.

Ericka's hands were trembling so hard she dropped her phone as she pointed Tim and Clarke to the screen. They screamed and clapped each other on the back. It took her three tries to dial the number. Four rings. "Abara here."

A few seconds to gather herself and get the words out. Her voice croaked with emotion. "Got him. He's in São Paulo, resolved to within five hundred yards."

Ericka jumped, not realizing the old woman was behind her. Duffel bag open on her bed, she'd been stuffing it full of whatever clean clothes were at hand before Tim picked her up to race for the airport. A stab of guilt lanced through her at the expression on Mrs. Donnelly's face, worry and hurt. Tim must have called her. It was 5:30 AM and she stood there watching Ericka in housecoat and slippers. She'd let herself in without making enough noise to distract Ericka from her packing.

Mrs. Donnelly didn't smile. "So, this is it then? You've caught him?"

Ericka stood next to her bed, not moving. "If we can get there before he figures it out and moves. I'm sorry, with all the rushing to get out of here, I didn't think to wake you."

There was a hint of reproof in the old woman's tone. "That's all right, our Tim did." She leaned against the doorjamb, folding her arms. "Have you made up your mind if you're coming back?"

Ericka's eyes widened, genuinely surprised by the question. "Of course I'm coming back!"

"Are ye? This was the last one, remember? After this one's in prison, all you've got left on your list is to find those men and hand them over to the police wherever they are?" Mrs. Donnelly's mouth curled into a tiny sarcastic smile, waiting for Ericka to deny it. "Or do you have other plans?"

Ericka let the smallest hint of defiance creep into her tone.

"Depends where they are. You want me to let them go? Let their gangs relocate them while they wait for trial?"

Mrs. Donnelly stepped forward, taking both Ericka's hands in hers, eyes locked together. "Nothing about this is what I want. Are you willing to pay the price you might have to if yer planning what I think you are? Can you come back and live with yourself if you don't? Can you come back at all? Think carefully, girl!"

Ericka couldn't maintain eye contact. "Not if they don't suffer for what they've done. They can't live on in peace. I can't live with that whatever the price."

The old woman drew her into a hug, whispering in her ear. "So, you have found them then?"

"I'll know soon."

Mrs. Donnelly drew back to look at her again. "Be sure. You'll not get a chance to reconsider."

Ericka gripped her shoulders, the worn flannel soft under her fingers, staring straight into the watery green eyes. "It's not a choice I want to make, but I can't win either way. The best I might be able to do is get rid of them and live with whatever comes. And you were right, this is just about me now."

"I understand. It isn't fashionable thinking these days, but a blood debt pollutes the soul until paid."

Ericka pulled her back close, burying her nose in the old woman's hair, the returned embrace tight. "Thank you. I only made it this far because of you. I'll be back when I can." She turned to snatch up her bag, zipping it up as she walked, forcing herself to not look back.

25

Exorcizamus Te, Draco Maledicte

The van rattled over another series of potholes, jarring her back to the world. Abara in front of her next to the driver, his posture erect as always, scanning the passing slums. Tim sat beside her with two members of the Brazilian Federal Police on the bench seat behind. Both men were huge, wearing black body armor and cradling automatic weapons between their knees. She adjusted her armor, doing inventory on her equipment in the back, field data acquisition, jammers, Faraday bags and cases. They would only get one brief shot at this. She closed her eyes and took a deep, shuddering breath, forcing her muscles to relax. It would be over soon, then she could finally rest.

Malware isolation had to be their first priority. If any of his code got into the wild as he'd threatened, the damage would be catastrophic. If it was gone already, they'd need as much as they could get of his tools to develop countermeasures. And yet she couldn't repress the thought: thirty pieces of silver. Would it be there? Could she leave it lying there if it was?

The rest of the local arrest team were already prepositioned in the upscale Morumbi neighborhood. Hard men, more soldiers than police, veterans of dozens of high-risk takedowns of local gangsters. All sitting now in vans in the stifling evening heat around the twenty-story condominium, waiting for their American guests to arrive. If they were following her instructions, all phones were off, leaving communication by radio only. Any clustering of cell signals around the building could tip him off. The flight down had been long, on one of Homeland's jets, arranged in short order by Director Riley. In blatant violation of normal air traffic rules, they arrived without filing a flight plan, a Brazilian police officer in the control tower to smooth things over as they made their approach. The local police would make the arrest, the FBI team would move in with them to secure the data. Extradition would follow.

Clarke and Maxwell sweated in their lab, leaning into their monitors, ready to coordinate their attempts to isolate his computers at the point of takedown. Ericka had no confidence they could succeed, but the plan she had crafted involved taking a portion of the city of eleven million people briefly offline and shutting down all cell towers within range of the building. The first direct action would be to land a helo on the roof and physically disable the four satellite dishes visible from an earlier reconnaissance pass. No way to be sure he wasn't hard-wired to dishes all over the city. If he had made good on his threat, countermeasures could take weeks or months if they didn't have his malware itself to work with.

As they crested a hill, one of the federal troopers behind her touched her shoulder and pointed ahead. "*É isso!*" A tall, glass building was visible set into the side of the next hill, standing proud of several smaller, low-rise structures. She chewed on her lip, her throat dry, hardly daring to believe he was in there, the weight of the endless hunt a crushing mass on her shoulders.

She turned to look over her shoulder. "How long?" The man shook his head—she was rusty. "*Quão mais?*"

"*Dez minutos.*"

She took out her encrypted mobile and powered it down, watching Tim do the same. The others in the van followed suit. From here on in, communication would be by scrambled radio signals piped through the Brazilian police system. The locals maintained full radio silence.

Ericka keyed her mic hailing Clarke by the home-base call sign. "Almighty, Echo one, over."

"Have you five by five, Echo one, over."

"Set?"

"Good as it's going to get."

"Five minutes, then we bring it down. Not sure we'll have radio reception once we're inside."

"Understood."

She pulled out her copy of the floor plan for one last look. All Clarke had been able to find from local sources were construction blueprints and some old advertisements for the condos. Local records showed three suites, each taking half of a floor on the eighteenth to twentieth floors registered to different numbered companies but filed by the same law office on the same day. The local authority had granted various building permits for modifications, but she had no doubt they would be stepping into the unknown once through the door. He was obviously hiding his power consumption somehow or he would have flagged himself to police long before now. Before they kicked in the doors, they intended to cut all power

347

to the top five floors of the building, but she fully expected he would have a backup system.

The sun set in a flourish of blood-red light, a fitting background. Ericka peered up the side of the building, hoping their best guess about where he was in there was right. No light came from the target suites. If they had it wrong and had to do a door-to-door search, he'd have all the time in the world. Three elevators would take a team to each floor. As soon as they were in position in the lobby, the containment team would cut the power and block the stairways down. The power to the elevators would remain on, so each floor team was responsible for containment on their level. Adrenaline coursing through her, her heart hammered against her ribs. She checked the slide on her pistol. Tim extended his hand to her and they gripped each other's wrists in the traditional warrior handshake, eyes locked, saying nothing. Their last one together. She bit her lip and looked down.

She turned to Abara. He nodded and she keyed her headset mic. "Almighty, and Bravo one, this is Echo one, Jericho, I say again, Jericho!"

The Brazilian commander responded in accented English. "Bravo one, we are on the move."

Clarke's voice crackled with static. "Almighty, walls are coming down now."

Ericka stepped out after Tim, craning her neck to look up as the armored Brazilian police sprinted past them. Seconds later the top quarter of the building went dark. A helicopter swooped onto the roof, hovering a few seconds before climbing a few hundred feet to hold station. Explosions lit the roof, leaving small clouds of smoke drifting away.

Clarke again. "Walls are down."

She ran, following the arrest team into the lobby, lunging for the waiting elevator, shouting to the squad leader commanding the team for the top floor to hold for them. The man nodded, his expression grim, snapping off the safety on his IMBEL IA2 weapon, careful to keep the muzzle down while he issued his orders to his four-man squad.

As they rode up in silence, two of the men dropped to one knee in front of the doors, ready to fire. Two more took positions at the front on both sides of the doors, also in position to fire. Ericka, Tim, Abara, and the squad commander went on one knee behind riot shields, weapons drawn. Sweat trickled down her back as she forced herself to take slow, deep breaths. The rank smell of well-used uniforms accompanied the sounds of deep breathing as the troopers prepared themselves.

Let the troops do the shooting, the data was more important. She brought to mind the horrors of the Idaho murder, making her stomach churn. There would be no more. Not from him. This was his end; she had him. The elevator slowed.

The doors parted to reveal blackness. The troopers snapped on their headlamps and gun-lights. The beams from their lights appeared almost solid in smoke, crisscrossing, scanning the short hallway and closed double doors. The Brazilians moved in unison, taking up position to cover the man who stepped forward with a ram, battering one side of the door to hang off its hinges revealing the dark wood floors behind. Nothing moved.

The city lights cast a dim glow through the floor-to-ceiling windows. Their information had been wrong. On this level, he had the whole top floor. Her skin crawled at the thought she might be leading these men into a trap. The assault team fanned out, clearing each room while she listened on the radio to the teams on the floors below call out as they did the same. Tim and Abara had their firearms out, scanning the central room where the FBI team waited. The whole floor was filling with smoke, billowing up the stairs connecting the three levels. Her eyes stung. *Jesus, he's torched the place.* Next to the stairs was a small internal elevator. The squad leader appeared at her side shaking his head, eyes bloodshot.

"*Computadores?*"

He shook his head again. "*Nada.*"

The eerie stillness shattered to the sound of rapid gunfire echoing up the stairs, deafening in the confined space. One man remained while the others ran for the internal stairs, the drumming of their boots making the metal structure ring. More gunfire, and screams of downed men.

She started for the stairs, arrested by Abara's hand gripping her shoulder. "You can't get shot. And I lead from the front— you know that." He disappeared down the steps with Tim close behind. Swearing, she followed close on their heels. They had to find the computers. If he had another way to transmit his tools out, it was long gone, too much time. The shooting started again, a bullet ricocheting off the railing next to her head, making her belatedly duck.

She scanned the floor below. Several of the Brazilian troops lay still, limbs flung in odd postures where they fell, pools of blood spreading under them. Between them sprawled several civilians still clutching their weapons. Nothing moved. She held her headset tight, listening to the remaining troops. Two males were out and down the stairs, the remaining police calling out their positions as they pursued. If Dantalion were one of them, he had no way out. Tim and Abara checked the remaining rooms, emerging to shake their heads. Both were breathing hard, eyes wide as they scanned their surroundings down the barrels of their guns.

Tim pointed his weapon down the last flight of the internal staircase. "No computers up here, nothing burning. Must be on eighteen." A flickering glow lit the stairs down, a pulsing red heart belching smoke like a gateway to Hell itself.

Abara nodded. "Let's go." He led the way down.

The lowest floor of the suite was ablaze. Industrial-looking, furnished with spartan tables, servers lined the walls. Red flames and sparking equipment lit the stacks, crackling and shorting, creating strobe lighting, illuminating the entire half-floor in brief flashes. In the center, a huge array of monitors stood on a U-shaped table facing towards the glass doors leading to an outer deck. Several of the screens were still live, displaying code and what looked to her like messaging systems. Ericka dove under the table, tearing off a device stuck to one of the towers and flinging it against the wall. One of his incendiaries had failed. She still had a chance.

Popping open the case on the portable acquisition unit, she pushed the connectors in with fumbling hands, snapping on the switches. The unit's screen began reading out as it pulled all available data from the arrayed computers. No time to be choosy, they could shut down at any time. The fire would leave nothing. Acquire it now and sift through it later. Her coughing fit sent shooting pains through her ribs and back as she watched the unit work. The smoke had a strong chemical odor, making her eyes water and sting. Excited voices over the radio announced one man who had run down the stairs was dead on the fourth floor. Three more civilian casualties. Where the hell were the firefighters? Pulsing light in her peripheral vision drew her attention to one of the side monitors, the small window's contents making her gasp. The system couldn't transmit. Containment had worked.

Intent on her task, she didn't see when he dropped from his hiding place in the hung ceiling, crashing through to the screech of bending metal and tearing panels, landing like a cat on his bare feet. The man was enormous, precision movements lightning fast, speed defying belief. He was over six and a half feet tall and must have weighed close to three hundred pounds. Dressed in black clothing, his dark skin left him little more than a flickering wraith in the dense smoke. His first shot went through the left temple of the last trooper, before backhanding Tim with a closed fist, sending him sprawling, his gun clattering off into the darkness.

He leveled his gun at her, blinding red laser sight now fixed on the center of her forehead. A shadow lunged between them as he fired, blocking her view. A wet sound like a fist smacking into raw meat accompanied the sharp report of the gun. Abara took the shot meant for her in the base of his neck. Sagging to the ground, he clutched his throat, arterial blood pulsing between his fingers, covering her face. She leaned over his face as life's light faded, fleeting eye contact, the slightest nod and he was gone. *Jesus, Abs, no!* The smell of blood brought bile to the back of her throat.

As he leveled his gun to fire again, Tim's flying kick took the behemoth full in the face, dropping him to his knees. Before he could stand, Tim lunge-kicked him again, catching him in the shoulder as the man tried to dodge the attack. The man's gun flew from his hand, sliding under one of the burning stacks. Unbelievably he stood, assuming a fighting posture. *Jesus, Capoeira trained. How the fuck is he still standing after that kind of punishment?* He glanced at Ericka, his glistening face lit by another shower of sparks, no doubt the model for Dantalion's avatar. She swallowed hard. *Jesus Christ, this could be him. I might be looking at him right now. What if Homeland was right?*

Avatar took a few quick steps backwards, his left hand fumbling for something on the wall she couldn't see, keeping his eyes trained on Tim who circled for an opening. Finding it, Avatar yanked upwards filling the room with a loud hissing sound. Crackling fires roared, the sound like a nearby waterfall, flaring bright enough she squinted. Curved metal shapes mounted to the wall behind him, oxygen? A second's hesitation, then everyone moved at once. Avatar lunged towards Tim as Ericka dove for Abara's gun, the metal reflecting flickering red light under the table of monitors. Tim took a step back, giving himself time to assess the attack.

Classic Capoeira move, a split second before reaching Tim, he dropped with unbelievable speed, spinning low to the ground, dodging Tim's kick while hooking his legs out from under him. Tim slammed into the floor, taking a kick to the face as his attacker continued to spin. Without rising Avatar placed his bare foot against Tim's cheek, pressing his face into the scorching stack behind him. Tim shrieked with pain as smoke rose from his bubbling skin, filling the room with the stench of charred flesh. Cold steel in her hand now as she gripped the gun, spraying bullets at the center of Avatar's hulking mass but he was already moving.

Her shots plowed grooves in his flesh, his right arm, and chest wall. Not slowing at all, he made no sound, didn't even flinch. He rolled low, her view blocked by a table, heading for his gun. He came up with the machine pistol in his right hand before slamming face first into the floor, Tim's hand clasped on his ankle. She lunged across the table, sending a monitor flying, and emptied the magazine into the back of Avatar's head, the grey of brains mixing on the floor with the destroyed remains of his face. *That was for Abs, motherfucker.* Rising to a surge of adrenaline-driven elation, she stepped over Avatar's still form. Hacking coughs doubled her over as she pulled Tim away from the fire, staying as low as she could where there was still air. Blood-red flesh, highlighted with blackened bits of skin, his left arm, chest and half his face charred by the flames.

The unburnt side of Tim's face twisted in pain. "Was it him?"

She grasped his good hand, squeezing hard. "I don't think so. Just going to grab the data, then we're going." He nodded, watching while she pulled the cables from the acquisition unit and slung it over her shoulder. She crawled back, shouting over the roaring fire. "Take a deep breath and try to stand!" He nodded, gasping in agony as he pushed himself onto his hands and knees. Tim's good arm draped over her shoulder, she dragged him the rest of the way up, and they staggered towards the only door she could see. A glimmer of light from a small object on his monitor table caught her eye through the smoke, a small silver thumb drive, the number "30" written on it. Damn him. She paused for only a second, instantly cold all over, squeezing her eyes shut, nodding her head.

She saw the face of Mrs. Donnelly flash in her mind's eye, before shutting it out, guilt and self-doubt dropping away from her like wet curtains, replaced with the cold anger, her trusted companion for so many years. She slid it into her pocket. *Decide what to do with it later. There might never be another chance to find them.*

She kicked the door open, pulling Tim, staggering. There was less smoke in the hallway. He dropped to his hands and knees, a quivering groan of agony forcing its way through his clenched teeth. She yanked him to his feet, bent under his weight, staggering towards the stairs, knowing without help she would never get him down alive. Light from the open elevator doors lit the gloom, an elderly couple huddled inside peering further down the hall as if waiting. *Christ, the power's still on here.* She followed the old man's stare. Past the elevator, a heavy-set woman was struggling to right a tipped wheelchair, the man in it trying in vain to right himself. His wasted legs strapped together, he was unable to twist his body under him, his features contorted with effort.

She lowered Tim to the ground, and ran stooping under the smoke, racked by more heavy coughs. None of them would be conscious much longer. Grasping the man's gaunt hand, she hauled the chair upright, guiding the woman and her charge to the waiting elevator. Ericka gestured to her with an open hand to hold for a moment while she ran back, putting her hands under Tim's arms, dragging him down the hall. A mechanical sound and she spun, checking the doors were still open. The man in the wheelchair had his hand out of view on the control panel, leaning forward, his head bowed.

"Wait!" His head snapped up and their eyes locked. Oddly familiar features, his forehead and left cheek engraved with deep scars. She stopped short, halted by the sheer, utter malevolence of his gaze. Then it softened. He smiled, a melancholy smile, holding her stare then a slow nod, his index finger rising to touch his right temple. The doors shut and he was gone.

London. That's why he never came up.

She screamed, a high-pitched howl of anguish, pounding both fists on the metal doors, then slumped to the floor. Tim groaned again. Staggering now, hacking coughs, her lungs burning, Ericka tried to drag Tim towards the stairs, maybe less smoke there. Her legs buckled under her, vision going dark and she fell across his prone form, her weight on his burns enough to draw gasps of pain. She dragged herself off, so they were face to face, touching his cheek, knowing they had only a few minutes to live. "Thank you, brother." Another violent fit of coughing and then nothing. Five minutes later she felt nothing as heavily suited firefighters lifted her from the floor.

The panoramic view of Rio de Janeiro's snowy-white beaches didn't register as Ericka stared over the balcony railing. She was aware of the unaccustomed scent of the place, salt air blended with the smells of the city. The ever-present low rumble felt rather than heard, the city's heartbeat gaining pace as night approached. Another long drink of the coconut fruit drink, fighting the terrible dehydration since being discharged from hospital. She looked down, turning the small thumb drive over and over in her hand, so often now his writing was faded almost to nothing, not yet ready to see the contents. She had no doubt Dantalion was as good as his word. He would have it no other way. It would diminish him to have lied about this.

They'd gotten what was left of his data, his tools. Clarke and Homeland had used what she'd recovered to track down and freeze some of his money. No one knew how he'd gotten out past the cordon, but then no one was looking for him, expecting a gang to try and shoot their way out. Such was their loyalty, his men had died for him. Not hired goons, but rather disciples, they'd stood and fought knowing they were going to die, like samurai defending their lord. What gave him such a hold on his followers? Dantalion was long gone now, and it would likely be years before they picked him up again, but they would, of that she had no doubt.

Ericka held up the tiny drive. The moment she opened it her long search was over and her reality forever altered. *What's changed, Patty? I used to feel like you were always with me, and we would do this last thing together, make it right, restore balance. To free you, give you your peace, rid us of your pain. Now you're gone. Ever since I picked this thing up, there's nothing but a vast, echoing silence in my head and I'm just talking to myself. I was always just talking to myself. No tears this time. You were never there at all, gone years and years ago. I recreated another you in my head because I couldn't let the real one go. A new Patty who wanted what I did, but kept me restrained, forcing me to live up to your memory, your imagined pride in me, my conscience personified as you. Nothing left of you now but what I remember, and that passes into oblivion when I'm gone.*

What's changed? Now, I'm truly alone. The years of anger, the decade-long war of obsession on reason, all done now. But something remains. Time to bring myself back. Mrs. Donnelly, Steiner, Fowler, you were all right. It was for me, just for me. So be it. I accept that and this is how I find my peace, if I ever find peace. How can I live with myself when I open it? You, Patty, so long in the ground and them out there, living, loving, every day having what they took from you. If they were within the reach of a justice system that cared, then that would have to be revenge enough. If, as I suspect, they are protected, there was no living with that, no way at all. If I hand it to police and they won't suffer, then nothing will change, no balance. That was it then. Decision made.

She stood, stepping over the rail of the sliding door into the hotel room. *Stop fighting who I am, trying to convince myself of my higher motives. I need this and that's all there is to it. The three of you bastards took her, took everything I had, and I need this to make it right. Even with the guilt gone, there must be balance.* Her heart was slow, her breathing deep and rhythmic, her shoulders free of tension, a calm that had escaped her for her entire adult life. No anger, just purpose. She pulled the laptop lid open and slid the drive into a slot, Dantalion's faded writing catching the evening light. Her thoughts were so much clearer, like someone had opened all the windows and let sunlight and a fresh breeze blow through her mind, allowing a long-buried part of her to awaken.

Tim sat next to O'Brien, his elbows on his knees, leaning forward as he stared out at the sparkling blue water of the Pacific. The rock wall they sat on perched just back from the clifftops, providing an endless vista of the incoming wave trains. Neahkahnie viewpoint in Oswald State Park, Oregon. The view was stunning. O'Brien leaned back, his jacket open, dark sunglasses obscuring his eyes. He turned his head to stare at Tim before speaking, pulling folded sheets of paper from his jacket pocket. "We safe up here?"

Tim nodded. "It's safe. No line of sight. Ericka showed me this place. She used to come here sometimes. She used to spend summers here when she was a kid. We can talk."

O'Brien nodded. "Her kind of place. How're you feeling?" His gaze traveled over Tim's left side, his gaze resting on the gloved left hand, twisted like a bird's claw, a blackened crow's foot, the scarring on his face creating an almost reptilian texture.

"Healing, my left hand is permanently fucked though."

O'Brien glanced again at Tim, who stared out into the distance. "Heard from her?"

Tim shook his head. "Not a peep. No sign of her online. Like she never existed. When she checked herself out of the hospital in Rio, she came into my room. They had me so doped up I can barely remember it. I just remember her leaning over me. Said she'd be in touch, but it might be a while. Something she had to do first, then we'd go after him again. Taking a leave of absence. She said she could find him. Left me a hard drive with the stuff she got from his computers, some thoughts about countermeasures."

"The suits still looking for her?"

"Oh yeah. They're scared shitless. Upstairs is starting to ask questions about why she was left to run this. No one knows what happened. I was unconscious; Abara's dead. Talking about congressional subpoenas now."

O'Brien handed Tim the papers. Tim took them with his right hand, trying to hold them steady in the breeze. "Where'd these come from?"

"Sent to one of her old dark web personas as well as

directors of several departments. I got them as they want to wire up all those accounts and see if either she or Dantalion turn up. Think they're talking?"

Tim leaned back, his spine rigid. "You think she's following him on her own? No, where she went has nothing to do with Dantalion."

O'Brien nodded at the papers. "Read. Then I burn."

Tim began to read, swearing under his breath.

This is the last time I will give any warning. If I am left alone to the world I have created, no one will hear from me again. Do not take comfort now just because the planes are flying again. Ericka, if you are there, please explain to your masters the consequences of trying my patience. I wish you contentment. Dantalion.

O'Brien took the papers back, lit the edge with his lighter, then dropped them on the rock at his feet, watching while the flames consumed them. "So, the fucker is alive. Sounds a little scared to me. How much was she talking to him while this was going on?"

Tim gazed off to the horizon, his jaw set. "Just three times, but I don't know everything he said to her."

O'Brien's voice carried his anguish. "How does she think she'll come back after this? A leave is one thing, but it can't be forever. People will think the worst."

Tim nodded. "Who knows if she wants to come back. There were things that girl held on to, parts of her she was never going to let anyone see. You know what happened to her sister years ago?" He looked down, watching the ashes disperse in the breeze.

O'Brien nodded. "She told me. Ericka wore that every minute I knew her. Always burning inside, never free from it for a minute."

"She never stopped looking for them, ever. Never found a thing." Tim paused, turning to look at O'Brien. "Dantalion found them for her."

"Jesus Christ! Did he tell her where to find them?"

"I don't know, I think he must have."

"Mother of God, I wouldn't want to be them now if he did."

Tim turned his head to look at him, his left eye disfigured, pressed half-shut, the scarring holding his expression rigid. He nodded several times, then turned back to stare out over the wave-flecked expanse.

Epilogue

Carlos Sousa, once Frederico Martinez, knew now with absolute certainty that he was going to die by degrees without ever knowing who had killed him or why. He had grown soft over the last decade, a paunch the inevitable result of indulgence. His ragged clothes were stained, smelling of sweat and urine and did not hide the dirt or slouched posture. He sat with his back against the wall of the old hut, cracks in the plaster digging into his skin, gaze fastened on the splintered door in front of him. He had wedged the pieces back together after breaking in, fragments propped up with a rusted chair. Each breath drew into his nose the stench of unseen rats lurking somewhere in the long-unused structure. Shuddering, nauseous at the reek, back aching from crouching so long, he considered the last few days, the final ones of his life.

Eleven days on the run and he had nowhere else to go. He pressed his eyes shut like it would take him back to his home, a place of marble floors, mountain views and safety, back to his beautiful if long-suffering wife, his three young children. A small palace bought with blood and money, the rightful lot of a man so well-connected. A fallen prince of the cartels. Gone now forever. Everything gone.

He opened his eyes, cocking his head to listen, but there was nothing but the night sounds of the nearby Baja village, the faint rhythmic sound of waves the town's pulse. His head nodded forward, fighting sleep, remembering the moment it all changed. When he arrived home, pulled into a doorway by his brother-in-law, Jorge's hand gripping his jaw, so angry he spat as he hissed his words.

"You bastard, my sister, your children, what the fuck were you doing? They know, they're coming for all of you!"

Carlos shook his hand off, snarling his response, a stab of fear gnawing at his guts. "What the fuck are you talking about?"

Jorge's eyes widened before flashing with rage. "Don't play stupid with me! You gave it all up. They know. You think you give up a year's profits to the fucking gringos and they aren't going to know? What did they promise you?" Jorge's fist slammed into his belly, taking him to the ground, followed by a kick to the ribs, leaving him in breathless agony, unable to scream his pain. "I'll get your family somewhere safe, but get the fuck out, lead them off, give me some time."

The tickle of blood from where his head hit the ground drew him back from staring at the concrete under his nose. By the time he pulled himself to his feet, Jorge was gone, his last memory of his family the panicked voice of his wife demanding to know where they were going and the wailing of his children as they were stuffed into a car. Next, the muted roar of Jorge's Mercedes spraying gravel against the house, then gone. Gone forever now.

Gasped air surged into his lungs, his mouth hanging open as he surveyed his home, no longer safe, his fortress, now a place he would die, his disfigured corpse displayed as a warning to others. The next breath came out as an unbidden moan of anguish, beginning a frantic dash through his house for money, guns, a safe phone, and his computer.

His grip was a vice on the wheel, jaw tight as he made the short drive to a farm where he had an old Hilux stashed. Carlos drove north for sixteen hours through the desert before stopping, before daring to turn on his laptop, and there it was. Transferred to a drop box in the States, the locations of the organization's offshore accounts, the circuitous route that moved the money, sent from his machine, a file transfer from his computer. He hadn't done it and no one could open this computer but him. He stifled a whimper knowing what to expect at the hands of his former colleagues.

The rising sun streamed through the back window of the old Toyota, making him squint as he tried to look through the files. At every touch a picture flashed on the screen, a pretty young woman, vaguely familiar but forgotten, no significance to him. No matter what he tried, nothing would stop it popping up. Someone not him was controlling it. He crushed the computer under the wheels of his truck, throwing the pieces into a gully beside the road.

Fatigue drained him, robbing him of focus so he almost missed them as he pulled into the badly lit station for fuel. Two men hunched in a car tucked behind the booth. The attendant was gone and he was the only customer. Madre de Dios, he'd driven right into an obvious ambush. The computer, the fucking computer had tracked him! He'd survived in this business by being quick and the men must have been dozing. He shot both in the head as they drew their weapons. No time to get rid of the bodies or the car and now they would know which direction he was going. He filled his tanks and jerry cans and left the main highway, doubling back on himself, trying for the coast to steal a boat.

They found him again the next day, in the middle of nowhere, like they knew where he would go. He pushed their car off the road, crushing the fender on his truck, climbing down to the wreckage to cut the throats of both men as they lay unconscious. Carlos was not going down without a fight. He torched the truck—it must have been bugged—leaving it to burn beside a deserted road before walking all night to climb aboard a ragged bus at daybreak.

They found him the third time as he stepped from the toilet at the bus station. Police arrived just as the shooting began, allowing him to run, through alleys to the edge of town to hide the night in a car repair shop. He smashed his phone, clutching his arm where a bullet grazed him, wincing as he tightened the bandages to staunch persistent bleeding. The mobile was a burner he had never used before, and he thought it untraceable. He paid most of his remaining cash to a fisherman returning to this shithole village to bring him here.

The old fishing shed was the only shelter Carlos could find. He came out at night for food, but now his mind was going. Hoping to find a tourist to rob, he waited by the town's only bank, but a whirring sound made him look up, imagining for a moment the security camera over the main door was tracking him. He moved and it followed him again, pointing right at him as he walked away. He hadn't come out since, his fear a prison. It wouldn't be long now. He had nowhere to go and nothing left to fight with.

He sat on the dirt floor in the hut, stinking, lips cracked with thirst, starting at every sound. Someone was killing him and doing it slowly, like they were savoring it and he had no idea who. He was not short of enemies, but none who killed like this, no one who could do such things, a watching eye that was always on him. Carlos sobbed, his head sinking between his knees, nostrils filled with his own stench.

At first, he couldn't tell what had changed—it was just a perception. Goose bumps rose all over him despite the sticky heat. He held his breath to listen, but there was nothing, and that was it. The sounds of the village were gone, no music, no hum of distant voices, like the town held its collective breath, the absolute silence of the jungle when the jaguar stirs itself for the night's hunt.

Trembling, Carlos pushed himself to his feet. Time to face his end. Nothing moved, silence broken only by gentle surf. Placing each step with care, he crept to the door, afraid to look but compelled, almost welcoming the end he knew was coming. There was nowhere else to run. Eye pressed to a gap in the splintered wood, he was surprised to feel the calm, cooling and soothing him. His run was over and this was the almost welcome end to his fear. Mere shapes against the night, there were men outside the door.

Author's Note

Do criminals like Dantalion exist? All aspects from which to construct him are found in existing offenders. Nothing he does is beyond the hacking talents of state-sponsored or organised crime hacker teams. His psychopathy, being a violent pan-sexual sadist and an extreme narcissist, is not common, but not unknown either. Dantalion is what happens when someone highly intelligent and sociopathic moves online. He is what happens when a ruthless predator quickly adapts to a new and unrestrained environment, each success driving him to dare more. I don't know if he exists, but I think he could.

With the proviso that from here on there are plot spoilers, I will start on the technical underpinnings of the story. It is, of course, a work of fiction, but all the technology depicted is either real or a short step ahead of where it currently exists. Regarding police technology, I have restricted the content to things that I know to be already in the public domain. As to the technical feats of Dantalion, all of his technology either exists or is on the near horizon. For those who are interested in diving into details, my website includes a select bibliography of reference material. As this is not a textbook, I have focused on portraying what the technology does occasionally at the expense of scrupulous accuracy as to how it does it.

Any reader suffering from excessively raised eyebrows at the notion that cars and airliners might be hacked and controlled may wish to read *Smithsonian Air and Space Magazine*, February 2021, 'Will Your Airliner Get Hacked'? Meet the people who are making sure it won't. It is a real threat and the aerospace industry treats it as such. The hijack is facilitated by a man inside and the inside man is almost impossible to defend against. The king of Troy would agree.

The virtual reality and enhanced reality technology depicted are real, though I have moved things currently in development to the operational realm for Dantalion. Now it's all down to processing speed and network capacity before the metaverse becomes a reality.

Single entity resolution, on the scale depicted in this book, is entirely the product of my imagination. The inspiration comes from a manufacturer's claims about this type of software and my seeing no reason why, if the claims are correct, it couldn't scale up to this degree.

It goes without saying that the police investigators depicted here are completely fictitious and not based on real officers. The book seeks to portray some of the dedication and talents of the police officers with whom it has been my privilege to work and the conditions under which they operate. They suffer from their prolonged contact with this horrific element of society and some spend years dealing with the consequences such as PTSD. We all owe them a debt for that.

I would be remiss if I didn't make it clear that while I have been a criminal barrister for thirty-two years, this book and its sequel are not based on any particular case or cases.

Rather those years in the business, have given me hundreds and hundreds of anecdotes from which to build my stories and the people in them. You can't deal with criminals for that long without coming to understand them and their underlying motivations. I have dealt with every kind of criminal from thieves to thugs, to hackers, to gangsters, to sexual predators, to money launderers and murderers. I hope this has allowed me to successfully portray what they are and what moves them. I would hate to think I had read all of those psych reports for nothing.

Finally, I'd like to thank the people whose talent and dedication have contributed to this book; author, Eve Seymour, for helping me forge and temper the raw material, my agent, Ian Drury, for opening doors and believing in my writing, my editor, Greg Rees, along with all members of the Head of Zeus team for their thorough polishing, and finally, Ben Hitchcock, for his insightful technical review. Any bad writing and technical errors that remain are my fault entirely. Last but far from least, my heartfelt thanks to my family, particularly my wife Tiffany, for putting up with me while I worked my way through this project. It may have only been her proofreading that made the others believe I was even marginally literate in the first place.

Daniel Scanlan

About the Author

DANIEL SCANLAN is a lawyer who has practiced extensively in the areas of cybercrime, digital evidence, wiretap, smuggling and money laundering. He wrote the non-fiction *Digital Evidence in Criminal Law* and contributed to *The Lawyer's Guide to the Forensic Sciences*, winner of the Walter Owen Book Prize. He lives on Vancouver Island and enjoys ocean kayaking and hiking. When not outdoors, he is reading and will read almost anything, except books about lawyers. *The Hacker* is his first novel.

Follow Daniel on @DanielMScanlan
danielscanlanauthor.com